AFTER
LAMBANA

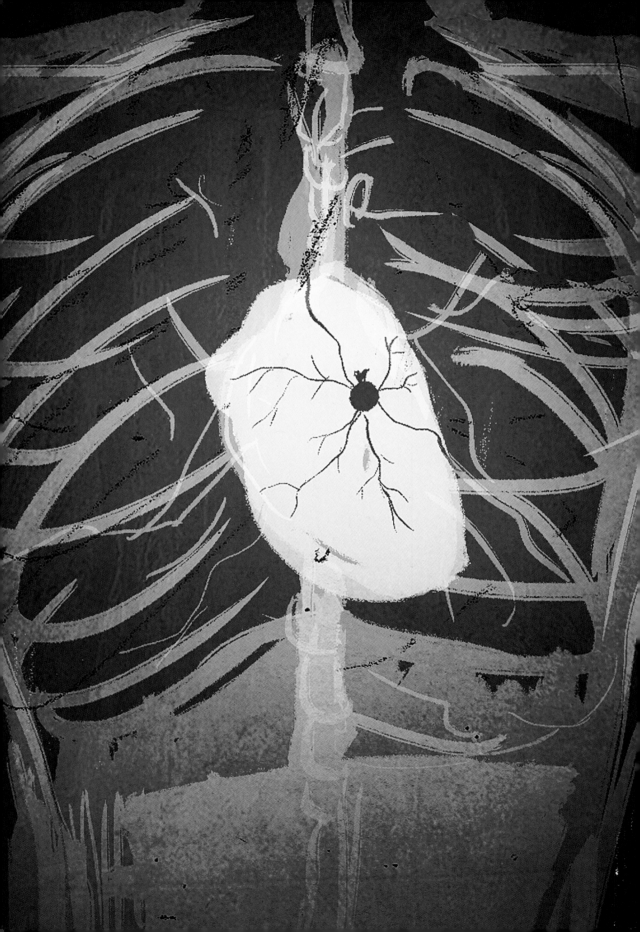

AFTER LAMBANA

Myth AND Magic IN Manila

A GRAPHIC NOVEL

ELIZA VICTORIA - MERVIN MALONZO

TUTTLE Publishing

Tokyo | Rutland, Vermont | Singapore

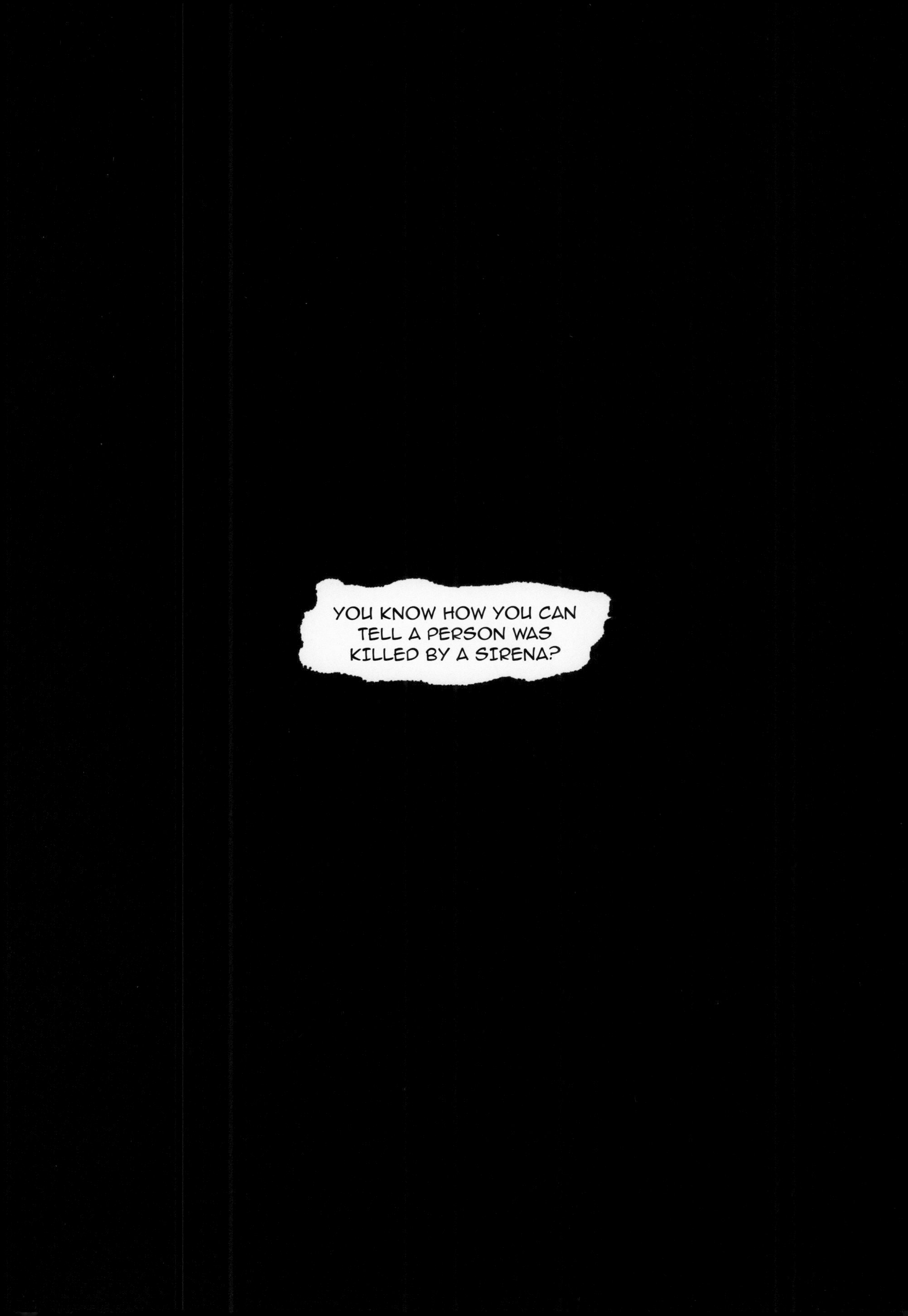
YOU KNOW HOW YOU CAN TELL A PERSON WAS KILLED BY A SIRENA?

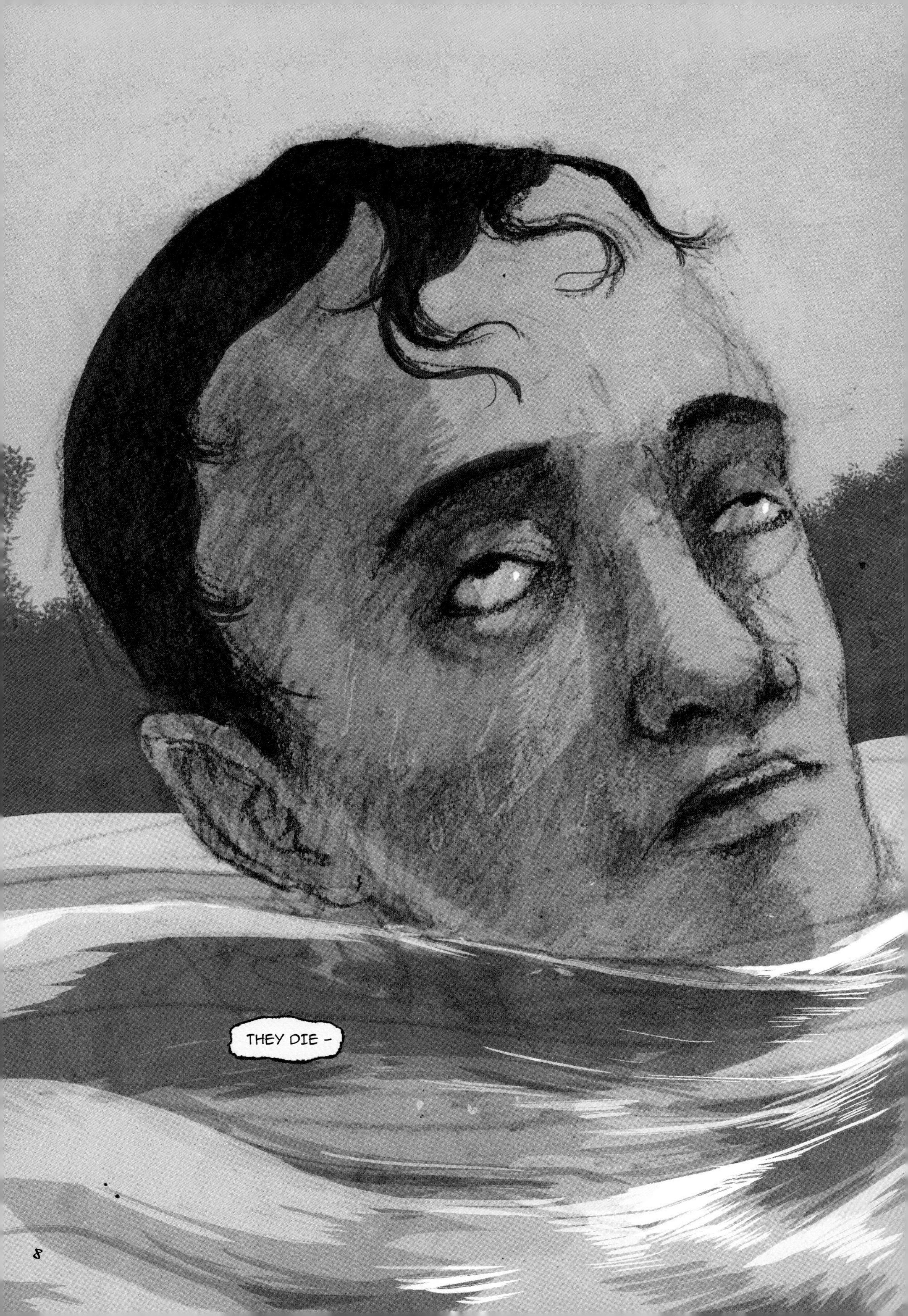
THEY DIE –

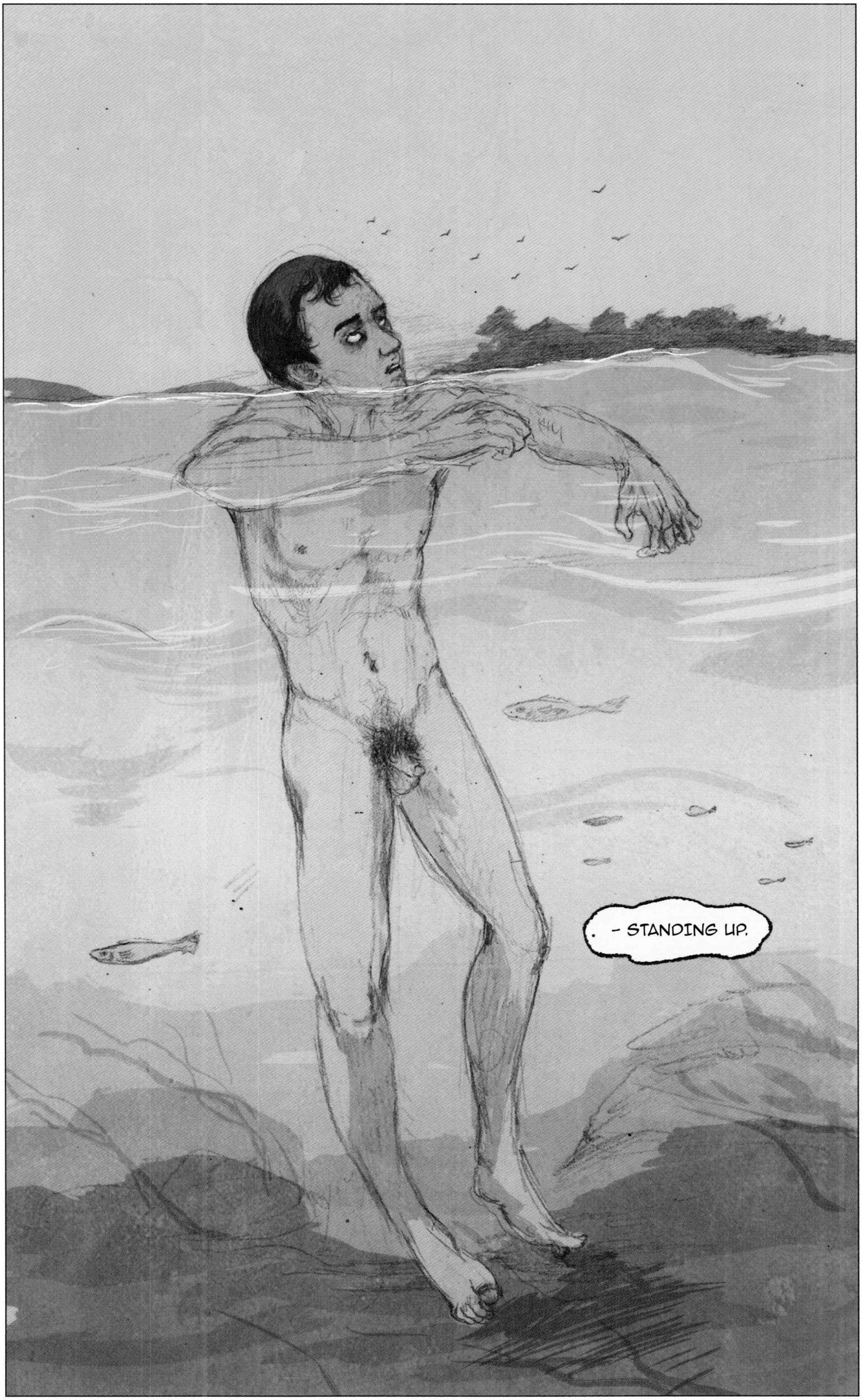
. - STANDING UP.

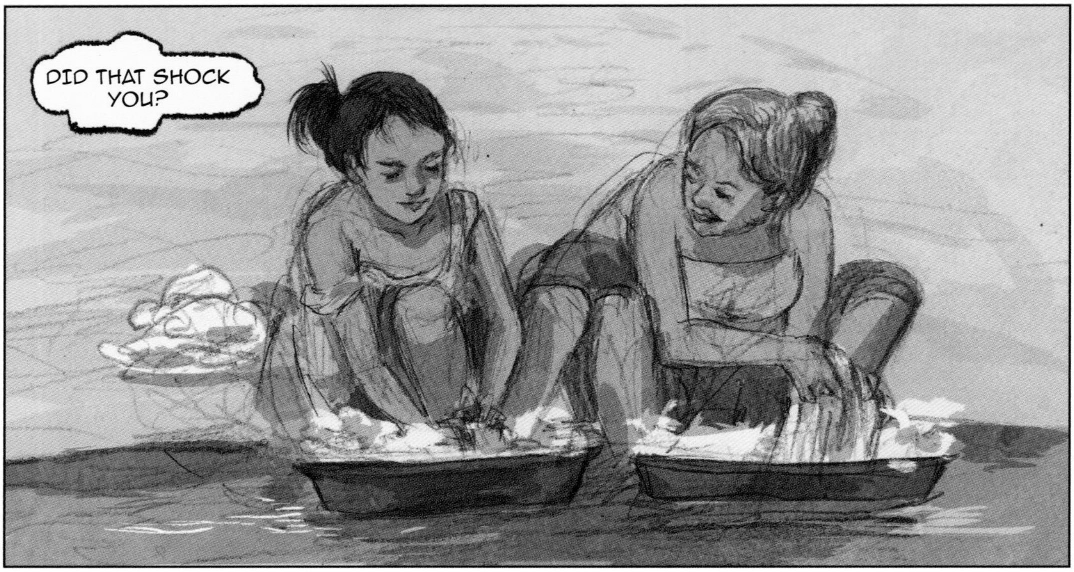
DID THAT SHOCK YOU?

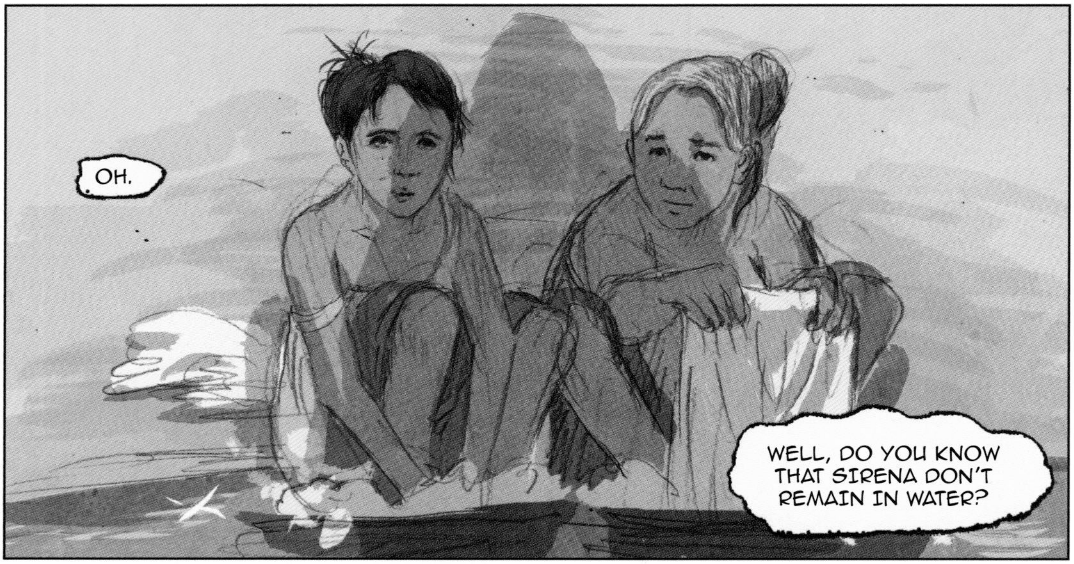
OH.
WELL, DO YOU KNOW THAT SIRENA DON'T REMAIN IN WATER?

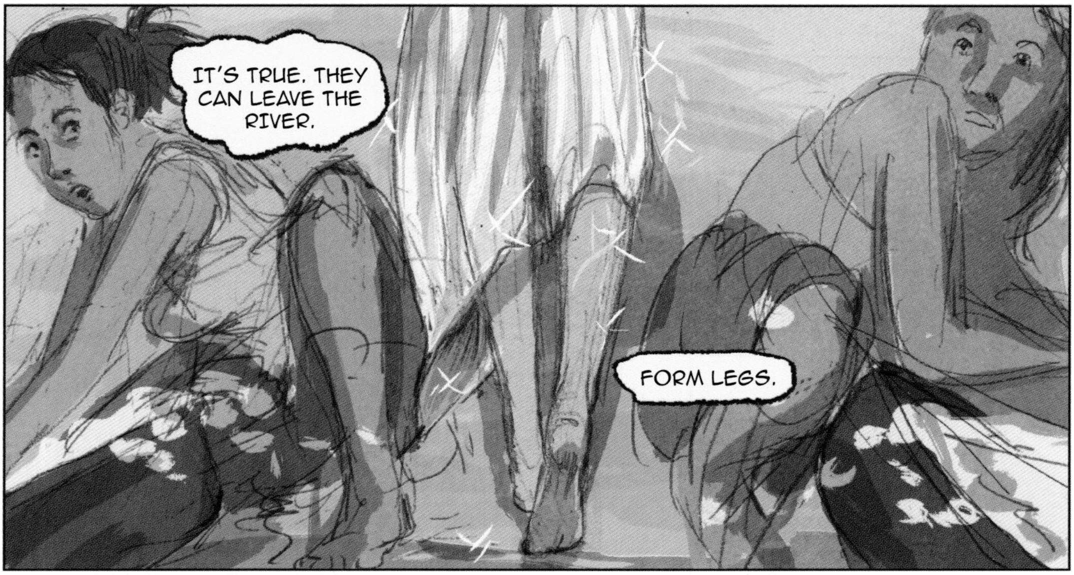
IT'S TRUE. THEY CAN LEAVE THE RIVER.
FORM LEGS.

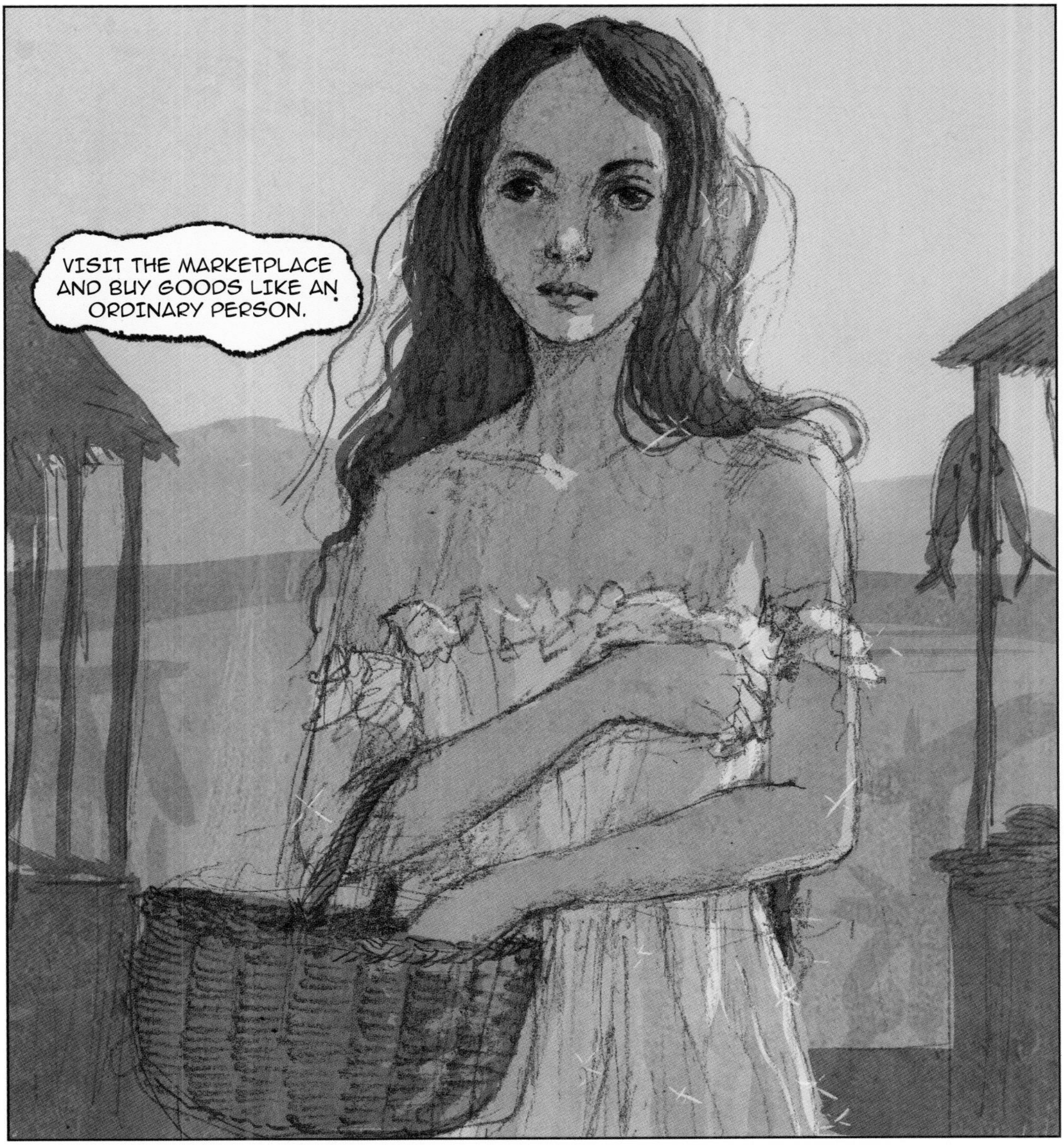
VISIT THE MARKETPLACE AND BUY GOODS LIKE AN ORDINARY PERSON.

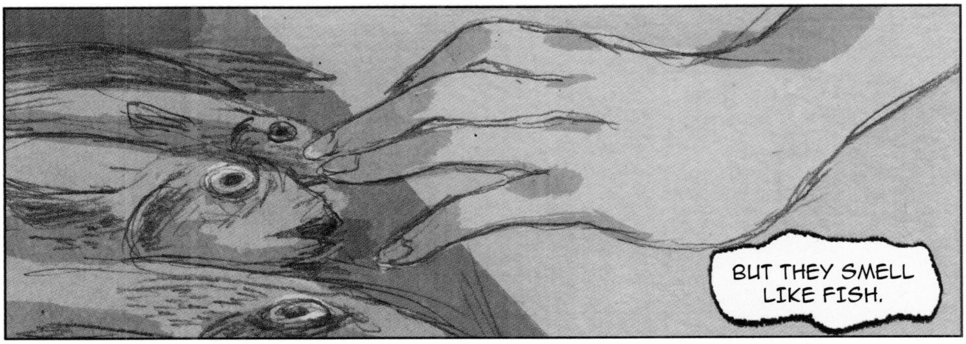
BUT THEY SMELL LIKE FISH.

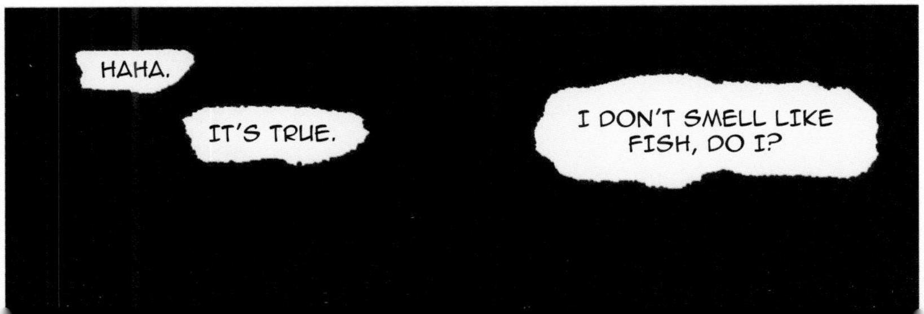
HAHA.
IT'S TRUE.
I DON'T SMELL LIKE FISH, DO I?

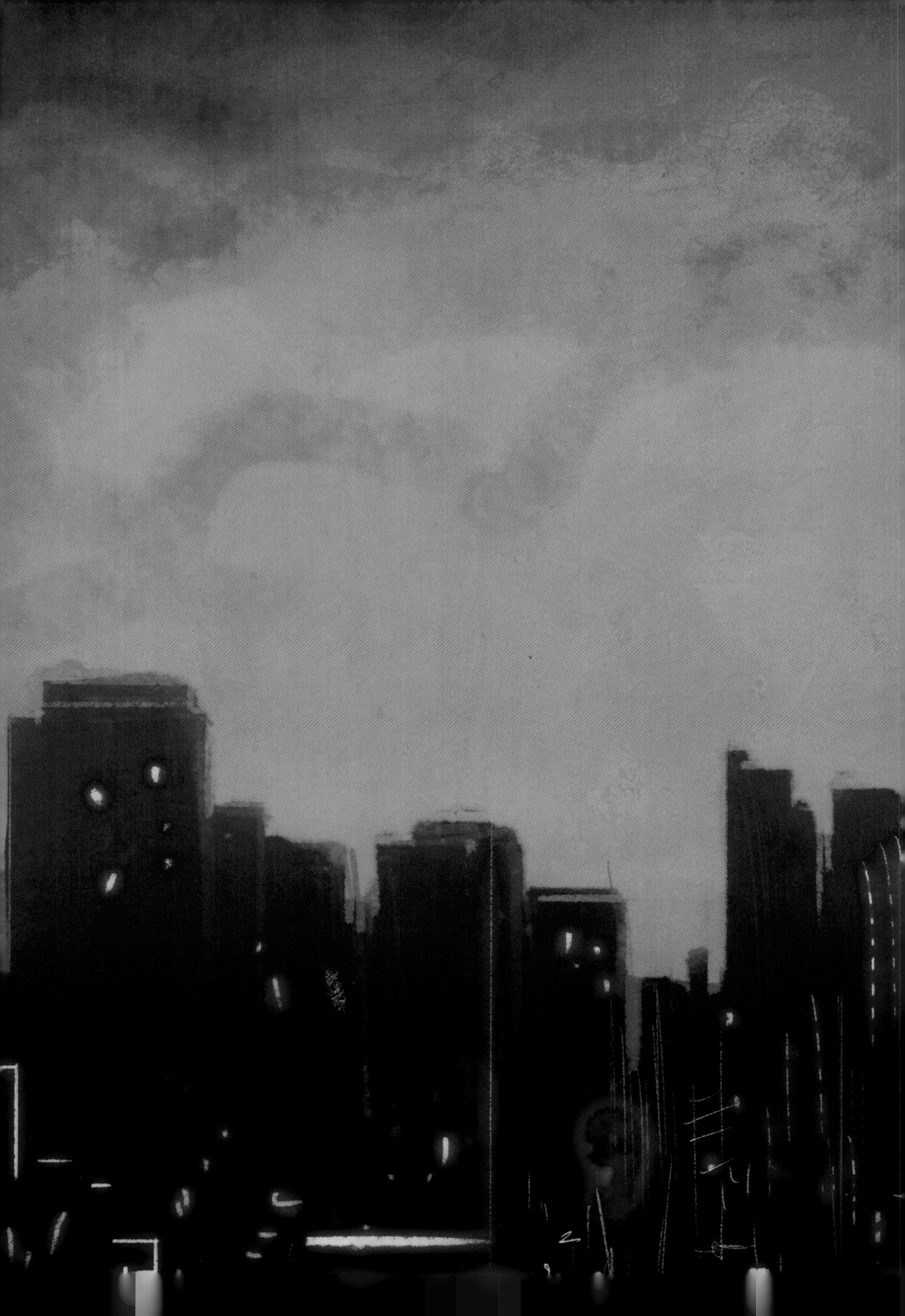

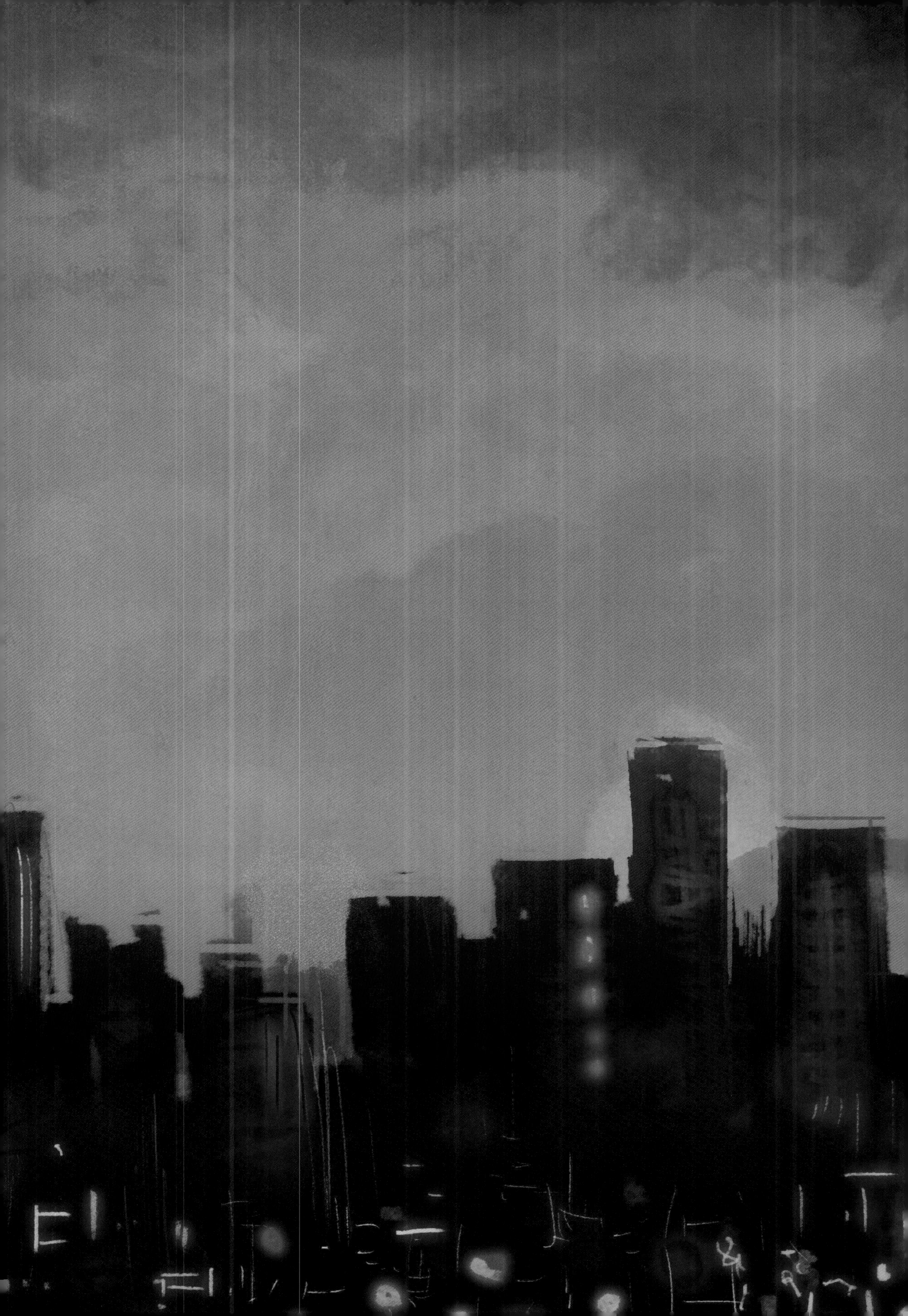

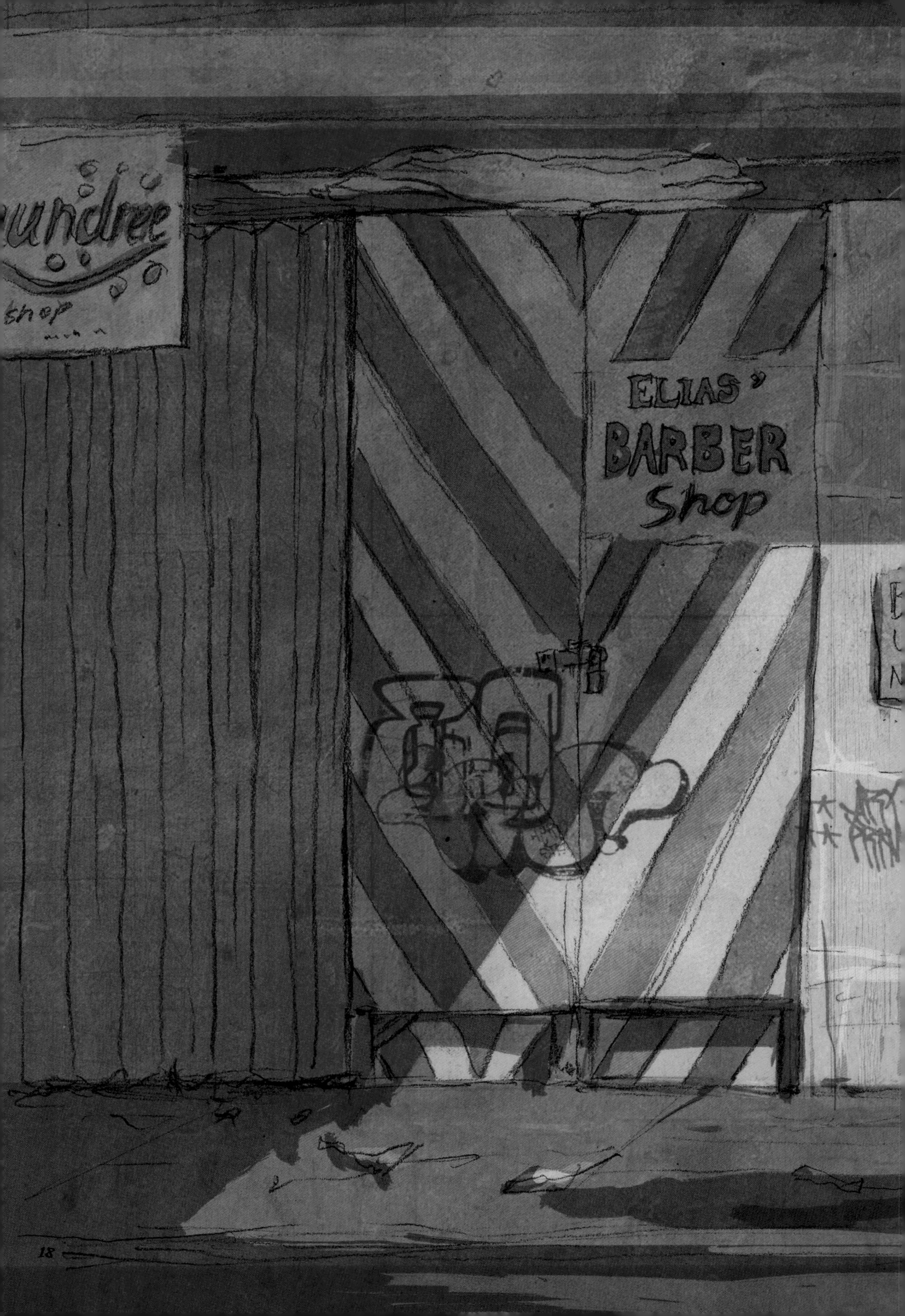
undree
shop
ELIAS'
BARBER
Shop

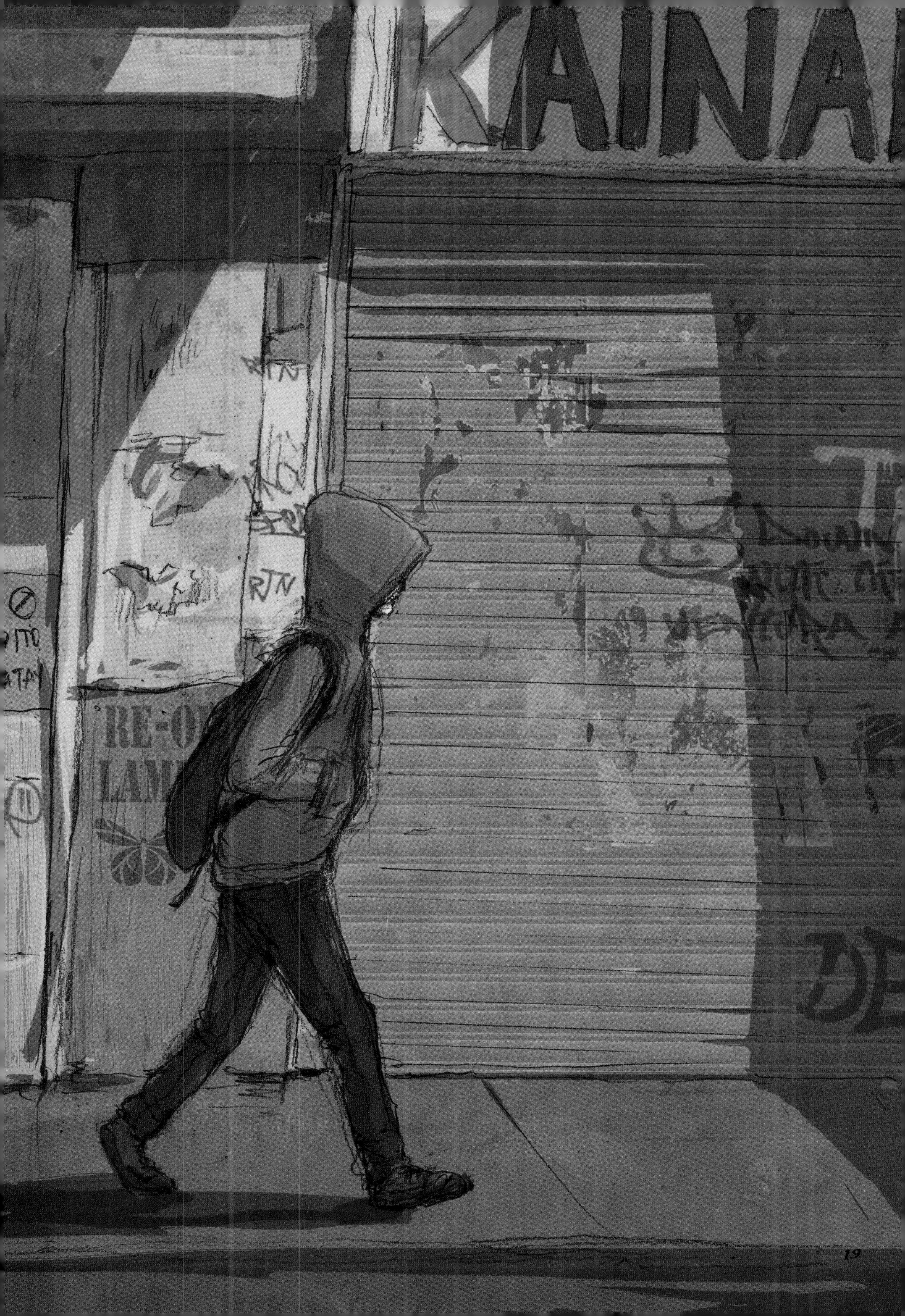

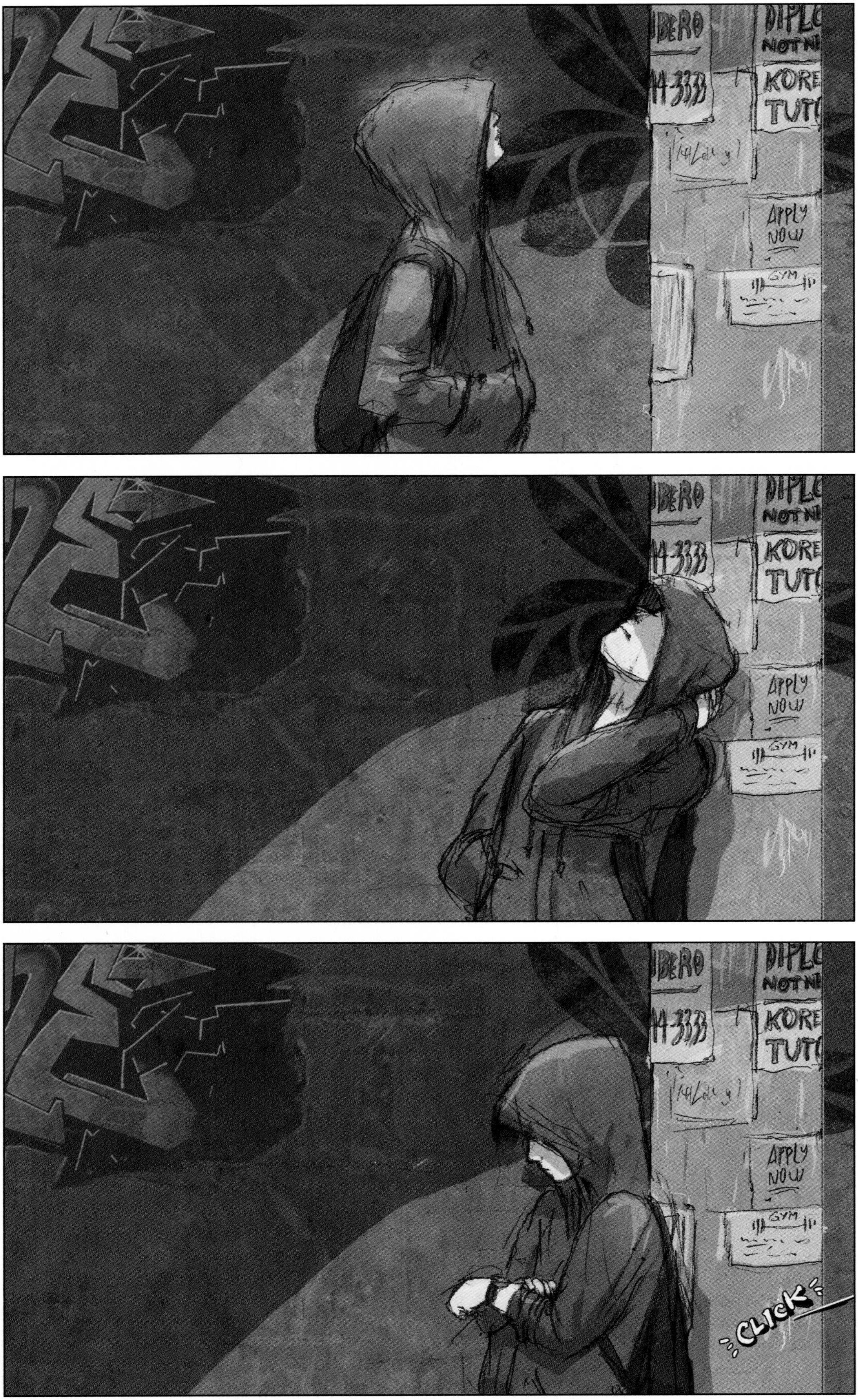
APPLY NOW
GYM
CLICK

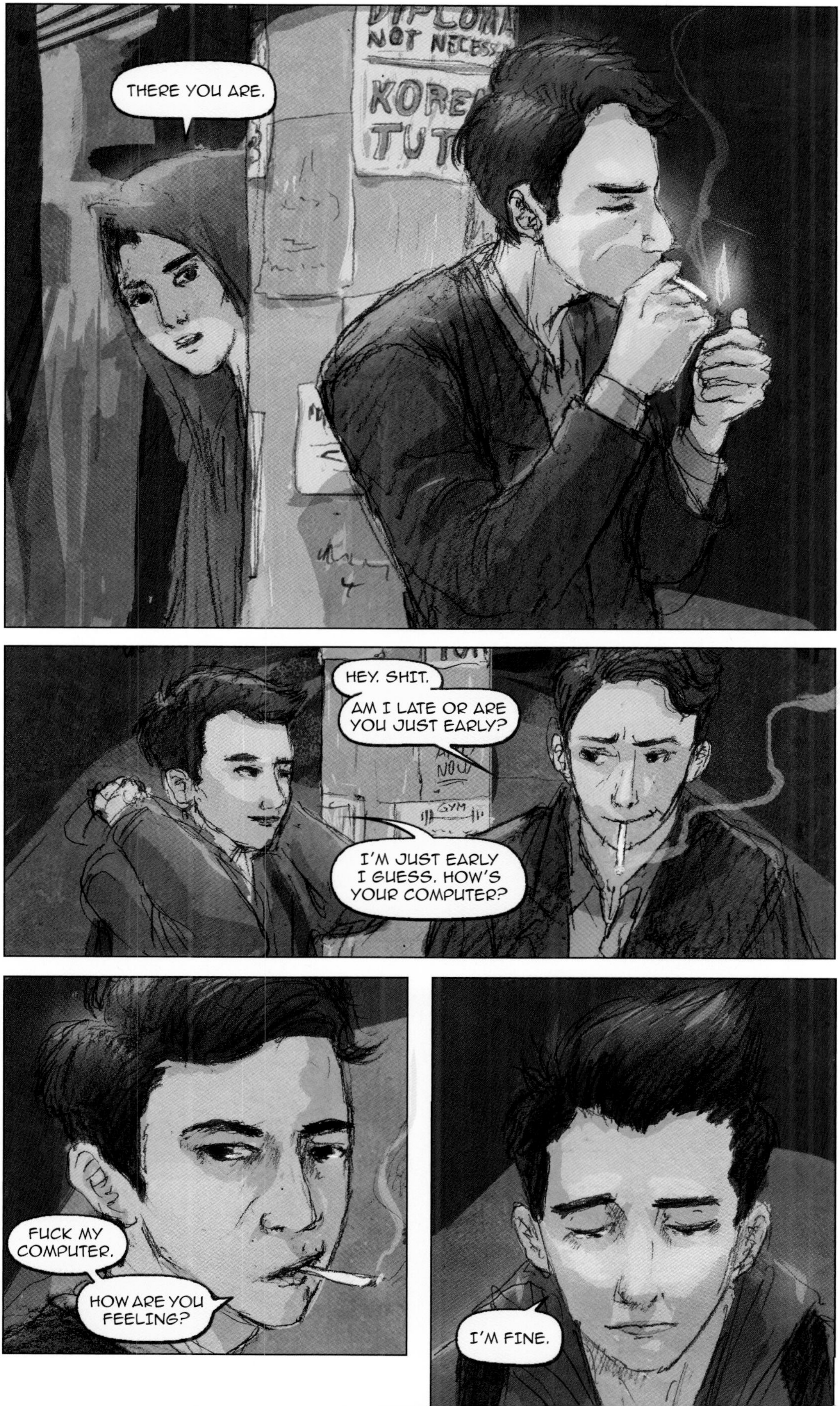
THERE YOU ARE.
HEY. SHIT.
AM I LATE OR ARE YOU JUST EARLY?
I'M JUST EARLY I GUESS. HOW'S YOUR COMPUTER?
FUCK MY COMPUTER.
HOW ARE YOU FEELING?
I'M FINE.

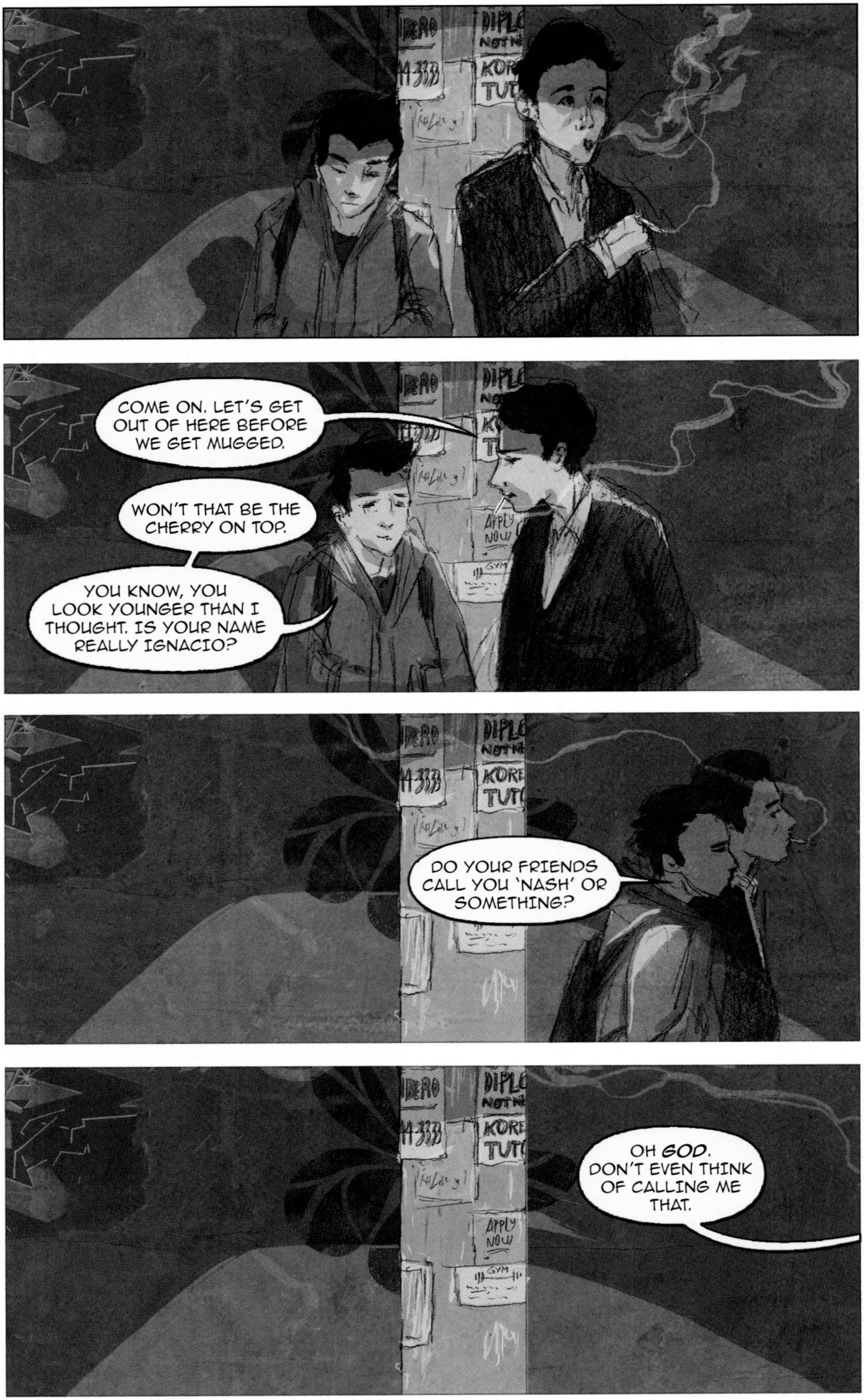
COME ON. LET'S GET OUT OF HERE BEFORE WE GET MUGGED.
WON'T THAT BE THE CHERRY ON TOP.
YOU KNOW, YOU LOOK YOUNGER THAN I THOUGHT. IS YOUR NAME REALLY IGNACIO?
DO YOUR FRIENDS CALL YOU 'NASH' OR SOMETHING?
OH *GOD*. DON'T EVEN THINK OF CALLING ME THAT.

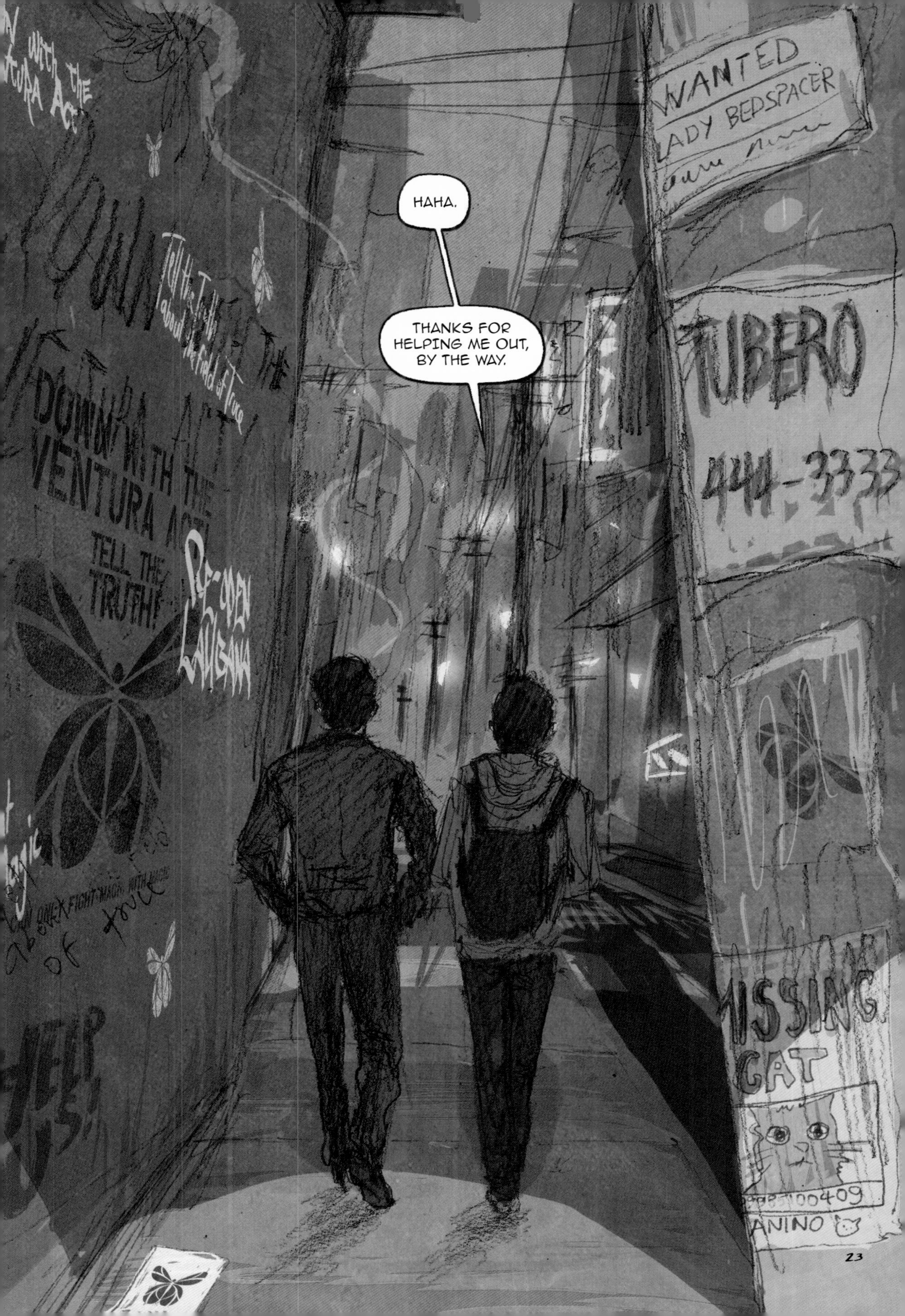
HAHA.
THANKS FOR HELPING ME OUT, BY THE WAY.
WANTED
LADY BEDSPACER
TUBERO
444-3333
DOWN WITH THE VENTURA ACT!
TELL THE TRUTH!
MISSING
CAT
ANINO

- IN THE NEST OF GRAY VEINS IS A WHITE SPHERE, LIT UP ON THE X-RAY PRINT LIKE A –

WITHIN 48 HOURS, THIS SPHERE – A BUD – WILL GROW LARGER, SLOWLY UNFOLDING...

...UNTIL IT BLOSSOMS INTO A FLOWER THAT BURSTS THROUGH TISSUE AND EPIDERMIS.

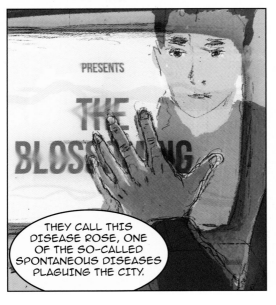

PRESENTS

THE BLOSSOMING

THEY CALL THIS DISEASE ROSE, ONE OF THE SO-CALLED SPONTANEOUS DISEASES PLAGUING THE CITY.

THIS HOSPITAL, SAN NICOLAS MEDICAL, HAS A GROWING COLLECTION OF ROSE BLOOMS, PRESERVED IN GLYCERIN.

NO TWO FLOWERS LOOK THE SAME. ONE, STRIKINGLY BEAUTIFUL, RESEMBLES A CHRYSANTHEMUM.

SURVIVAL FROM ROSE DEPENDS ON WHERE THE BUD APPEARS, AND HOW SOON IT IS DETECTED.

ROSE #457 — PATIENT Z. 11 YO, F, BRAIN

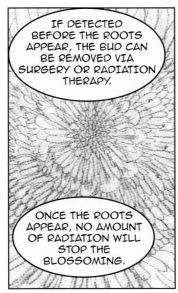

IF DETECTED BEFORE THE ROOTS APPEAR, THE BUD CAN BE REMOVED VIA SURGERY OR RADIATION THERAPY.

ONCE THE ROOTS APPEAR, NO AMOUNT OF RADIATION WILL STOP THE BLOSSOMING.

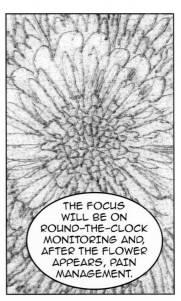

THE FOCUS WILL BE ON ROUND-THE-CLOCK MONITORING AND, AFTER THE FLOWER APPEARS, PAIN MANAGEMENT.

AH, KID. WHY BOTHER WATCHING THIS DEPRESSING DRIVEL?

MOST CASES SADLY END UP IN HOSPICES AND PALLIATIVE CARE, OR IN VOLUNTARY EUTHANASIA.

I THOUGHT THEY HAD SOMETHING NEW TO SAY.

YOU WANT TO SEE IT?

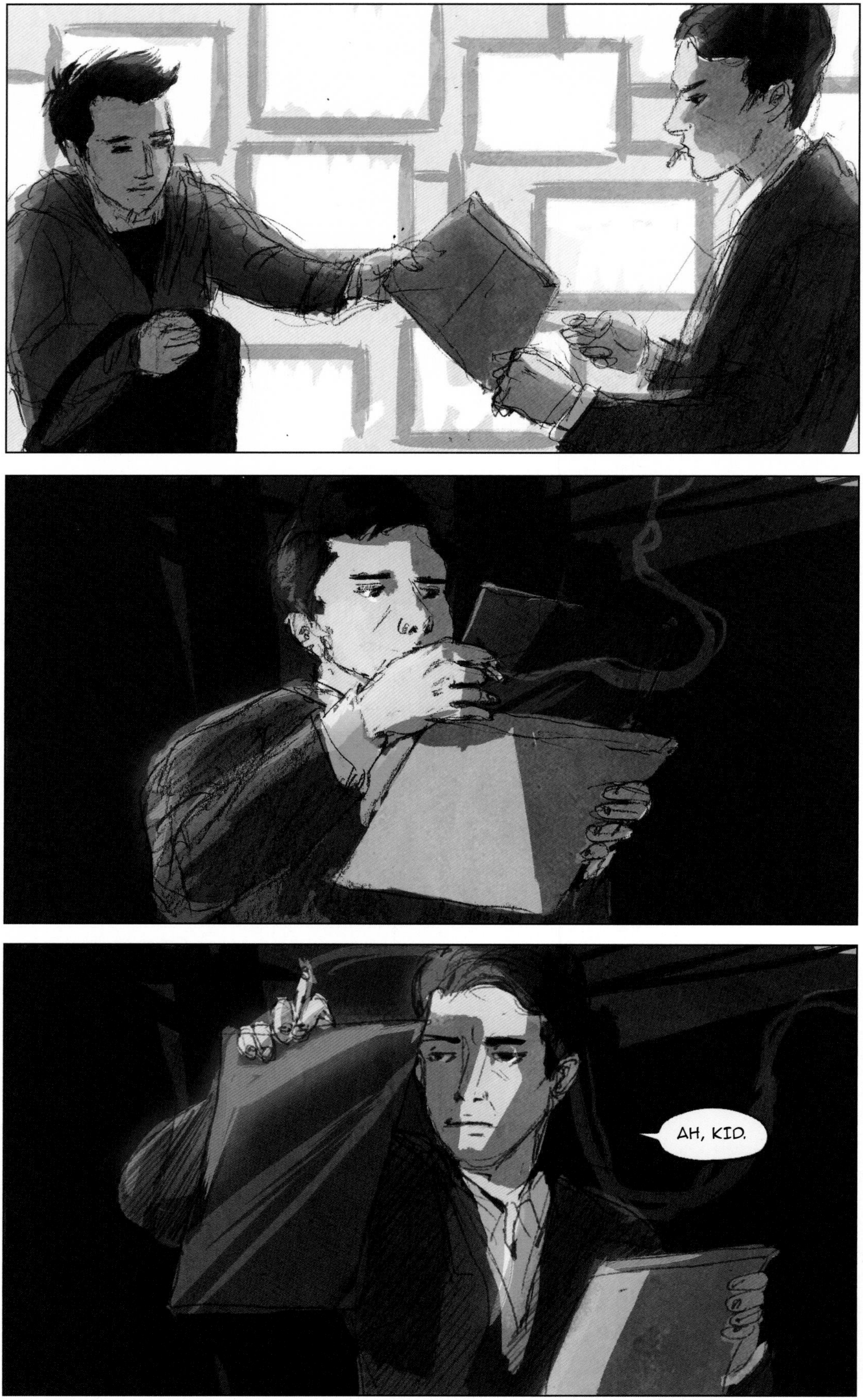
AH, KID.

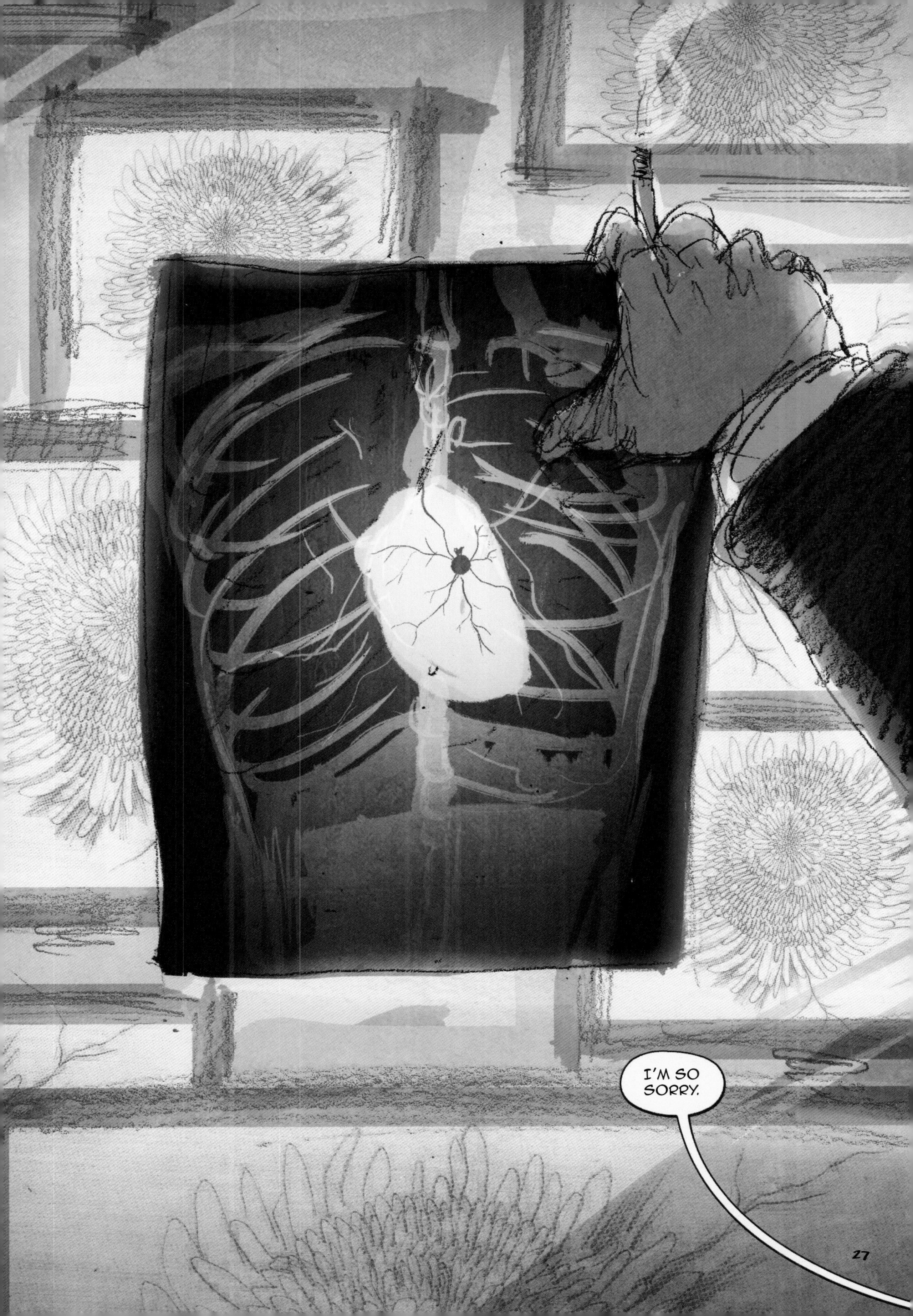
I'M SO SORRY.

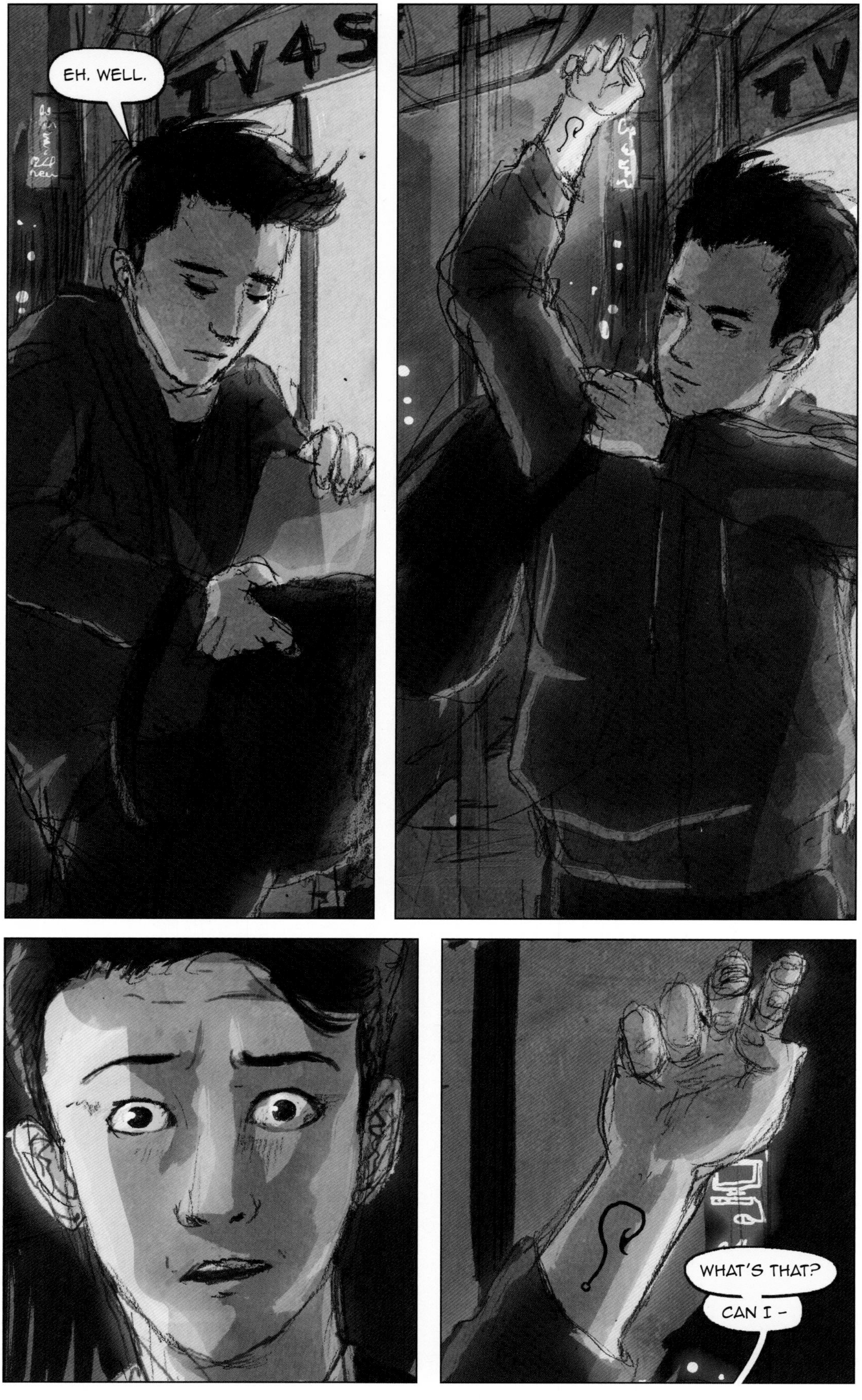
EH. WELL.
WHAT'S THAT?
CAN I -

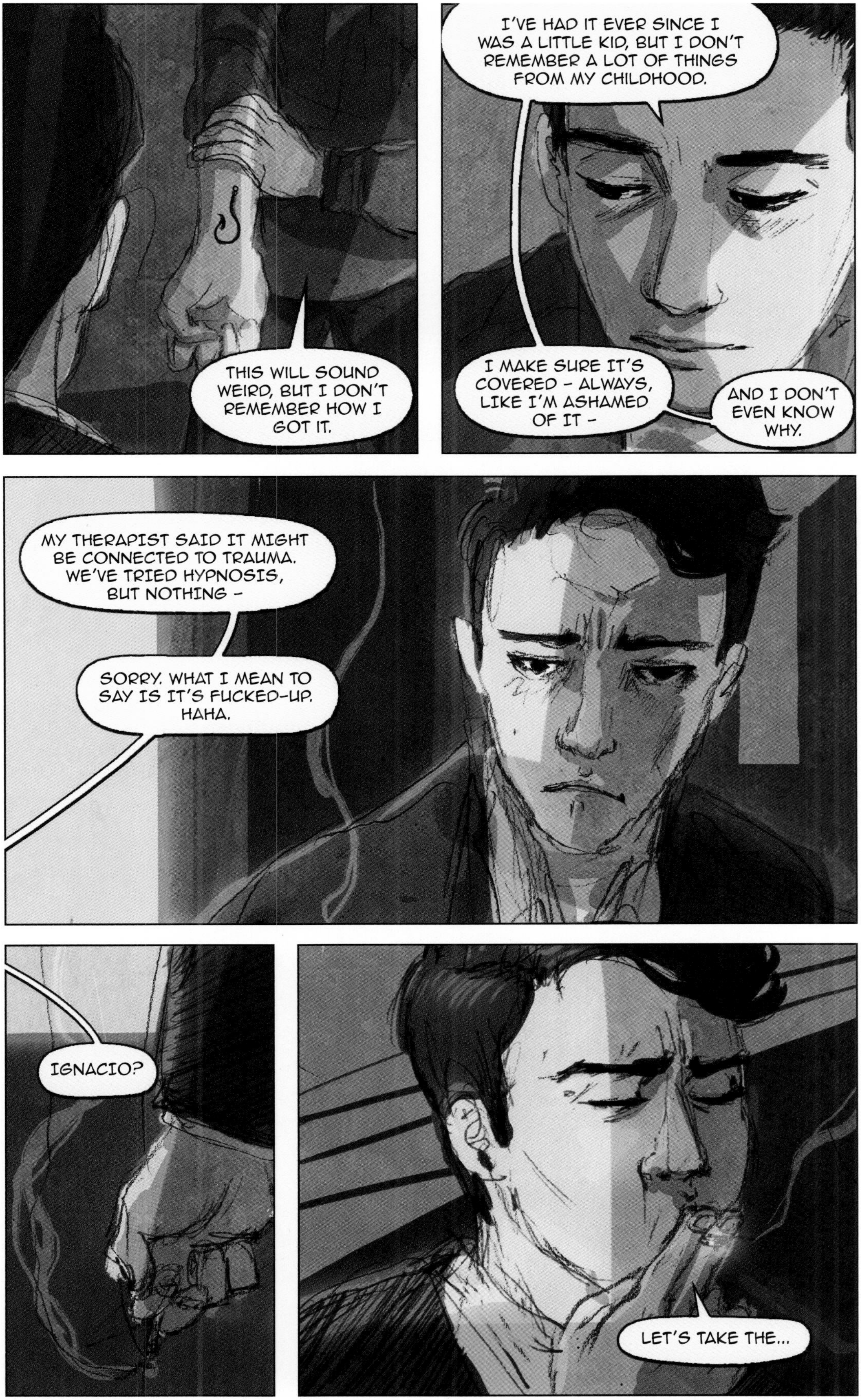
THIS WILL SOUND WEIRD, BUT I DON'T REMEMBER HOW I GOT IT.
I'VE HAD IT EVER SINCE I WAS A LITTLE KID, BUT I DON'T REMEMBER A LOT OF THINGS FROM MY CHILDHOOD.
I MAKE SURE IT'S COVERED – ALWAYS, LIKE I'M ASHAMED OF IT –
AND I DON'T EVEN KNOW WHY.
MY THERAPIST SAID IT MIGHT BE CONNECTED TO TRAUMA. WE'VE TRIED HYPNOSIS, BUT NOTHING –
SORRY. WHAT I MEAN TO SAY IS IT'S FUCKED-UP. HAHA.
IGNACIO?
LET'S TAKE THE...

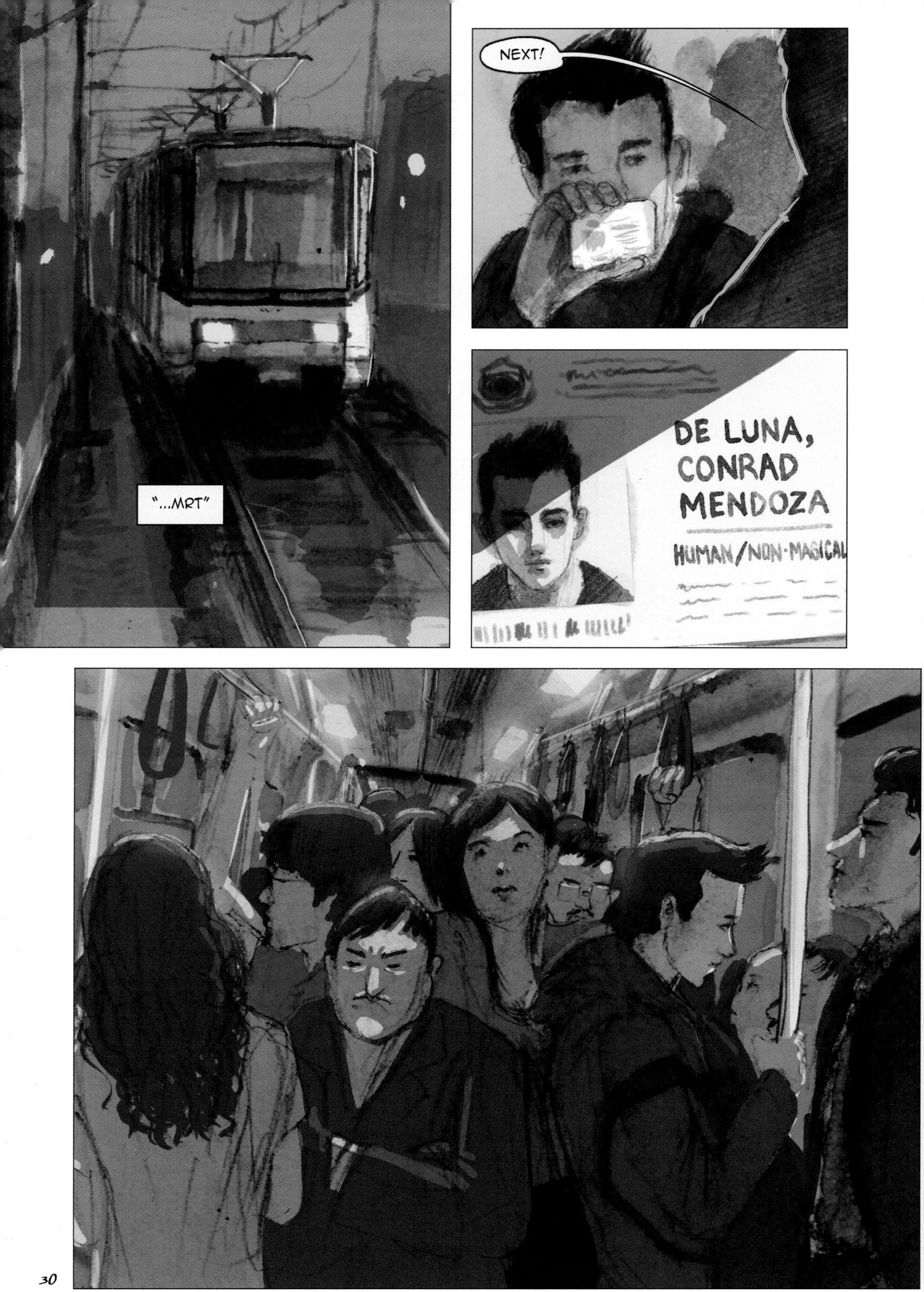
"...MRT"
NEXT!
DE LUNA,
CONRAD
MENDOZA
HUMAN/NON-MAGICAL

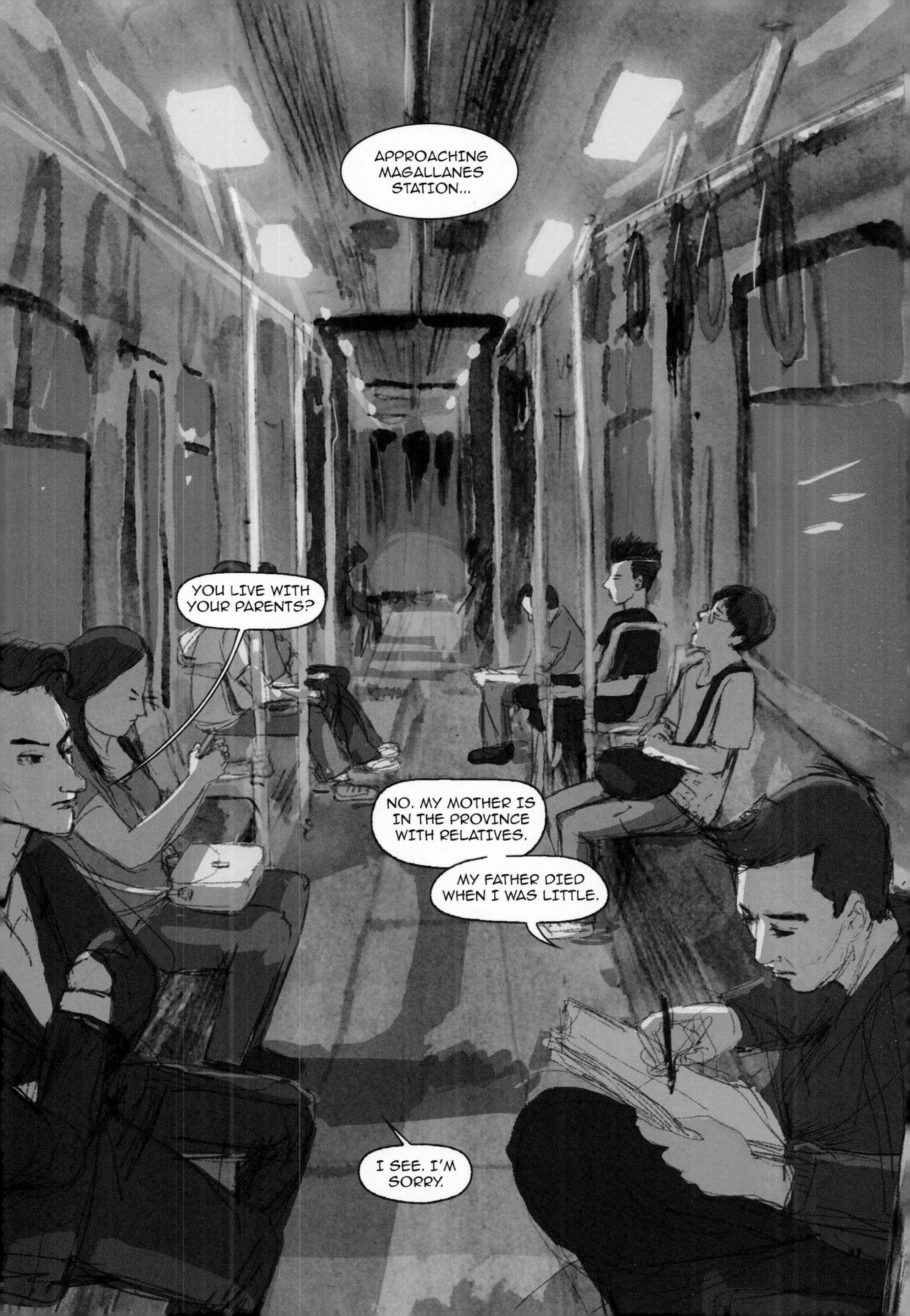
APPROACHING MAGALLANES STATION...
YOU LIVE WITH YOUR PARENTS?
NO. MY MOTHER IS IN THE PROVINCE WITH RELATIVES.
MY FATHER DIED WHEN I WAS LITTLE.
I SEE. I'M SORRY.

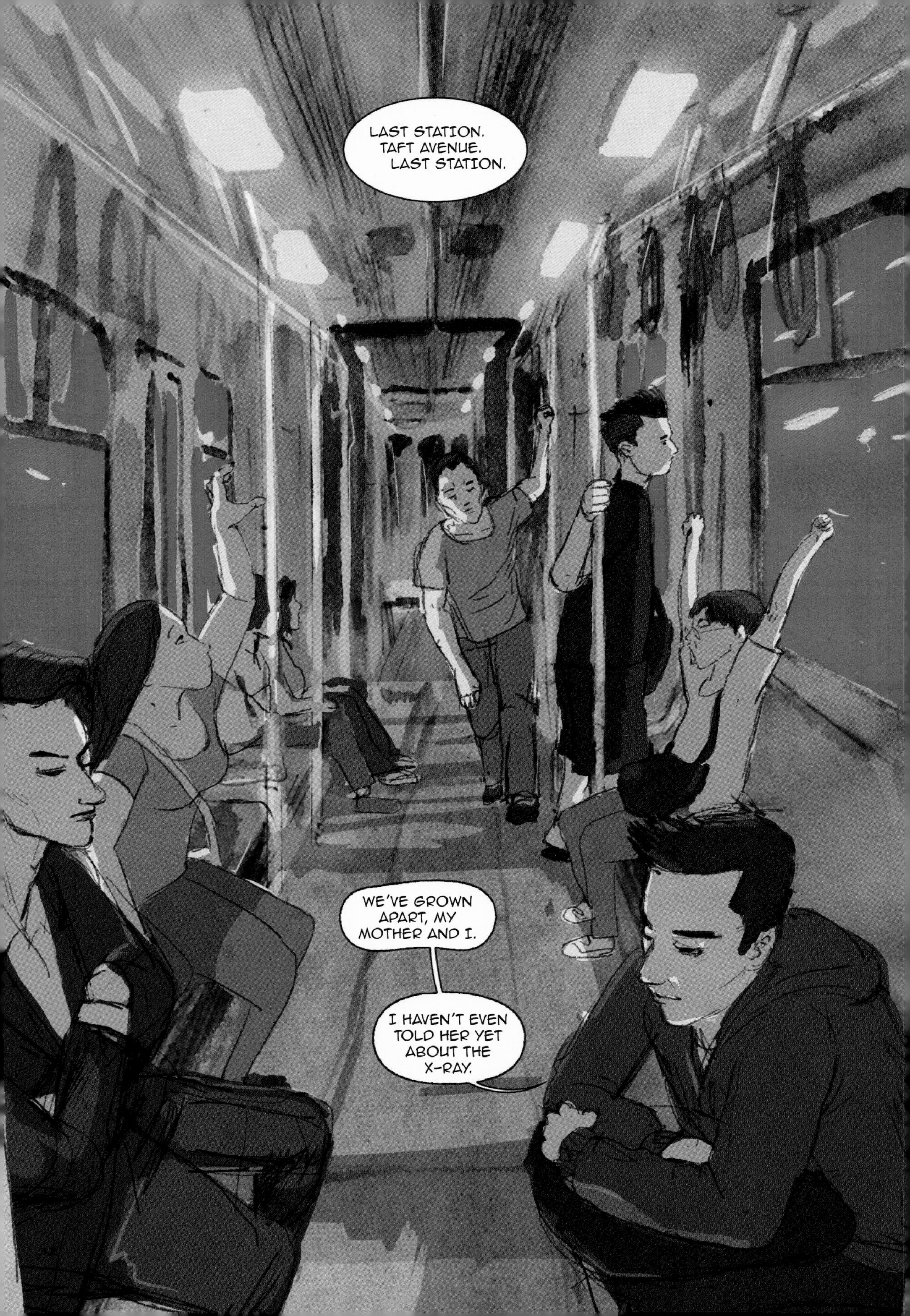
LAST STATION. TAFT AVENUE. LAST STATION.
WE'VE GROWN APART, MY MOTHER AND I.
I HAVEN'T EVEN TOLD HER YET ABOUT THE X-RAY.

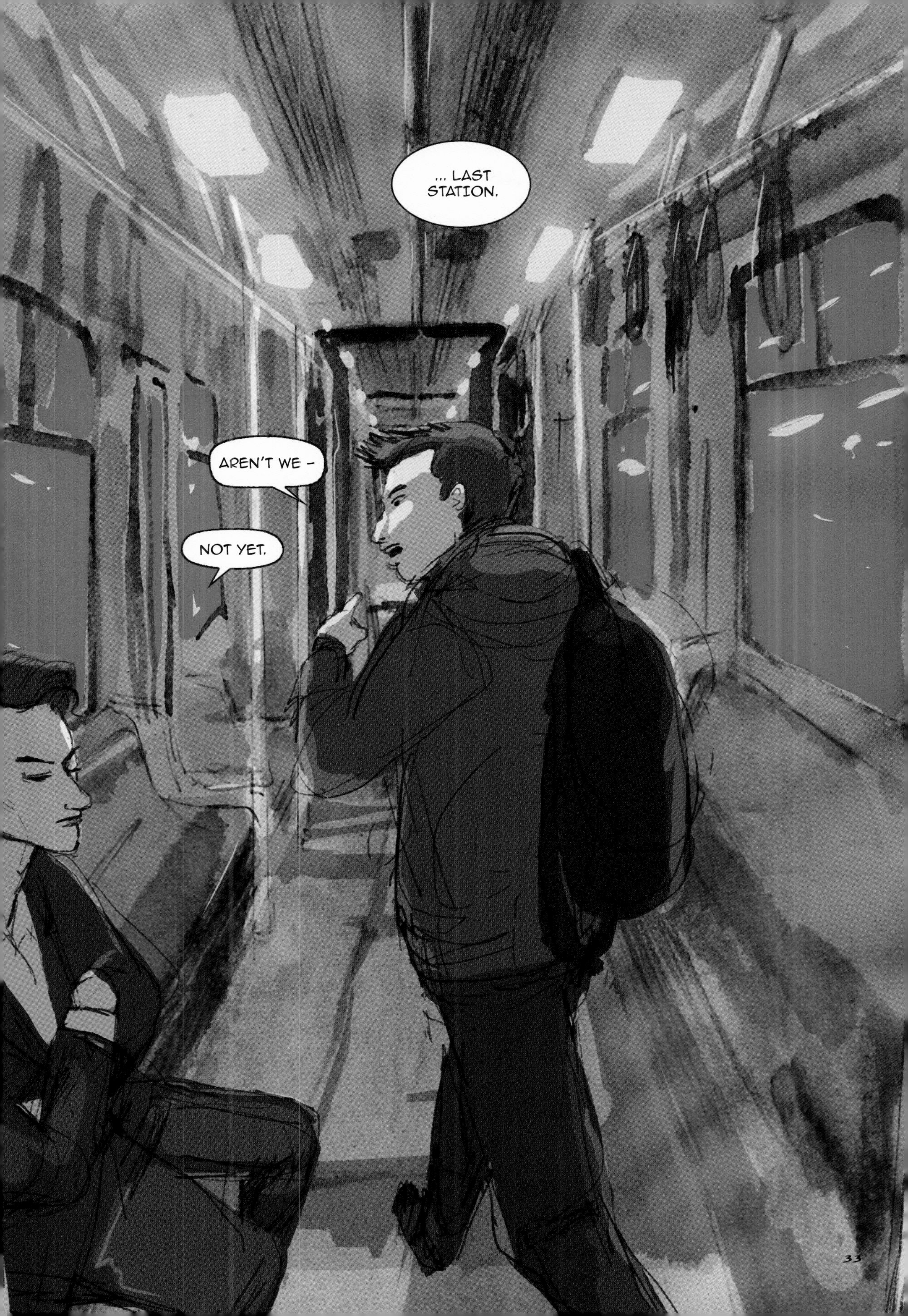
... LAST STATION.
AREN'T WE -
NOT YET.

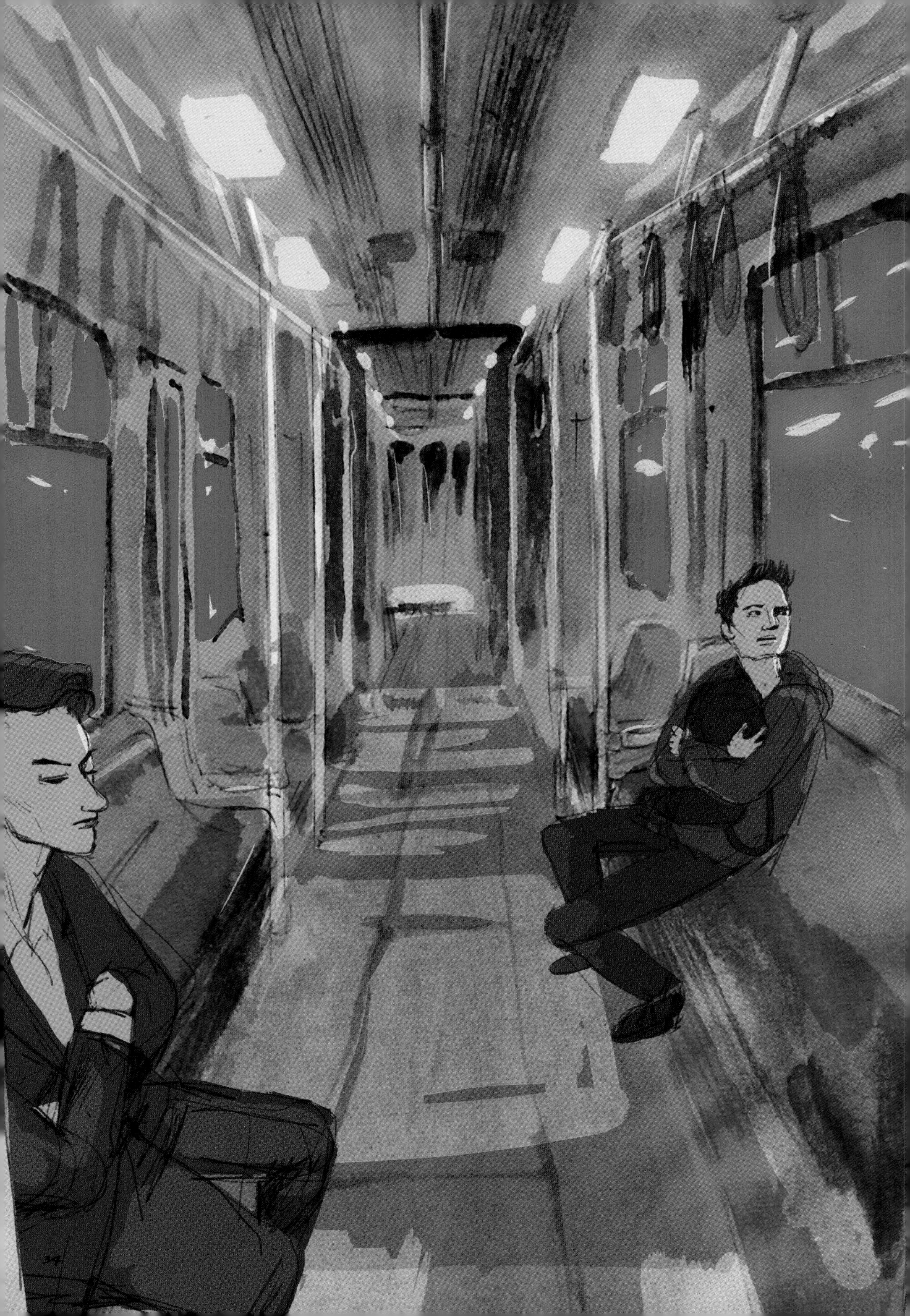

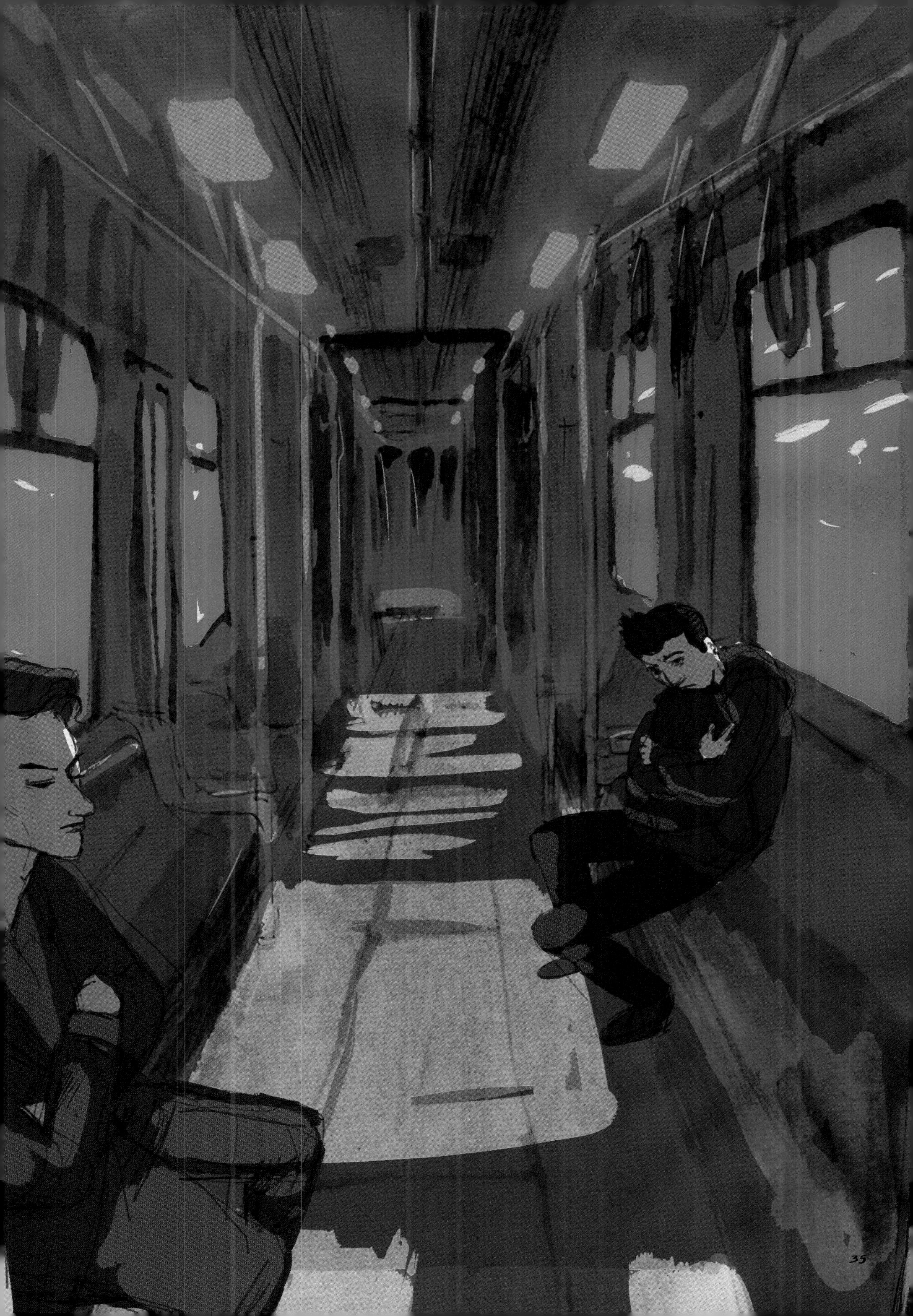

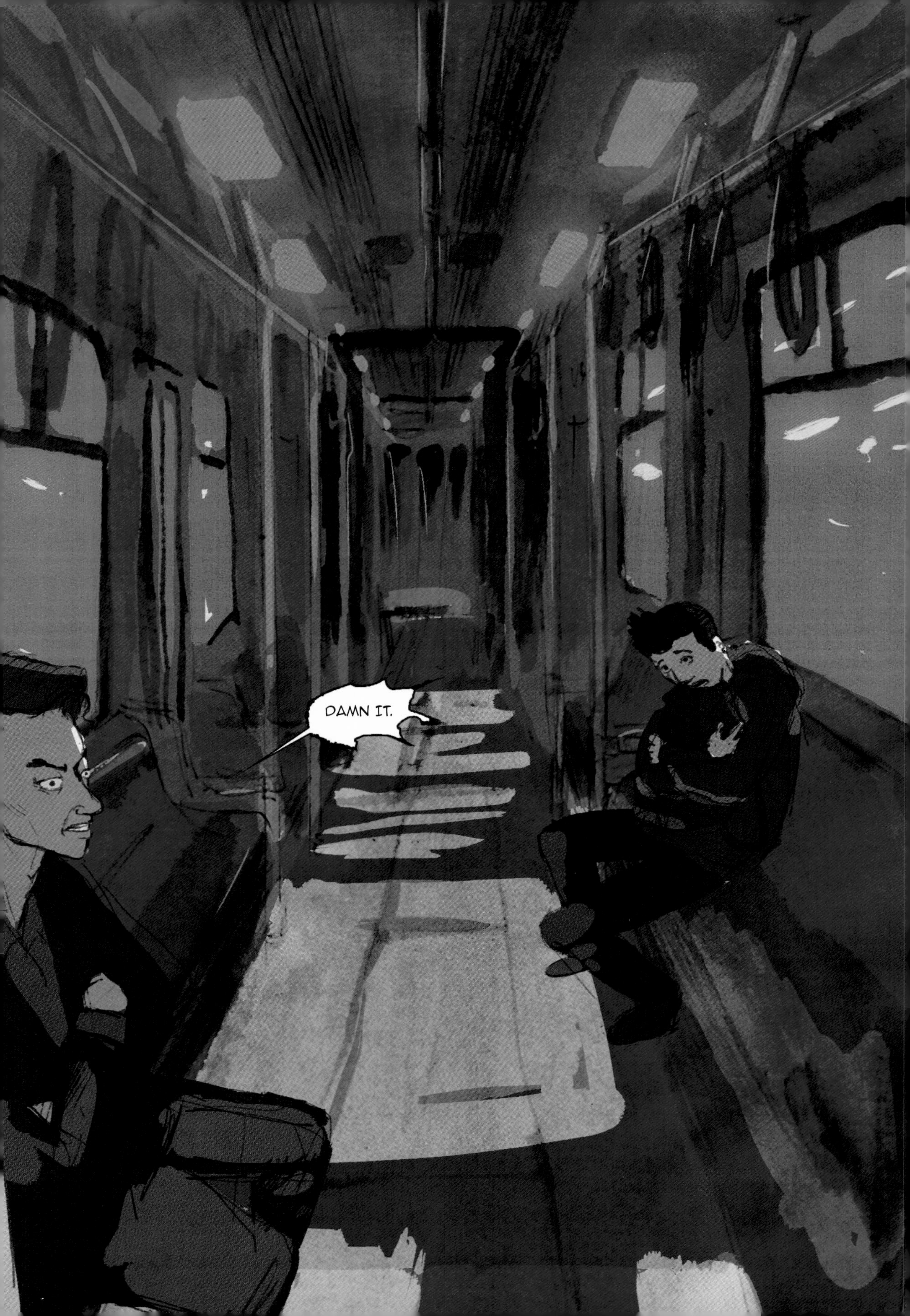
DAMN IT.

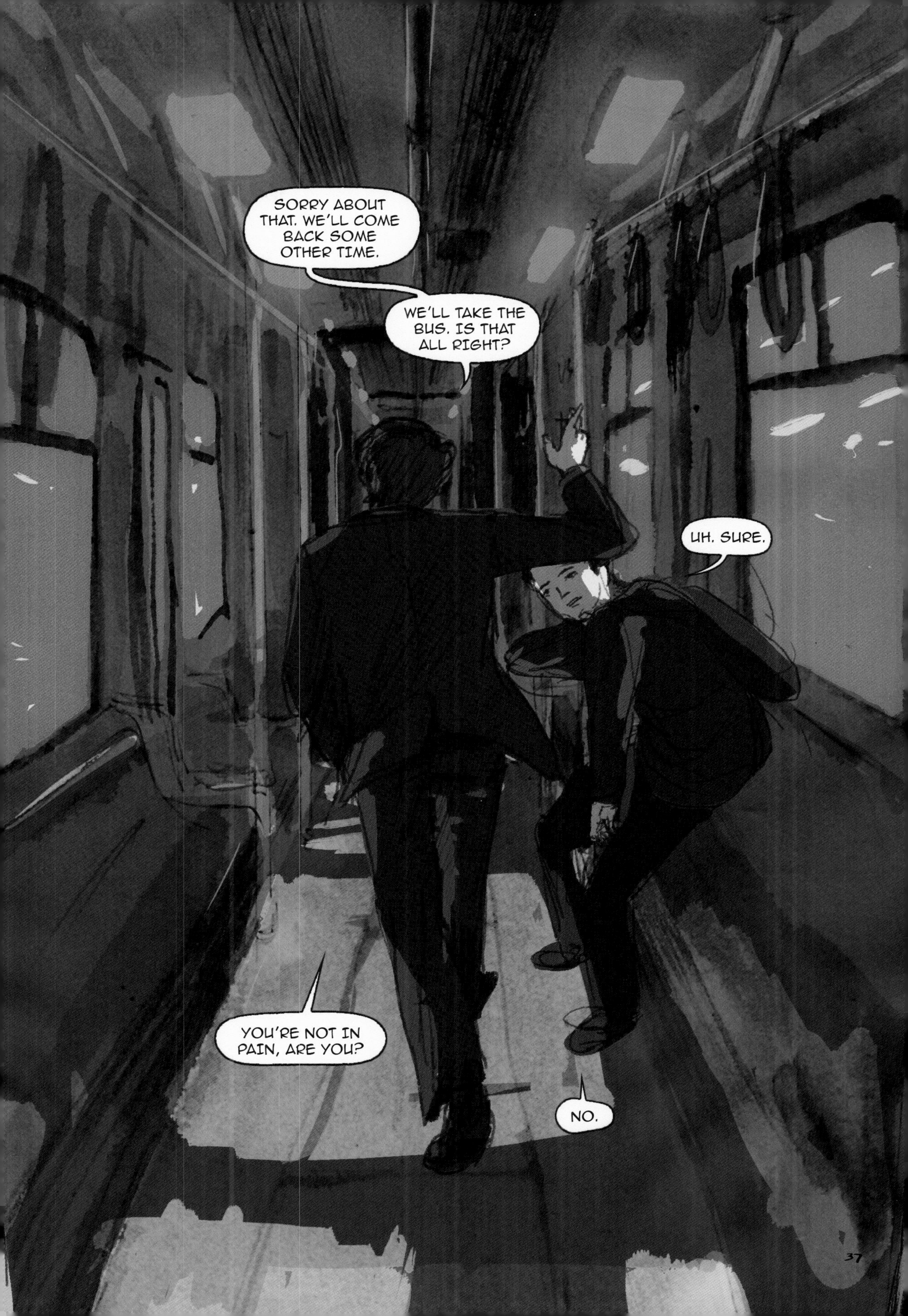
SORRY ABOUT THAT. WE'LL COME BACK SOME OTHER TIME.
WE'LL TAKE THE BUS. IS THAT ALL RIGHT?
UH. SURE.
YOU'RE NOT IN PAIN, ARE YOU?
NO.

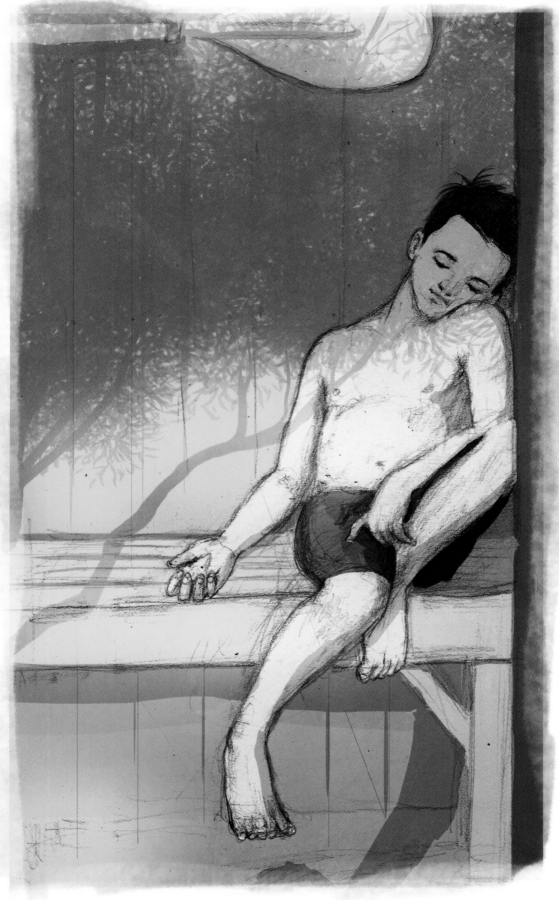

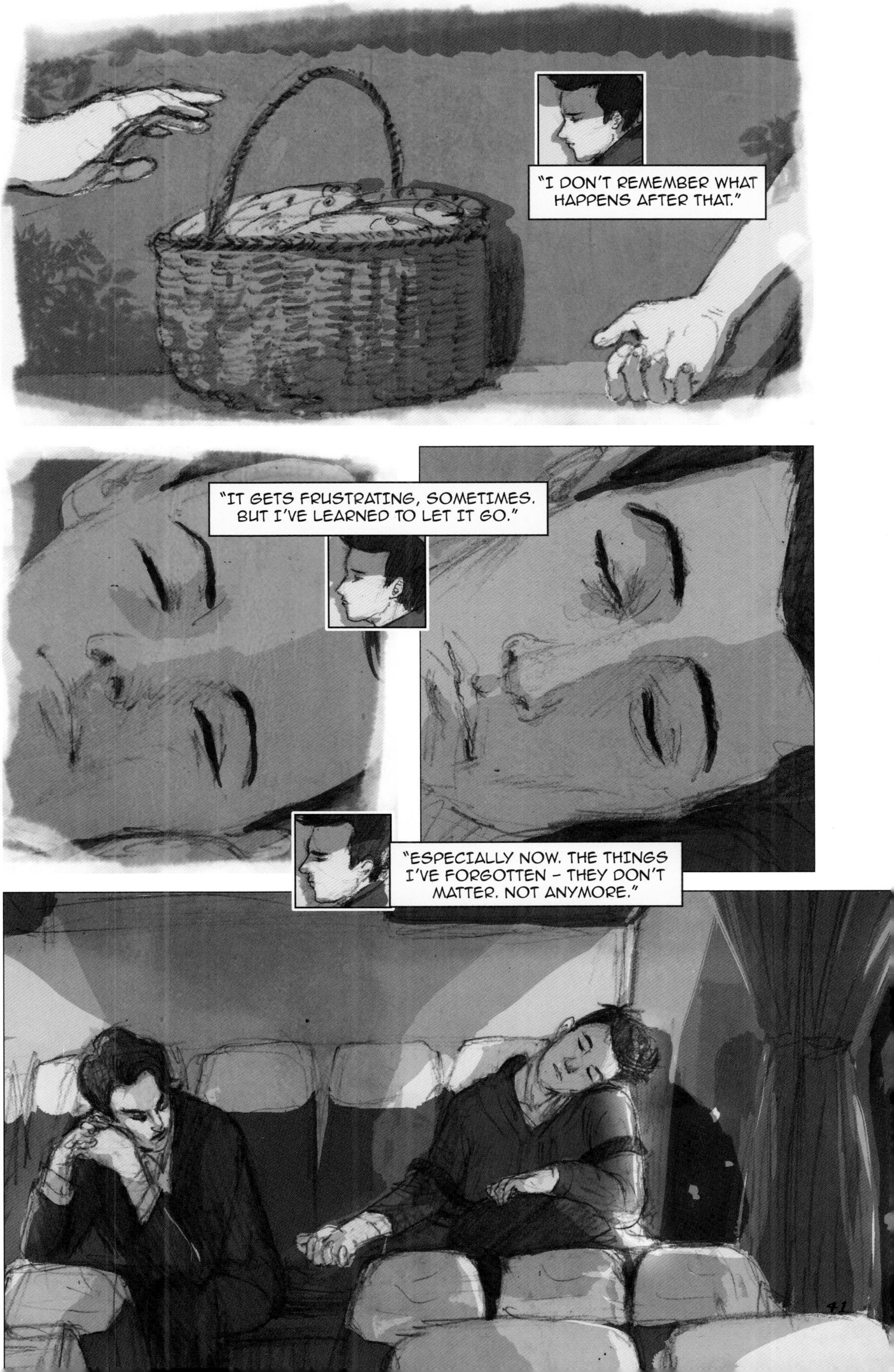
"I DON'T REMEMBER WHAT HAPPENS AFTER THAT."
"IT GETS FRUSTRATING, SOMETIMES. BUT I'VE LEARNED TO LET IT GO."
"ESPECIALLY NOW. THE THINGS I'VE FORGOTTEN – THEY DON'T MATTER. NOT ANYMORE."

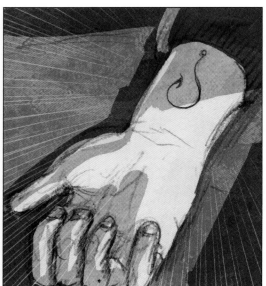

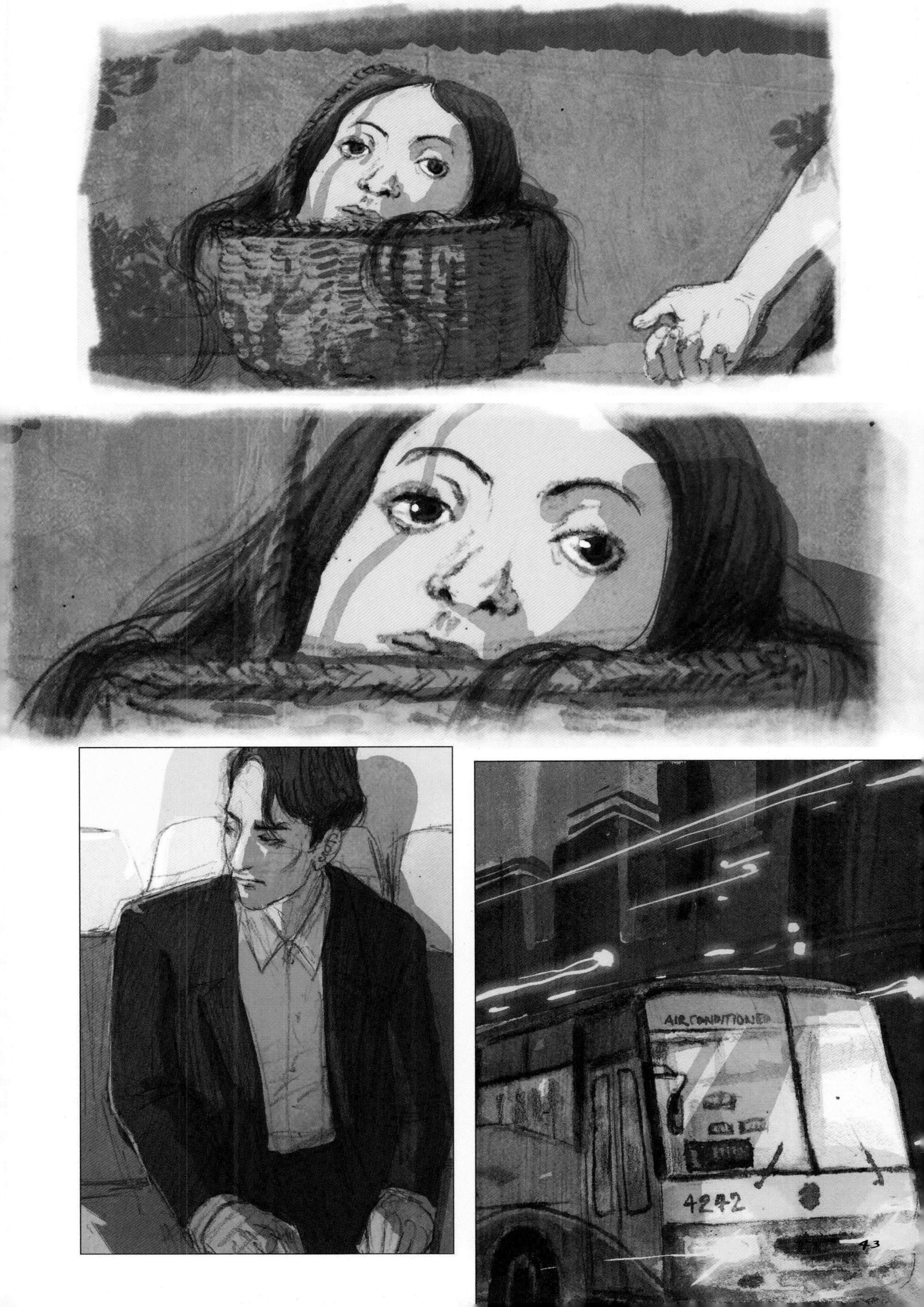
AIR CONDITIONED
4242

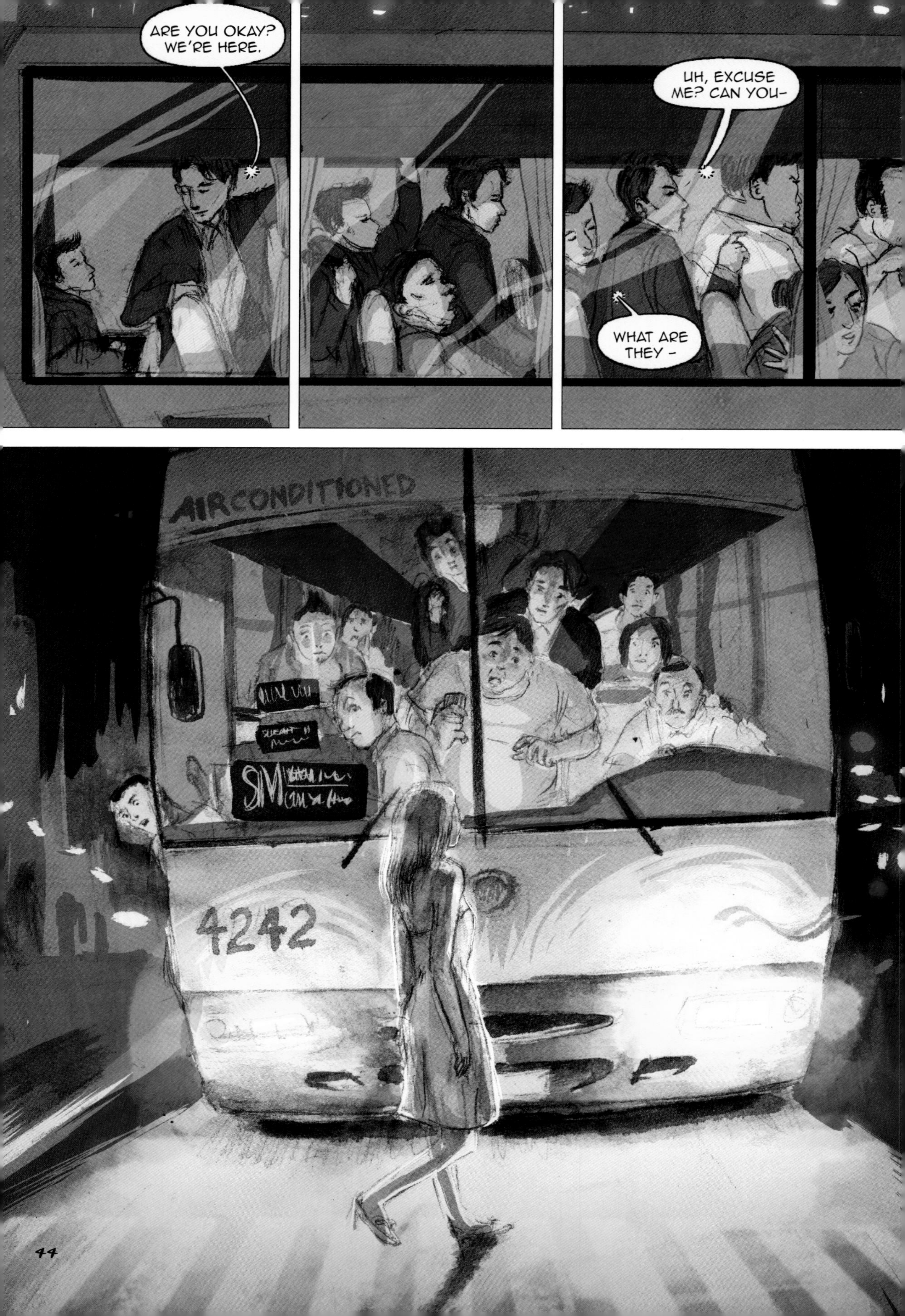
ARE YOU OKAY? WE'RE HERE.
UH, EXCUSE ME? CAN YOU-
WHAT ARE THEY -
AIRCONDITIONED
4242

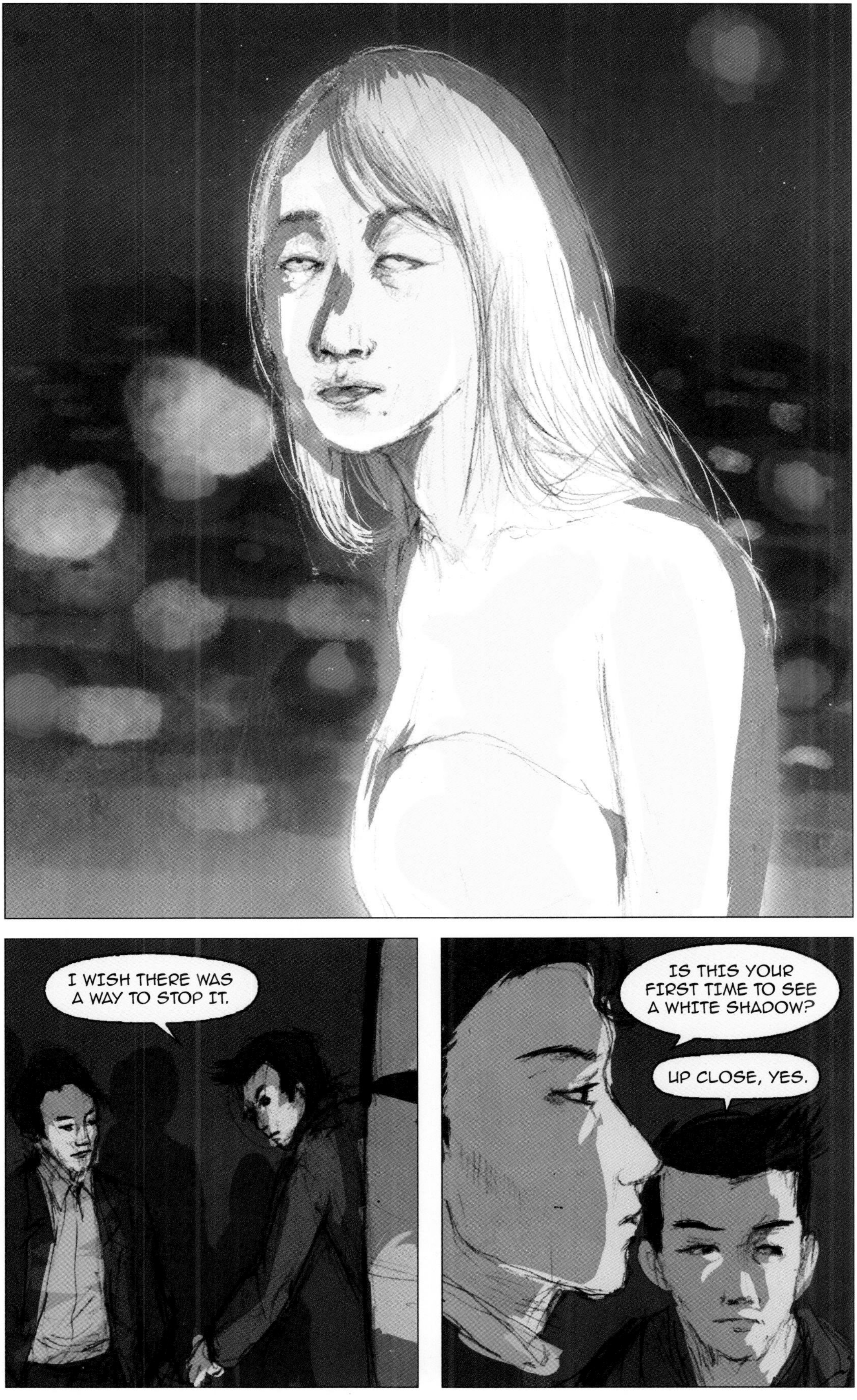
I WISH THERE WAS A WAY TO STOP IT.
IS THIS YOUR FIRST TIME TO SEE A WHITE SHADOW?
UP CLOSE, YES.

YOU CAN'T REALLY STOP THEM.

STOPPING THEM – IT'S LIKE ASKING A CANCER CELL TO STOP DIVIDING. AND IF YOU KILL IT, THE HOST DIES.

I WONDER WHO SHE IS. THE SHADOW'S HOST.

SHE'S WEARING A DRESS. SHE'S PROBABLY IN A PARTY.

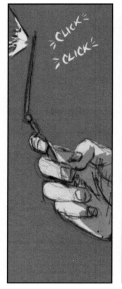

CLICK
CLICK

WHAT IN THE WORLD ARE THOSE PEOPLE DOING?

YOU HAVEN'T SEEN THAT DONE BEFORE?

THERE IS A FACEBOOK PAGE FOR THIS. AND A TWITTER ACCOUNT. FIND HOST.

YOU UPLOAD THE PHOTO, WITH THE DATE, TIME, PLACE.

PEOPLE VISIT THE PAGES EVERY DAY, HOPING THEY WON'T FIND A SHADOW THAT LOOKS LIKE THEM.

WELL – WHATEVER HAPPENS TO THE SHADOW HAPPENS TO THE HOST BODY, RIGHT?

AND IF THEY DO?

SOME OF THEM HUNT DOWN THEIR WHITE SHADOWS AND TIE THEM DOWN IN A SAFE PLACE.

FEEDING IT REGULARLY SO THE HOST WON'T DIE.

THERE HAVE BEEN STORIES OF WHITE SHADOWS DISAPPEARING AFTER WEEKS, SO THAT GIVES PEOPLE HOPE.

AND THESE STORIES HAVE BEEN VERIFIED?

WELL, NO. I DON'T THINK SO.

WELL, AT LEAST IT'S BETTER THAN HAVING A BLACK SHADOW, WHICH ACTS LIKE A PUPPET MASTER.

IT'S EASIER TO RESTRAIN SOMEONE THAN FORCE SOMEONE TO MOVE.

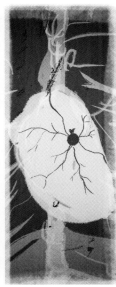

AH –

AH. OW.

DAMN IT.

FUCK. ARE YOU OKAY? LET ME –

IT'S OKAY. IT COMES AND GOES.

DAMN. ARE YOU TAKING ANY MEDICINE?

THE DOCTOR PRESCRIBED NITROGLYCERIN.

I – I THINK I CAN WALK NOW.

OKAY. LET'S GET YOU SOMETHING STRONGER.

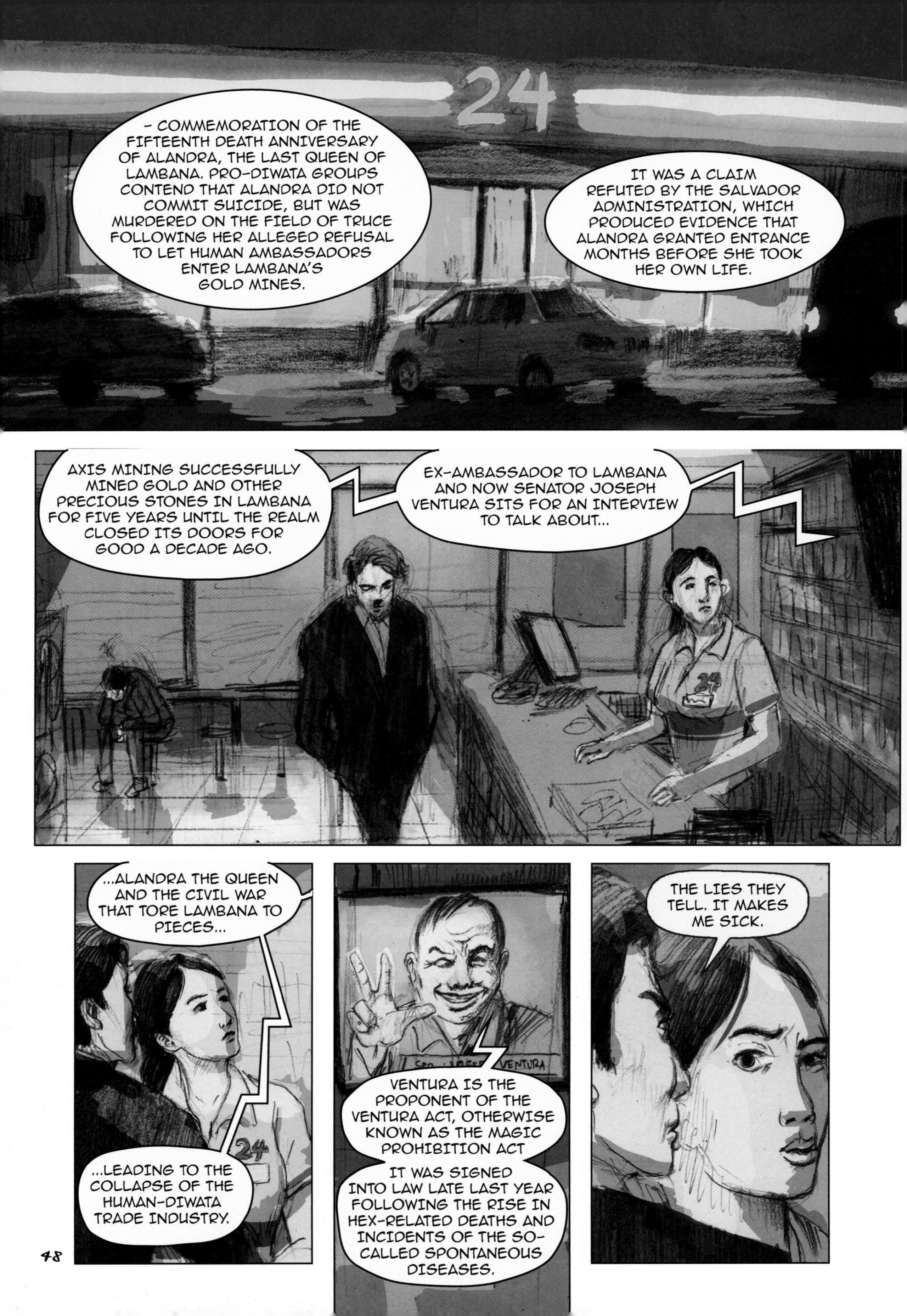

24
– COMMEMORATION OF THE FIFTEENTH DEATH ANNIVERSARY OF ALANDRA, THE LAST QUEEN OF LAMBANA. PRO-DIWATA GROUPS CONTEND THAT ALANDRA DID NOT COMMIT SUICIDE, BUT WAS MURDERED ON THE FIELD OF TRUCE FOLLOWING HER ALLEGED REFUSAL TO LET HUMAN AMBASSADORS ENTER LAMBANA'S GOLD MINES.
IT WAS A CLAIM REFUTED BY THE SALVADOR ADMINISTRATION, WHICH PRODUCED EVIDENCE THAT ALANDRA GRANTED ENTRANCE MONTHS BEFORE SHE TOOK HER OWN LIFE.
AXIS MINING SUCCESSFULLY MINED GOLD AND OTHER PRECIOUS STONES IN LAMBANA FOR FIVE YEARS UNTIL THE REALM CLOSED ITS DOORS FOR GOOD A DECADE AGO.
EX-AMBASSADOR TO LAMBANA AND NOW SENATOR JOSEPH VENTURA SITS FOR AN INTERVIEW TO TALK ABOUT...
...ALANDRA THE QUEEN AND THE CIVIL WAR THAT TORE LAMBANA TO PIECES...
...LEADING TO THE COLLAPSE OF THE HUMAN-DIWATA TRADE INDUSTRY.
VENTURA IS THE PROPONENT OF THE VENTURA ACT, OTHERWISE KNOWN AS THE MAGIC PROHIBITION ACT
IT WAS SIGNED INTO LAW LATE LAST YEAR FOLLOWING THE RISE IN HEX-RELATED DEATHS AND INCIDENTS OF THE SO-CALLED SPONTANEOUS DISEASES.
THE LIES THEY TELL. IT MAKES ME SICK.

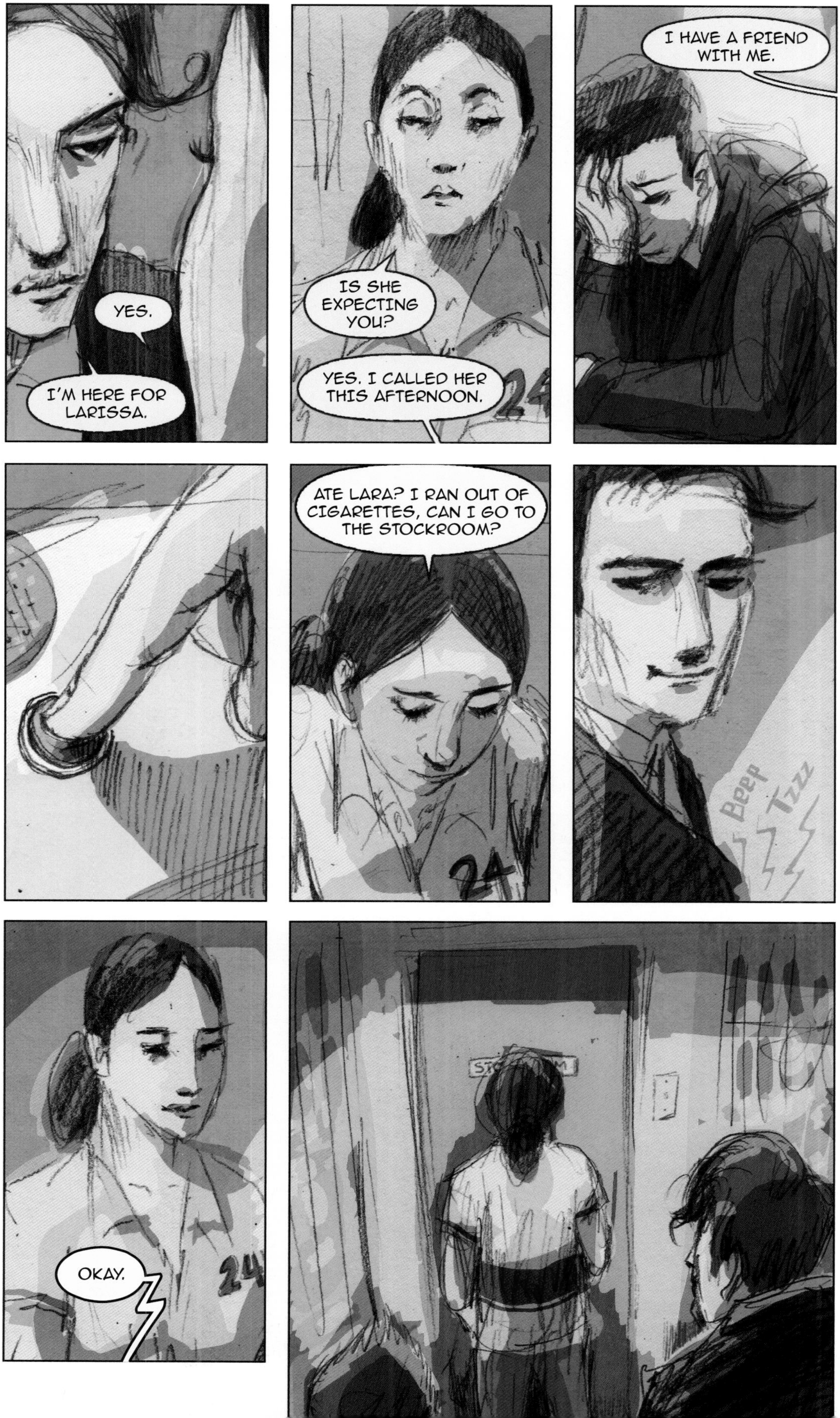
YES.
I'M HERE FOR LARISSA.
IS SHE EXPECTING YOU?
YES. I CALLED HER THIS AFTERNOON.
I HAVE A FRIEND WITH ME.
ATE LARA? I RAN OUT OF CIGARETTES, CAN I GO TO THE STOCKROOM?
Beep
Tzzz
OKAY.

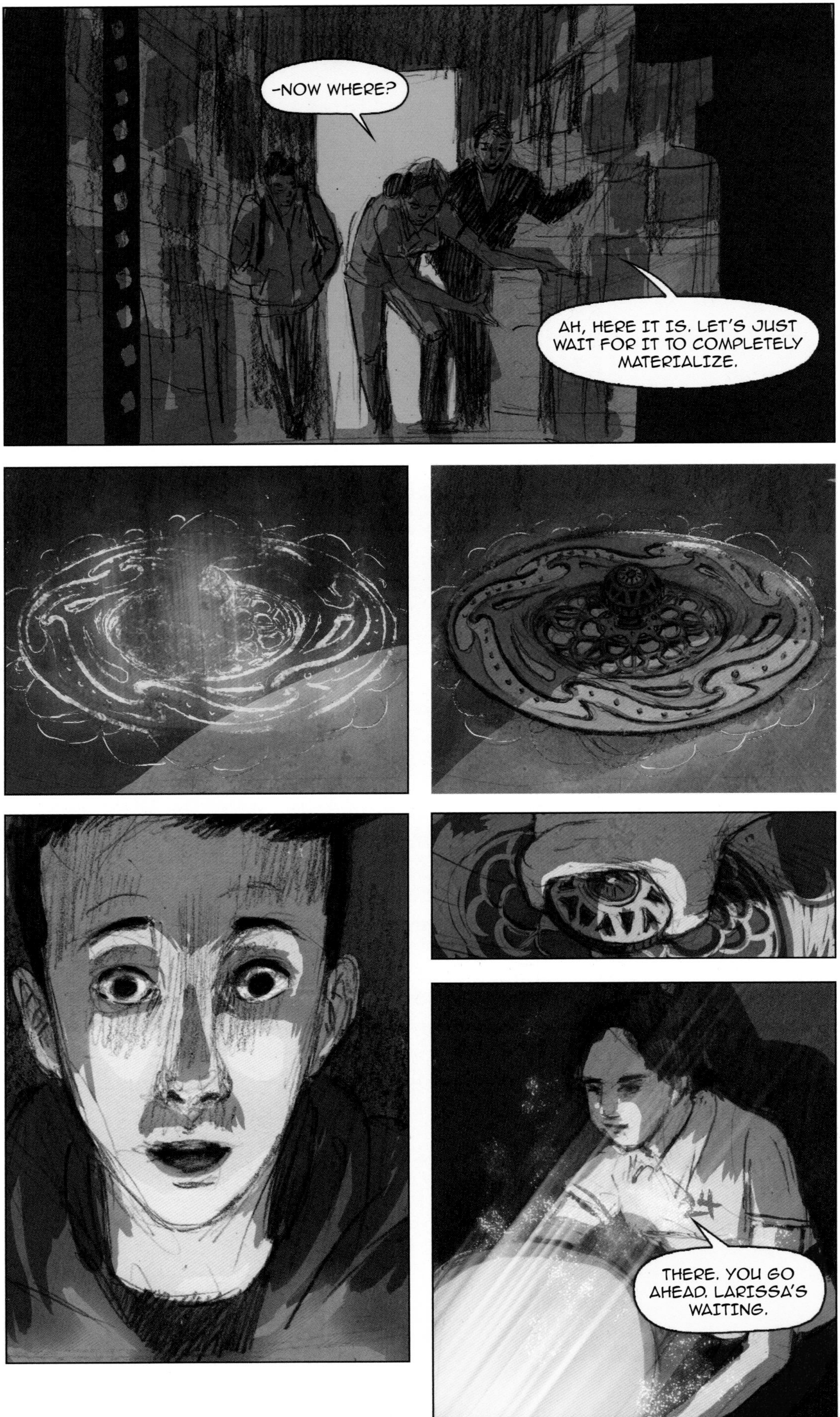
-NOW WHERE?
AH, HERE IT IS. LET'S JUST WAIT FOR IT TO COMPLETELY MATERIALIZE.
THERE. YOU GO AHEAD. LARISSA'S WAITING.

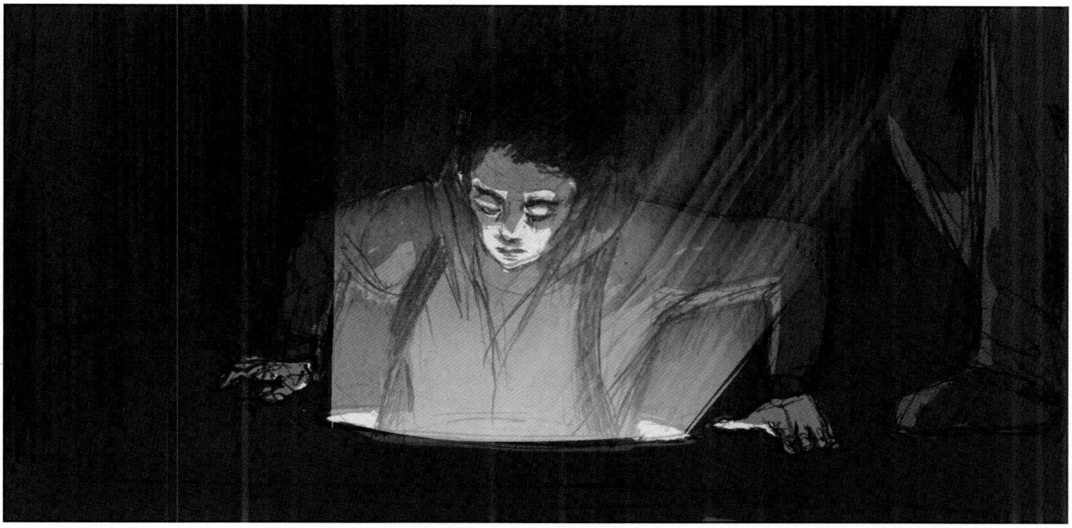

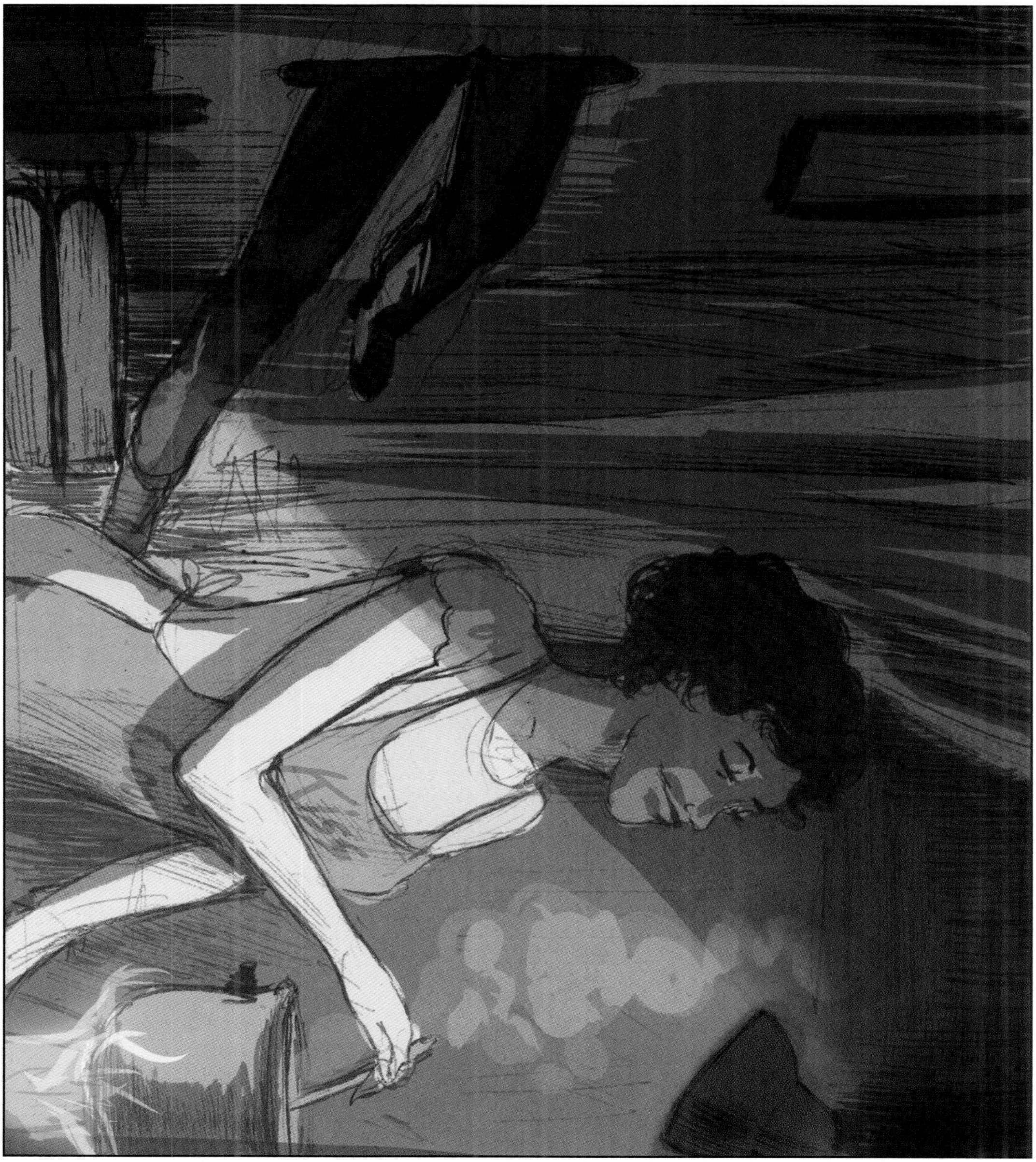

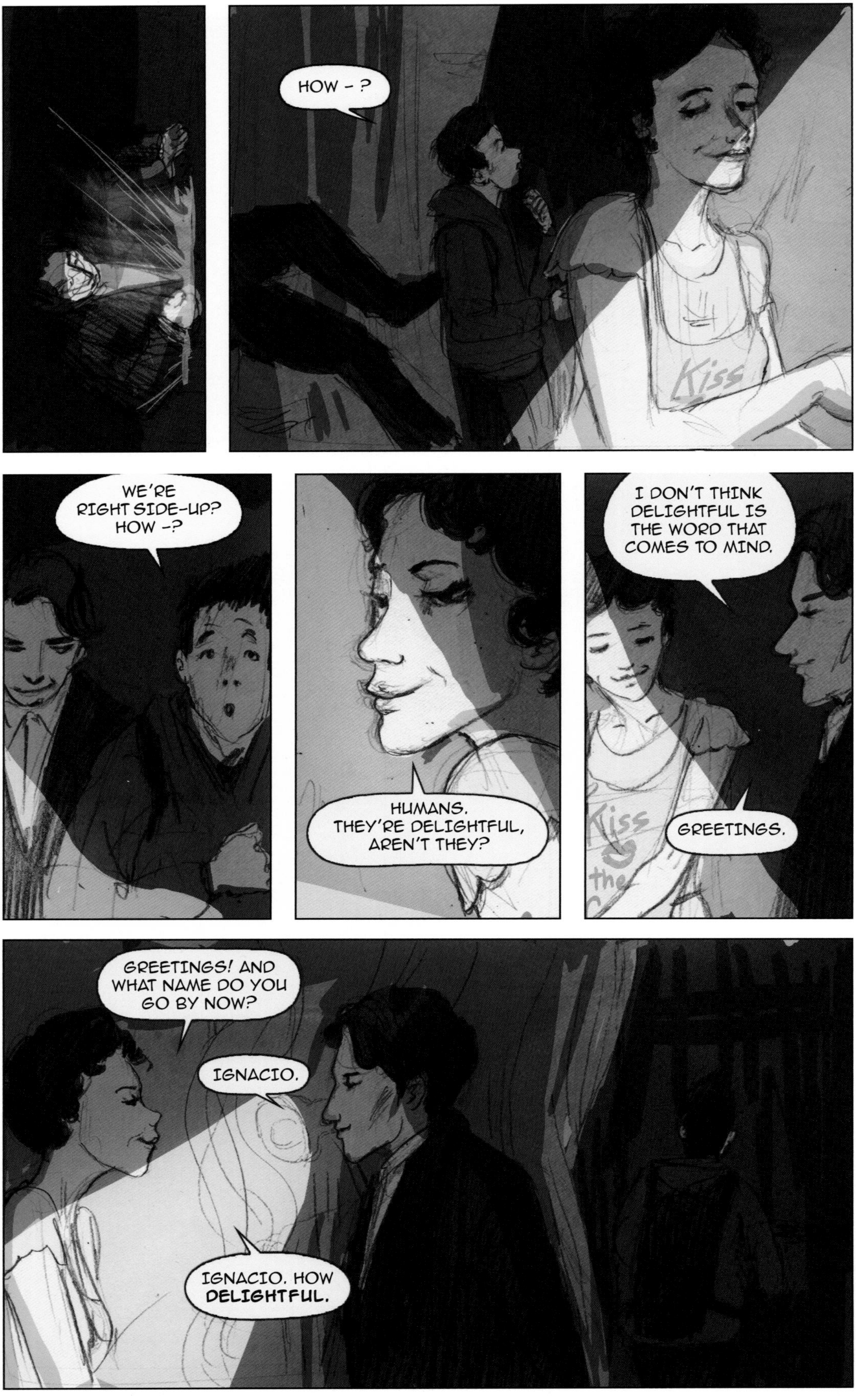
HOW - ?
WE'RE RIGHT SIDE-UP? HOW -?
HUMANS. THEY'RE DELIGHTFUL, AREN'T THEY?
I DON'T THINK DELIGHTFUL IS THE WORD THAT COMES TO MIND.
GREETINGS.
GREETINGS! AND WHAT NAME DO YOU GO BY NOW?
IGNACIO.
IGNACIO. HOW **DELIGHTFUL.**

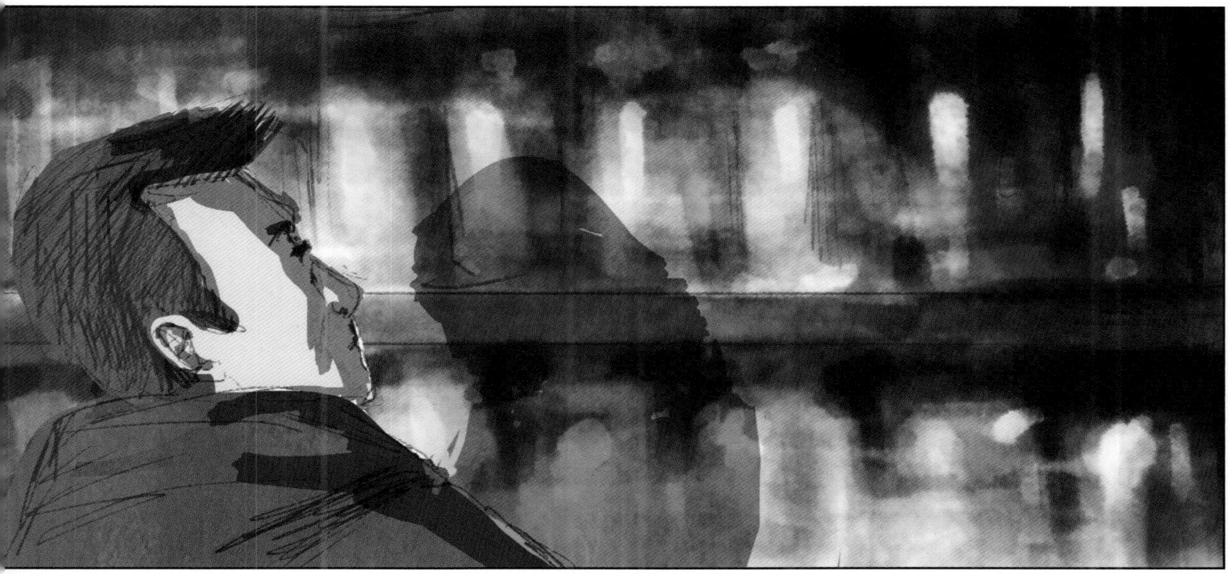
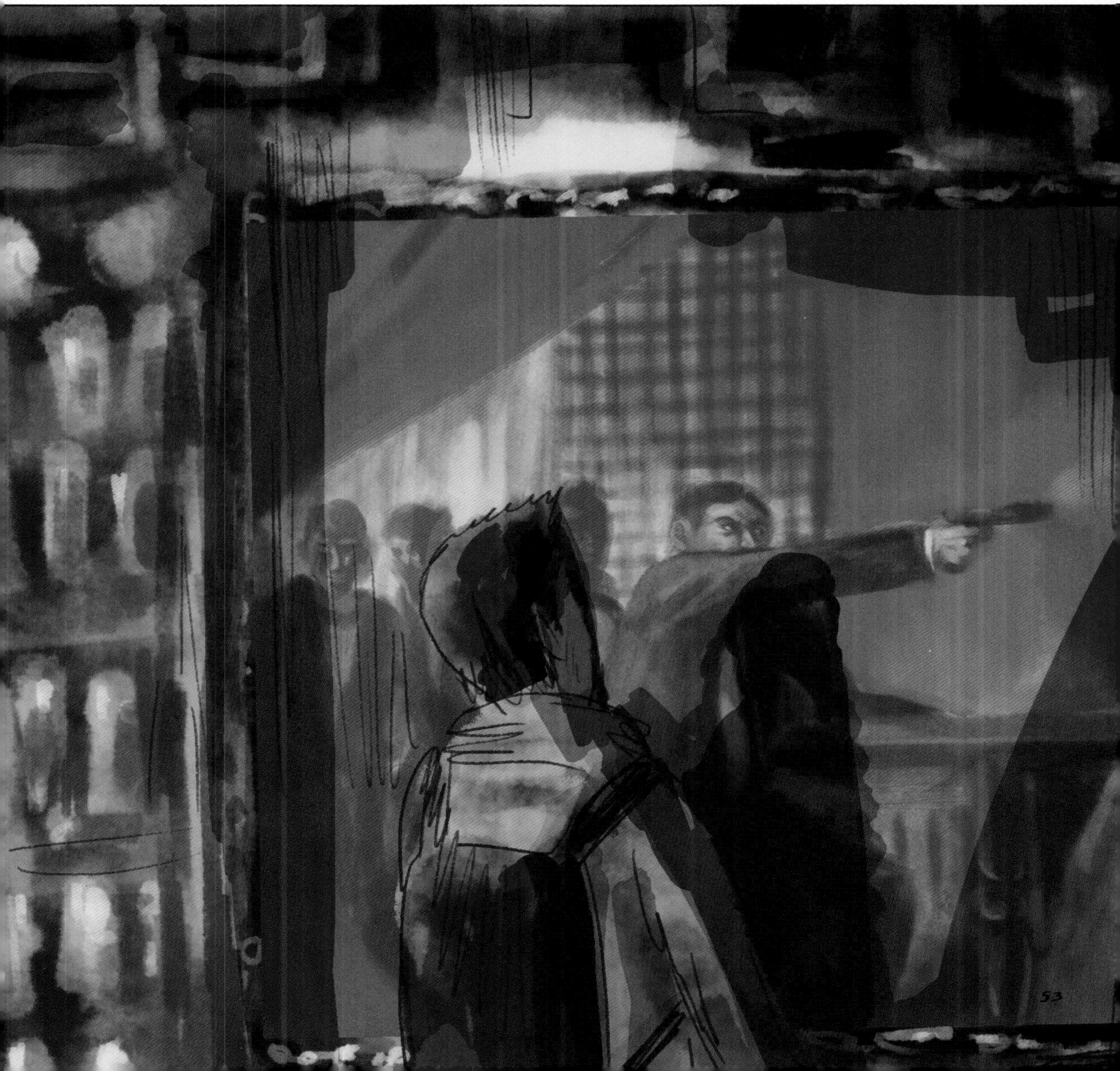

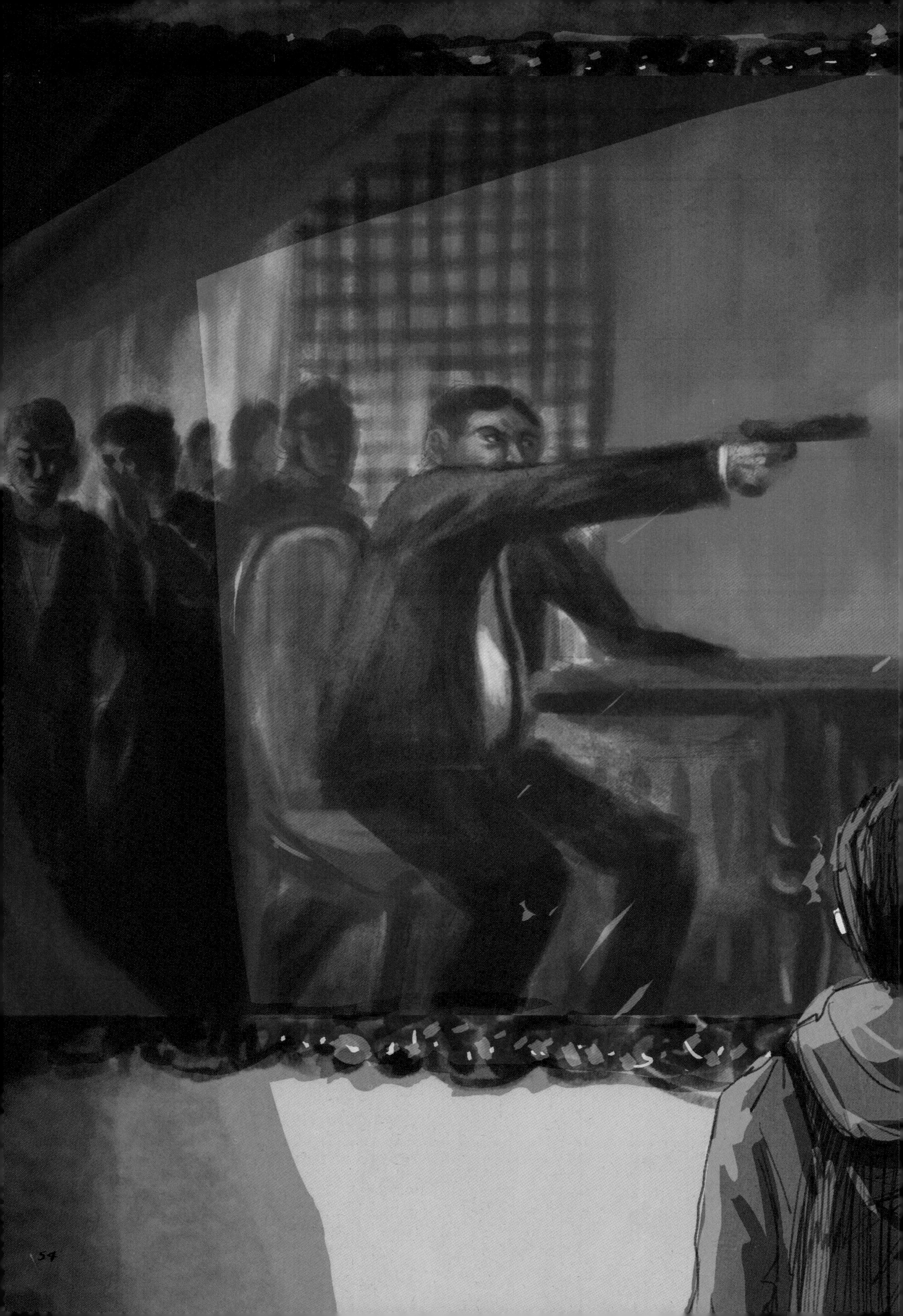

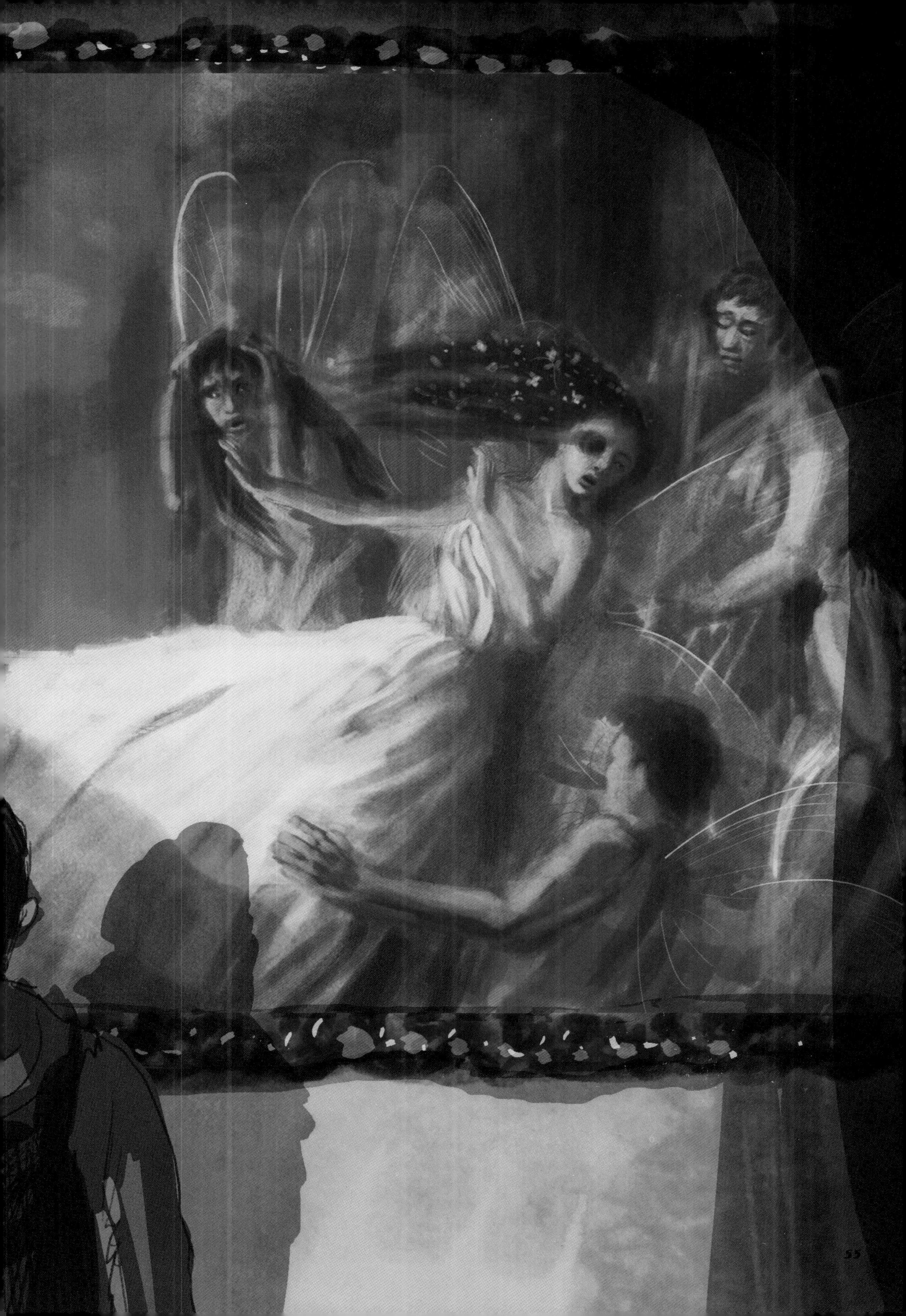

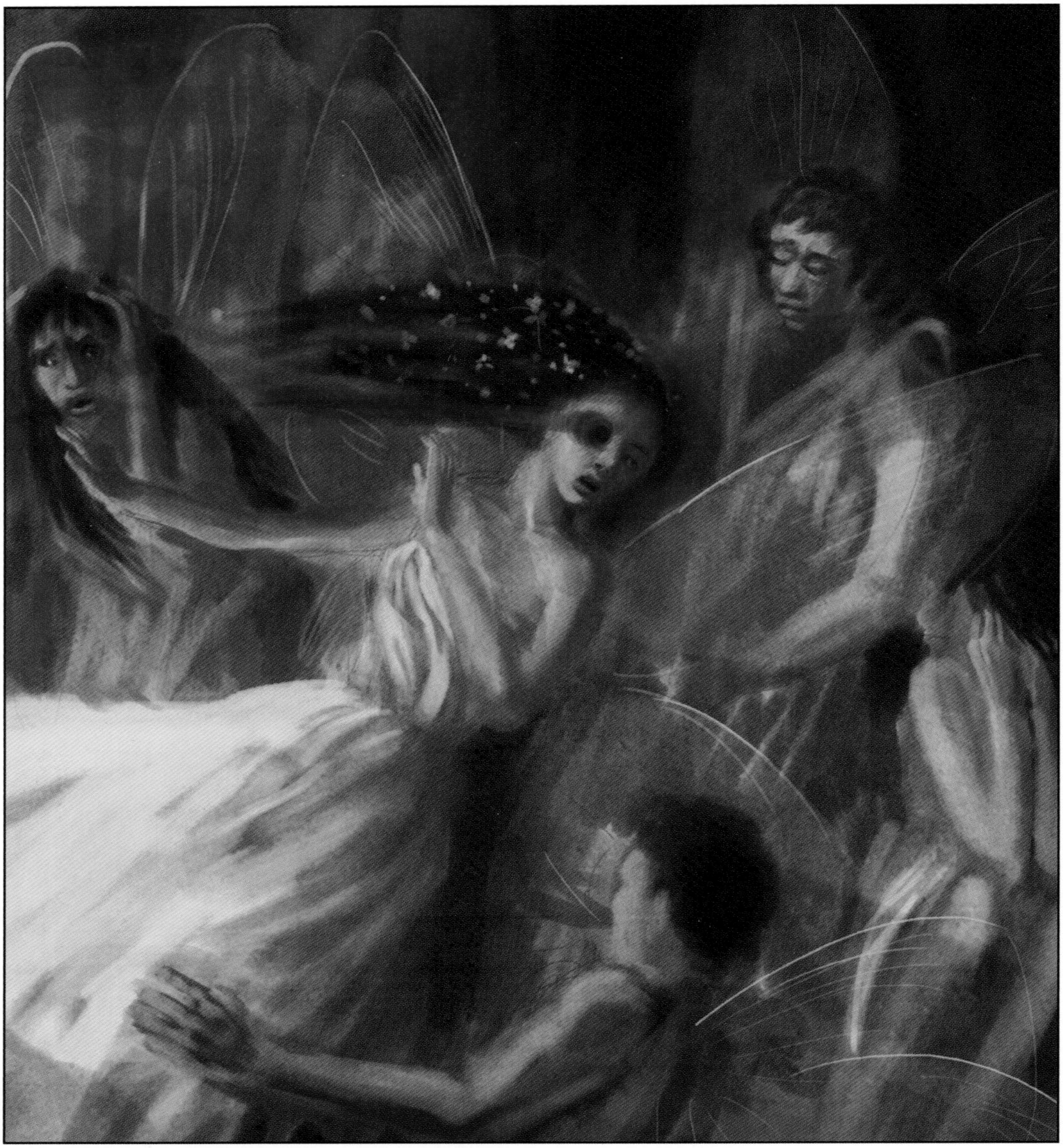

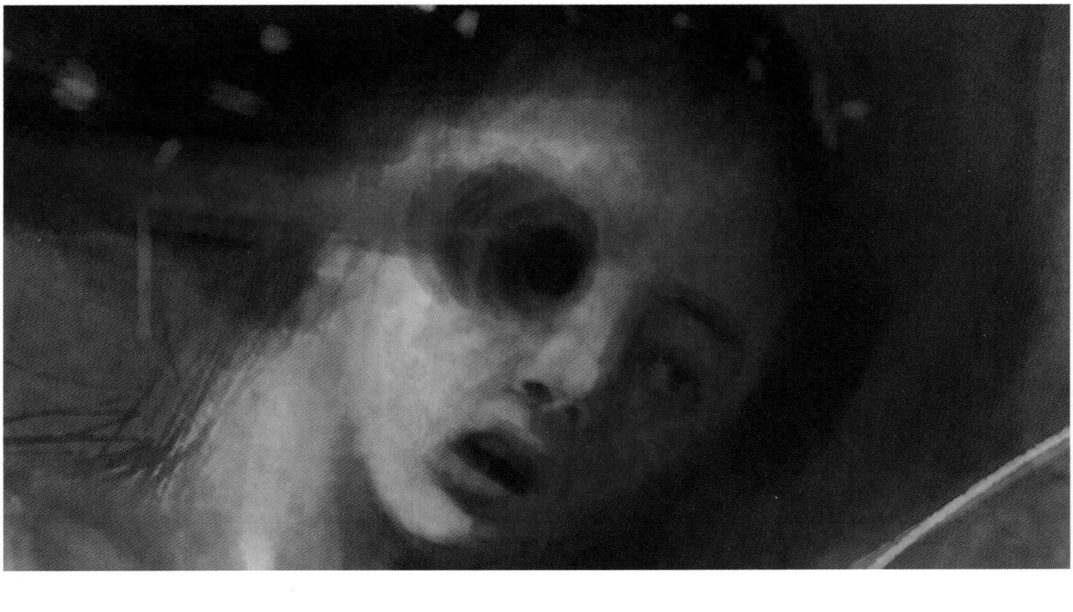

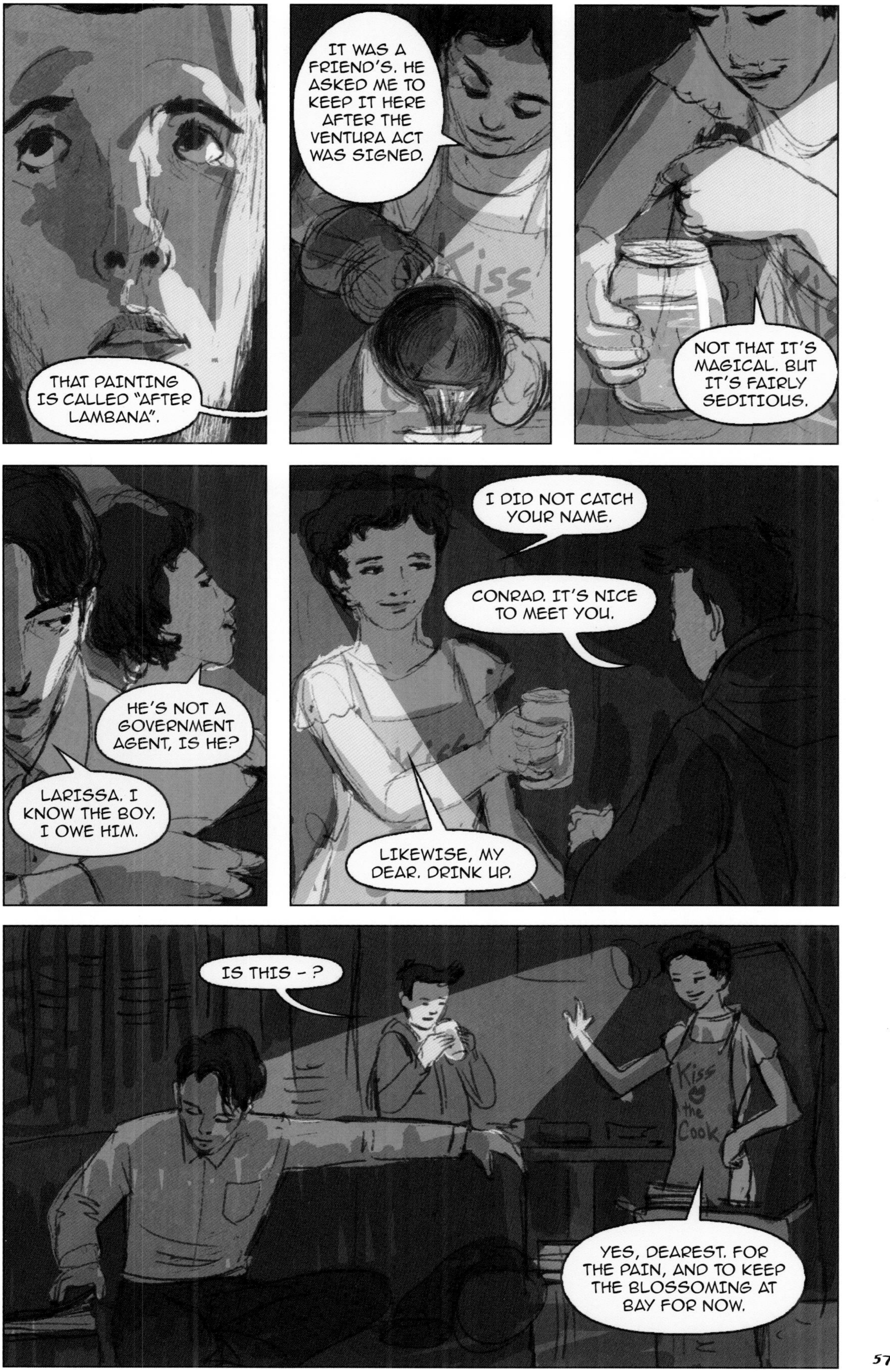
THAT PAINTING IS CALLED "AFTER LAMBANA".
IT WAS A FRIEND'S. HE ASKED ME TO KEEP IT HERE AFTER THE VENTURA ACT WAS SIGNED.
Kiss
NOT THAT IT'S MAGICAL. BUT IT'S FAIRLY SEDITIOUS.
HE'S NOT A GOVERNMENT AGENT, IS HE?
LARISSA. I KNOW THE BOY. I OWE HIM.
I DID NOT CATCH YOUR NAME.
CONRAD. IT'S NICE TO MEET YOU.
LIKEWISE, MY DEAR. DRINK UP.
IS THIS – ?
Kiss the Cook
YES, DEAREST. FOR THE PAIN, AND TO KEEP THE BLOSSOMING AT BAY FOR NOW.

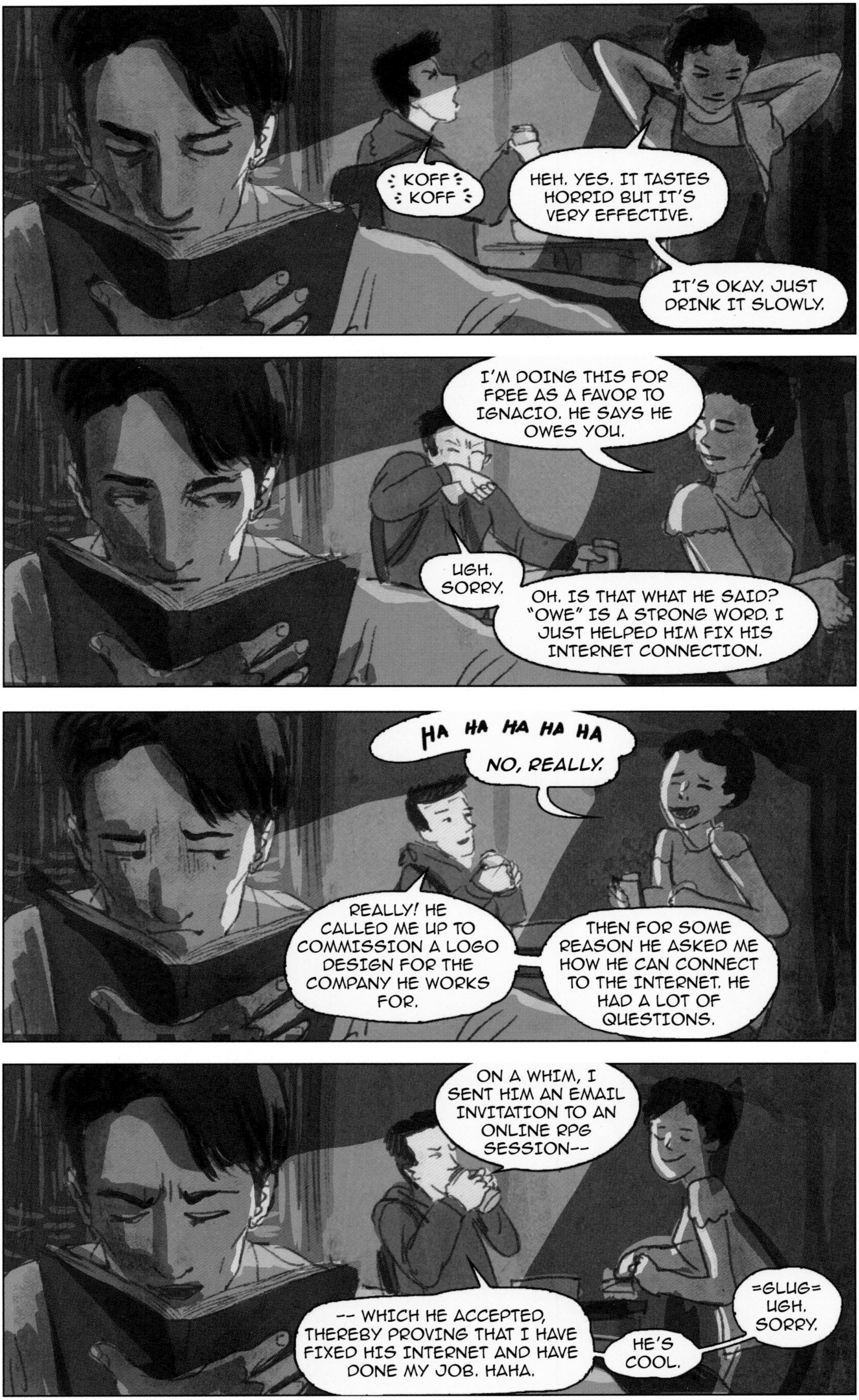
KOFF KOFF
HEH. YES. IT TASTES HORRID BUT IT'S VERY EFFECTIVE.
IT'S OKAY. JUST DRINK IT SLOWLY.
I'M DOING THIS FOR FREE AS A FAVOR TO IGNACIO. HE SAYS HE OWES YOU.
UGH. SORRY.
OH. IS THAT WHAT HE SAID? "OWE" IS A STRONG WORD. I JUST HELPED HIM FIX HIS INTERNET CONNECTION.
HA HA HA HA HA
NO, REALLY.
REALLY! HE CALLED ME UP TO COMMISSION A LOGO DESIGN FOR THE COMPANY HE WORKS FOR.
THEN FOR SOME REASON HE ASKED ME HOW HE CAN CONNECT TO THE INTERNET. HE HAD A LOT OF QUESTIONS.
ON A WHIM, I SENT HIM AN EMAIL INVITATION TO AN ONLINE RPG SESSION--
-- WHICH HE ACCEPTED, THEREBY PROVING THAT I HAVE FIXED HIS INTERNET AND HAVE DONE MY JOB. HAHA.
HE'S COOL.
=GLUG= UGH. SORRY.

IS THAT IT?

IT LOOKS SO SMALL.

LOOKS ARE DECEPTIVE.

ARE YOU SURE ABOUT THIS?

I CAN'T AFFORD THE HOSPICE.

UNLESS YOU HAVE A DRINK THAT CAN REMOVE THE BUD WITHOUT KILLING ME.

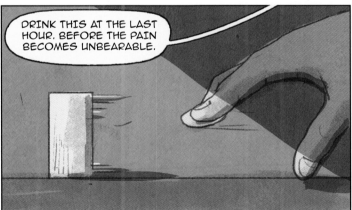

DRINK THIS AT THE LAST HOUR. BEFORE THE PAIN BECOMES UNBEARABLE.

DO SOMETHING FUN BEFORE THEN, WHY DON'T YOU.

SOMETHING BEAUTIFUL.

59

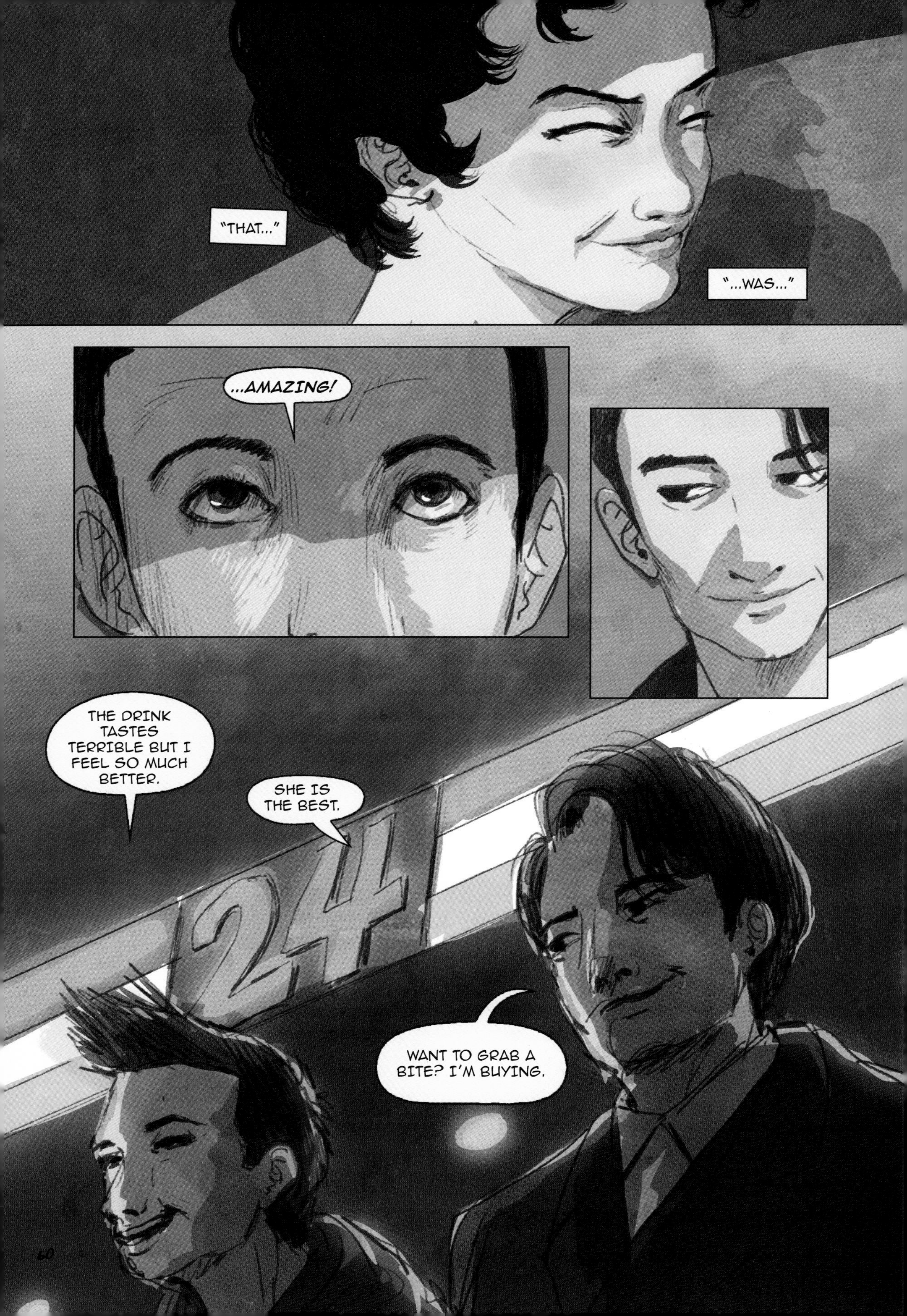
"THAT..."
"...WAS..."
...AMAZING!
THE DRINK TASTES TERRIBLE BUT I FEEL SO MUCH BETTER.
SHE IS THE BEST.
24
WANT TO GRAB A BITE? I'M BUYING.

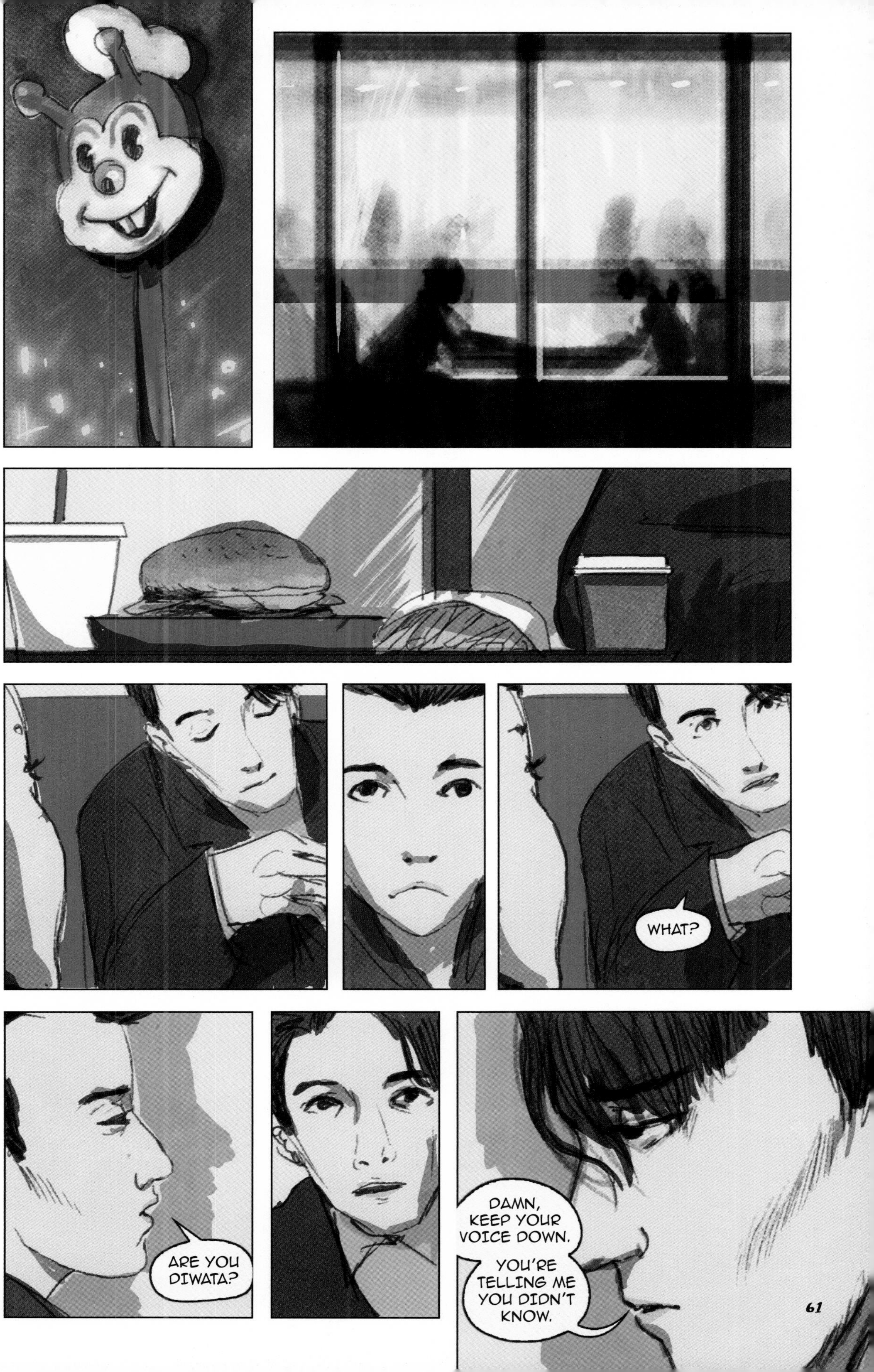
WHAT?
ARE YOU DIWATA?
DAMN, KEEP YOUR VOICE DOWN.
YOU'RE TELLING ME YOU DIDN'T KNOW.

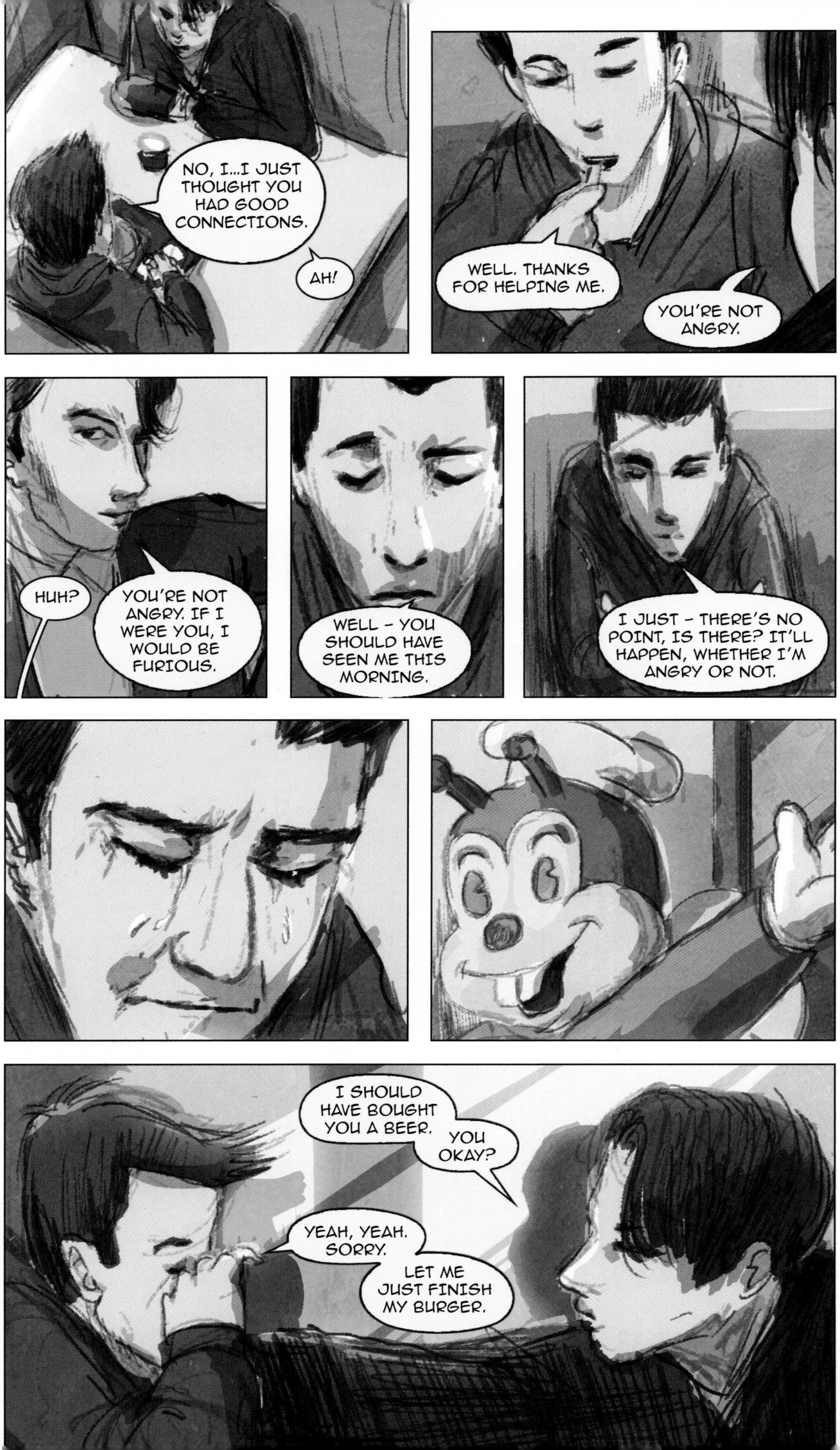
NO, I...I JUST THOUGHT YOU HAD GOOD CONNECTIONS.
AH!
WELL. THANKS FOR HELPING ME.
YOU'RE NOT ANGRY.
HUH?
YOU'RE NOT ANGRY. IF I WERE YOU, I WOULD BE FURIOUS.
WELL - YOU SHOULD HAVE SEEN ME THIS MORNING.
I JUST - THERE'S NO POINT, IS THERE? IT'LL HAPPEN, WHETHER I'M ANGRY OR NOT.
I SHOULD HAVE BOUGHT YOU A BEER.
YOU OKAY?
YEAH, YEAH. SORRY.
LET ME JUST FINISH MY BURGER.

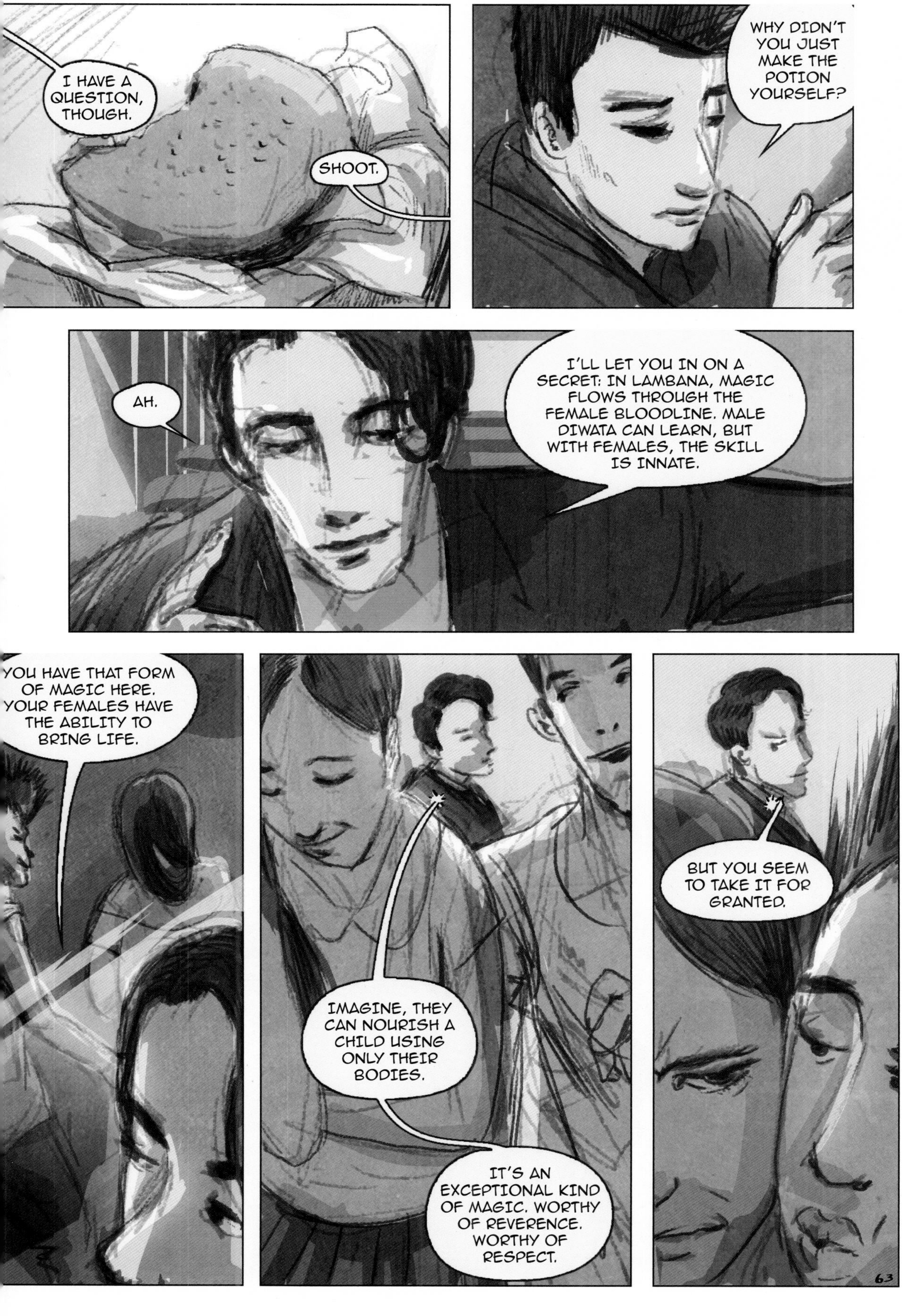
I HAVE A QUESTION, THOUGH.
SHOOT.
WHY DIDN'T YOU JUST MAKE THE POTION YOURSELF?
AH.
I'LL LET YOU IN ON A SECRET: IN LAMBANA, MAGIC FLOWS THROUGH THE FEMALE BLOODLINE. MALE DIWATA CAN LEARN, BUT WITH FEMALES, THE SKILL IS INNATE.
YOU HAVE THAT FORM OF MAGIC HERE. YOUR FEMALES HAVE THE ABILITY TO BRING LIFE.
IMAGINE, THEY CAN NOURISH A CHILD USING ONLY THEIR BODIES.
IT'S AN EXCEPTIONAL KIND OF MAGIC. WORTHY OF REVERENCE. WORTHY OF RESPECT.
BUT YOU SEEM TO TAKE IT FOR GRANTED.

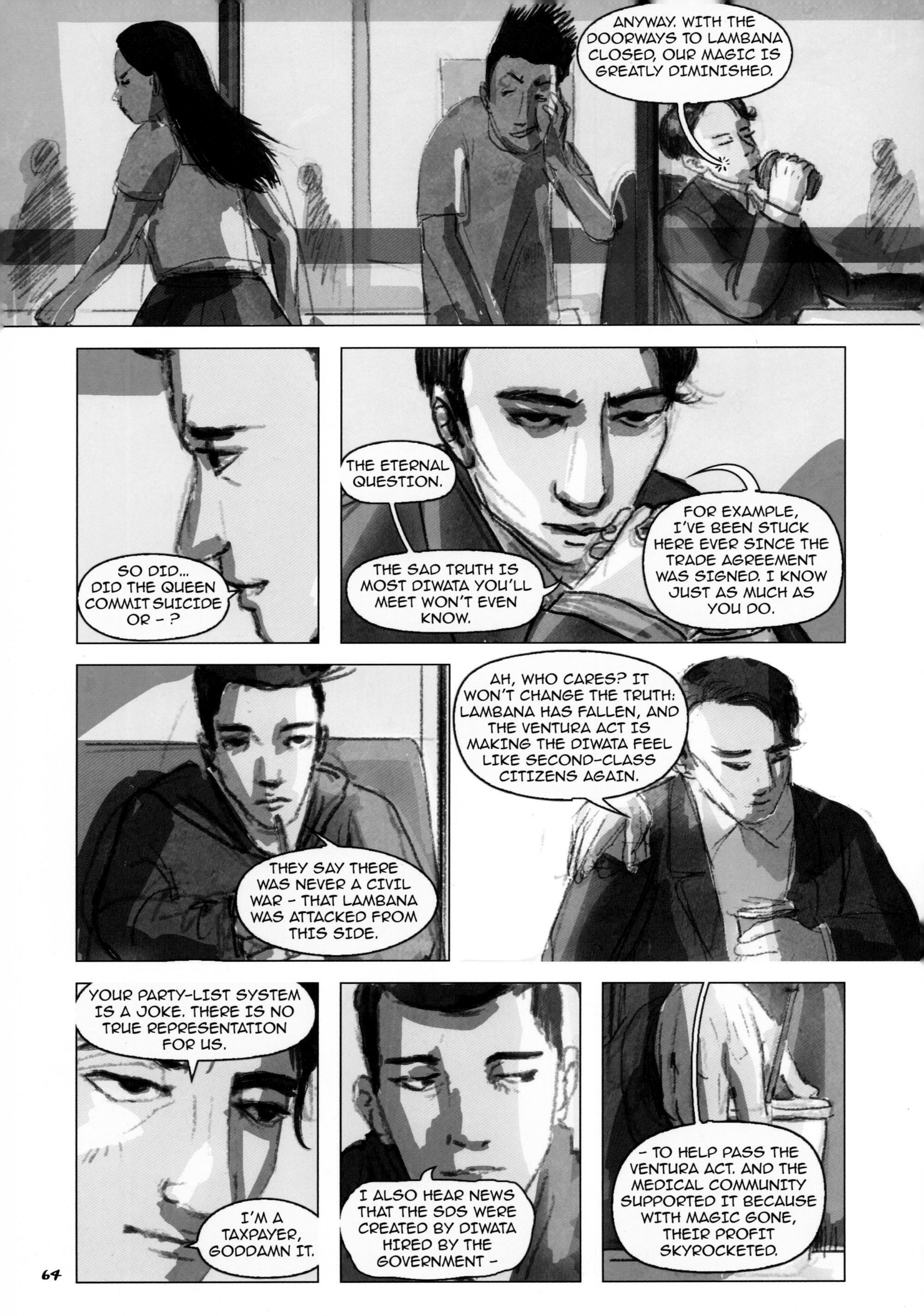
ANYWAY. WITH THE DOORWAYS TO LAMBANA CLOSED, OUR MAGIC IS GREATLY DIMINISHED.
SO DID... DID THE QUEEN COMMIT SUICIDE OR – ?
THE ETERNAL QUESTION.
THE SAD TRUTH IS MOST DIWATA YOU'LL MEET WON'T EVEN KNOW.
FOR EXAMPLE, I'VE BEEN STUCK HERE EVER SINCE THE TRADE AGREEMENT WAS SIGNED. I KNOW JUST AS MUCH AS YOU DO.
THEY SAY THERE WAS NEVER A CIVIL WAR – THAT LAMBANA WAS ATTACKED FROM THIS SIDE.
AH, WHO CARES? IT WON'T CHANGE THE TRUTH: LAMBANA HAS FALLEN, AND THE VENTURA ACT IS MAKING THE DIWATA FEEL LIKE SECOND-CLASS CITIZENS AGAIN.
YOUR PARTY-LIST SYSTEM IS A JOKE. THERE IS NO TRUE REPRESENTATION FOR US.
I'M A TAXPAYER, GODDAMN IT.
I ALSO HEAR NEWS THAT THE SDS WERE CREATED BY DIWATA HIRED BY THE GOVERNMENT –
– TO HELP PASS THE VENTURA ACT. AND THE MEDICAL COMMUNITY SUPPORTED IT BECAUSE WITH MAGIC GONE, THEIR PROFIT SKYROCKETED.

BECAUSE PEOPLE WENT TO DOCTORS AGAIN.

AH, POLITICS. I REALLY HAVE NO ANSWERS FOR YOU.

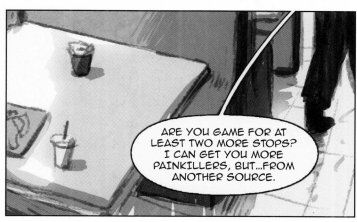

ARE YOU GAME FOR AT LEAST TWO MORE STOPS? I CAN GET YOU MORE PAINKILLERS, BUT...FROM ANOTHER SOURCE.

UNLESS YOU'D RATHER GO HOME AND REST.

NO, NO. I'LL JUST DRIVE MYSELF CRAZY SITTING ALONE IN MY APARTMENT.

TAXI

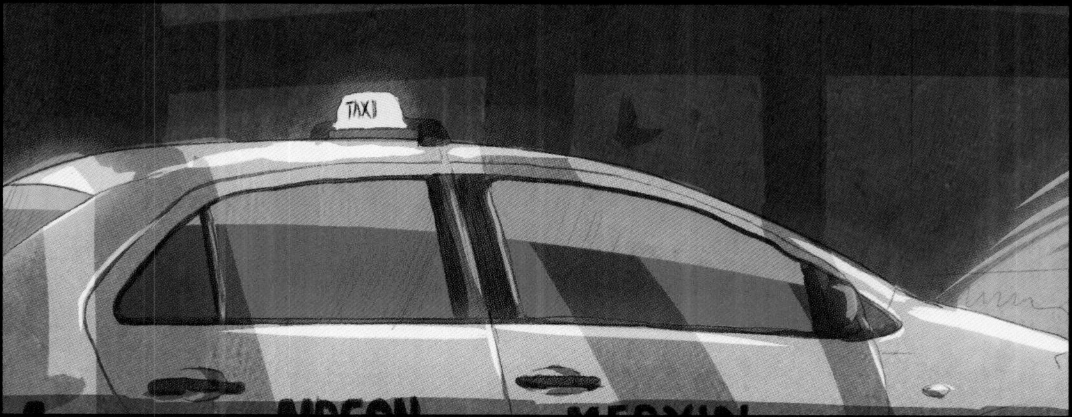
TAXI

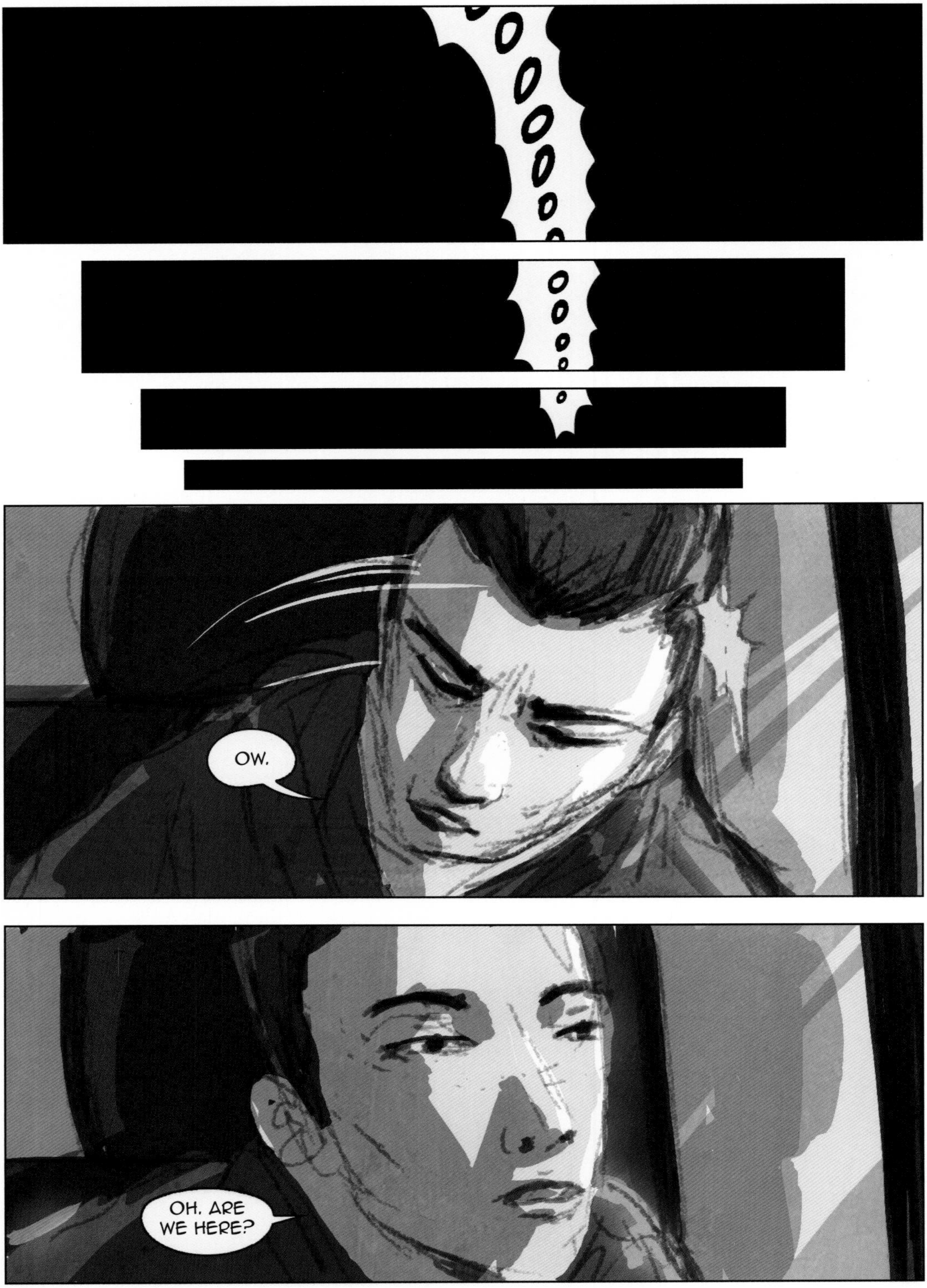
OW.
OH. ARE WE HERE?

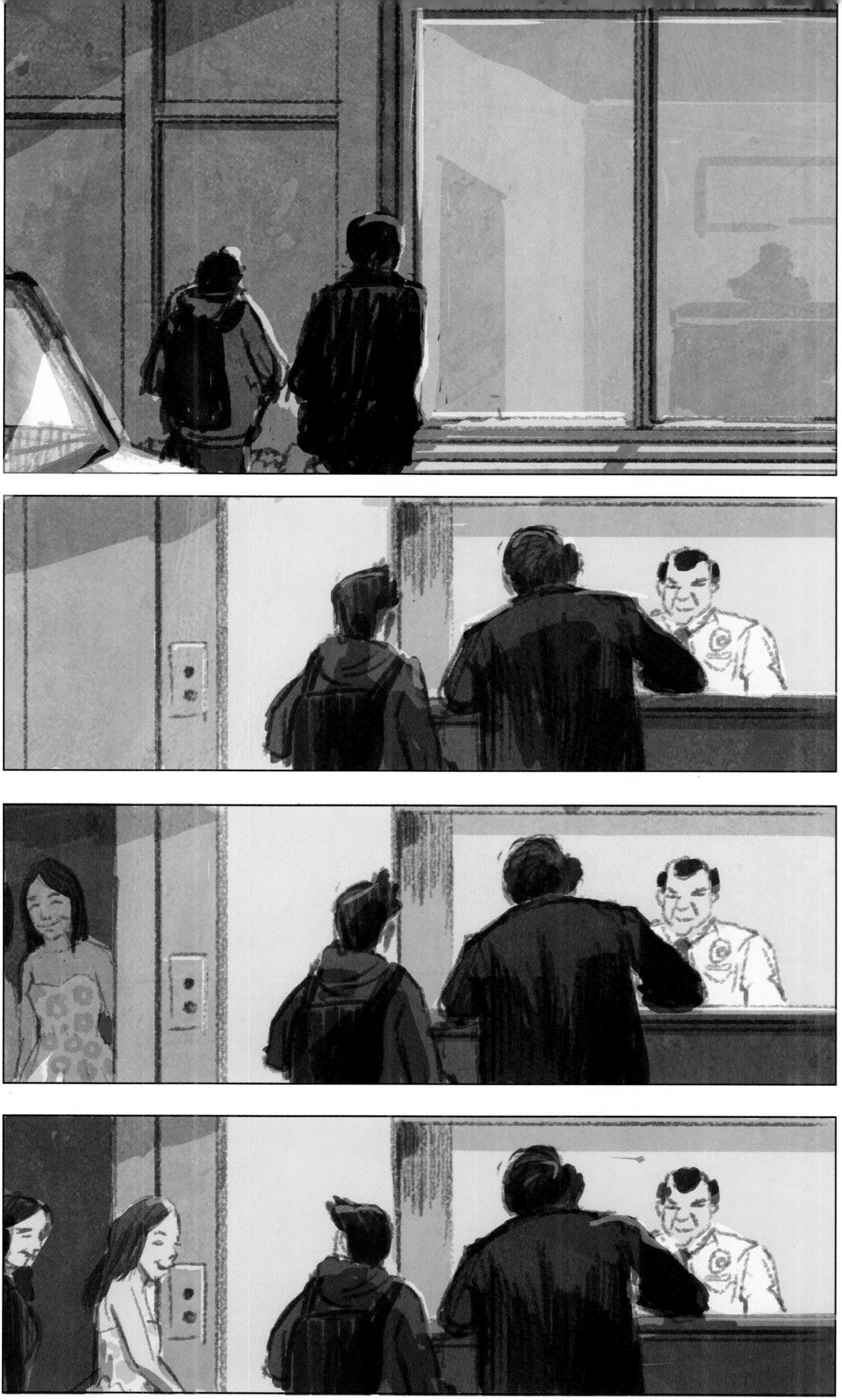

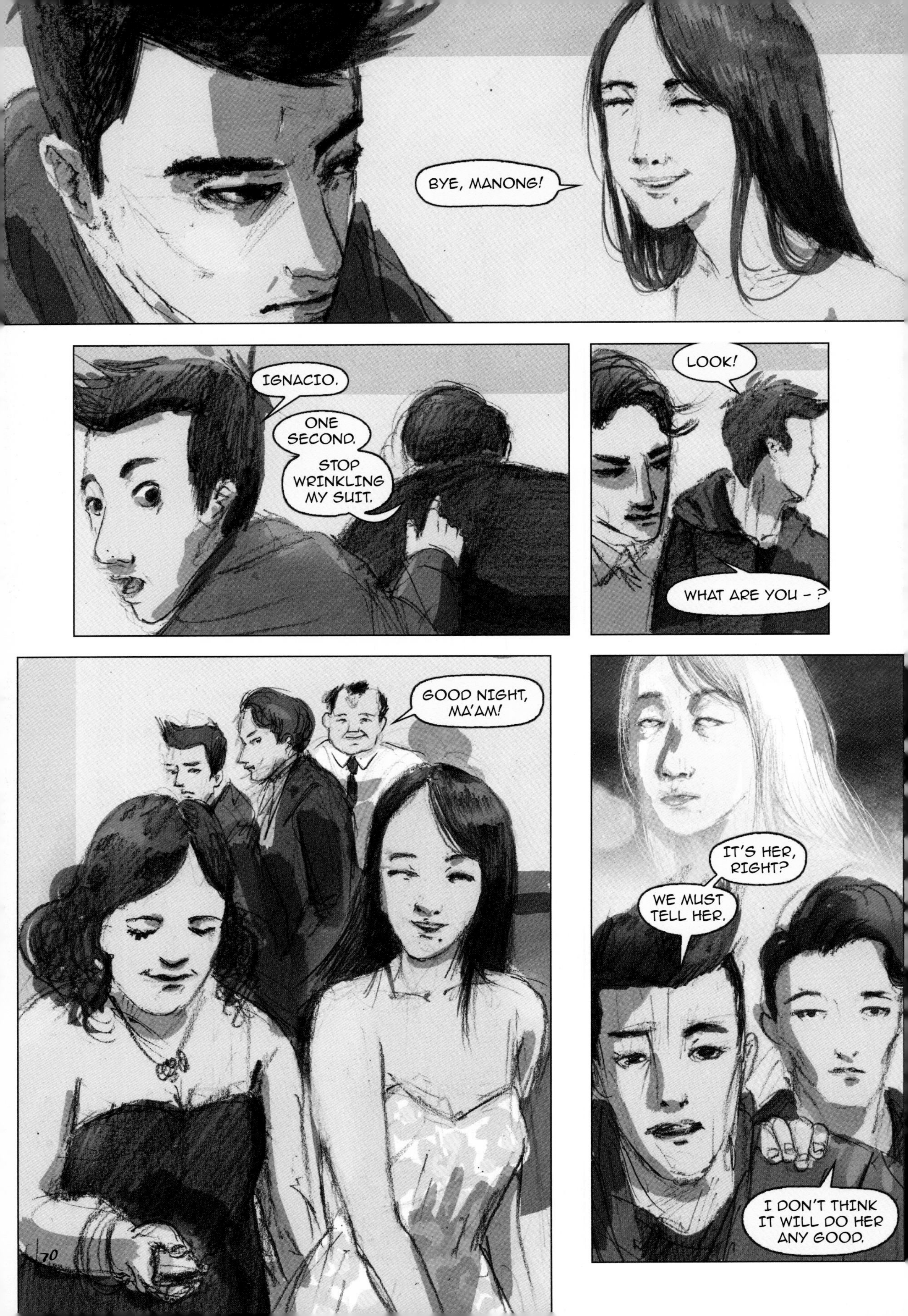
BYE, MANONG!
IGNACIO.
ONE SECOND.
STOP WRINKLING MY SUIT.
LOOK!
WHAT ARE YOU – ?
GOOD NIGHT, MA'AM!
IT'S HER, RIGHT?
WE MUST TELL HER.
I DON'T THINK IT WILL DO HER ANY GOOD.

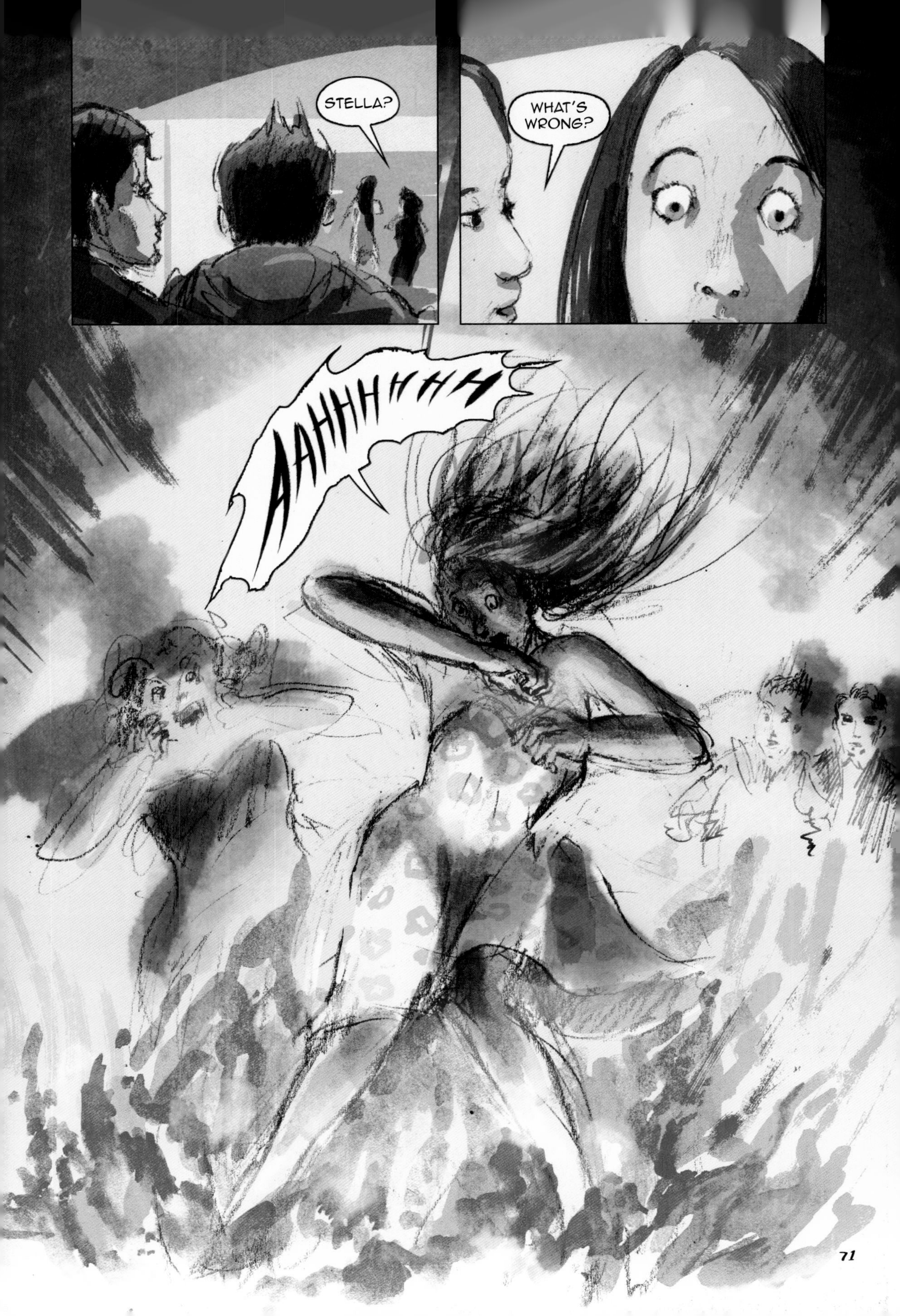
STELLA?
WHAT'S WRONG?
AAHHHHHHH

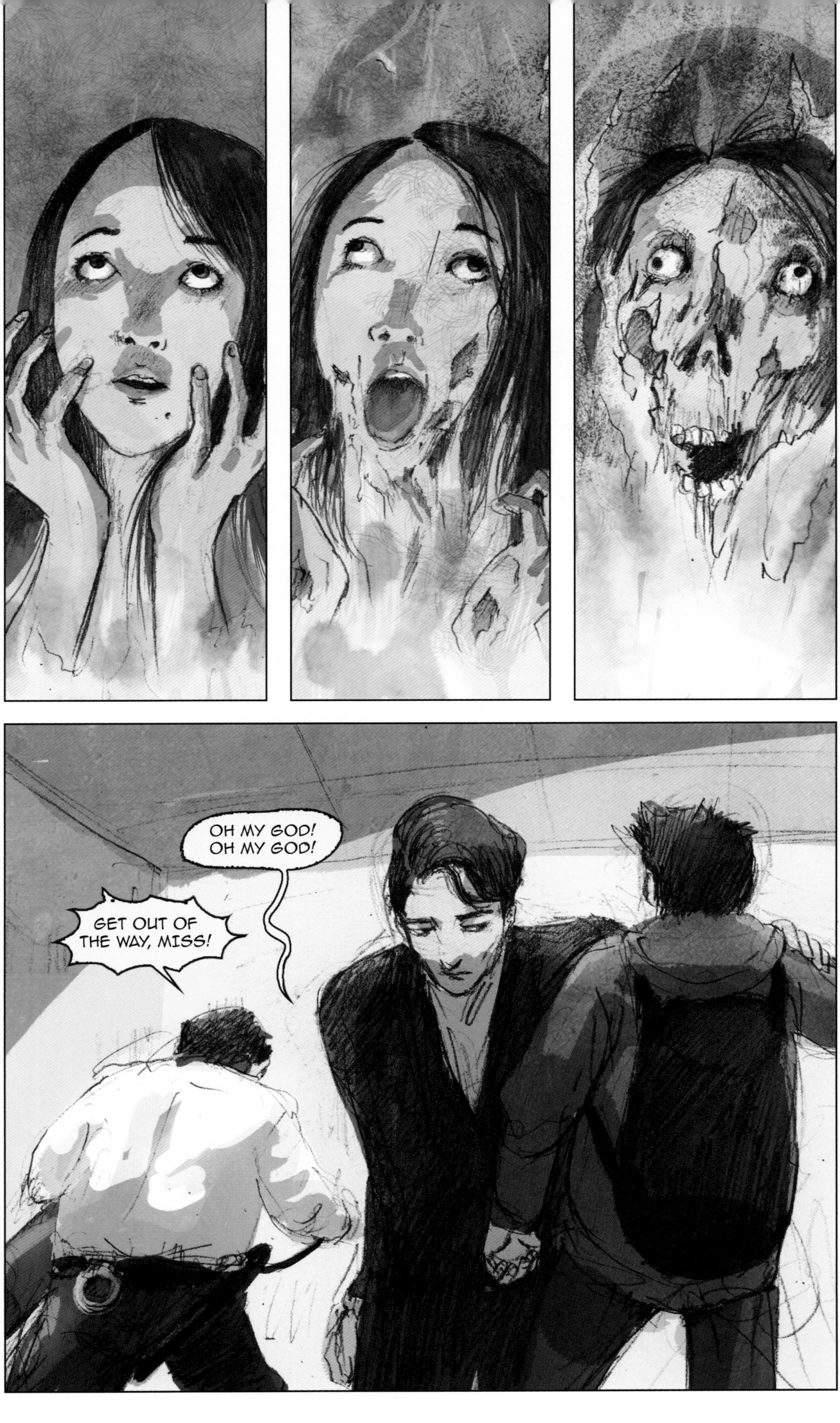
GET OUT OF THE WAY, MISS!
OH MY GOD! OH MY GOD!

WEEEOOOEEEWEEEEOOO

ARE YOU OKAY? YOU NEED A MINUTE?

NO... LET'S GO.

WEEEOOOEEEWEEEEOOO

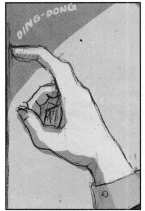

DING-DONG

HELLO?

IT'S ME.

73

MIRRA.
IT'S ME.

YOU DON'T NEED
TO LET ME IN. I
JUST NEED—

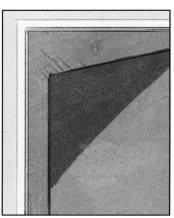

WHAT?

WHAT DO
YOU NEED
THIS TIME?

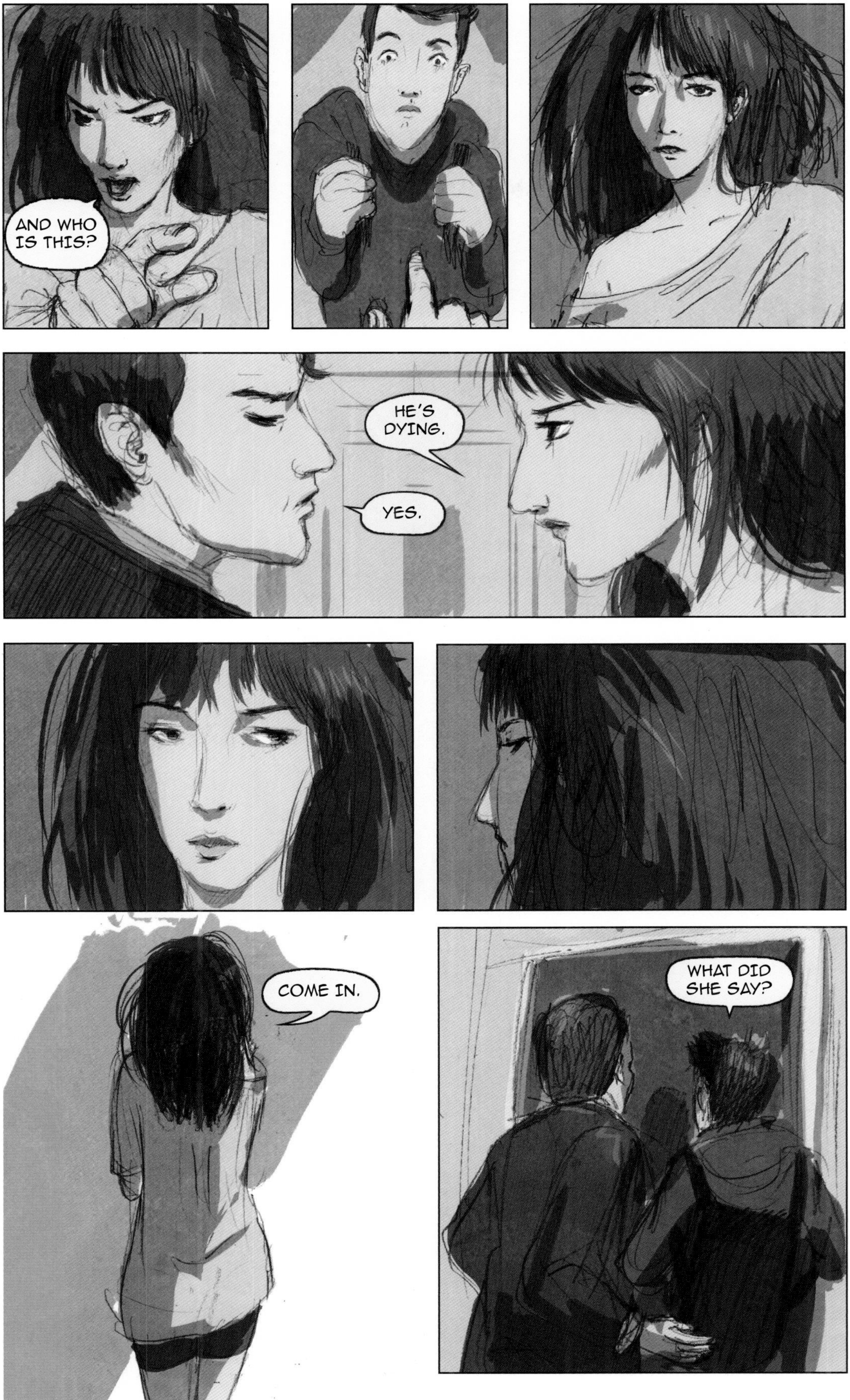
AND WHO IS THIS?
HE'S DYING.
YES.
COME IN.
WHAT DID SHE SAY?

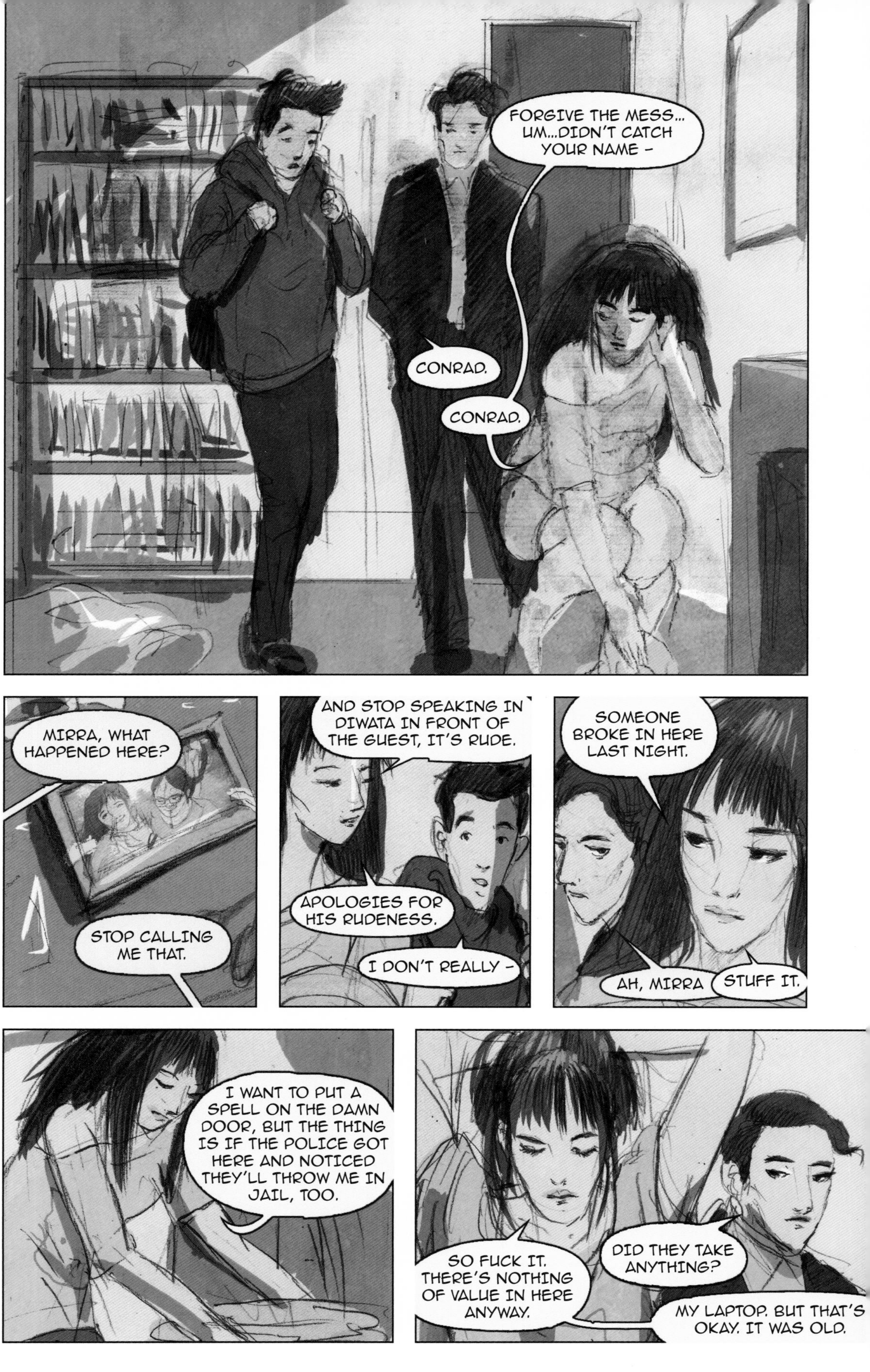
FORGIVE THE MESS... UM...DIDN'T CATCH YOUR NAME –
CONRAD.
CONRAD.
MIRRA, WHAT HAPPENED HERE?
STOP CALLING ME THAT.
AND STOP SPEAKING IN DIWATA IN FRONT OF THE GUEST, IT'S RUDE.
APOLOGIES FOR HIS RUDENESS.
I DON'T REALLY –
SOMEONE BROKE IN HERE LAST NIGHT.
AH, MIRRA
STUFF IT.
I WANT TO PUT A SPELL ON THE DAMN DOOR, BUT THE THING IS IF THE POLICE GOT HERE AND NOTICED THEY'LL THROW ME IN JAIL, TOO.
SO FUCK IT. THERE'S NOTHING OF VALUE IN HERE ANYWAY.
DID THEY TAKE ANYTHING?
MY LAPTOP. BUT THAT'S OKAY. IT WAS OLD.

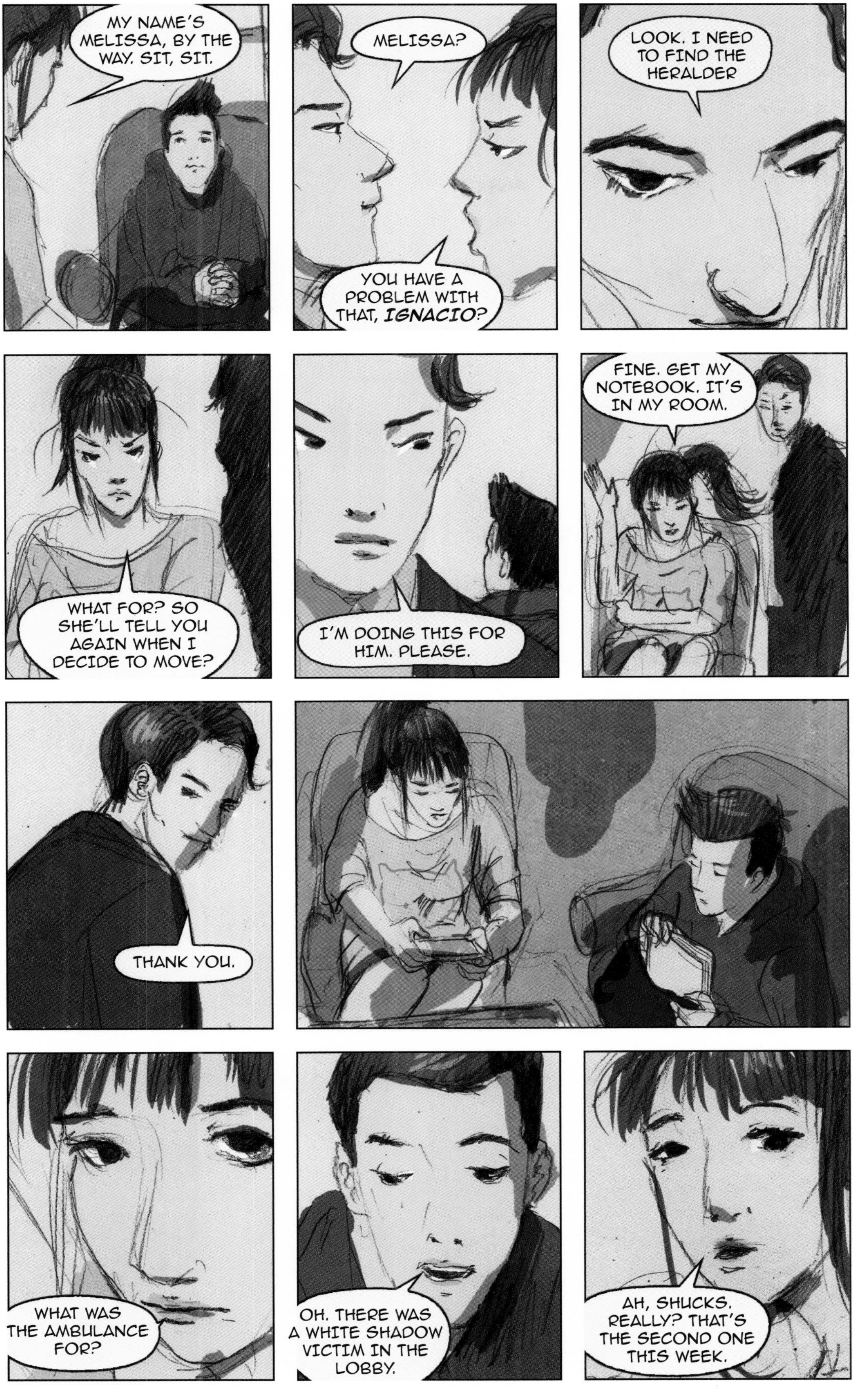
MY NAME'S MELISSA, BY THE WAY. SIT, SIT.
MELISSA?
YOU HAVE A PROBLEM WITH THAT, *IGNACIO*?
LOOK. I NEED TO FIND THE HERALDER
WHAT FOR? SO SHE'LL TELL YOU AGAIN WHEN I DECIDE TO MOVE?
I'M DOING THIS FOR HIM. PLEASE.
FINE. GET MY NOTEBOOK. IT'S IN MY ROOM.
THANK YOU.
WHAT WAS THE AMBULANCE FOR?
OH. THERE WAS A WHITE SHADOW VICTIM IN THE LOBBY.
AH, SHUCKS. REALLY? THAT'S THE SECOND ONE THIS WEEK.

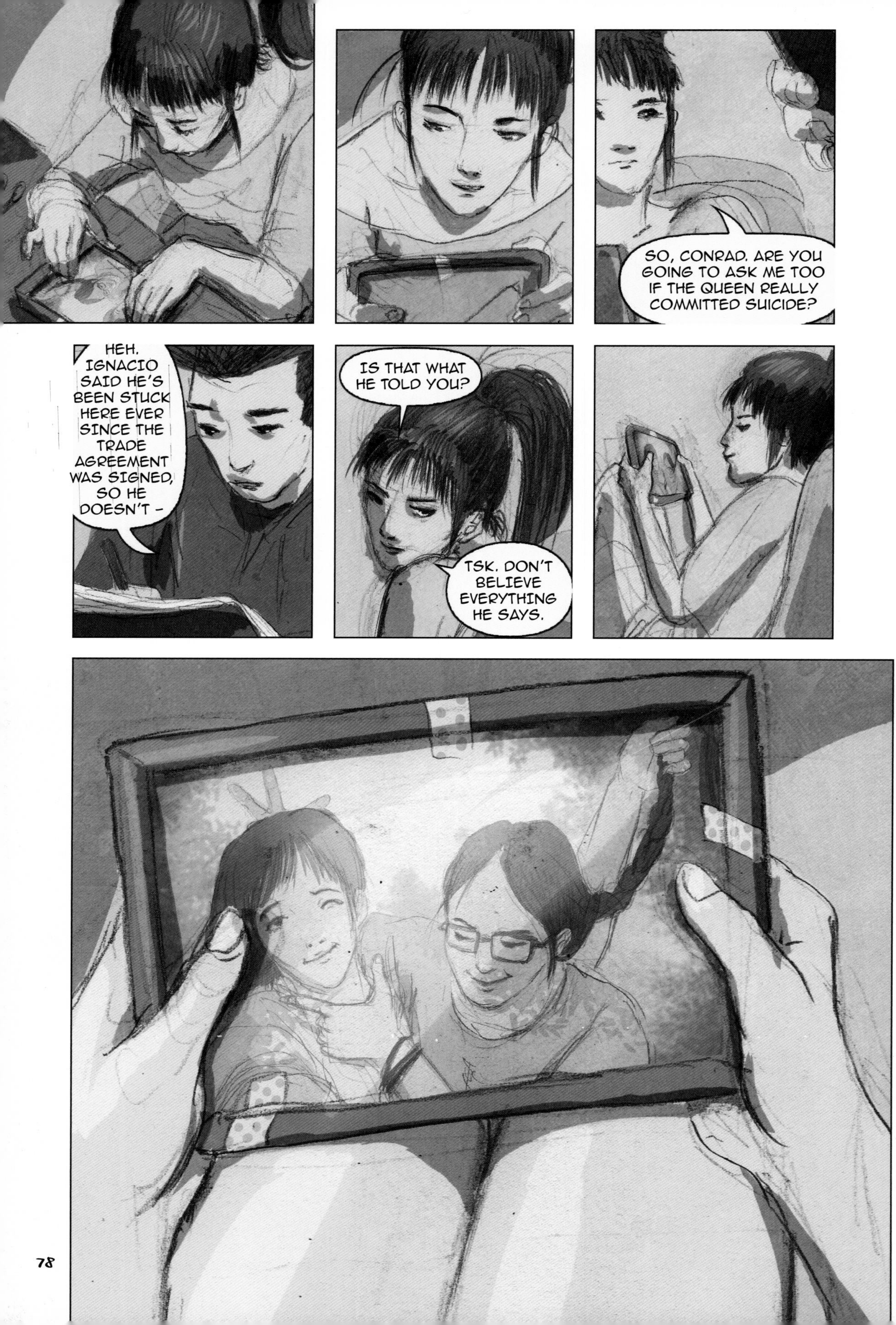
SO, CONRAD. ARE YOU GOING TO ASK ME TOO IF THE QUEEN REALLY COMMITTED SUICIDE?
HEH. IGNACIO SAID HE'S BEEN STUCK HERE EVER SINCE THE TRADE AGREEMENT WAS SIGNED, SO HE DOESN'T -
IS THAT WHAT HE TOLD YOU?
TSK. DON'T BELIEVE EVERYTHING HE SAYS.

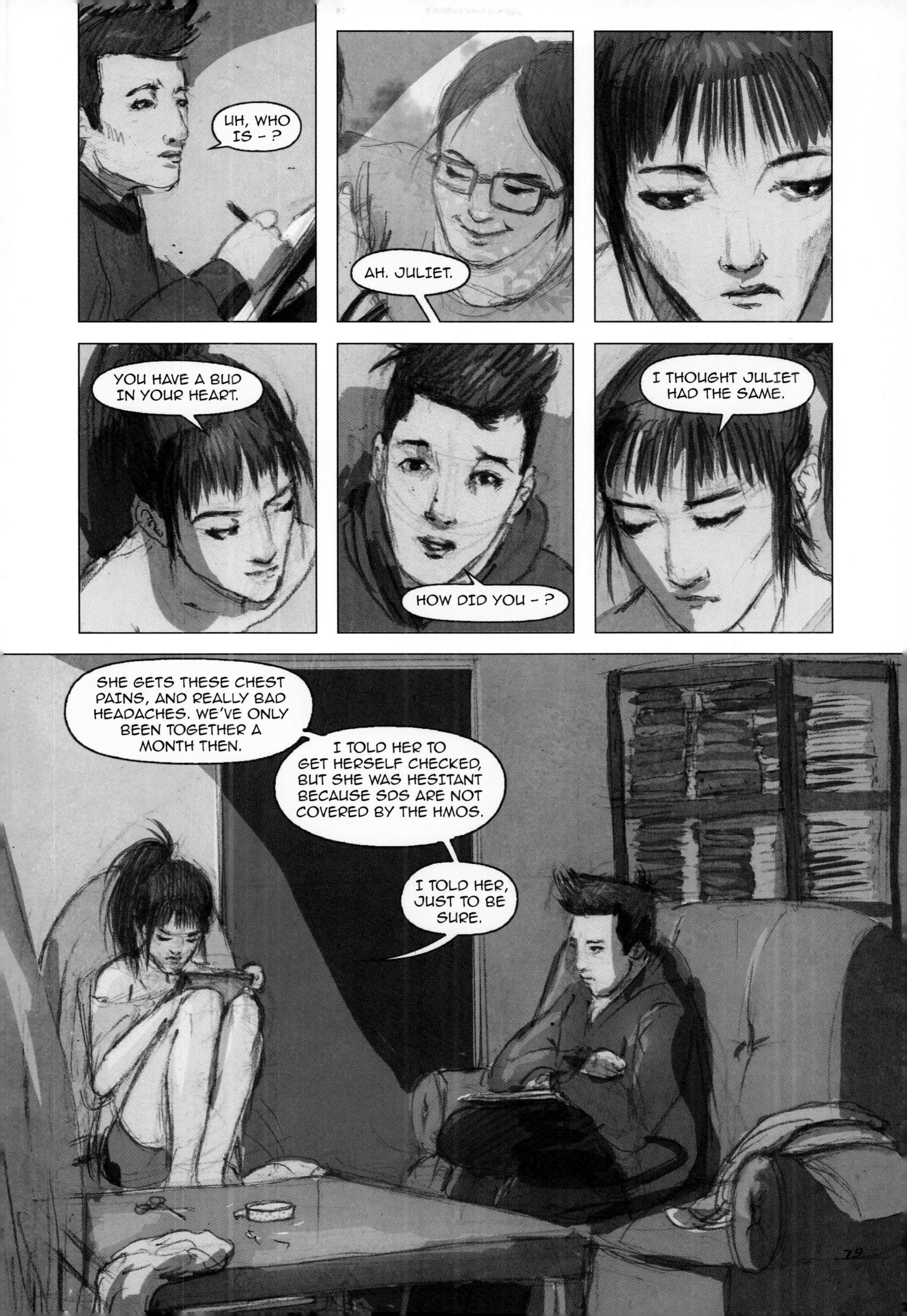
UH, WHO IS - ?
AH. JULIET.
YOU HAVE A BUD IN YOUR HEART.
HOW DID YOU - ?
I THOUGHT JULIET HAD THE SAME.
SHE GETS THESE CHEST PAINS, AND REALLY BAD HEADACHES. WE'VE ONLY BEEN TOGETHER A MONTH THEN.
I TOLD HER TO GET HERSELF CHECKED, BUT SHE WAS HESITANT BECAUSE SDS ARE NOT COVERED BY THE HMOS.
I TOLD HER, JUST TO BE SURE.

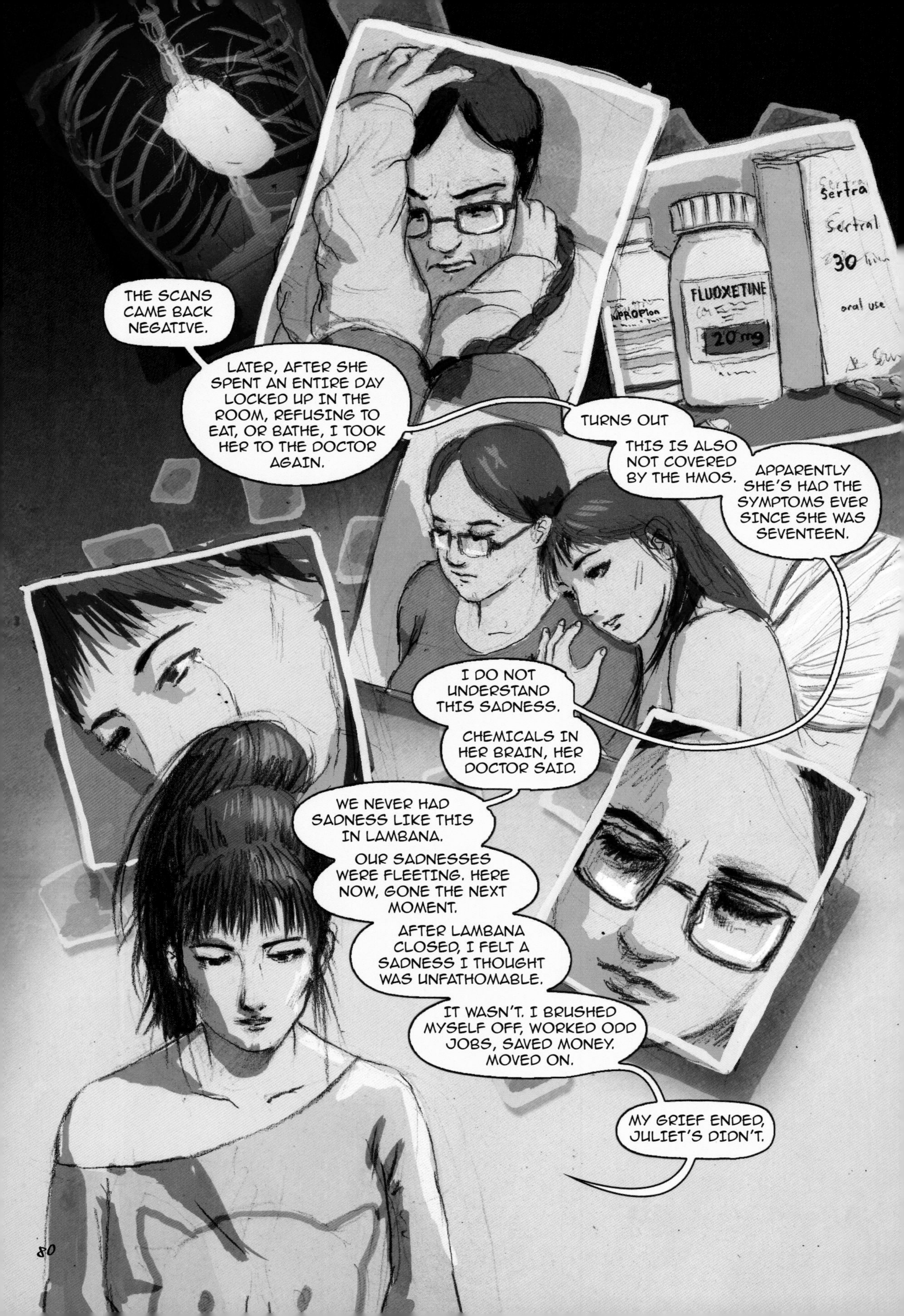

THE SCANS CAME BACK NEGATIVE.
LATER, AFTER SHE SPENT AN ENTIRE DAY LOCKED UP IN THE ROOM, REFUSING TO EAT, OR BATHE, I TOOK HER TO THE DOCTOR AGAIN.
TURNS OUT
THIS IS ALSO NOT COVERED BY THE HMOS.
APPARENTLY SHE'S HAD THE SYMPTOMS EVER SINCE SHE WAS SEVENTEEN.
FLUOXETINE
20 mg
Sertra
Sertral
30
oral use
I DO NOT UNDERSTAND THIS SADNESS.
CHEMICALS IN HER BRAIN, HER DOCTOR SAID.
WE NEVER HAD SADNESS LIKE THIS IN LAMBANA.
OUR SADNESSES WERE FLEETING. HERE NOW, GONE THE NEXT MOMENT.
AFTER LAMBANA CLOSED, I FELT A SADNESS I THOUGHT WAS UNFATHOMABLE.
IT WASN'T. I BRUSHED MYSELF OFF, WORKED ODD JOBS, SAVED MONEY. MOVED ON.
MY GRIEF ENDED, JULIET'S DIDN'T.

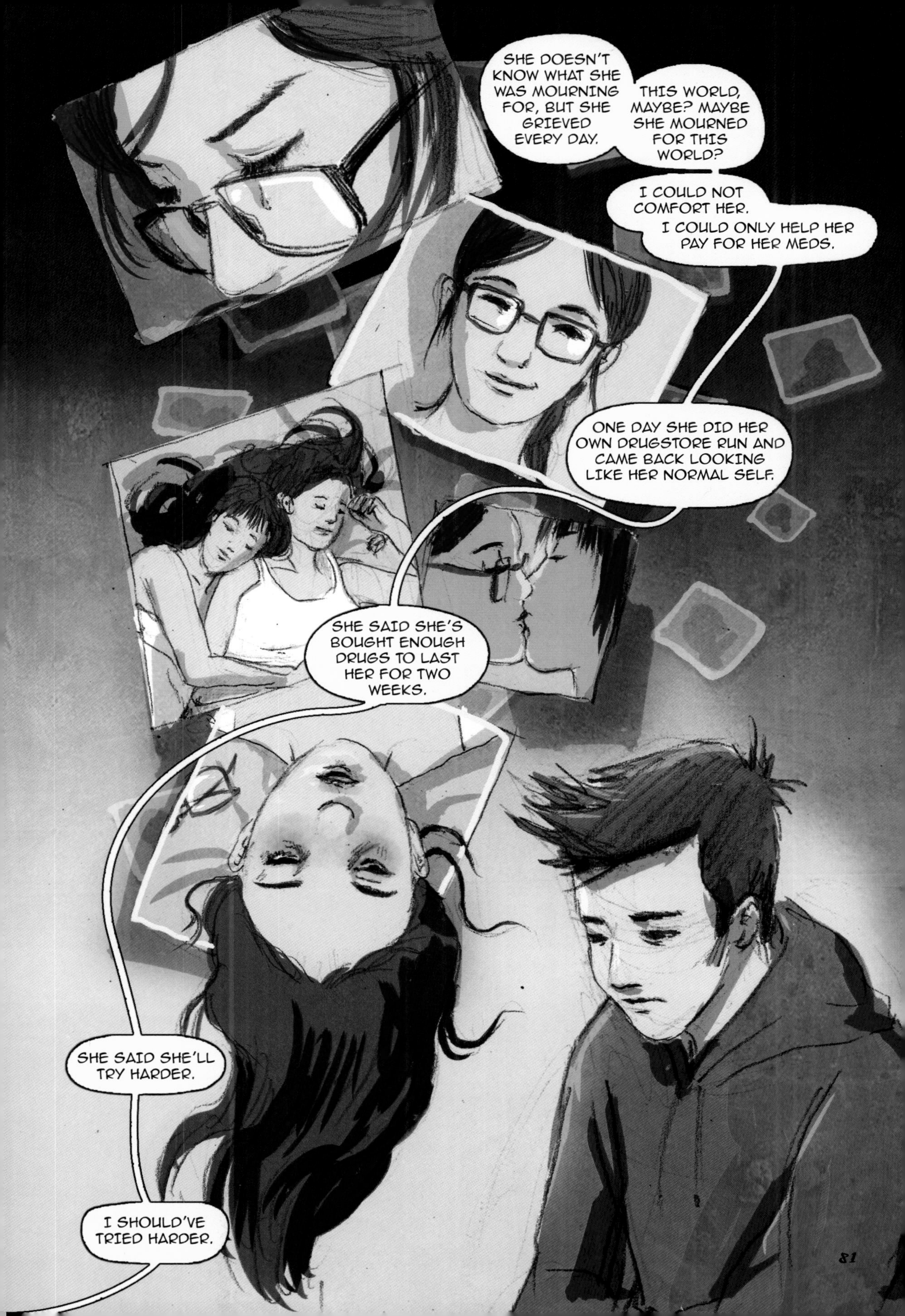
SHE DOESN'T KNOW WHAT SHE WAS MOURNING FOR, BUT SHE GRIEVED EVERY DAY.
THIS WORLD, MAYBE? MAYBE SHE MOURNED FOR THIS WORLD?
I COULD NOT COMFORT HER.
I COULD ONLY HELP HER PAY FOR HER MEDS.
ONE DAY SHE DID HER OWN DRUGSTORE RUN AND CAME BACK LOOKING LIKE HER NORMAL SELF.
SHE SAID SHE'S BOUGHT ENOUGH DRUGS TO LAST HER FOR TWO WEEKS.
SHE SAID SHE'LL TRY HARDER.
I SHOULD'VE TRIED HARDER.

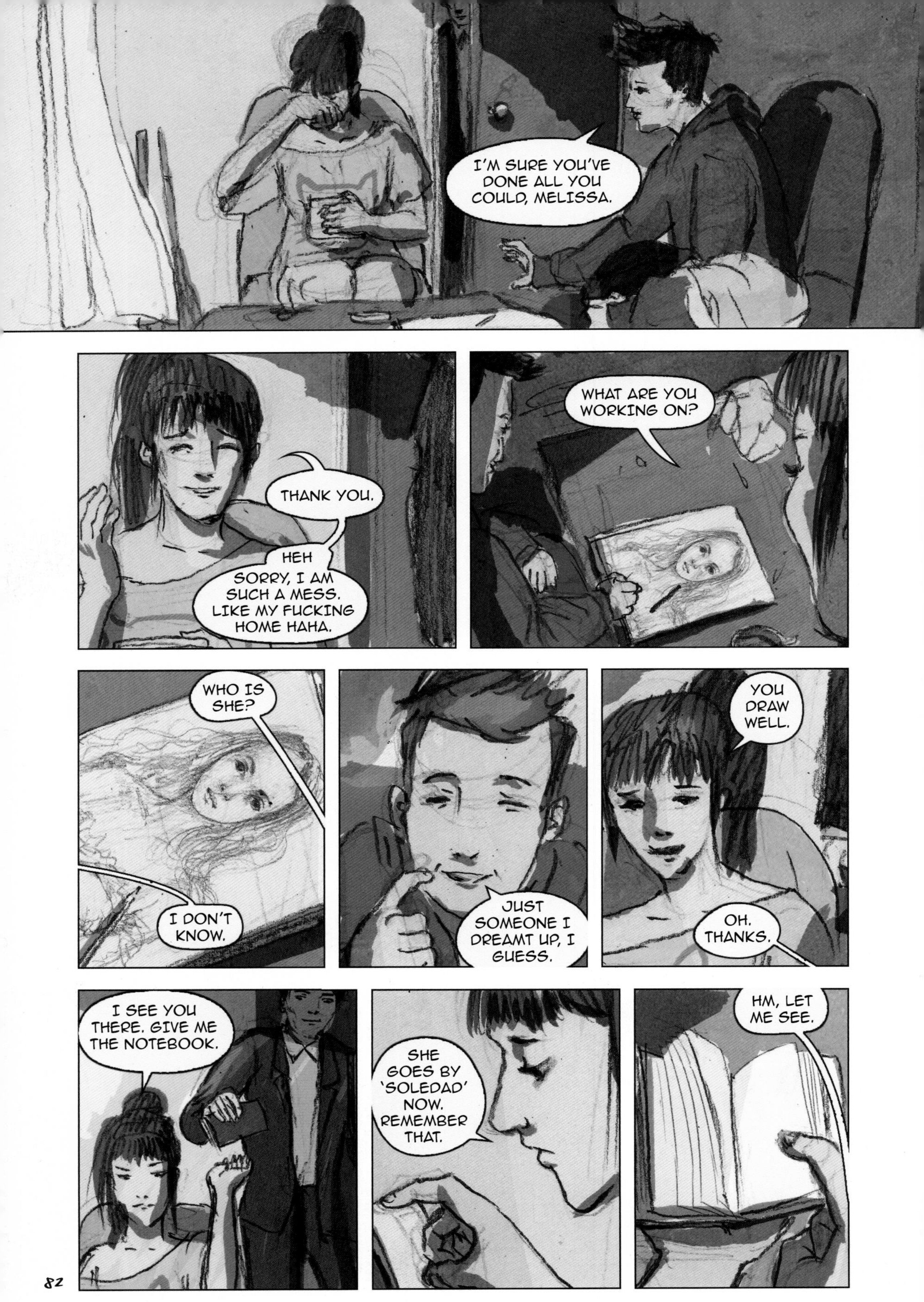

I'M SURE YOU'VE DONE ALL YOU COULD, MELISSA.
THANK YOU.
HEH SORRY, I AM SUCH A MESS. LIKE MY FUCKING HOME HAHA.
WHAT ARE YOU WORKING ON?
WHO IS SHE?
I DON'T KNOW.
JUST SOMEONE I DREAMT UP, I GUESS.
YOU DRAW WELL.
OH. THANKS.
I SEE YOU THERE. GIVE ME THE NOTEBOOK.
SHE GOES BY 'SOLEDAD' NOW. REMEMBER THAT.
HM, LET ME SEE.

THERE, YOU SEE?

I SEE.

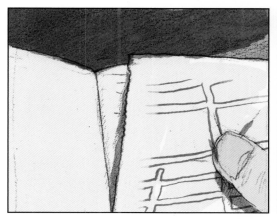

HERE. IN CASE YOU LOSE YOUR WAY.

THANK YOU.

CAN I TALK TO YOU? IN PRIVATE?

EXCUSE US, CONRAD.

OH, SURE. NOWORRIES.

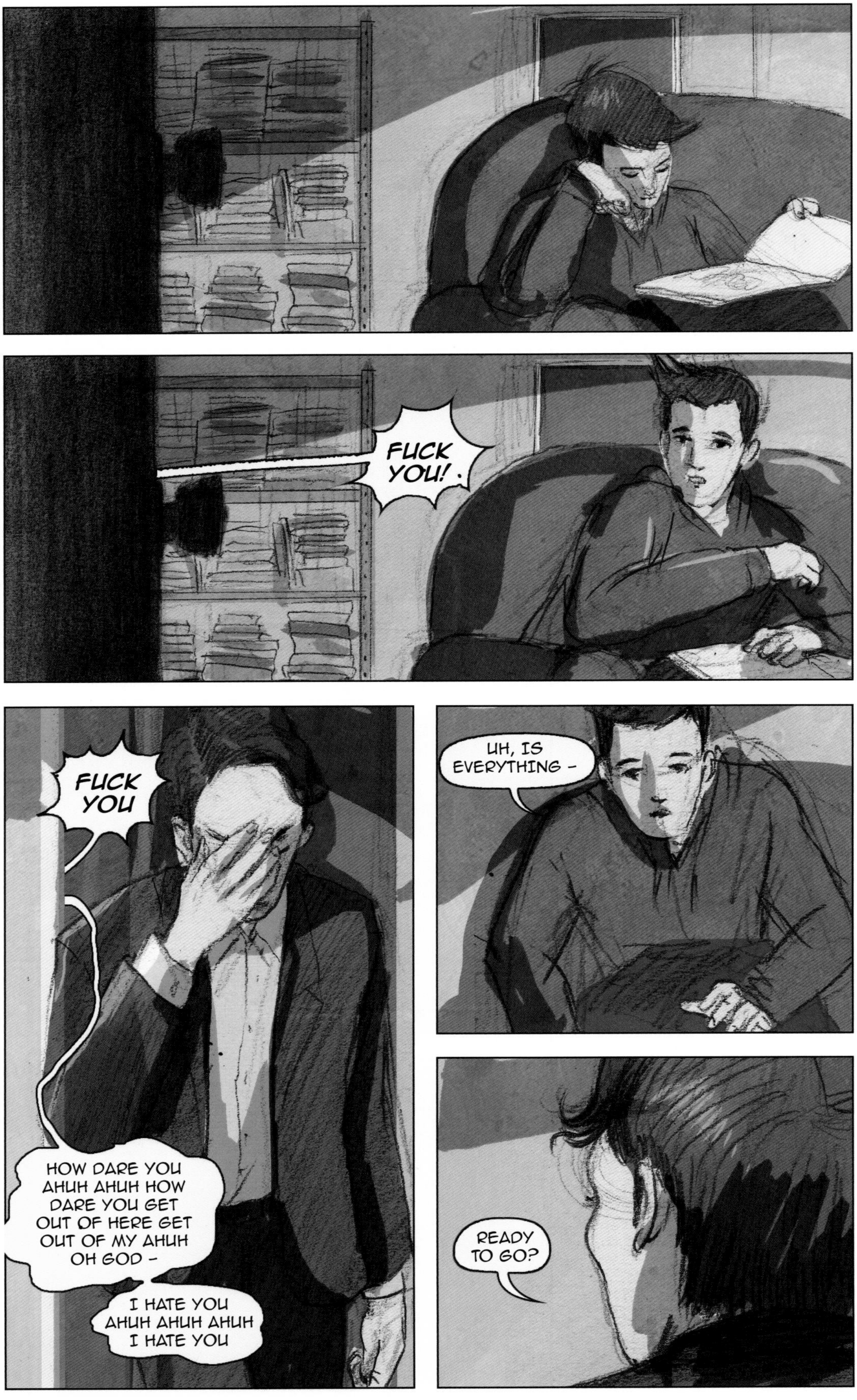
FUCK YOU!
FUCK YOU
HOW DARE YOU AHUH AHUH HOW DARE YOU GET OUT OF HERE GET OUT OF MY AHUH OH GOD -
I HATE YOU AHUH AHUH AHUH I HATE YOU
UH, IS EVERYTHING -
READY TO GO?

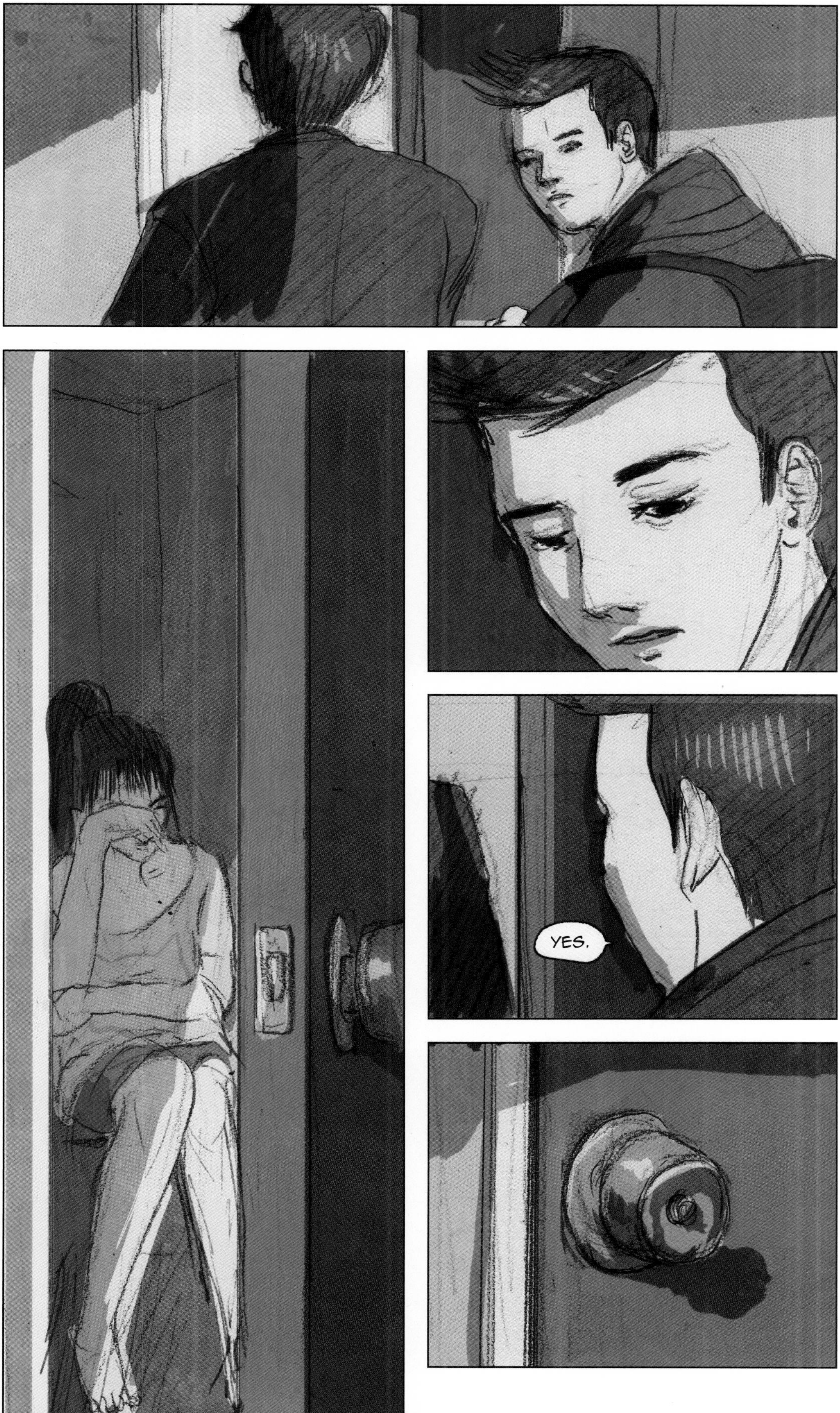
YES.

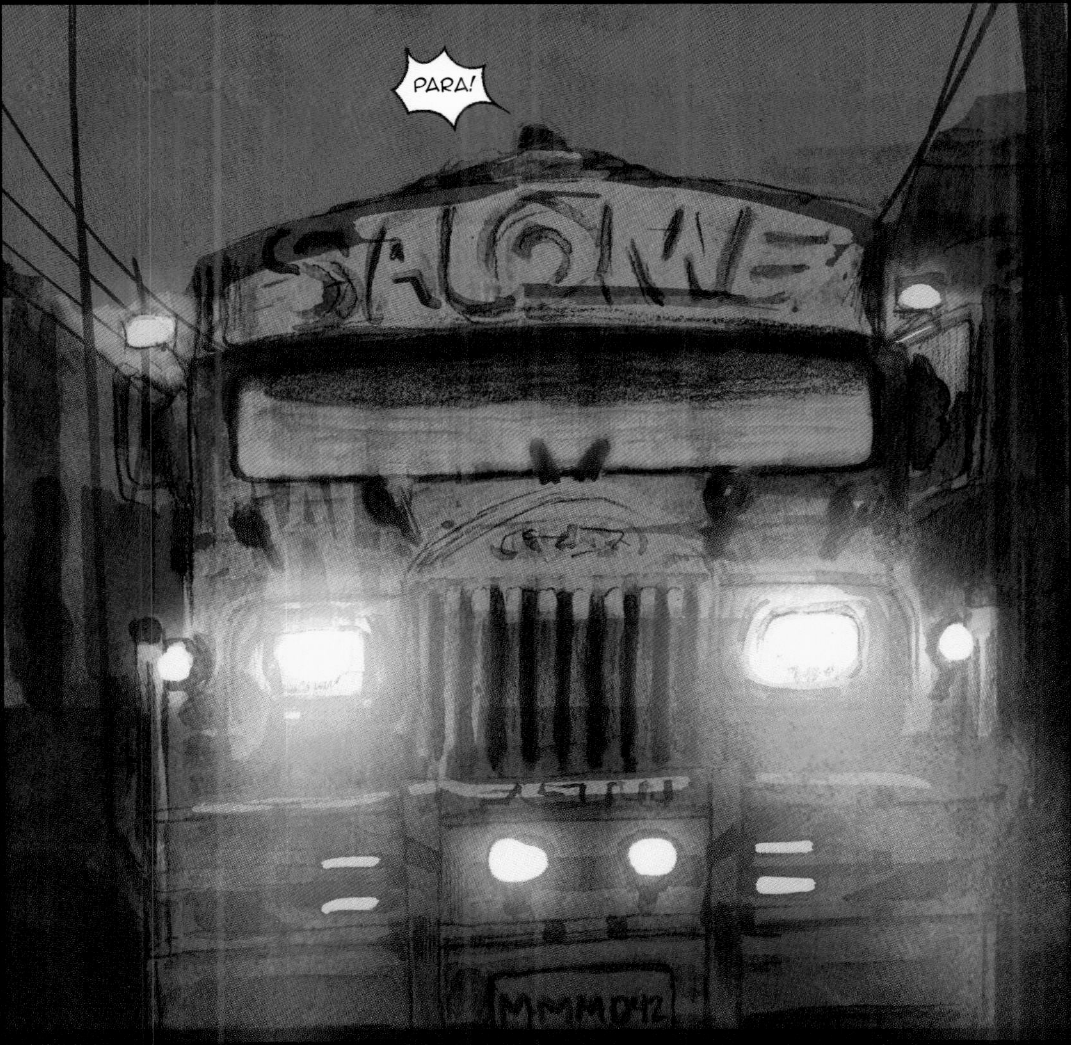
PARA!

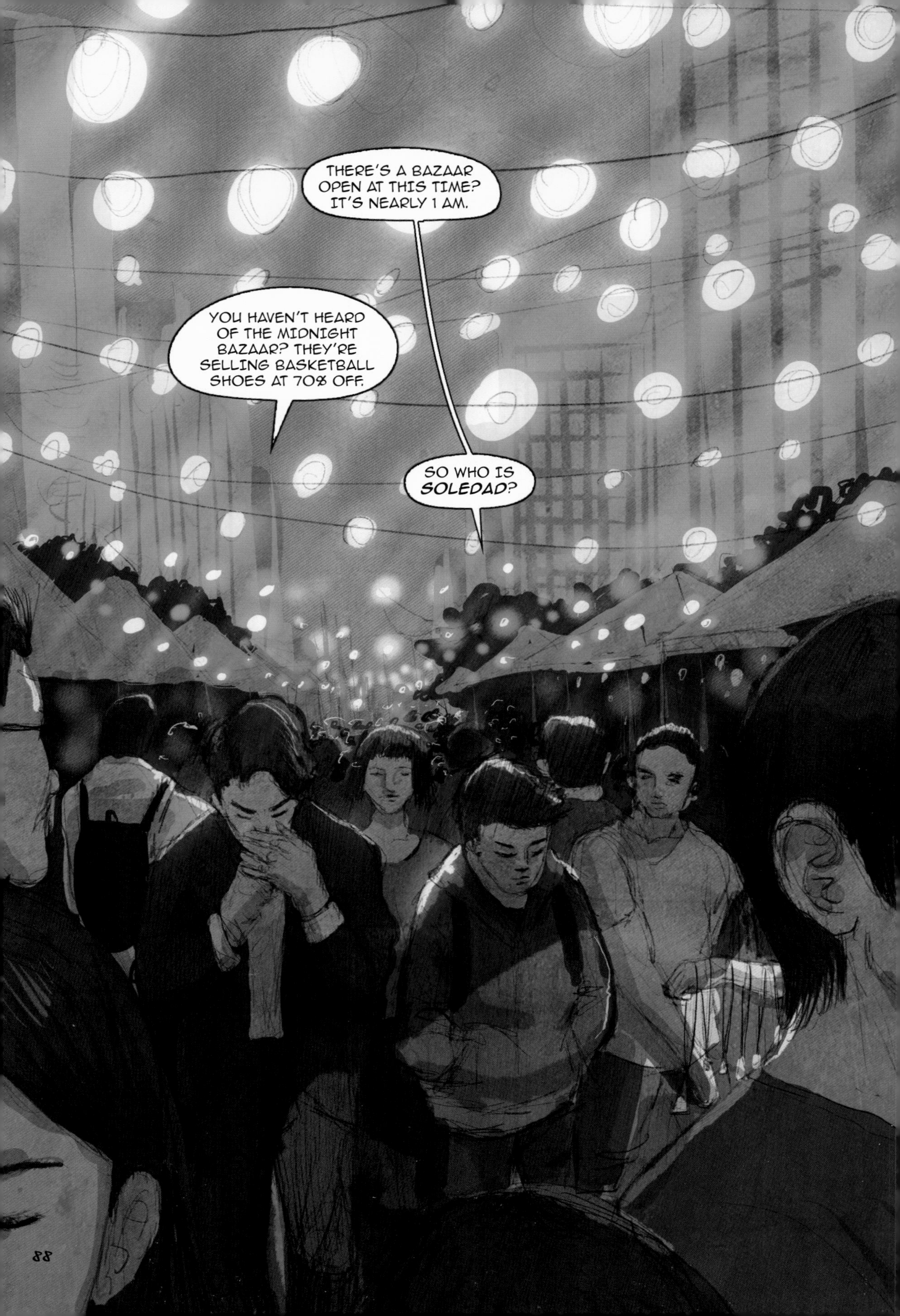
THERE'S A BAZAAR OPEN AT THIS TIME? IT'S NEARLY 1 AM.
YOU HAVEN'T HEARD OF THE MIDNIGHT BAZAAR? THEY'RE SELLING BASKETBALL SHOES AT 70% OFF.
SO WHO IS *SOLEDAD*?

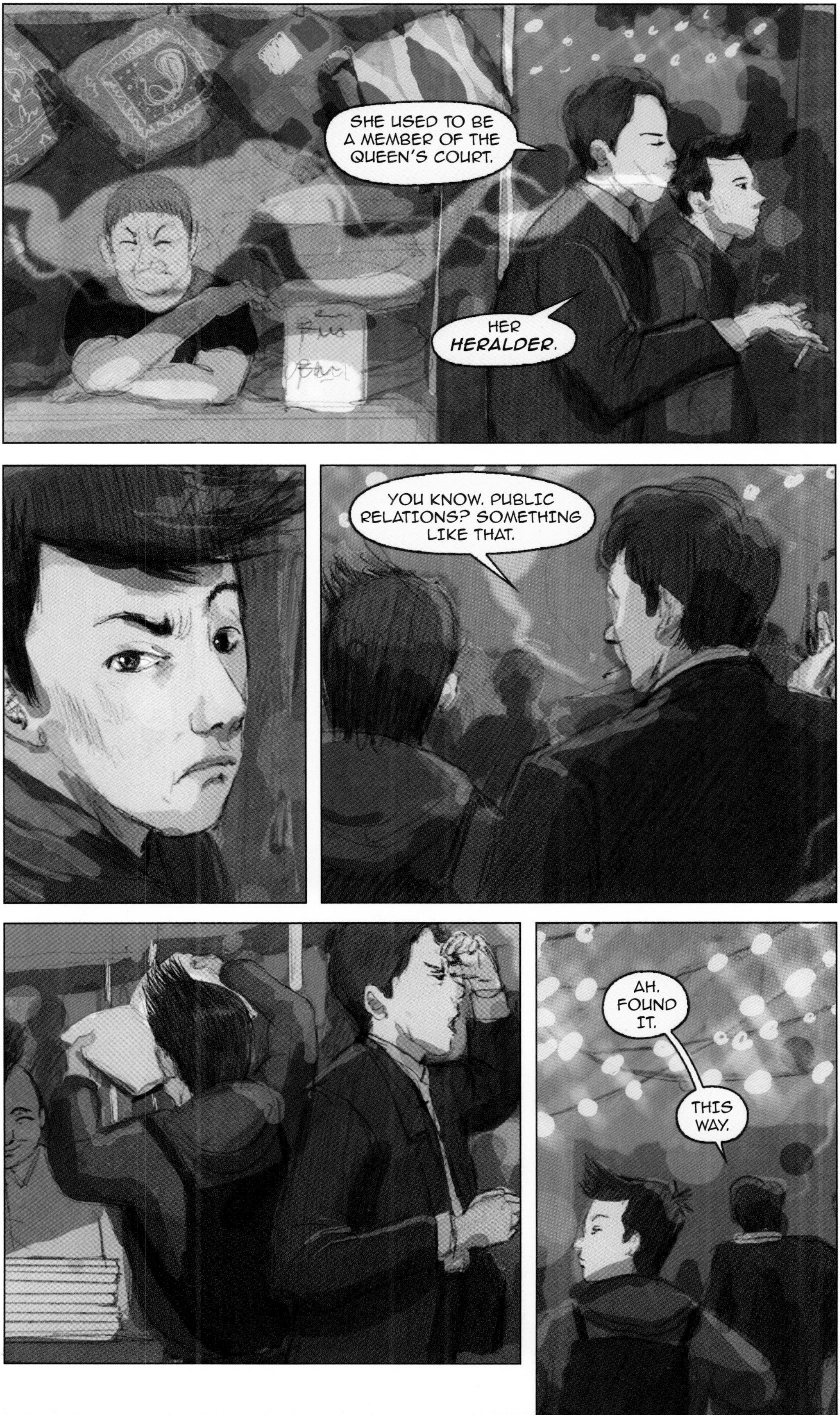

SHE USED TO BE A MEMBER OF THE QUEEN'S COURT.
HER ***HERALDER***.
YOU KNOW. PUBLIC RELATIONS? SOMETHING LIKE THAT.
AH. FOUND IT.
THIS WAY.

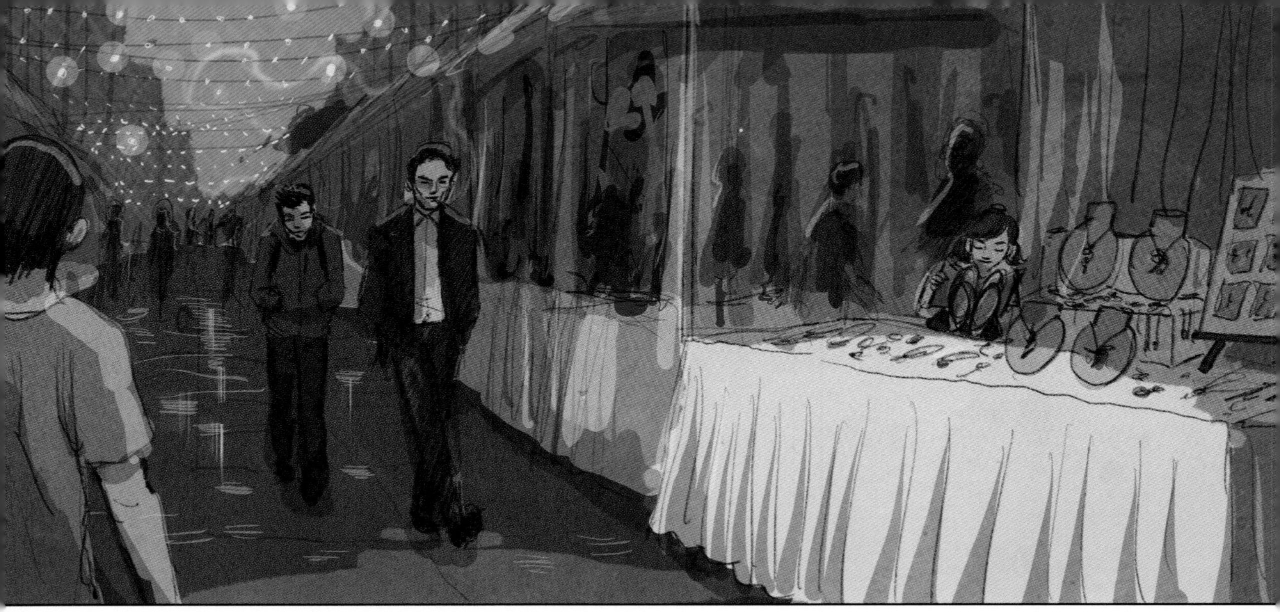

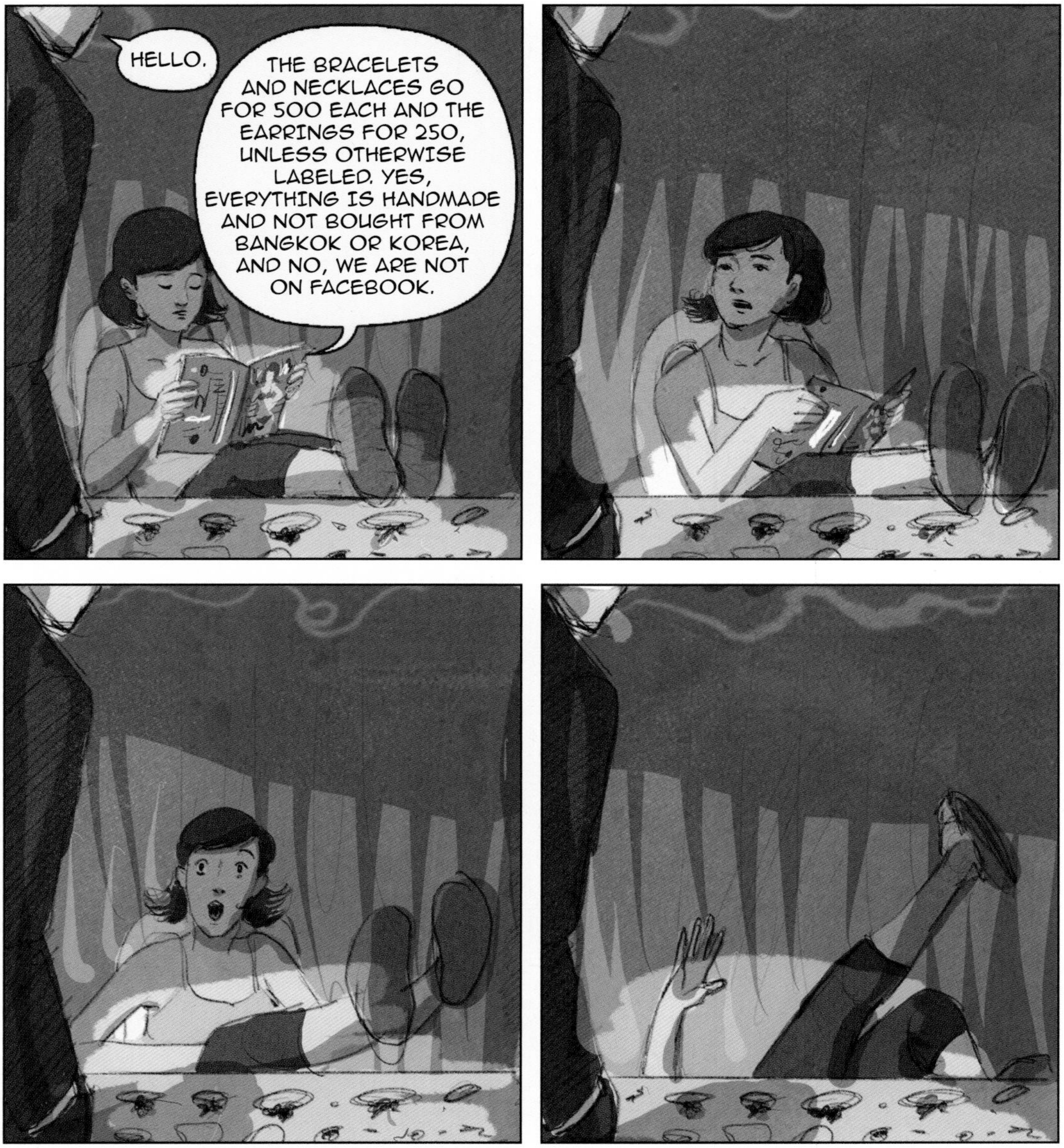
HELLO.
THE BRACELETS AND NECKLACES GO FOR 500 EACH AND THE EARRINGS FOR 250, UNLESS OTHERWISE LABELED. YES, EVERYTHING IS HANDMADE AND NOT BOUGHT FROM BANGKOK OR KOREA, AND NO, WE ARE NOT ON FACEBOOK.

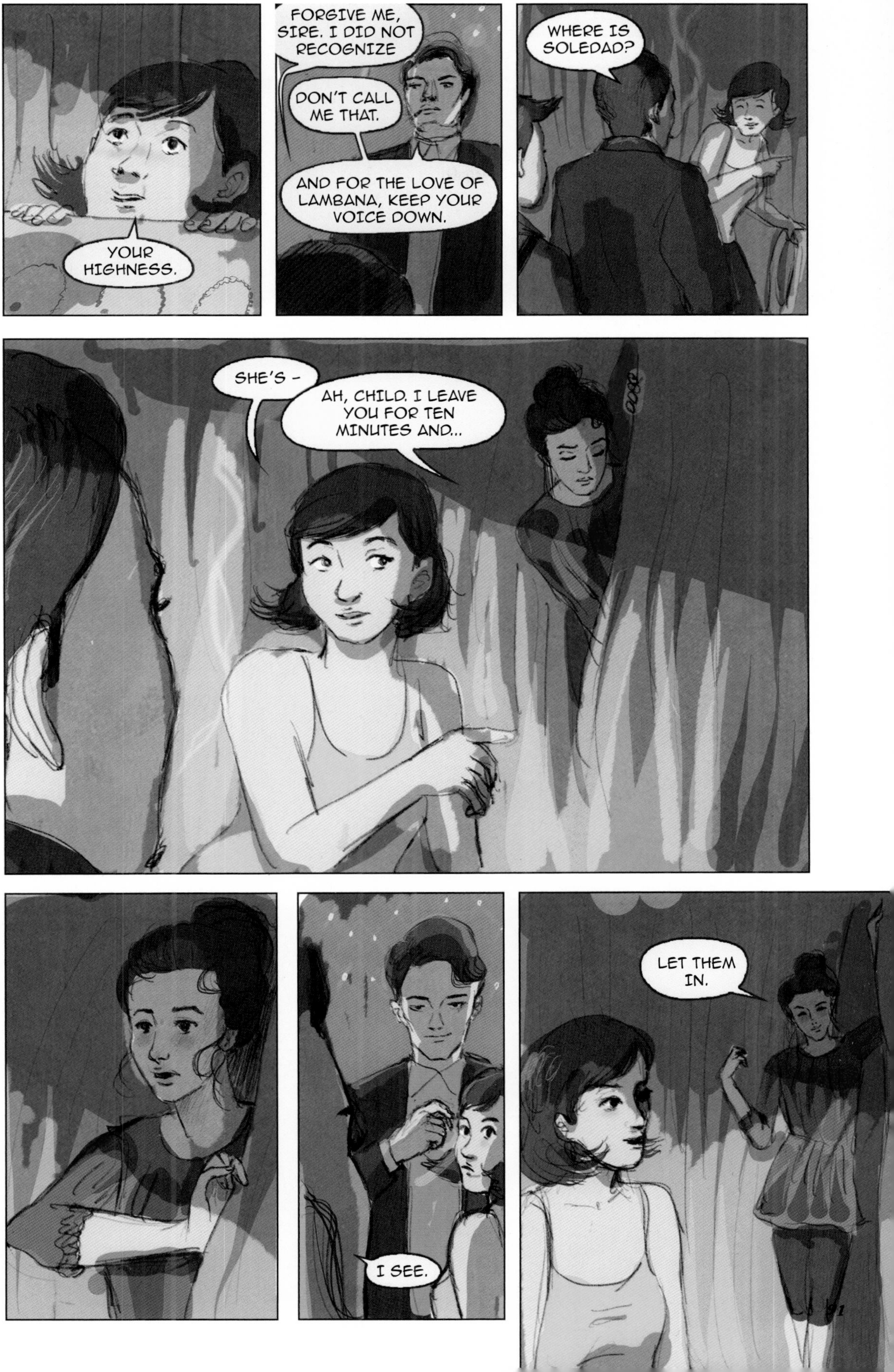
YOUR HIGHNESS.
FORGIVE ME, SIRE. I DID NOT RECOGNIZE
DON'T CALL ME THAT.
AND FOR THE LOVE OF LAMBANA, KEEP YOUR VOICE DOWN.
WHERE IS SOLEDAD?
SHE'S -
AH, CHILD. I LEAVE YOU FOR TEN MINUTES AND...
I SEE.
LET THEM IN.

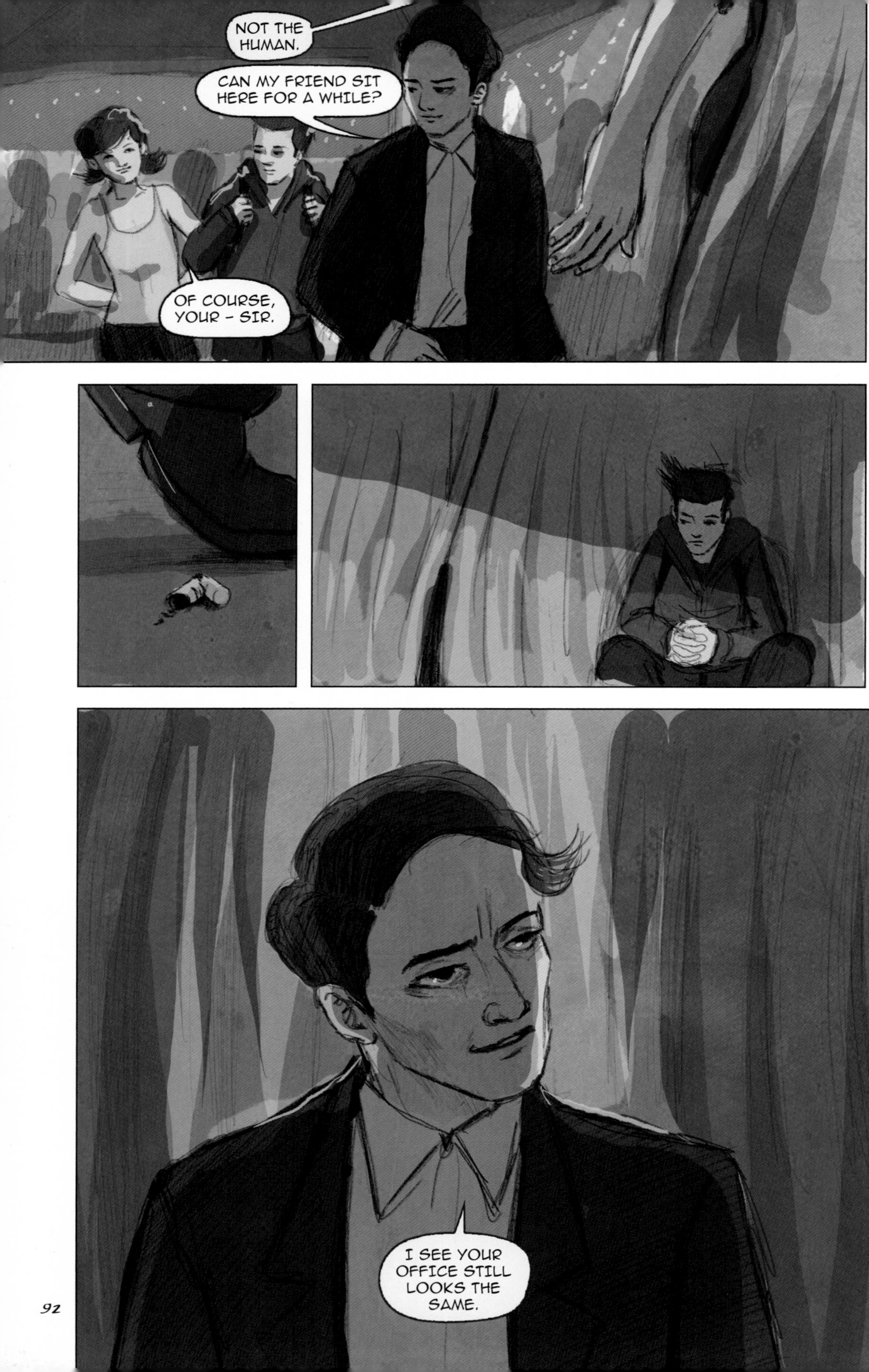
NOT THE HUMAN.
CAN MY FRIEND SIT HERE FOR A WHILE?
OF COURSE, YOUR - SIR.
I SEE YOUR OFFICE STILL LOOKS THE SAME.

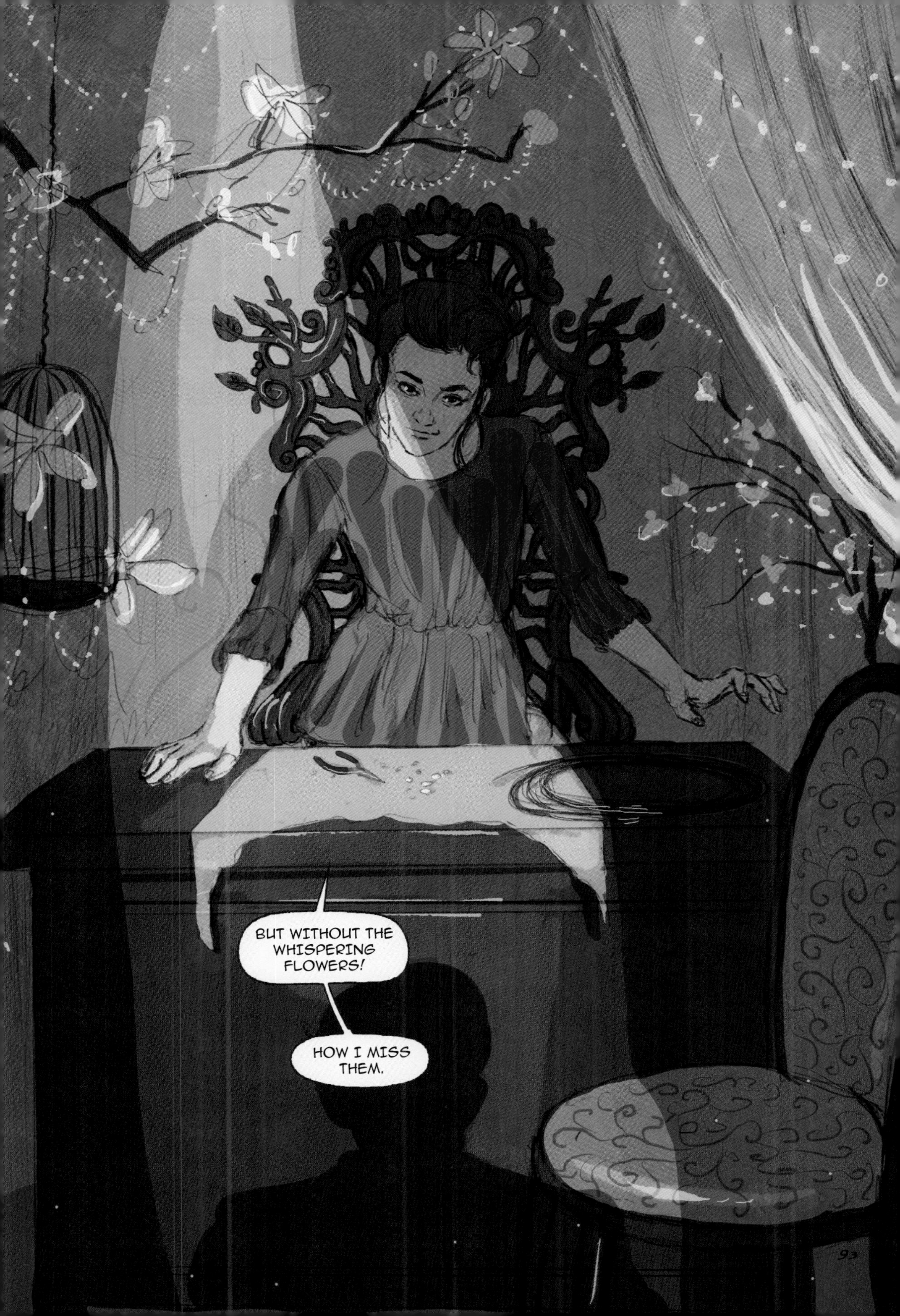
BUT WITHOUT THE WHISPERING FLOWERS!
HOW I MISS THEM.

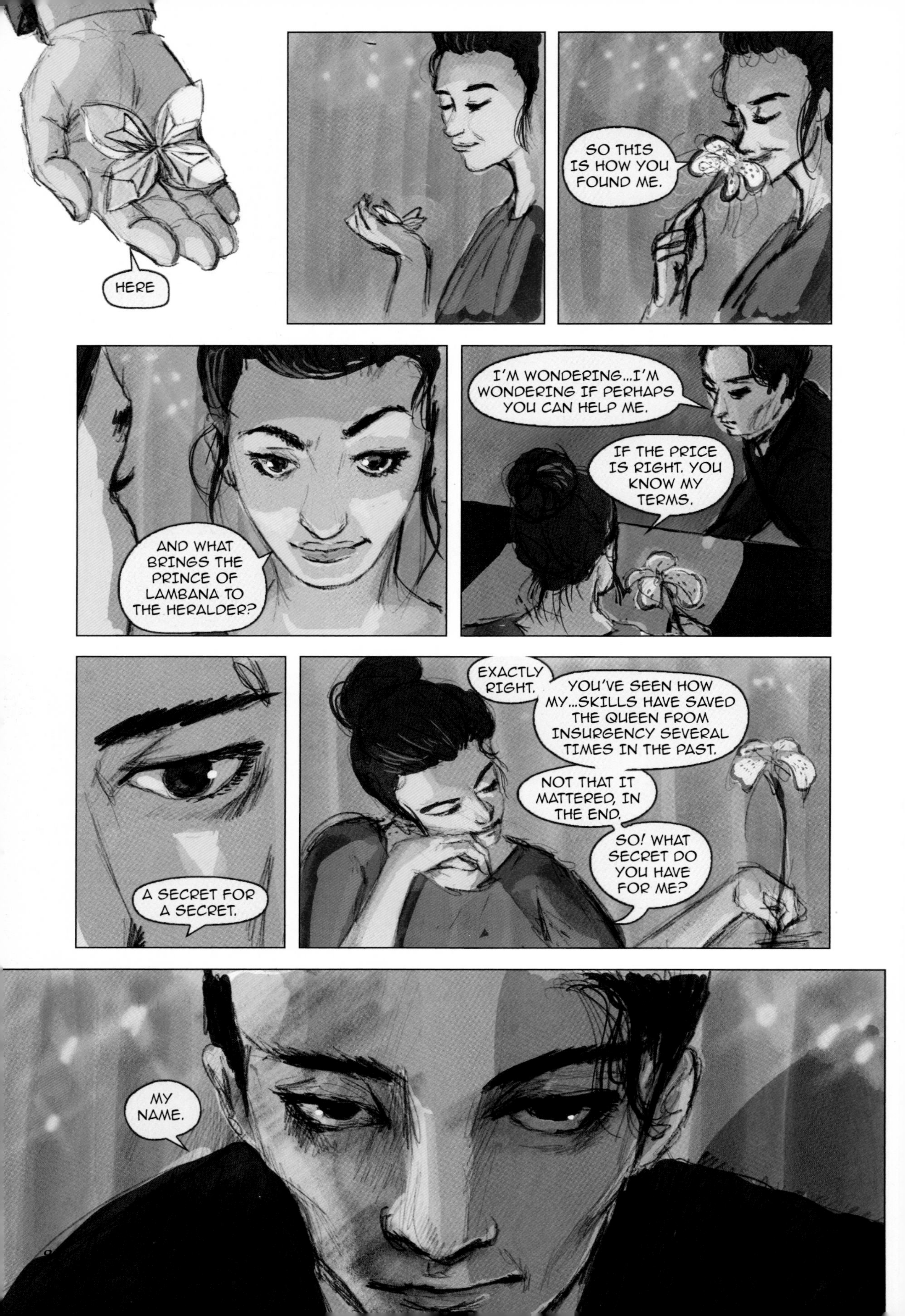
HERE
SO THIS IS HOW YOU FOUND ME.
AND WHAT BRINGS THE PRINCE OF LAMBANA TO THE HERALDER?
I'M WONDERING...I'M WONDERING IF PERHAPS YOU CAN HELP ME.
IF THE PRICE IS RIGHT. YOU KNOW MY TERMS.
A SECRET FOR A SECRET.
EXACTLY RIGHT.
YOU'VE SEEN HOW MY...SKILLS HAVE SAVED THE QUEEN FROM INSURGENCY SEVERAL TIMES IN THE PAST.
NOT THAT IT MATTERED, IN THE END.
SO! WHAT SECRET DO YOU HAVE FOR ME?
MY NAME.

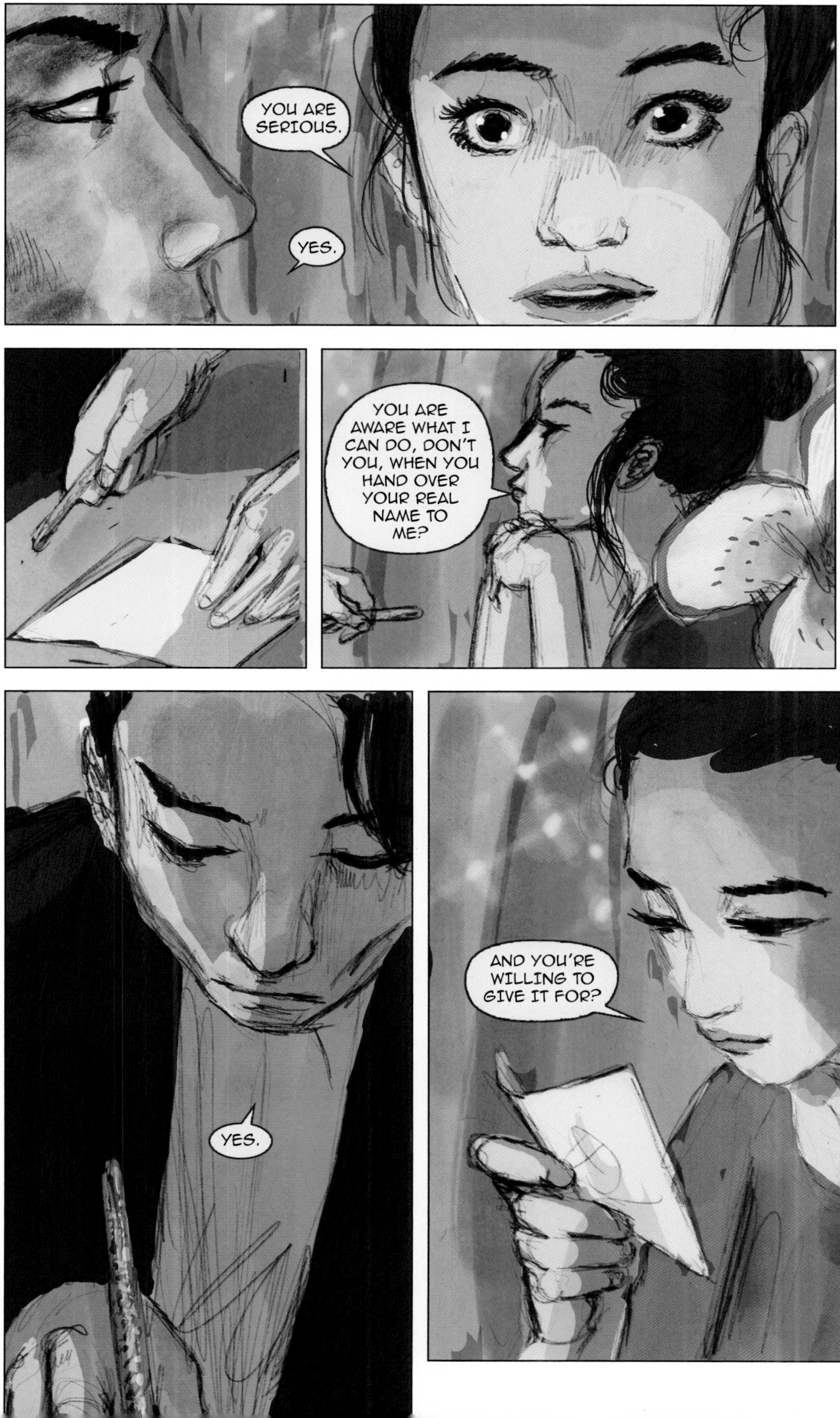
YOU ARE SERIOUS.
YES.
YOU ARE AWARE WHAT I CAN DO, DON'T YOU, WHEN YOU HAND OVER YOUR REAL NAME TO ME?
YES.
AND YOU'RE WILLING TO GIVE IT FOR?

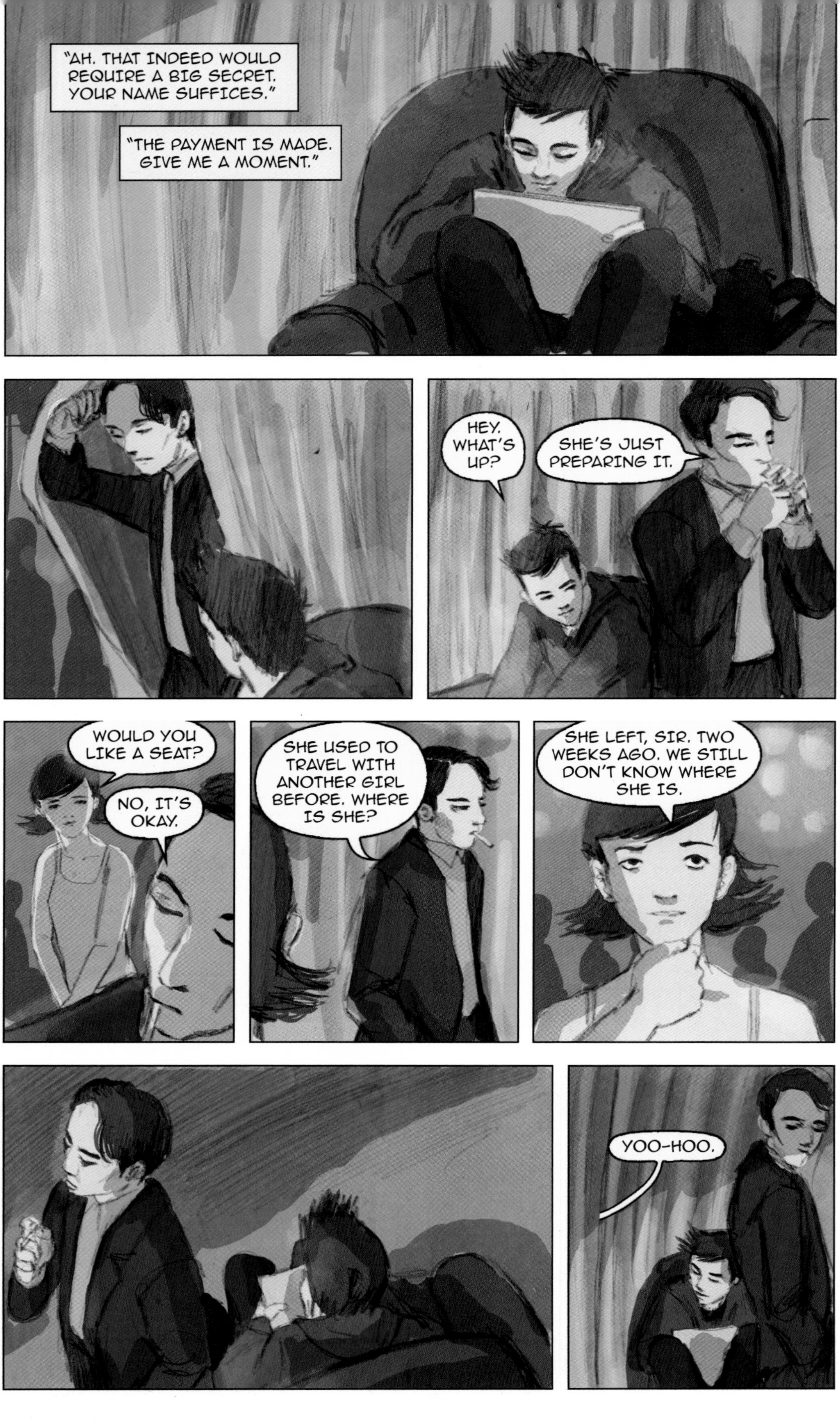
"AH. THAT INDEED WOULD REQUIRE A BIG SECRET. YOUR NAME SUFFICES."
"THE PAYMENT IS MADE. GIVE ME A MOMENT."
HEY. WHAT'S UP?
SHE'S JUST PREPARING IT.
WOULD YOU LIKE A SEAT?
NO, IT'S OKAY.
SHE USED TO TRAVEL WITH ANOTHER GIRL BEFORE. WHERE IS SHE?
SHE LEFT, SIR. TWO WEEKS AGO. WE STILL DON'T KNOW WHERE SHE IS.
YOO-HOO.

OH, HELLO. PLEASE HAVE A SEAT.

IGNACIO IS A FRIEND OF YOURS?

YOU CAN SAY THAT.

DO YOU TRUST HIM?

WELL, YES, HE – DID HE TELL YOU...WHAT WAS WRONG WITH ME?

YES. YES, HE DID.

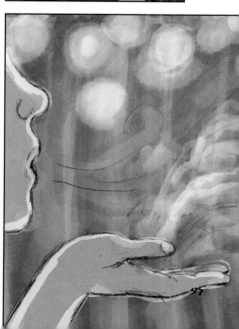

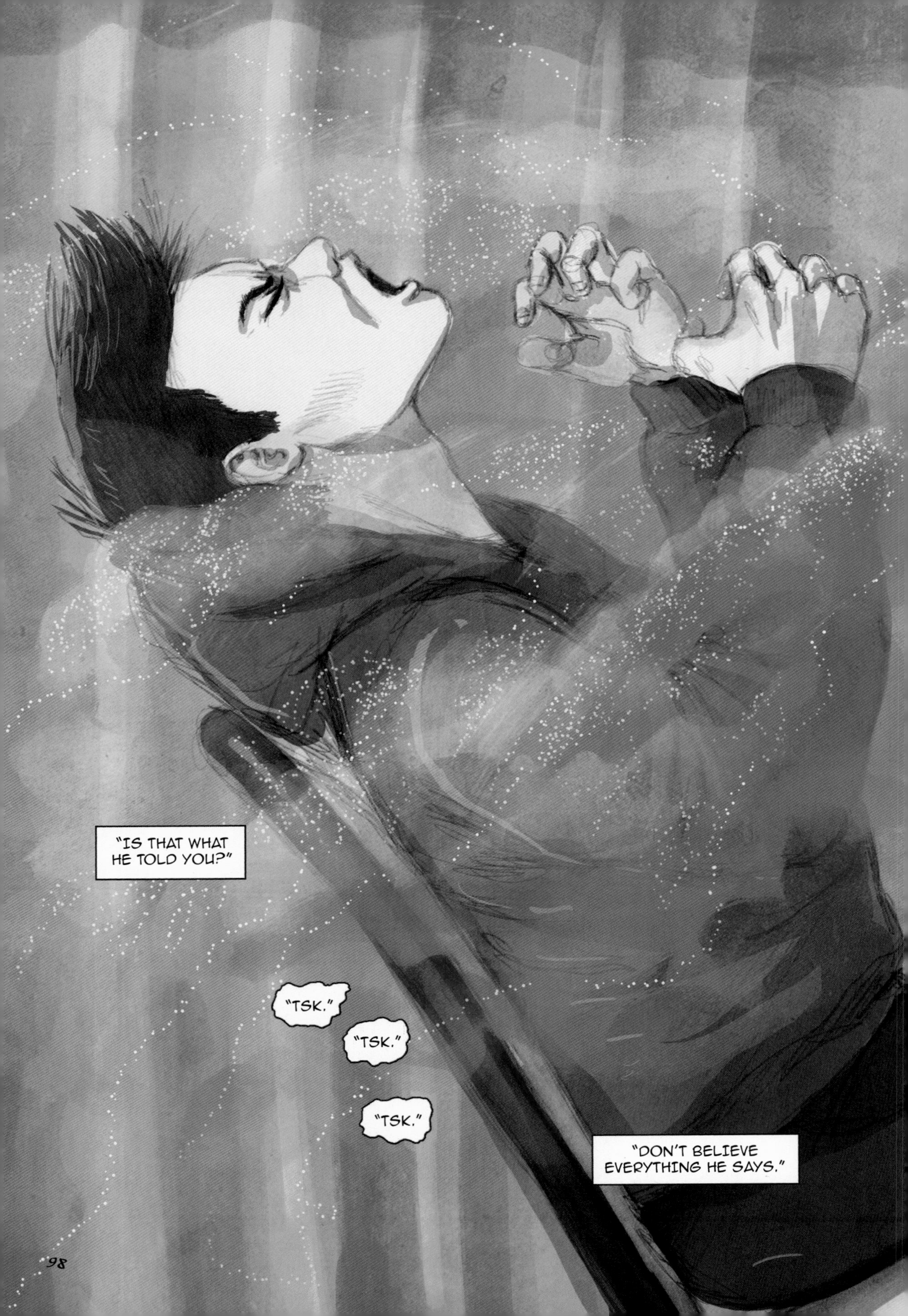
"IS THAT WHAT HE TOLD YOU?"
"TSK."
"TSK."
"TSK."
"DON'T BELIEVE EVERYTHING HE SAYS."

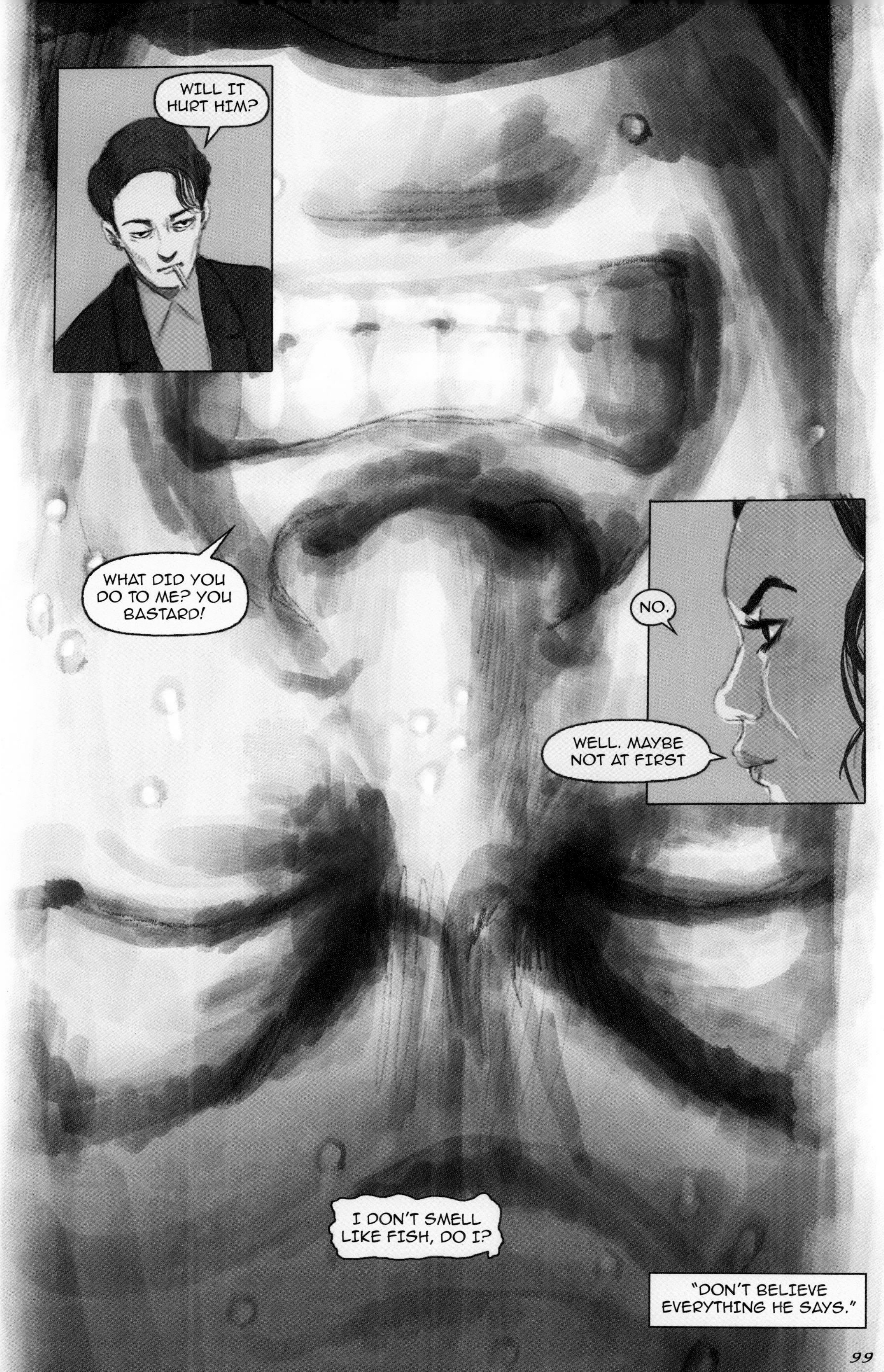
WILL IT HURT HIM?
WHAT DID YOU DO TO ME? YOU BASTARD!
NO.
WELL. MAYBE NOT AT FIRST
I DON'T SMELL LIKE FISH, DO I?
"DON'T BELIEVE EVERYTHING HE SAYS."

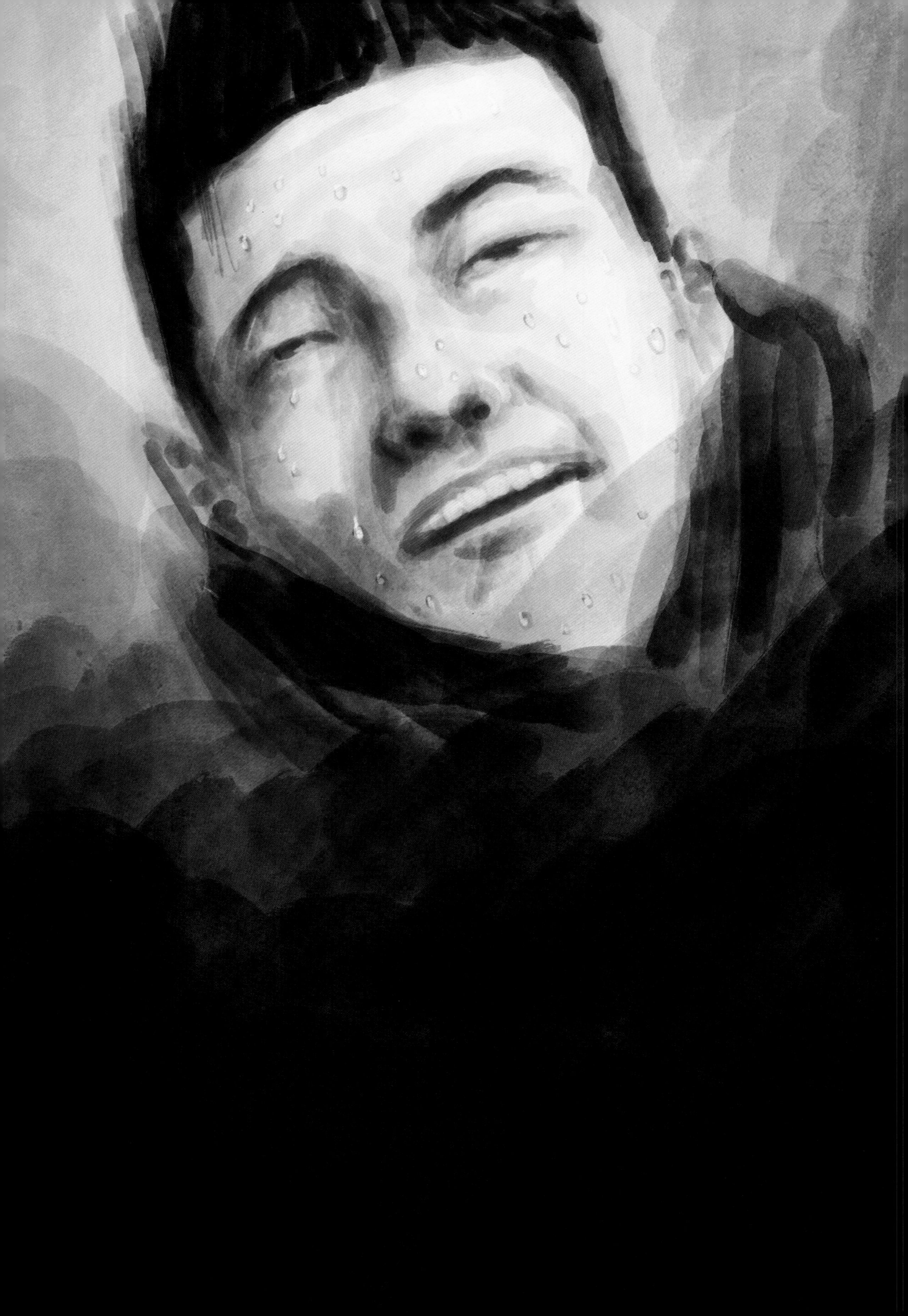

CONRAD?

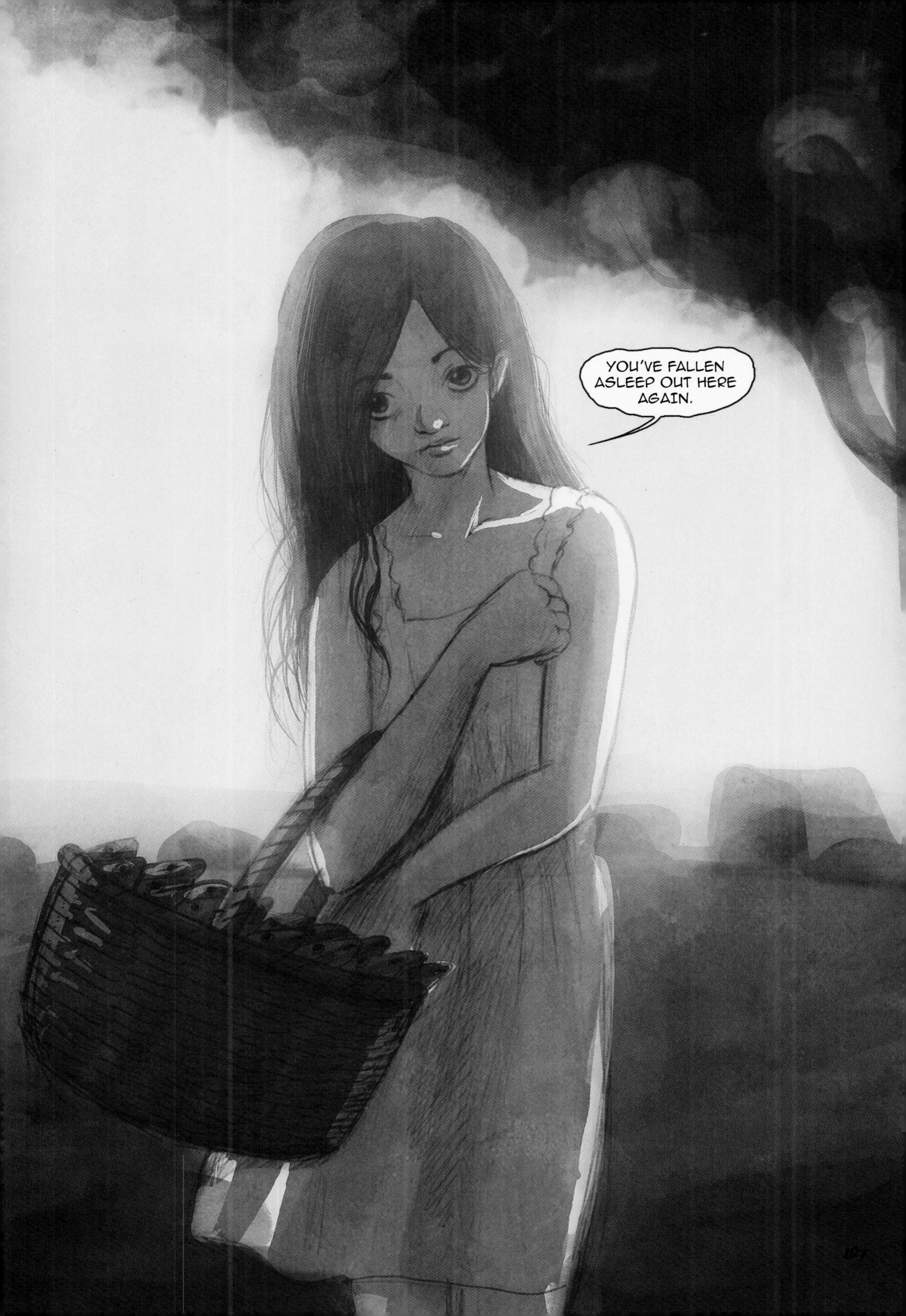
YOU'VE FALLEN ASLEEP OUT HERE AGAIN.

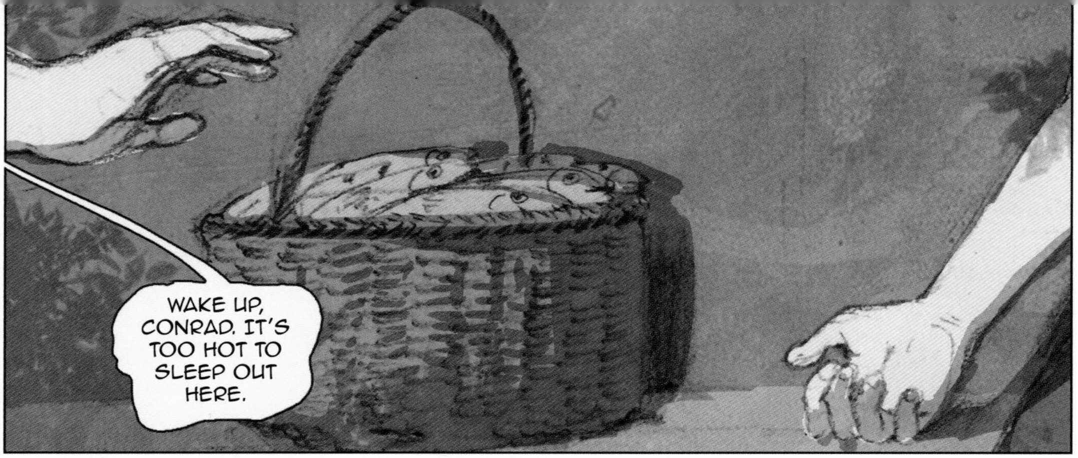
WAKE UP, CONRAD. IT'S TOO HOT TO SLEEP OUT HERE.

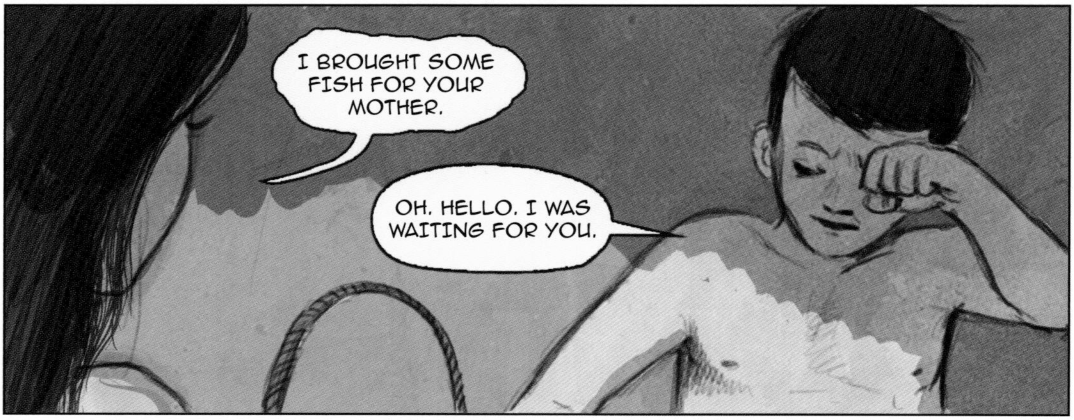
I BROUGHT SOME FISH FOR YOUR MOTHER.
OH. HELLO. I WAS WAITING FOR YOU.

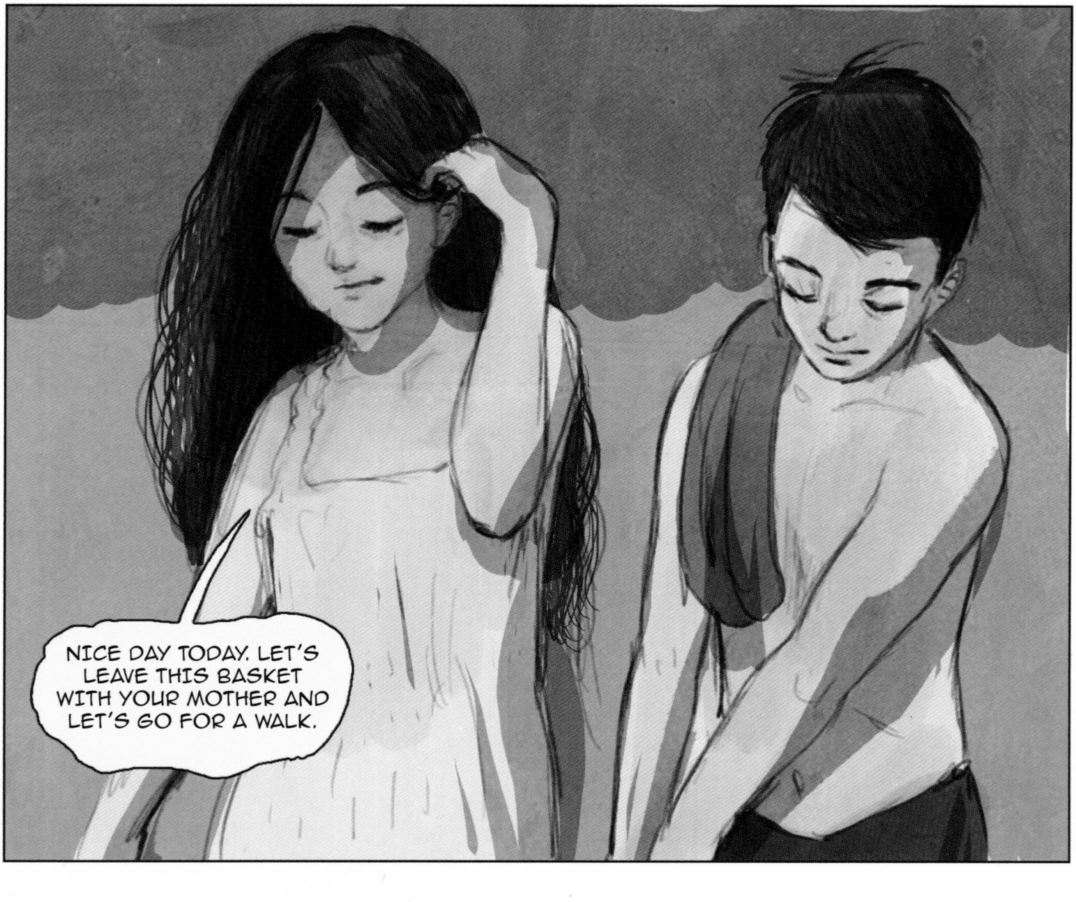
NICE DAY TODAY. LET'S LEAVE THIS BASKET WITH YOUR MOTHER AND LET'S GO FOR A WALK.

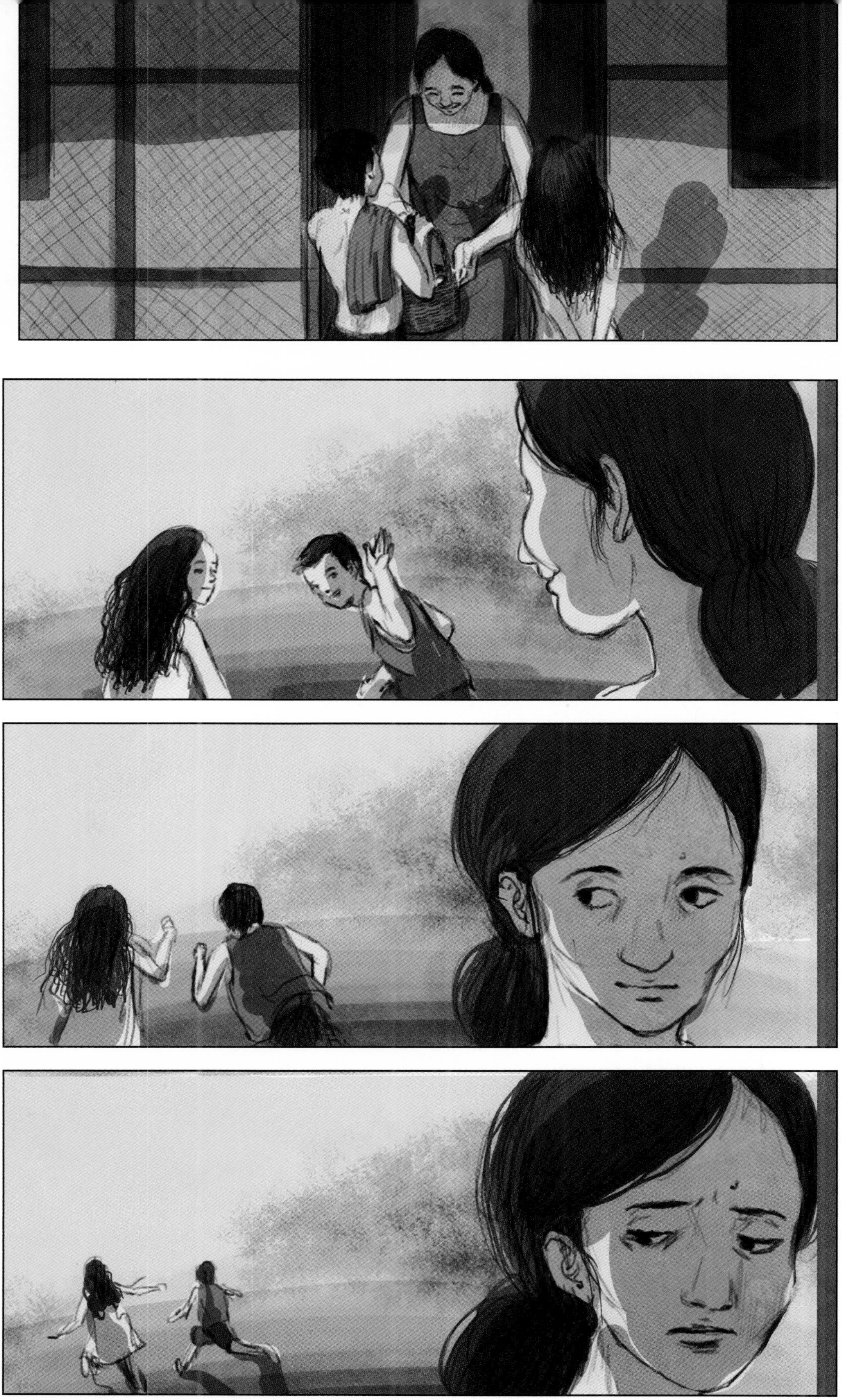

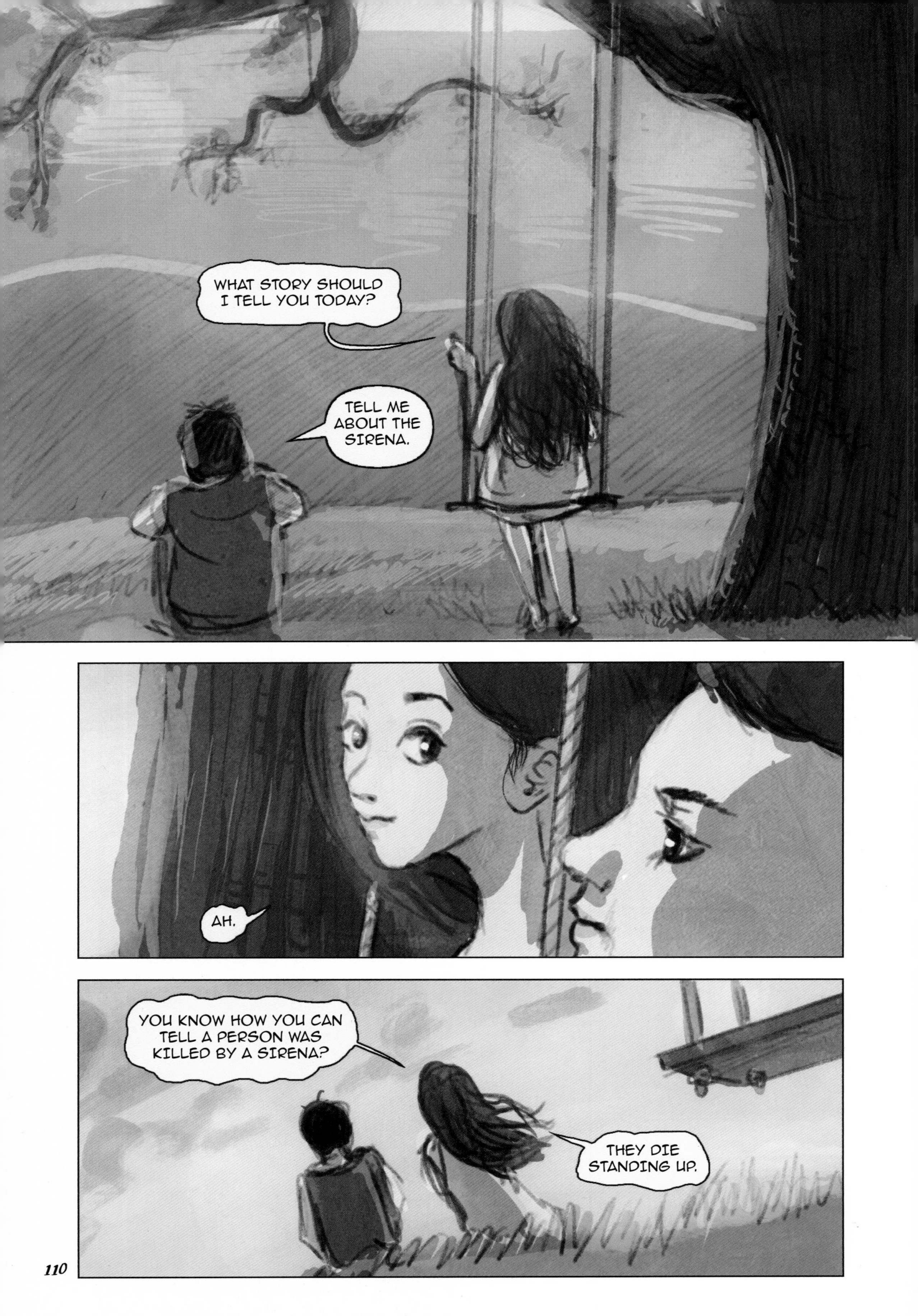
WHAT STORY SHOULD I TELL YOU TODAY?
TELL ME ABOUT THE SIRENA.
AH.
YOU KNOW HOW YOU CAN TELL A PERSON WAS KILLED BY A SIRENA?
THEY DIE STANDING UP.

DID THAT SHOCK YOU?

CONRAD?

MY FATHER DIED THAT WAY.

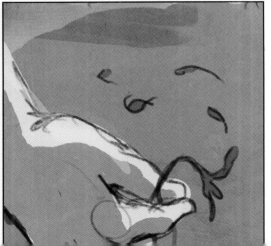

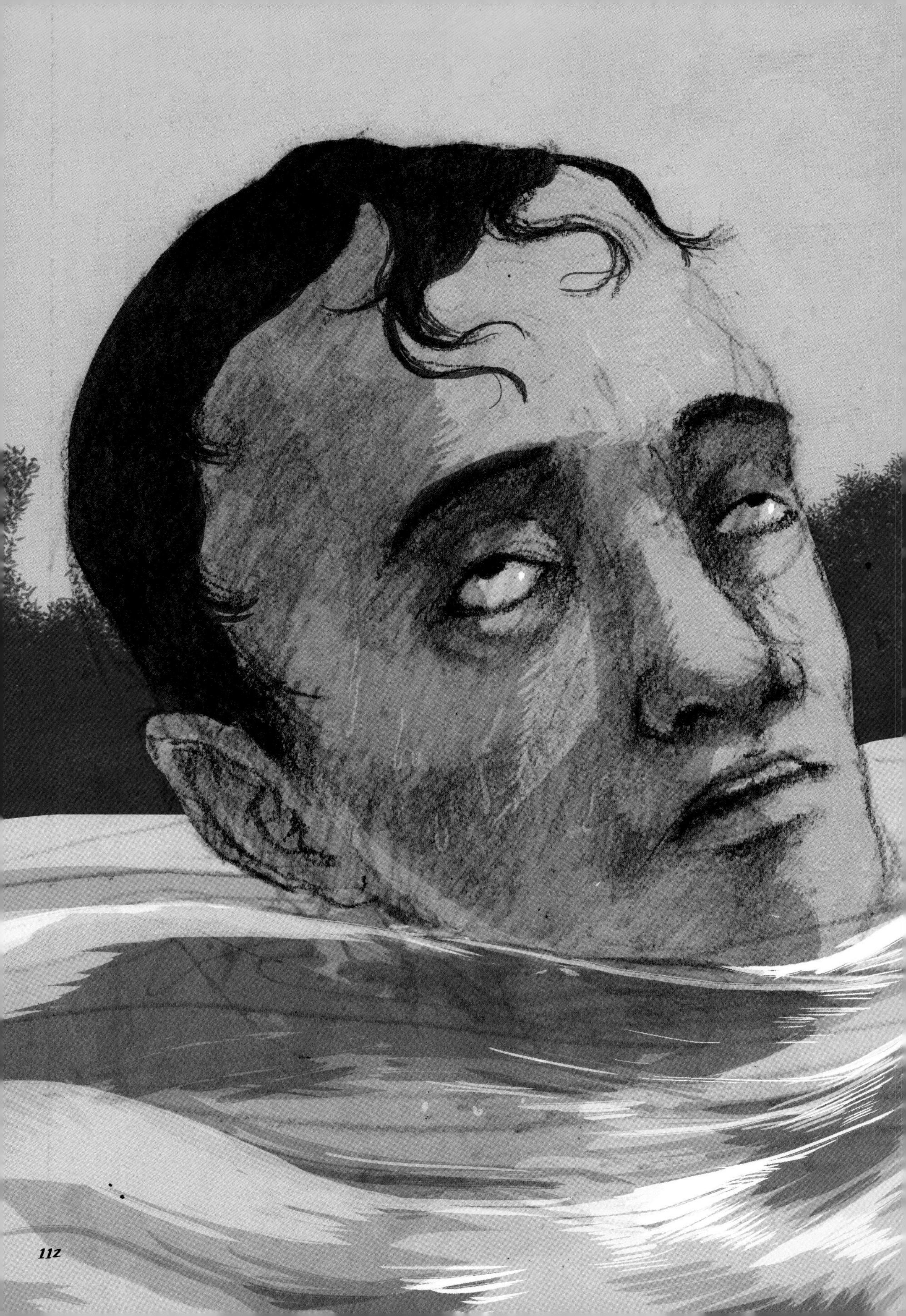

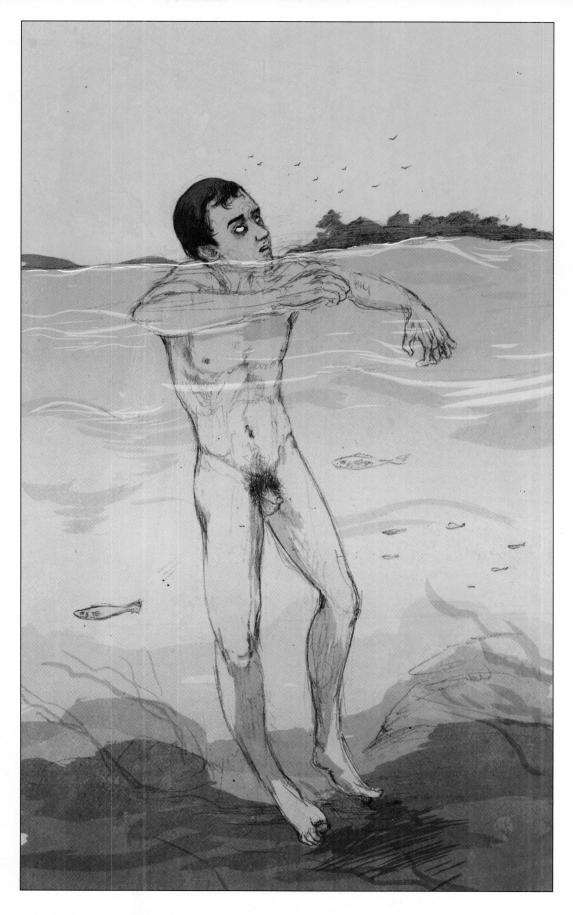

MOTHER SAID IT WAS BECAUSE FATHER FOUND SOMETHING IN THE RIVER THAT BELONGED TO THEM.

HE WOULD HAVE RETURNED IT! THE SIRENA NEED ONLY ASK.

THEY SOUND LIKE A SELF-CENTERED, HOTHEADED LOT.

BUT, IF YOU ARE WRONGED BY THE SIRENA—

THEY MAKE IT UP TO YOU.

THEY DO?

WELL, THEY HAVEN'T MADE IT UP TO US.

WELL, DO YOU KNOW THAT SIRENA DON'T REMAIN IN WATER?

LIAR.

IT'S TRUE! THEY CAN LEAVE THE RIVER. FORM LEGS.

VISIT THE MARKETPLACE AND BUY GOODS LIKE AN ORDINARY PERSON.

BUT THEY SMELL LIKE FISH.

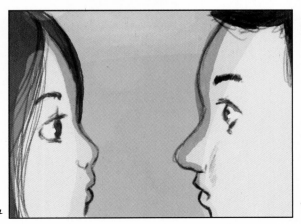

HA HA HA HA HA

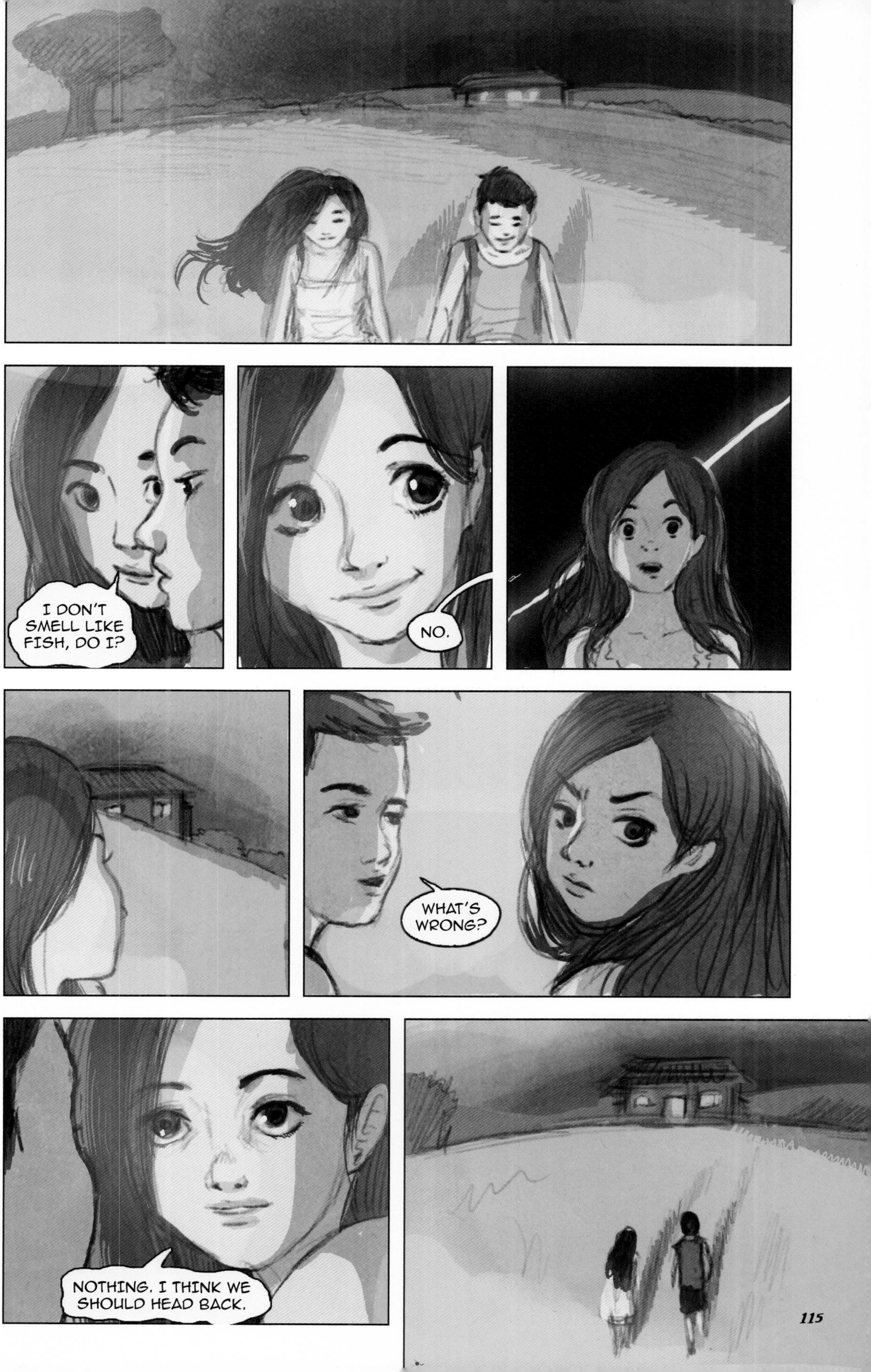
I DON'T SMELL LIKE FISH, DO I?
NO.
WHAT'S WRONG?
NOTHING. I THINK WE SHOULD HEAD BACK.

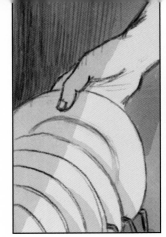

TOK TOK

TAO PO?

GOOD EVENING AGAIN! I'M SORRY, I FORGOT TO TELL CONRAD SOMETHING.

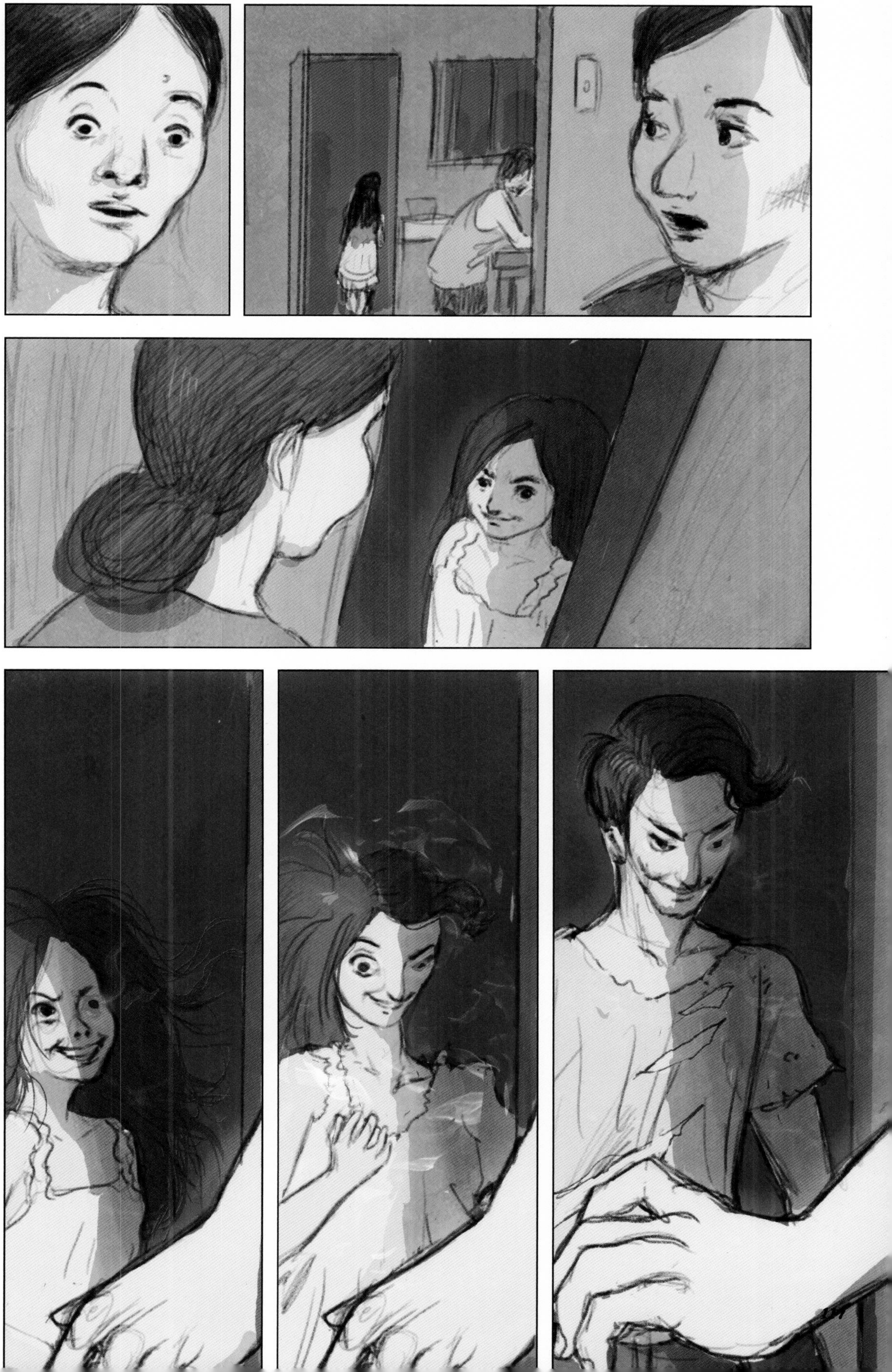

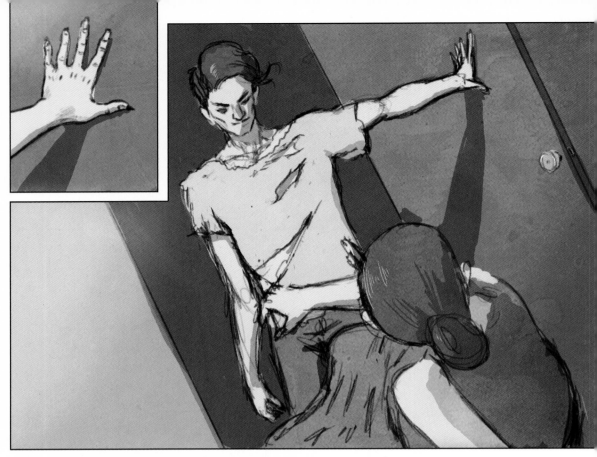

NANANG!

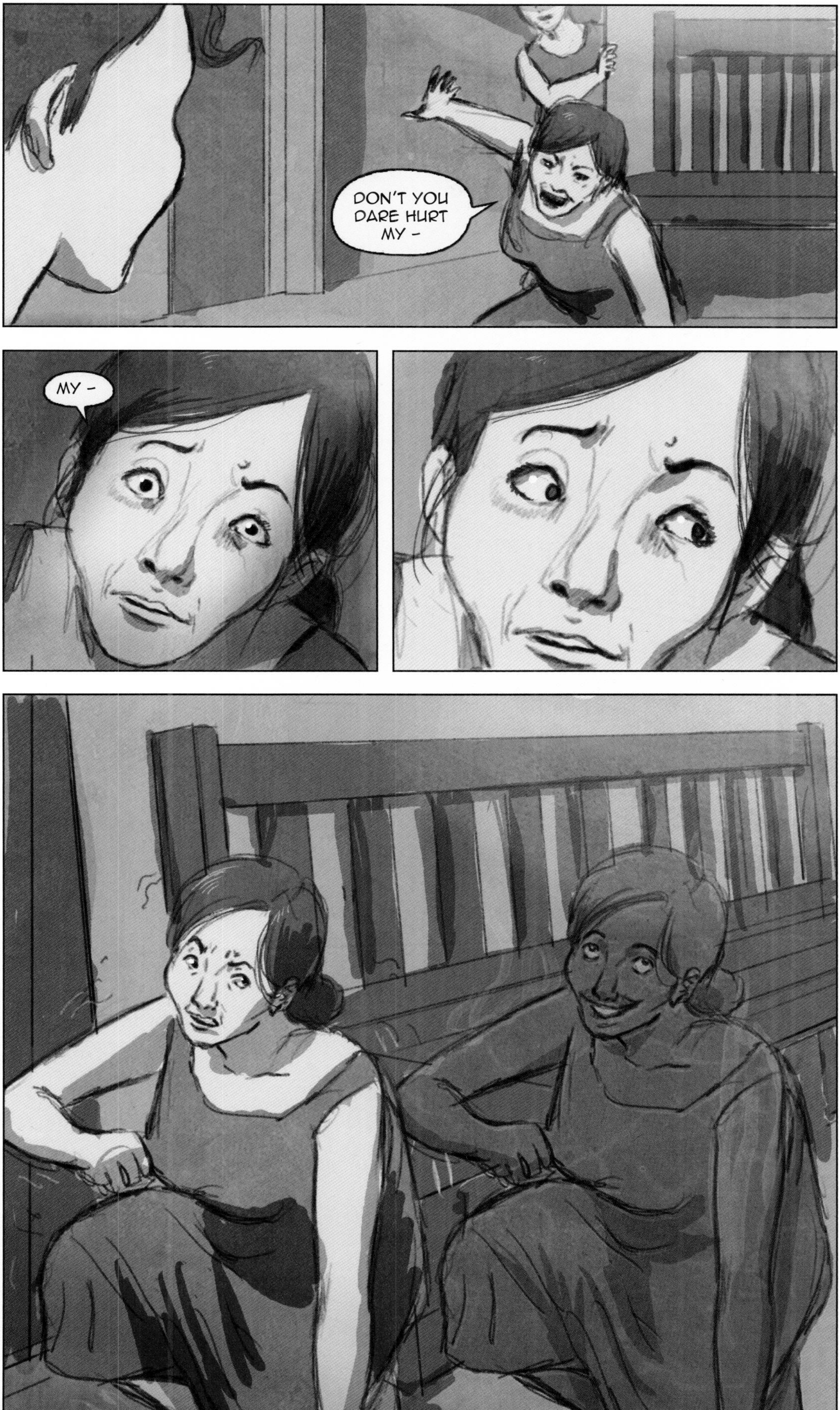
DON'T YOU DARE HURT MY -
MY -

N-NO, NO.

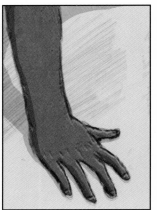

NO AHUH AHUH NO NO PLEASE –

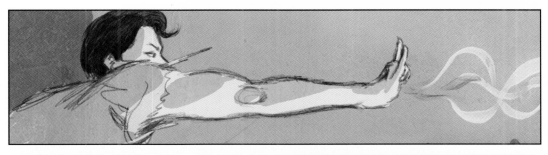

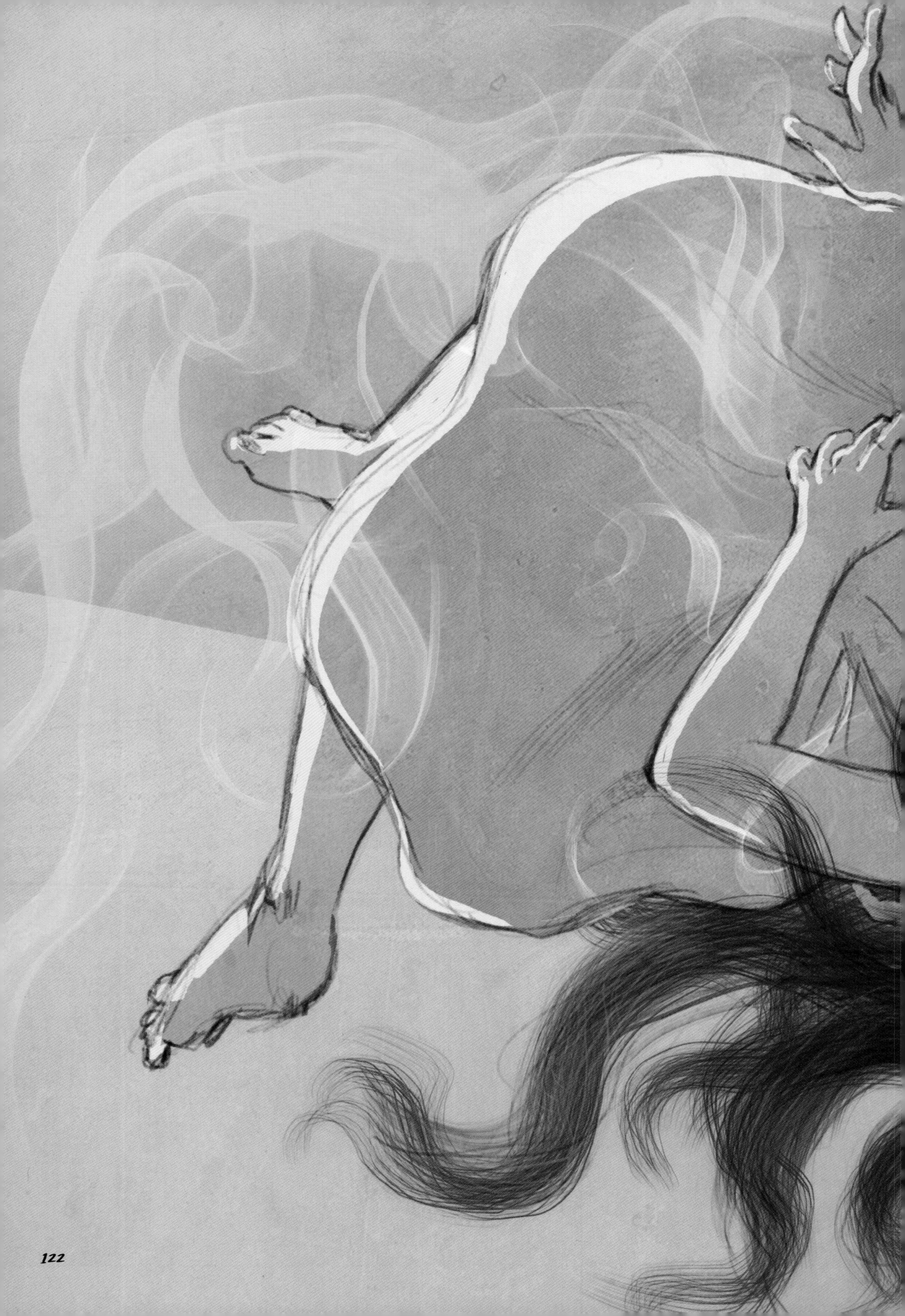

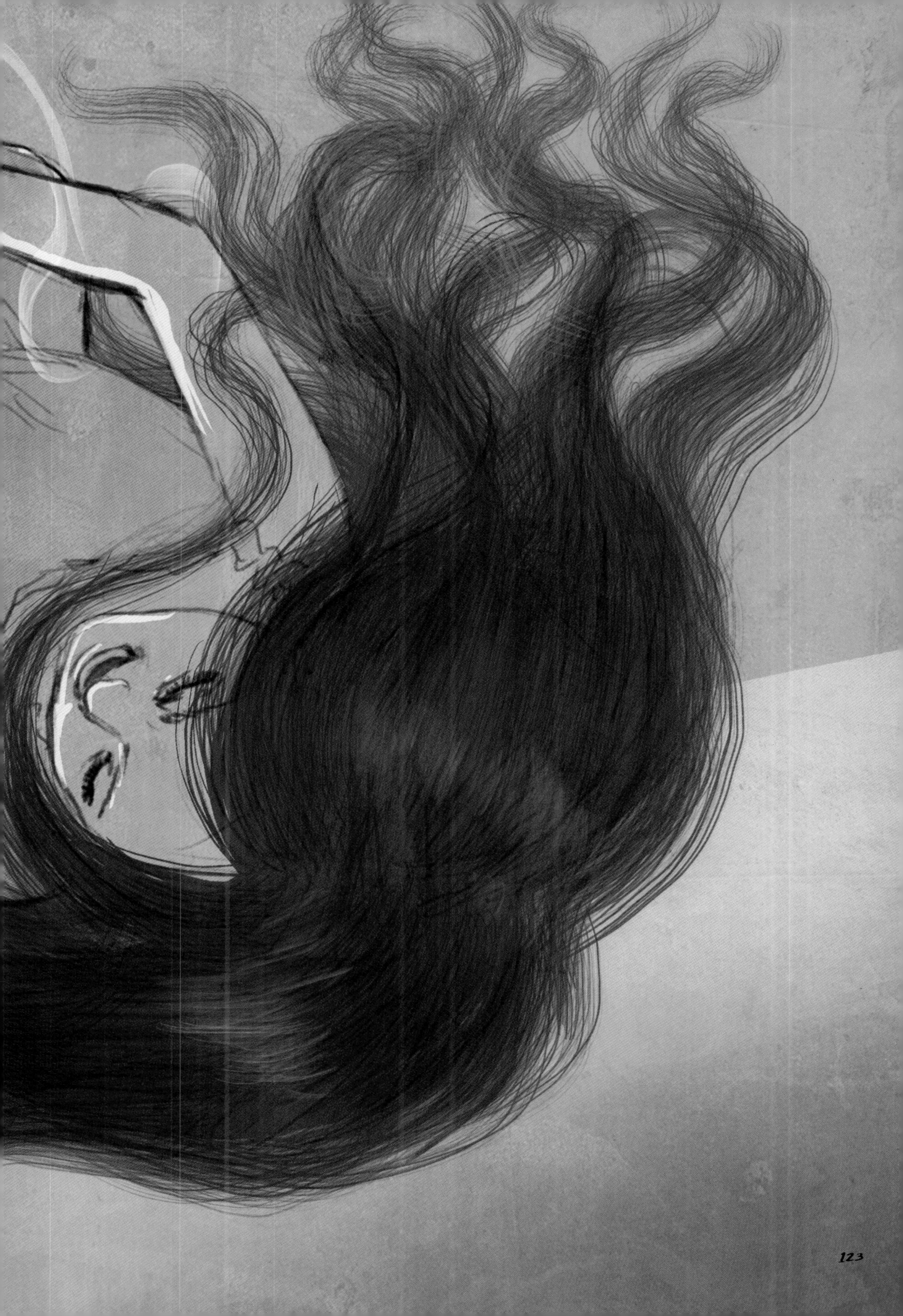

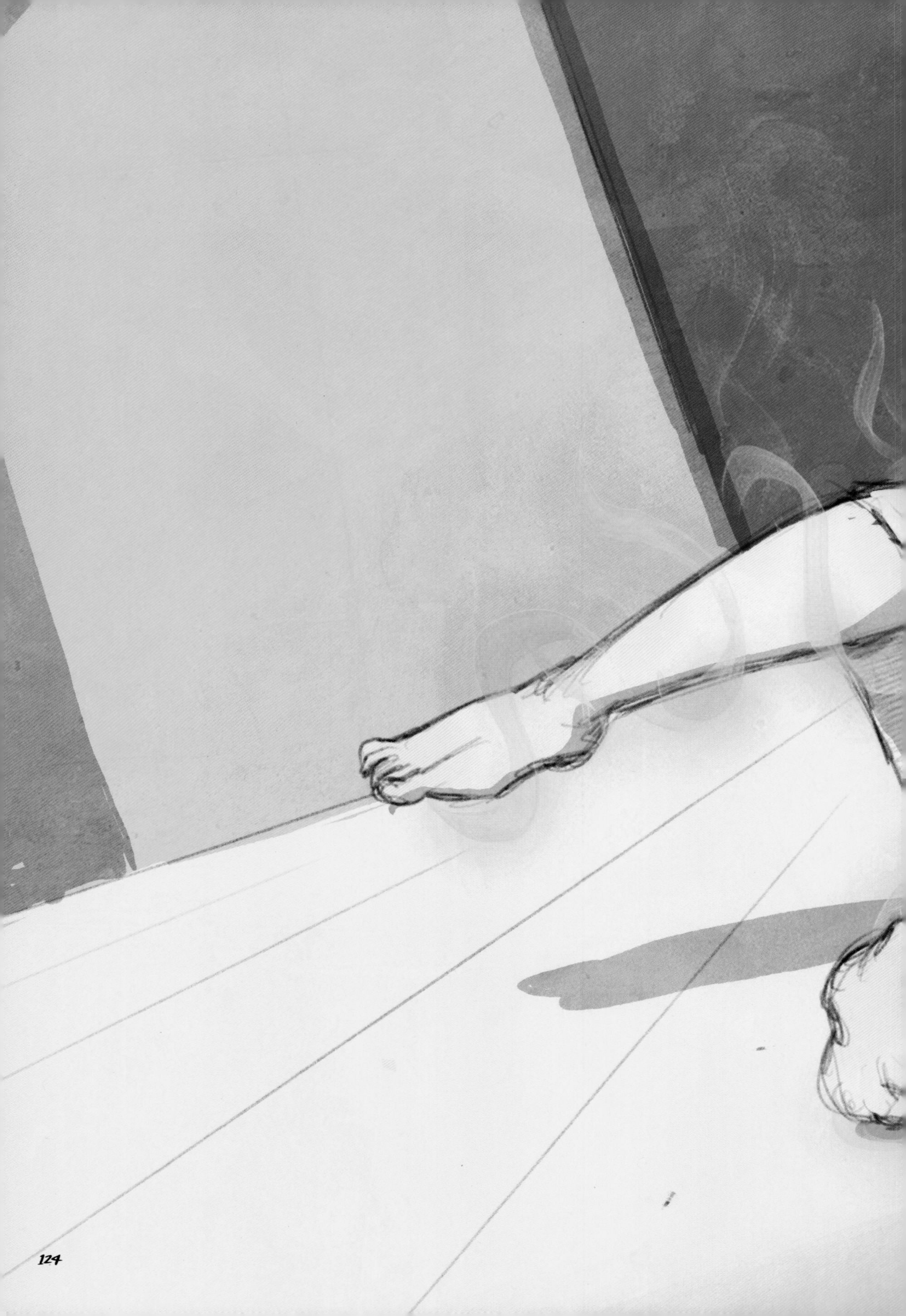

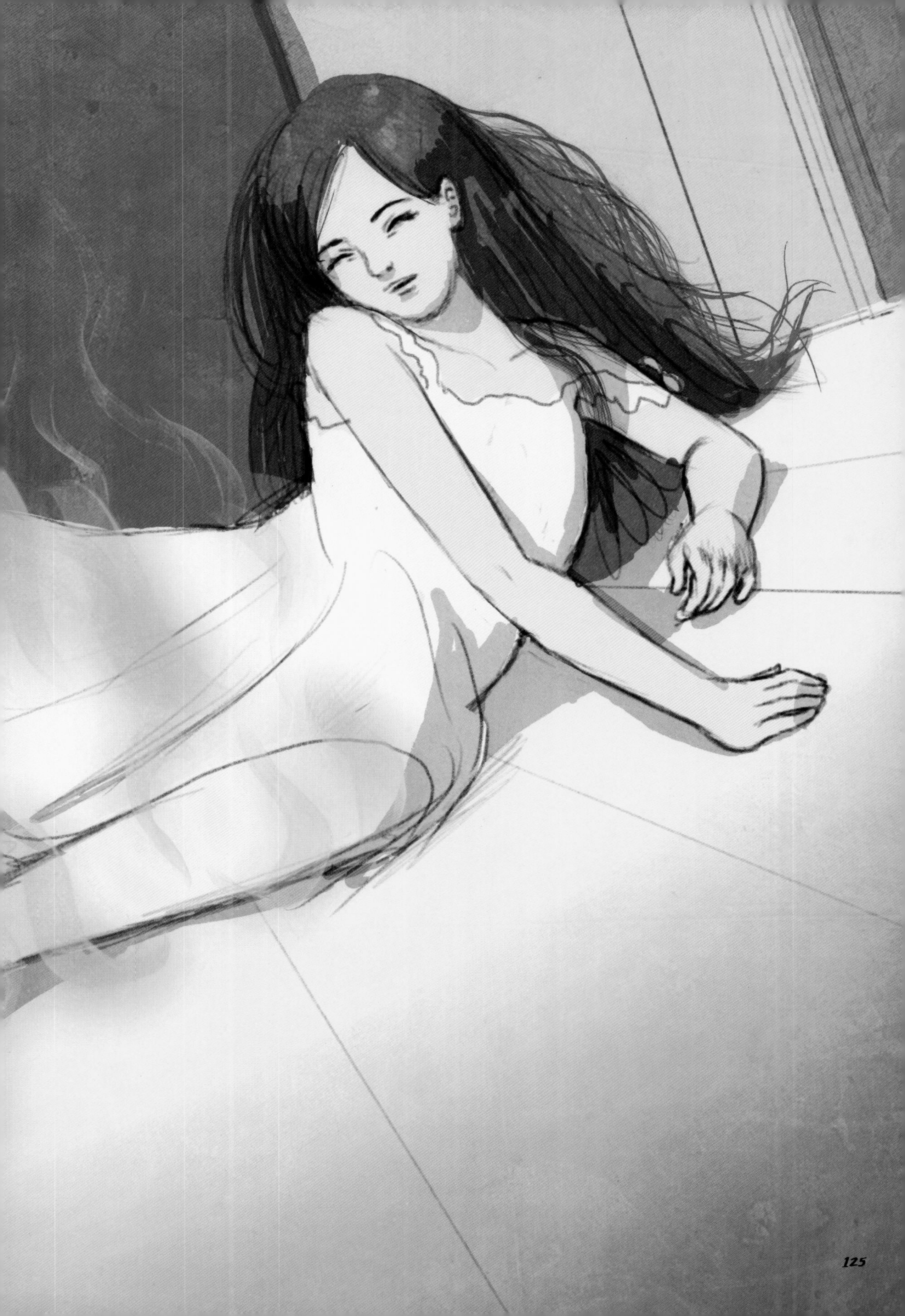

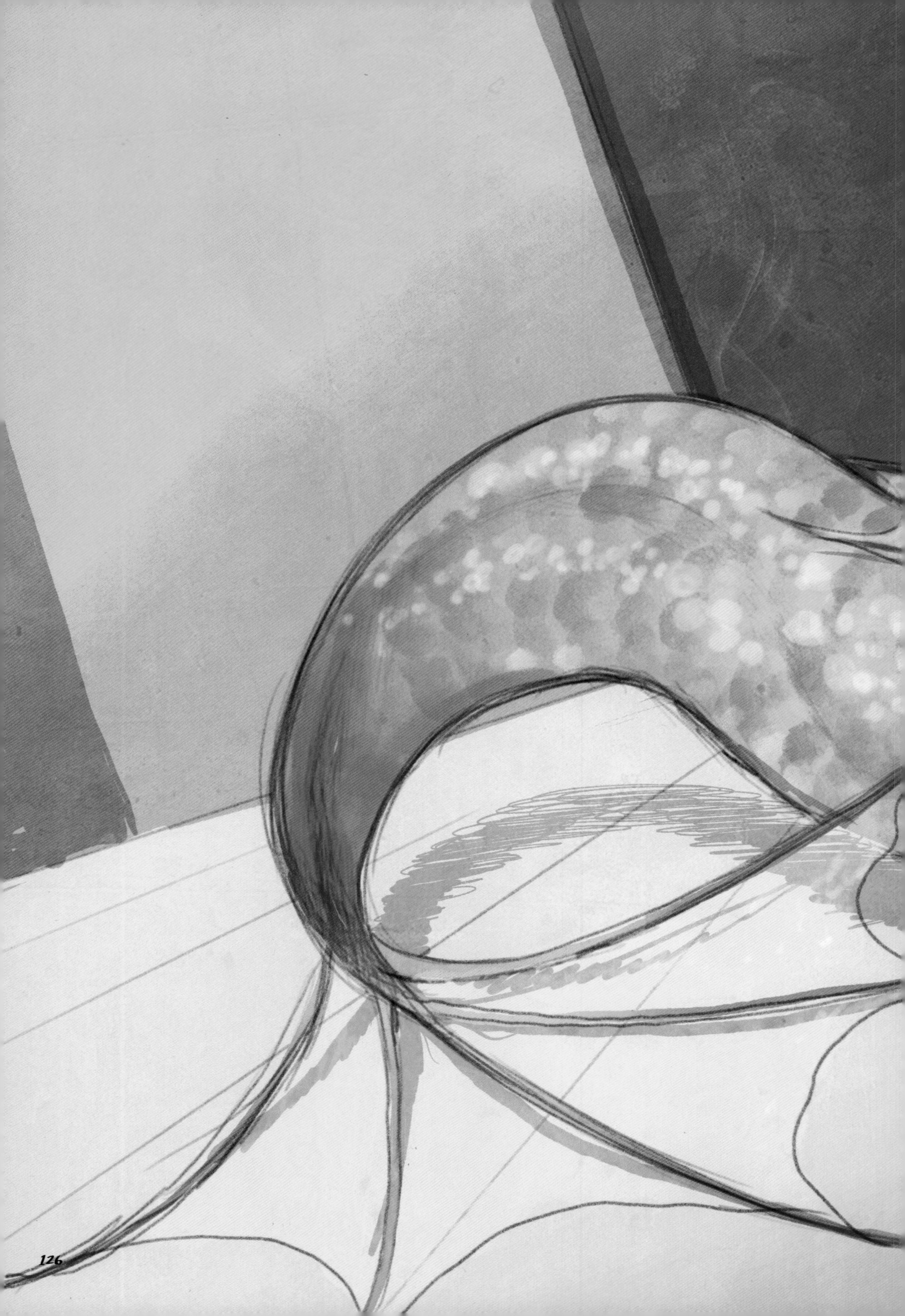

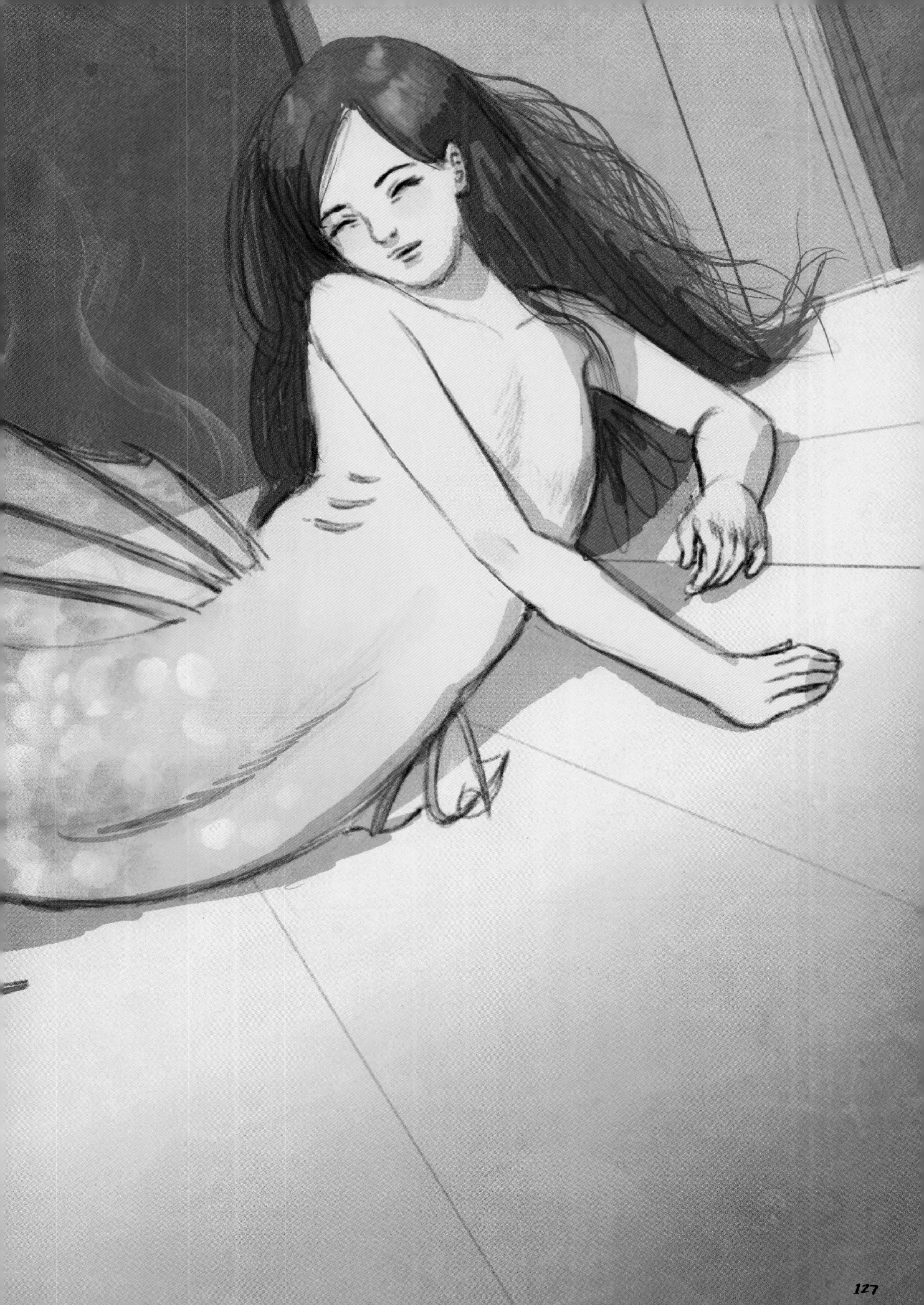

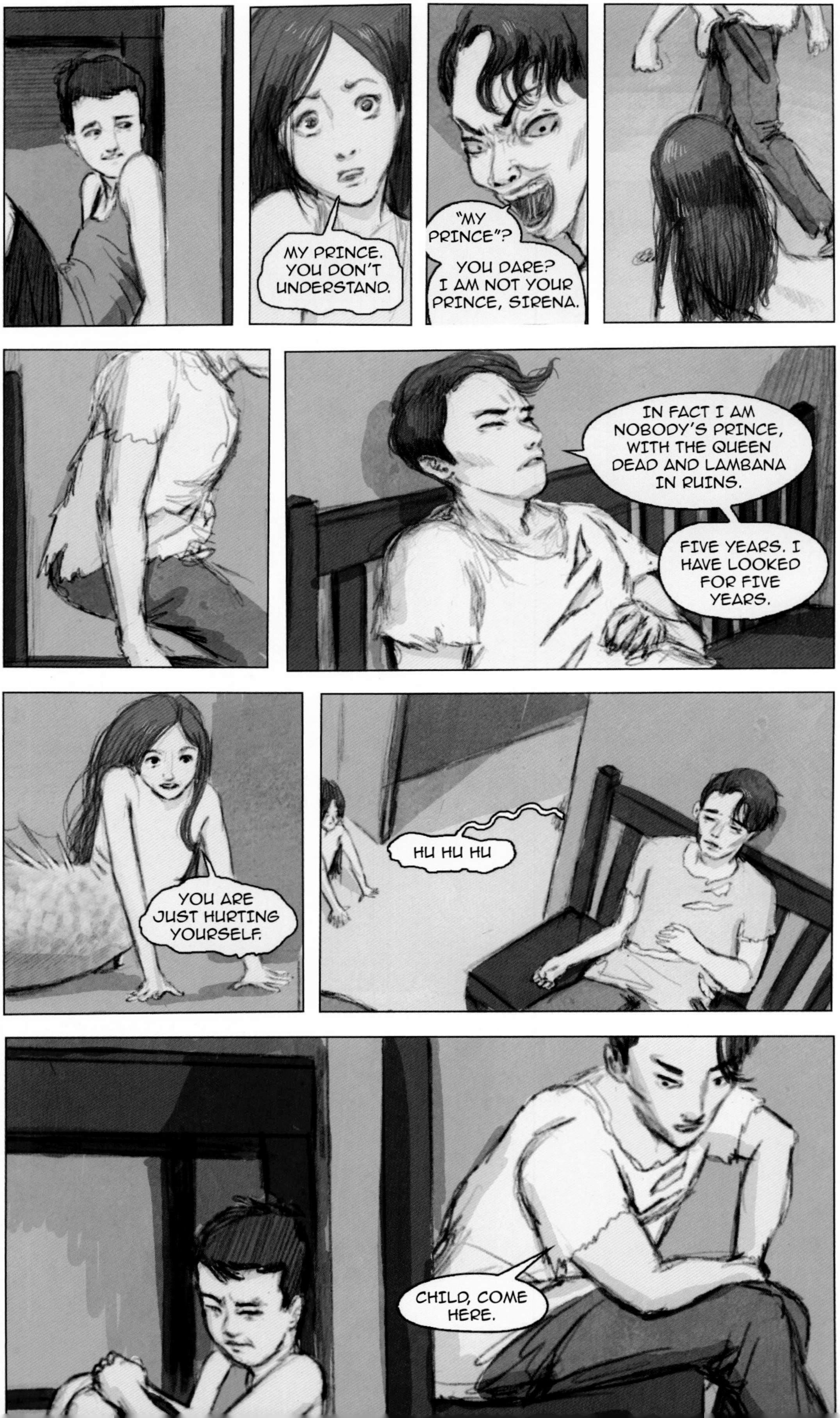
MY PRINCE. YOU DON'T UNDERSTAND.
"MY PRINCE"?
YOU DARE? I AM NOT YOUR PRINCE, SIRENA.
IN FACT I AM NOBODY'S PRINCE, WITH THE QUEEN DEAD AND LAMBANA IN RUINS.
FIVE YEARS. I HAVE LOOKED FOR FIVE YEARS.
YOU ARE JUST HURTING YOURSELF.
HU HU HU
CHILD, COME HERE.

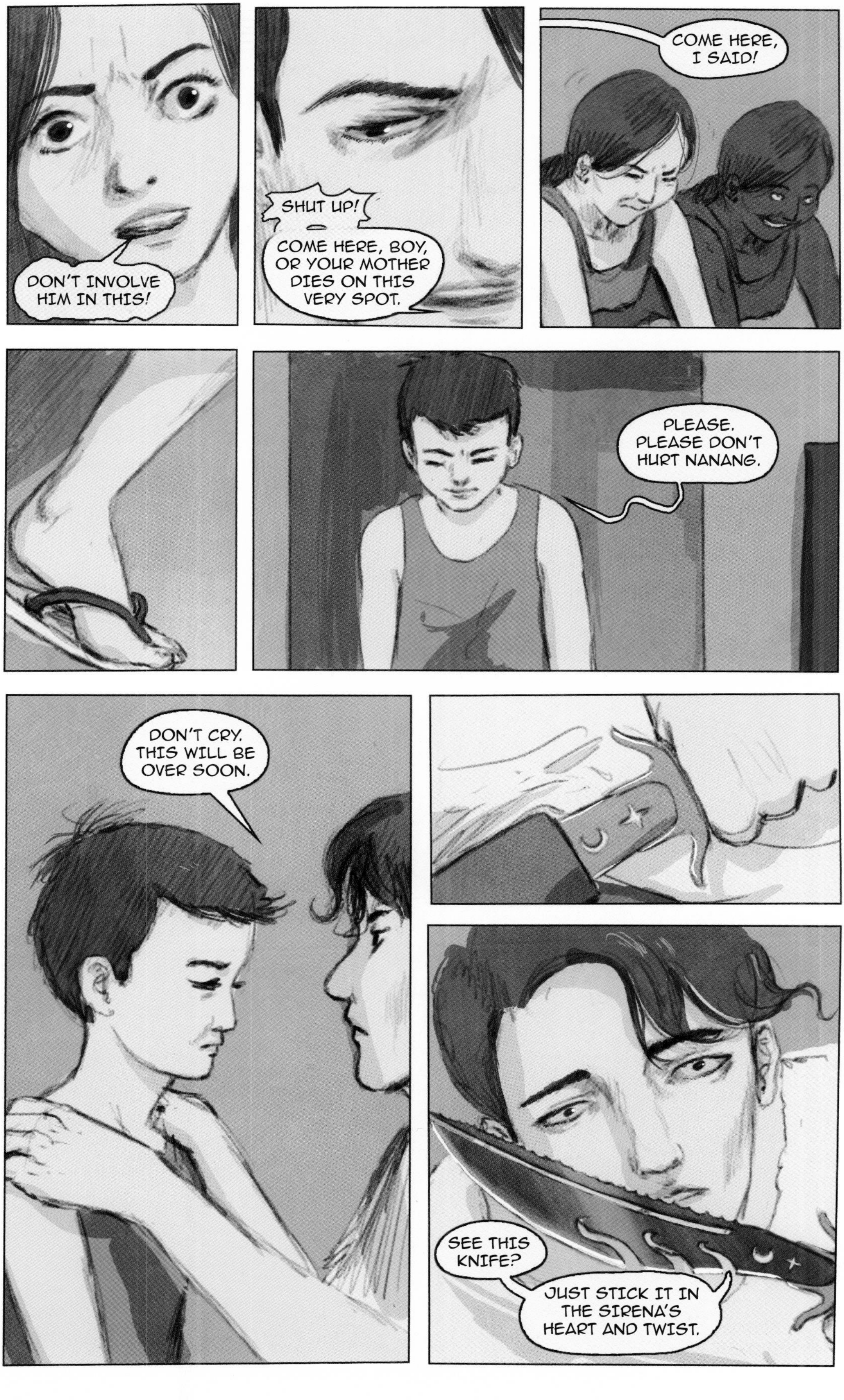
DON'T INVOLVE HIM IN THIS!
SHUT UP!
COME HERE, BOY, OR YOUR MOTHER DIES ON THIS VERY SPOT.
COME HERE, I SAID!
PLEASE. PLEASE DON'T HURT NANANG.
DON'T CRY. THIS WILL BE OVER SOON.
SEE THIS KNIFE?
JUST STICK IT IN THE SIRENA'S HEART AND TWIST.

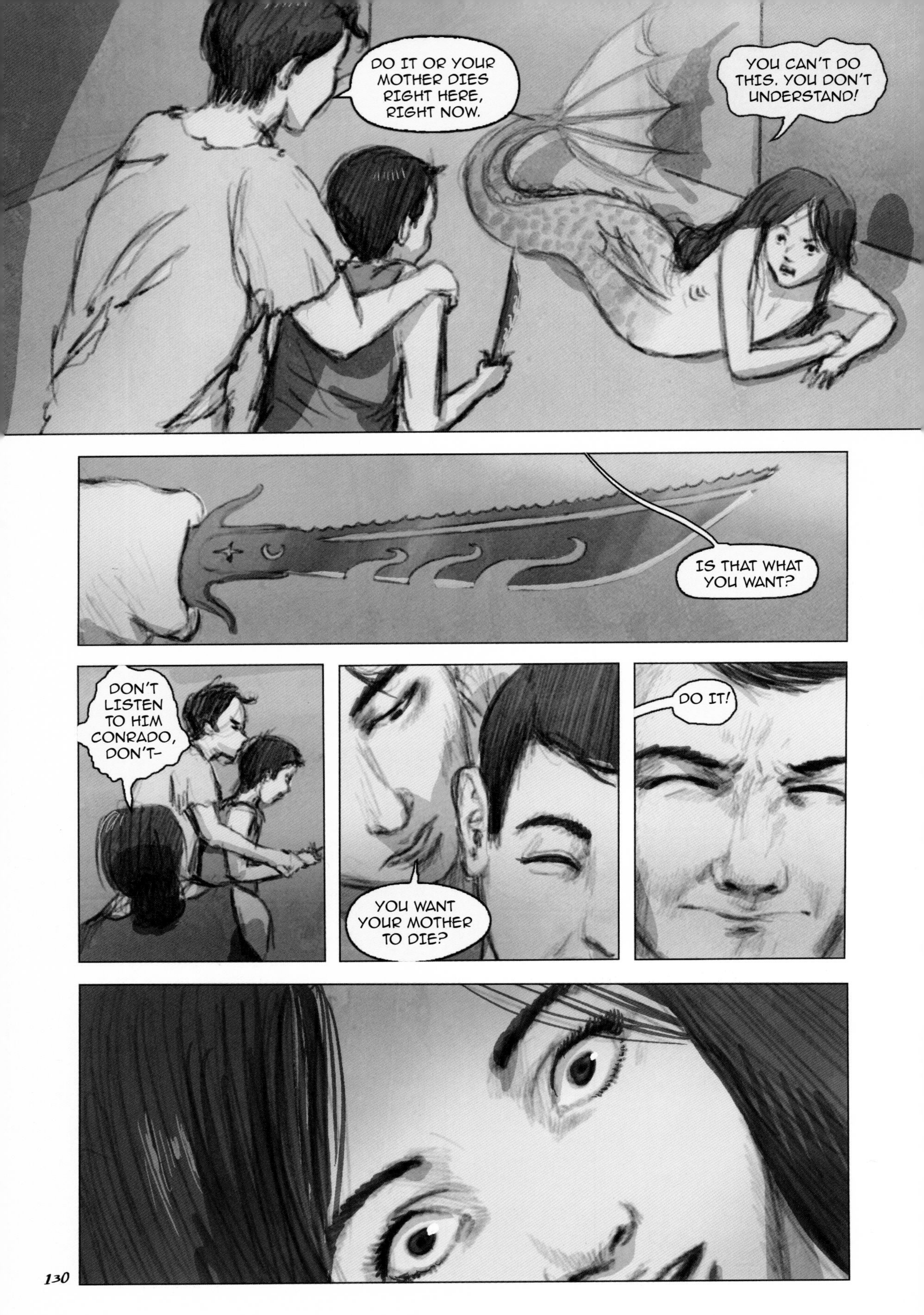
DO IT OR YOUR MOTHER DIES RIGHT HERE, RIGHT NOW.
YOU CAN'T DO THIS. YOU DON'T UNDERSTAND!
IS THAT WHAT YOU WANT?
DON'T LISTEN TO HIM CONRADO, DON'T-
YOU WANT YOUR MOTHER TO DIE?
DO IT!

AAAAAAAAAAAAAAAA

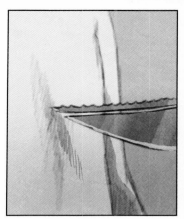

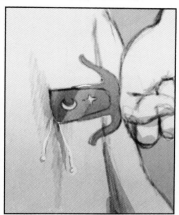

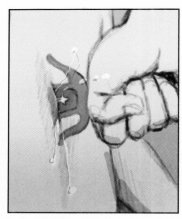

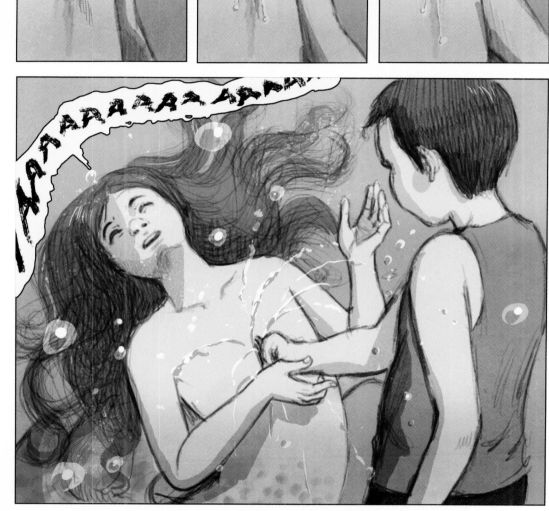

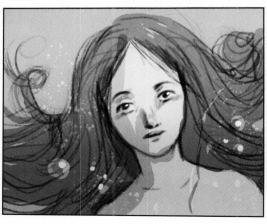

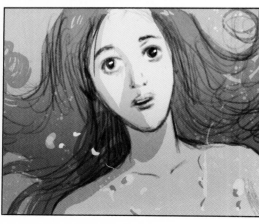

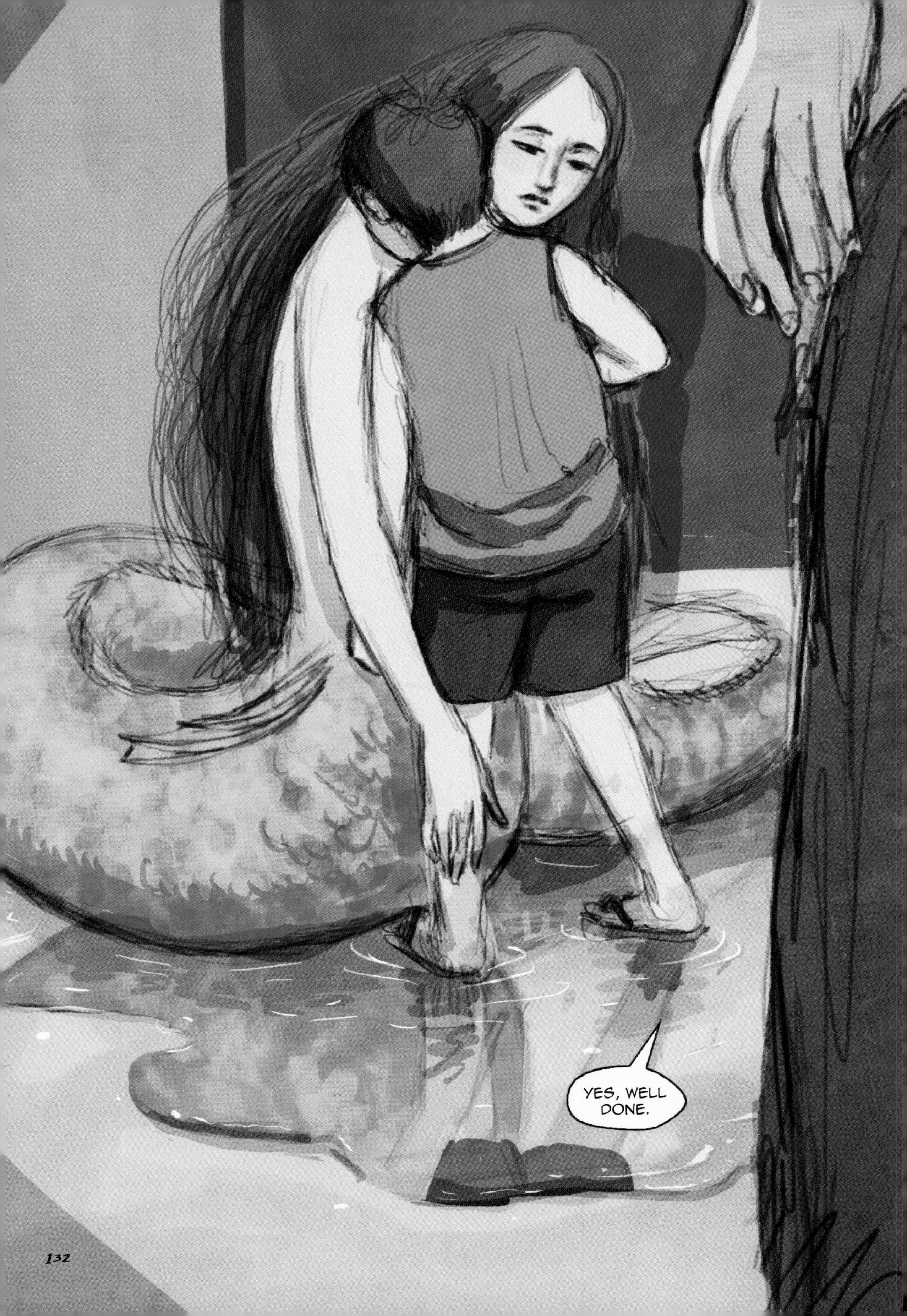
YES, WELL DONE.

NOW –

– TWIST –

– THE BLADE.

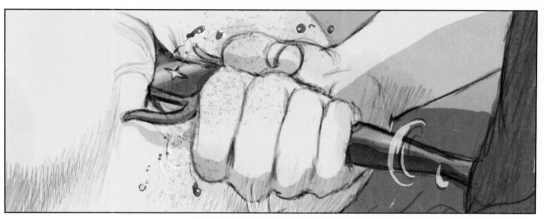

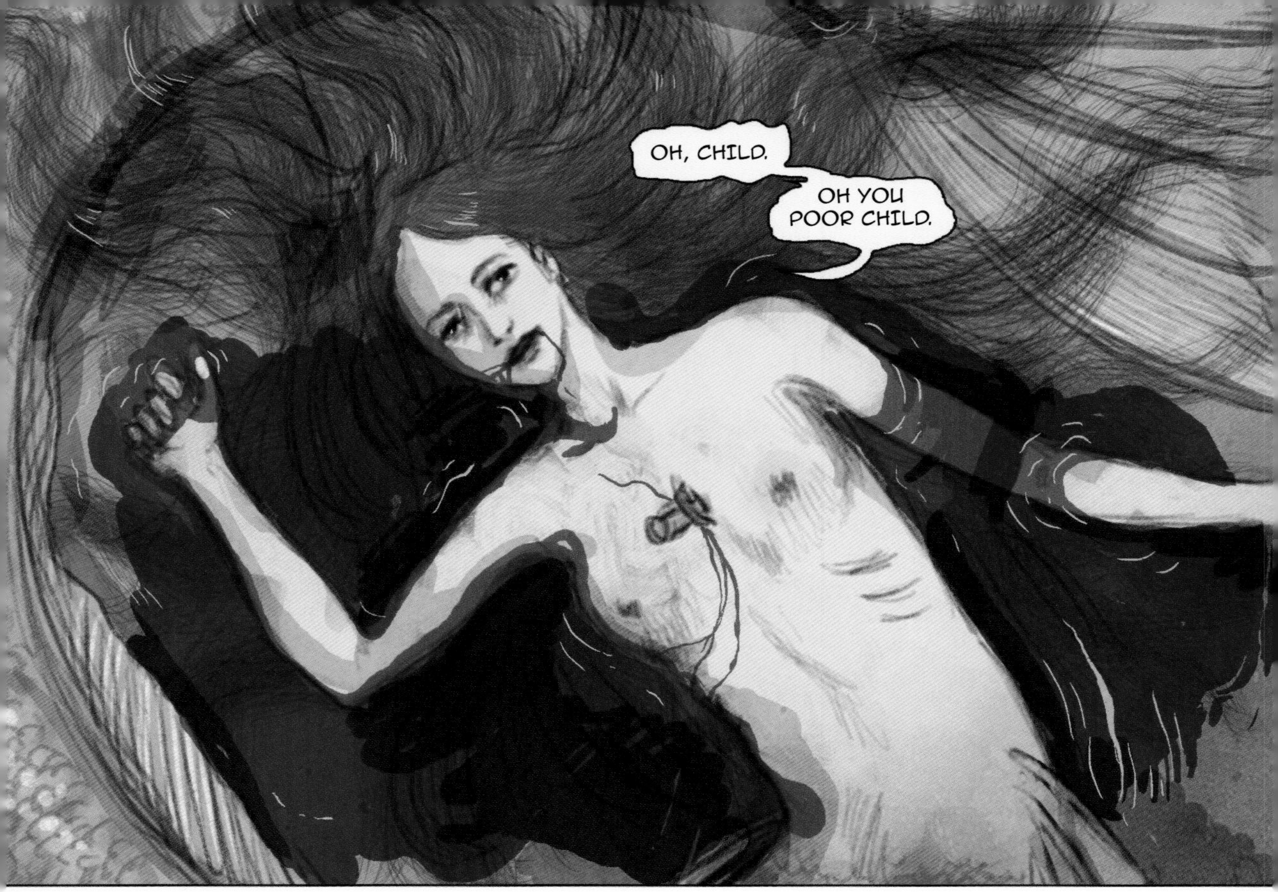
OH, CHILD.
OH YOU POOR CHILD.

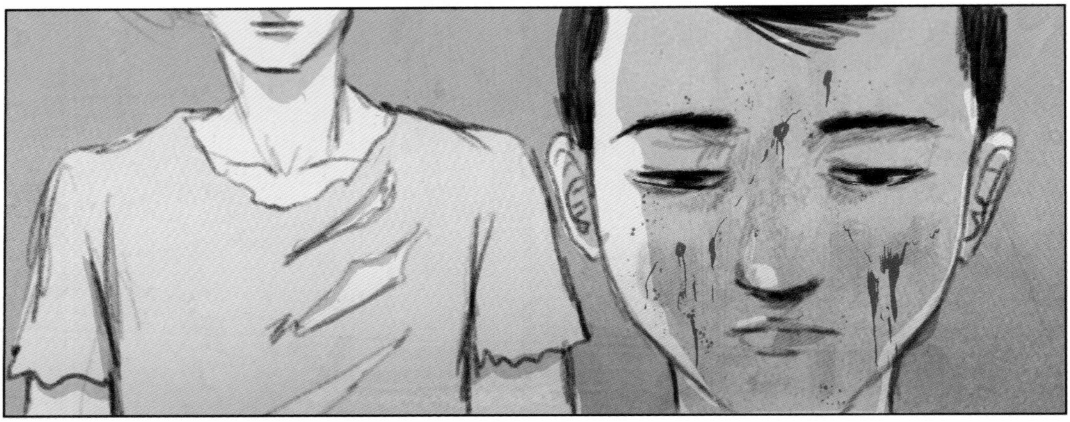

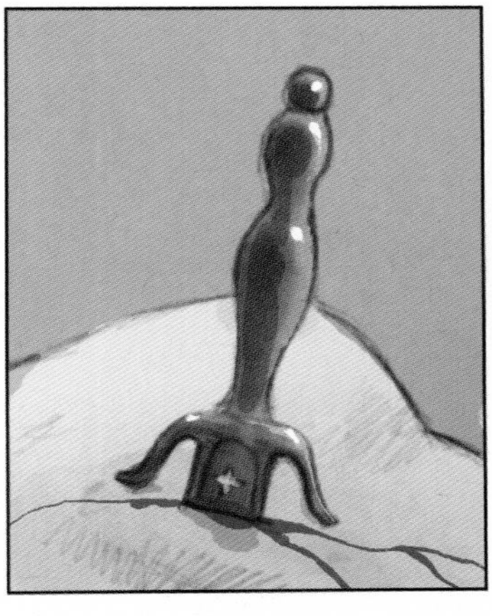

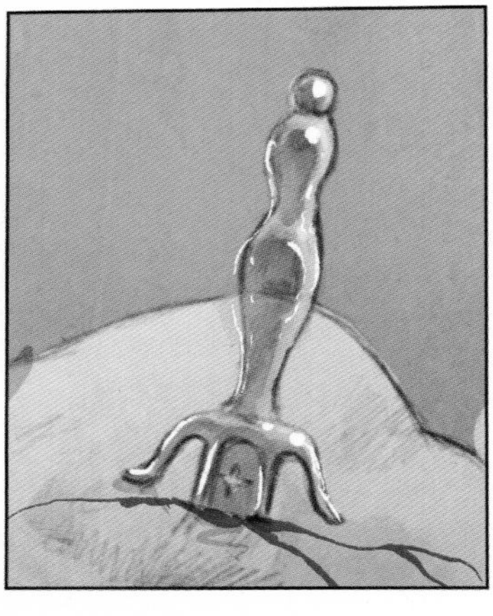

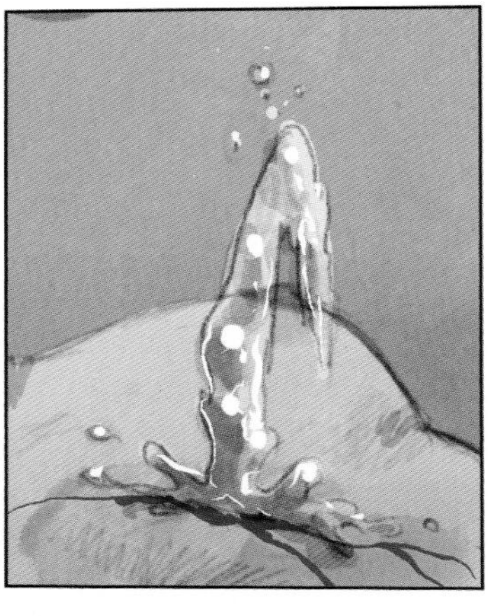

YOU DID WELL, CHILD. YOU ARE SAFE NOW.

AND I AM GOING HOME.

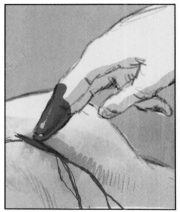

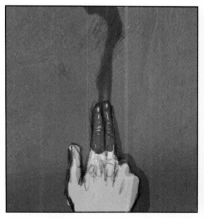

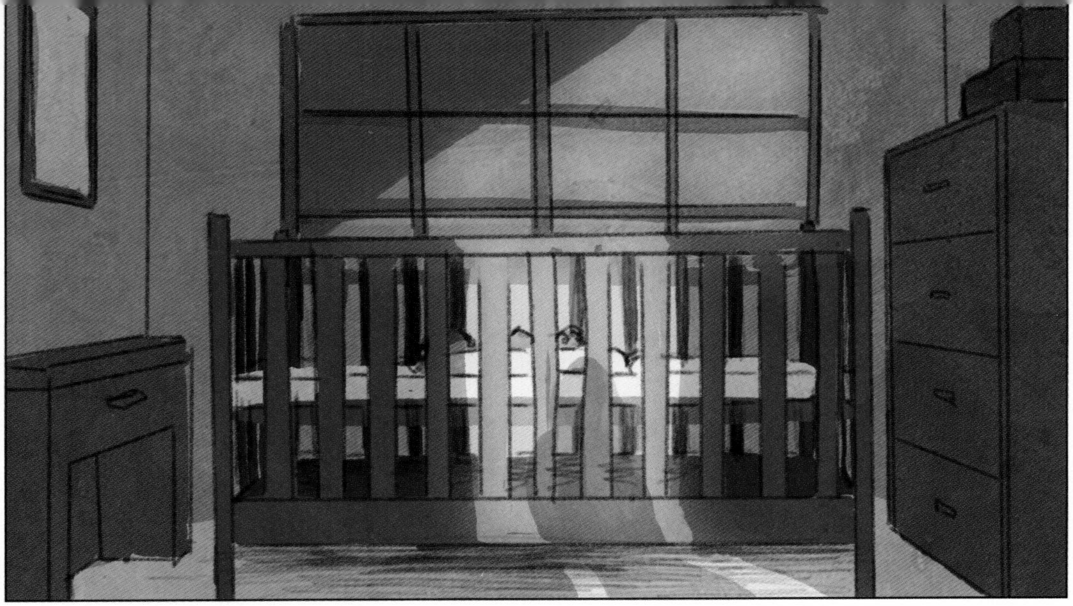

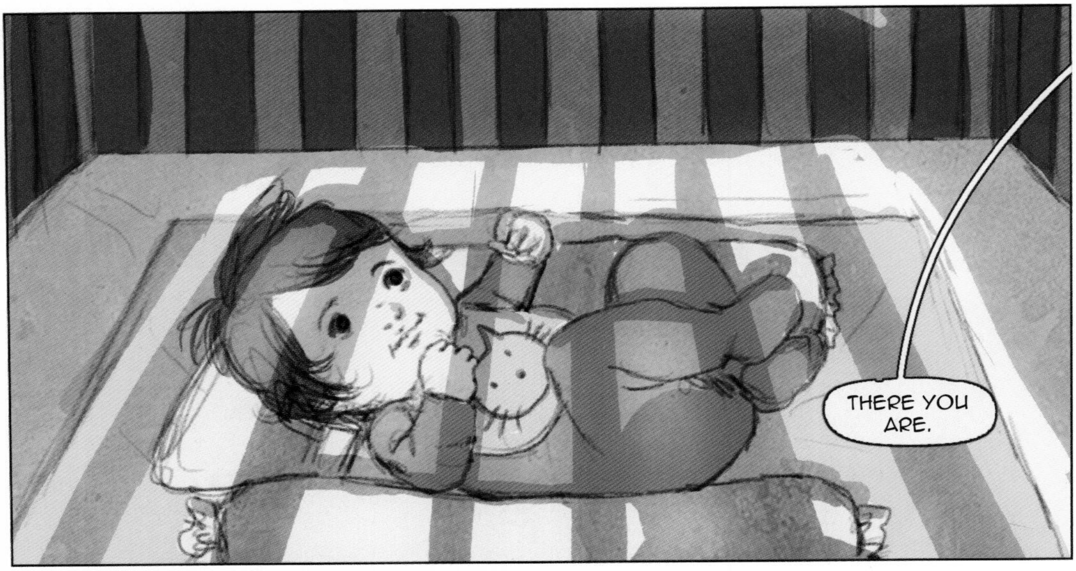
THERE YOU ARE.

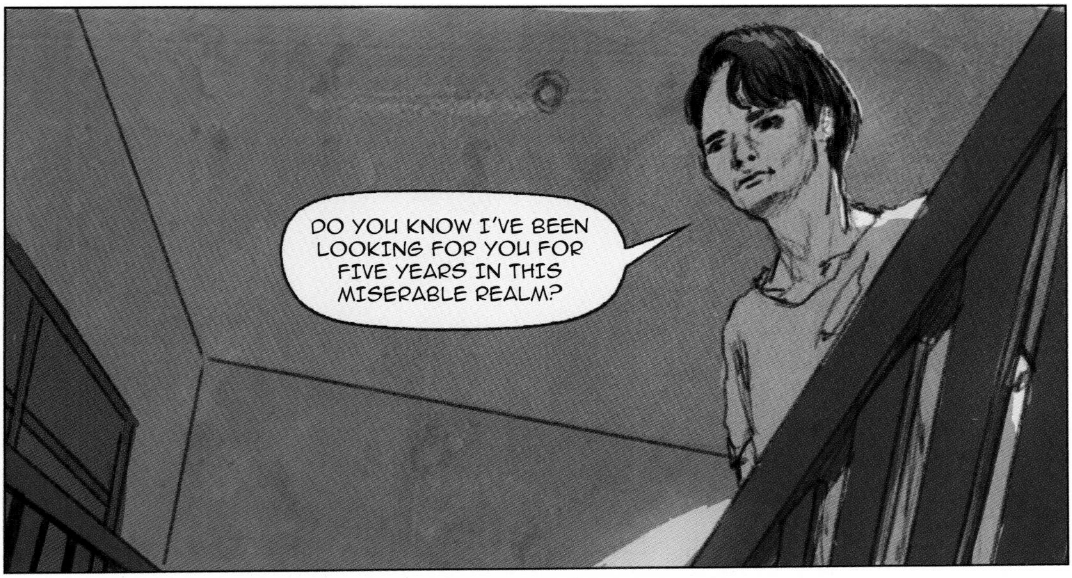
DO YOU KNOW I'VE BEEN LOOKING FOR YOU FOR FIVE YEARS IN THIS MISERABLE REALM?

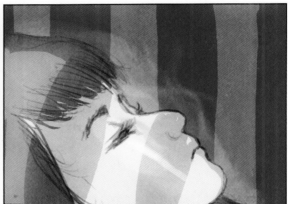

THE SIRENA THOUGHT THEY CAN KEEP THE RIGHTFUL HEIR FROM LAMBANA.

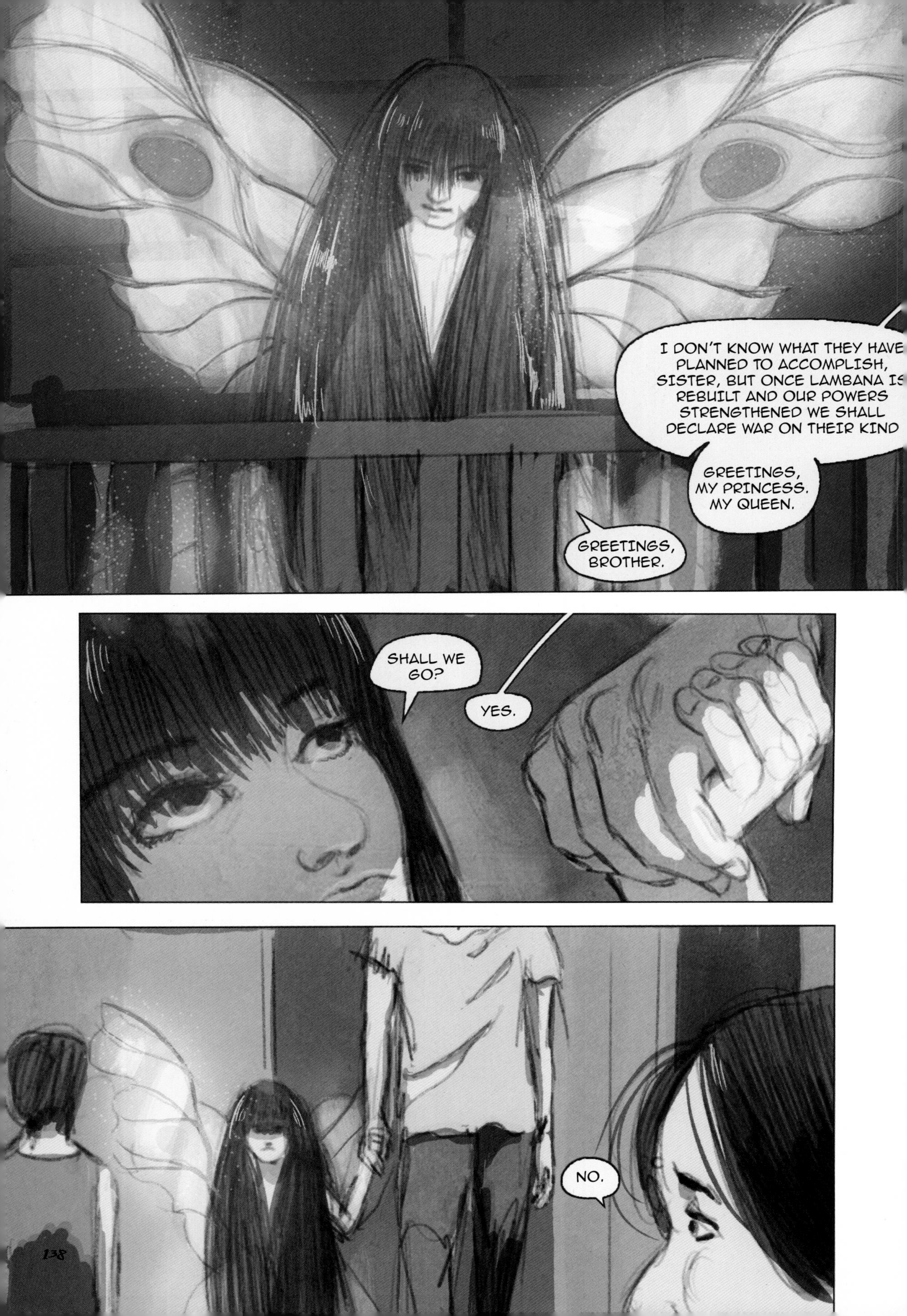
I DON'T KNOW WHAT THEY HAVE PLANNED TO ACCOMPLISH, SISTER, BUT ONCE LAMBANA IS REBUILT AND OUR POWERS STRENGTHENED WE SHALL DECLARE WAR ON THEIR KIND
GREETINGS, MY PRINCESS. MY QUEEN.
GREETINGS, BROTHER.
SHALL WE GO?
YES.
NO.

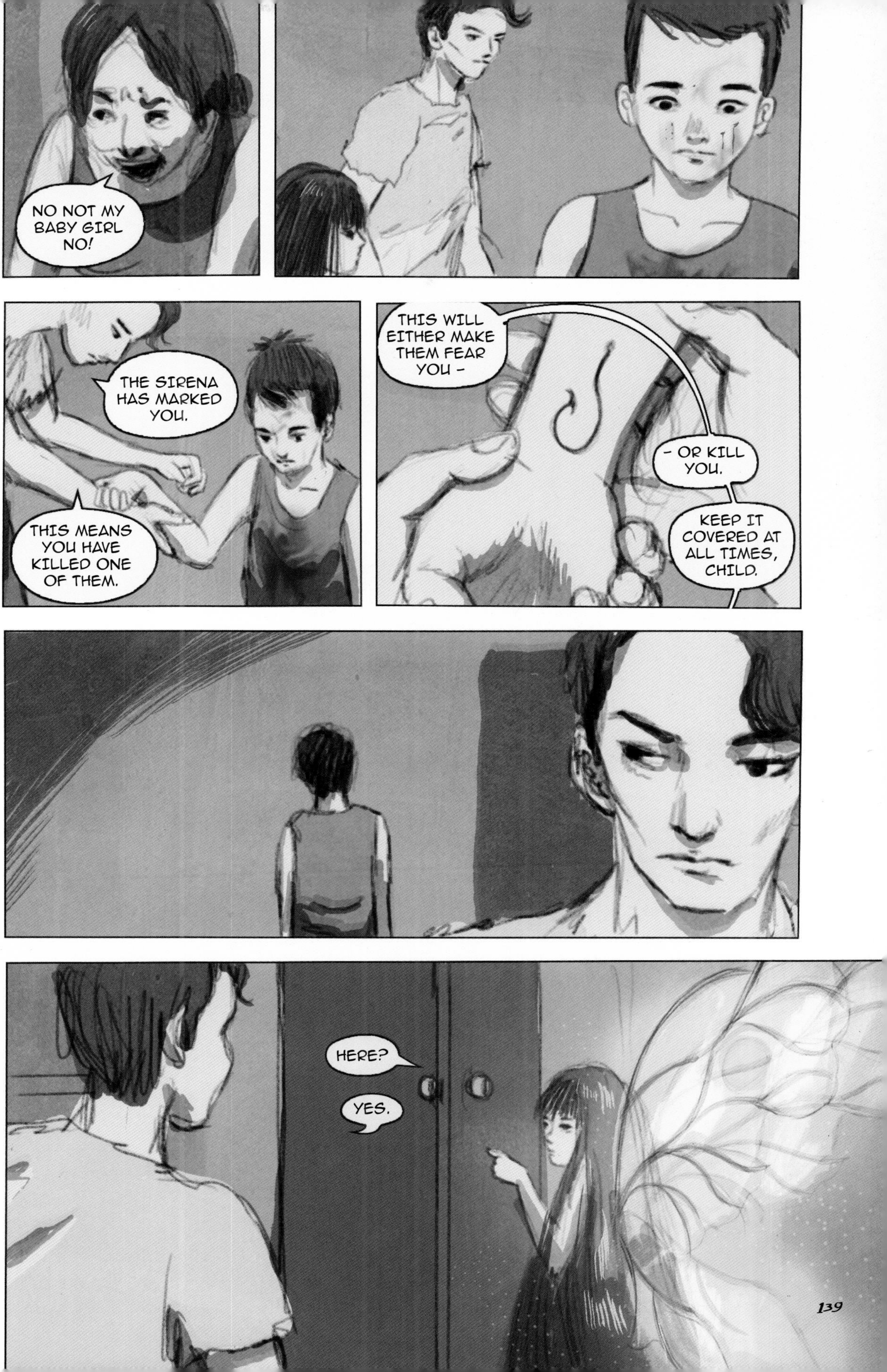
NO NOT MY BABY GIRL NO!
THE SIRENA HAS MARKED YOU.
THIS MEANS YOU HAVE KILLED ONE OF THEM.
THIS WILL EITHER MAKE THEM FEAR YOU -
- OR KILL YOU.
KEEP IT COVERED AT ALL TIMES, CHILD.
HERE?
YES.

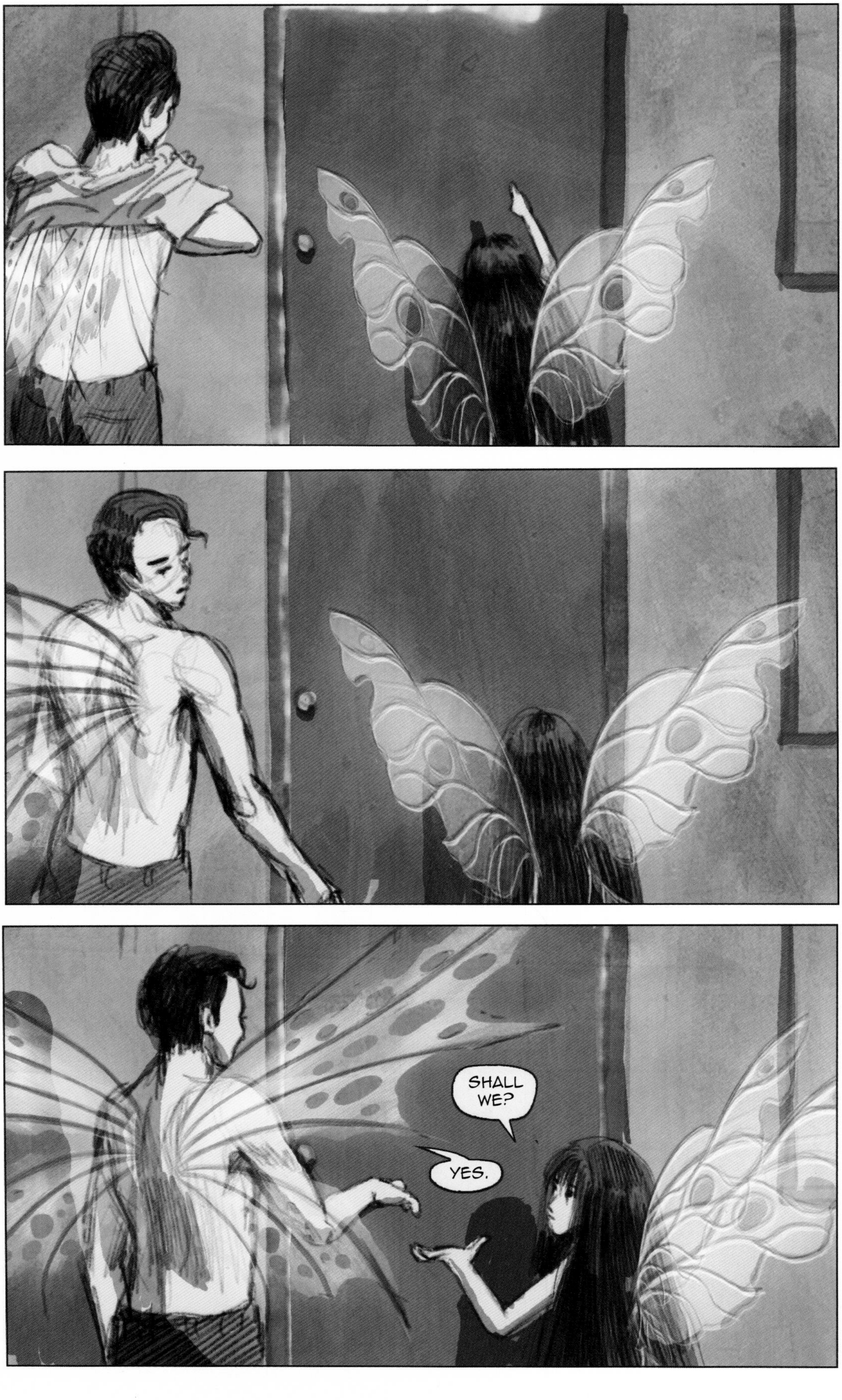
SHALL WE?
YES.

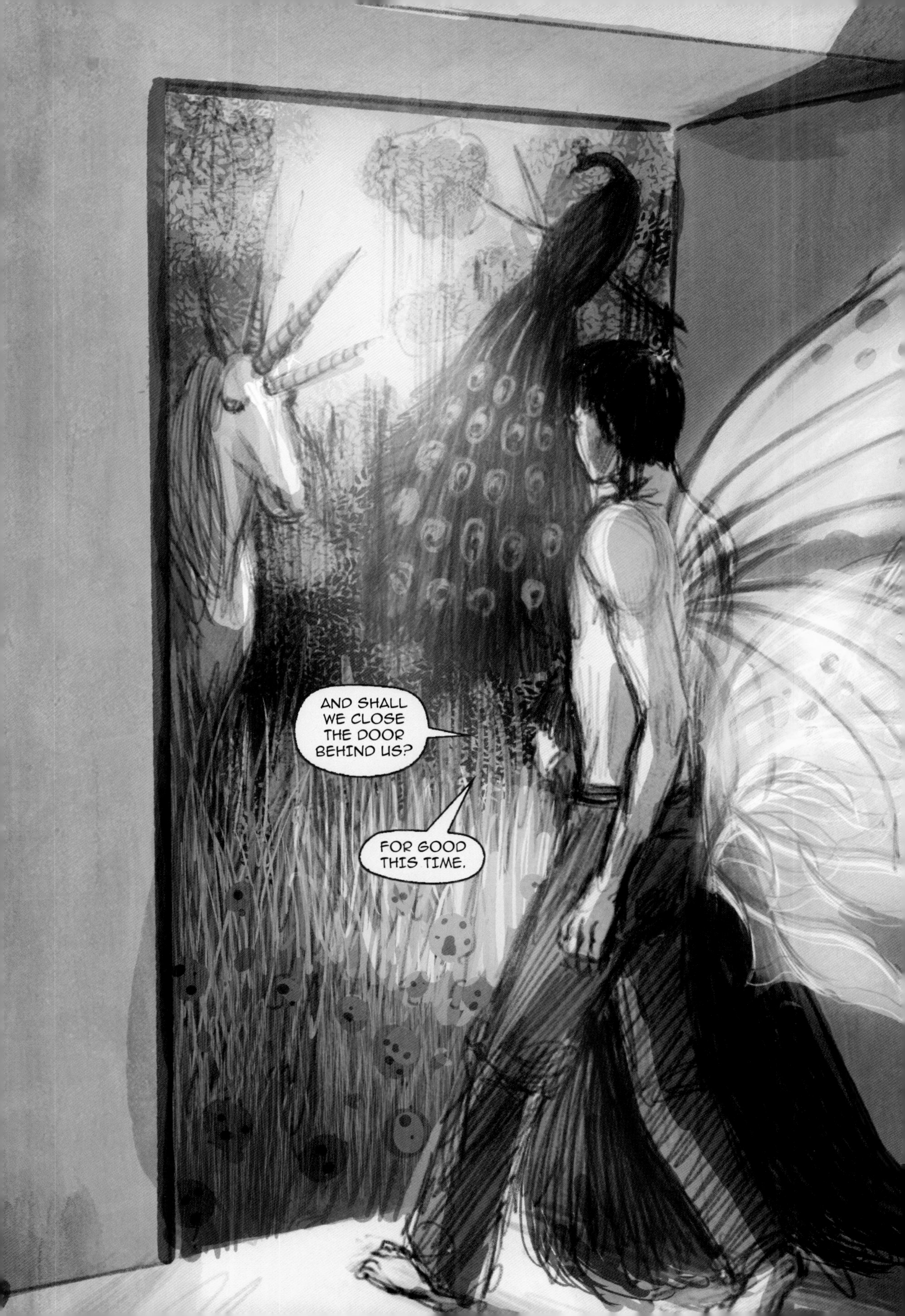
AND SHALL WE CLOSE THE DOOR BEHIND US?
FOR GOOD THIS TIME.

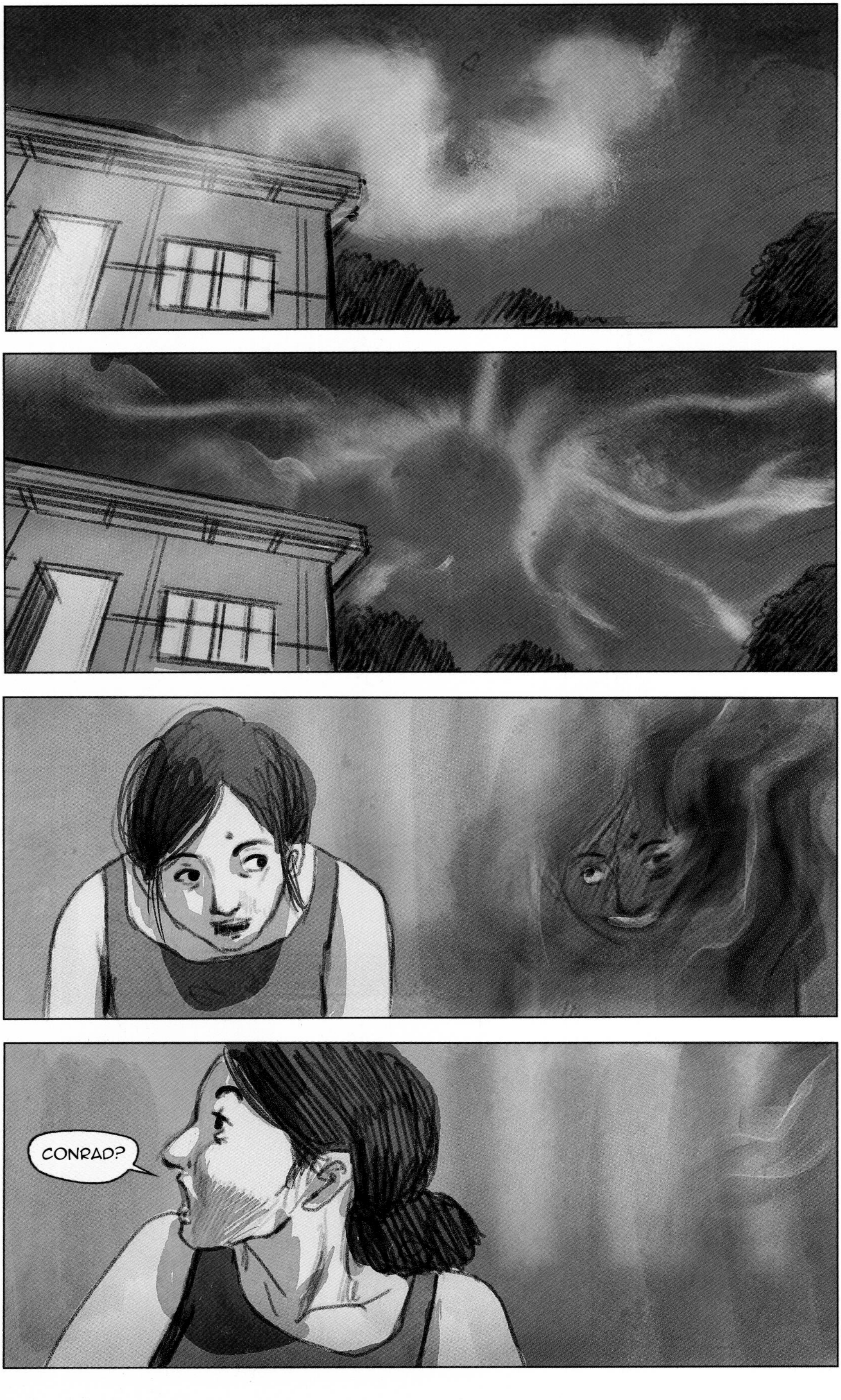
CONRAD?

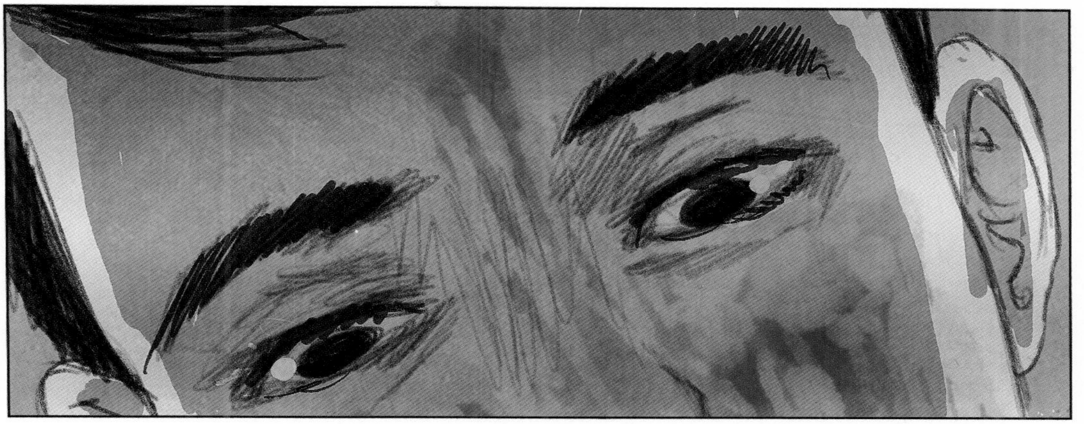

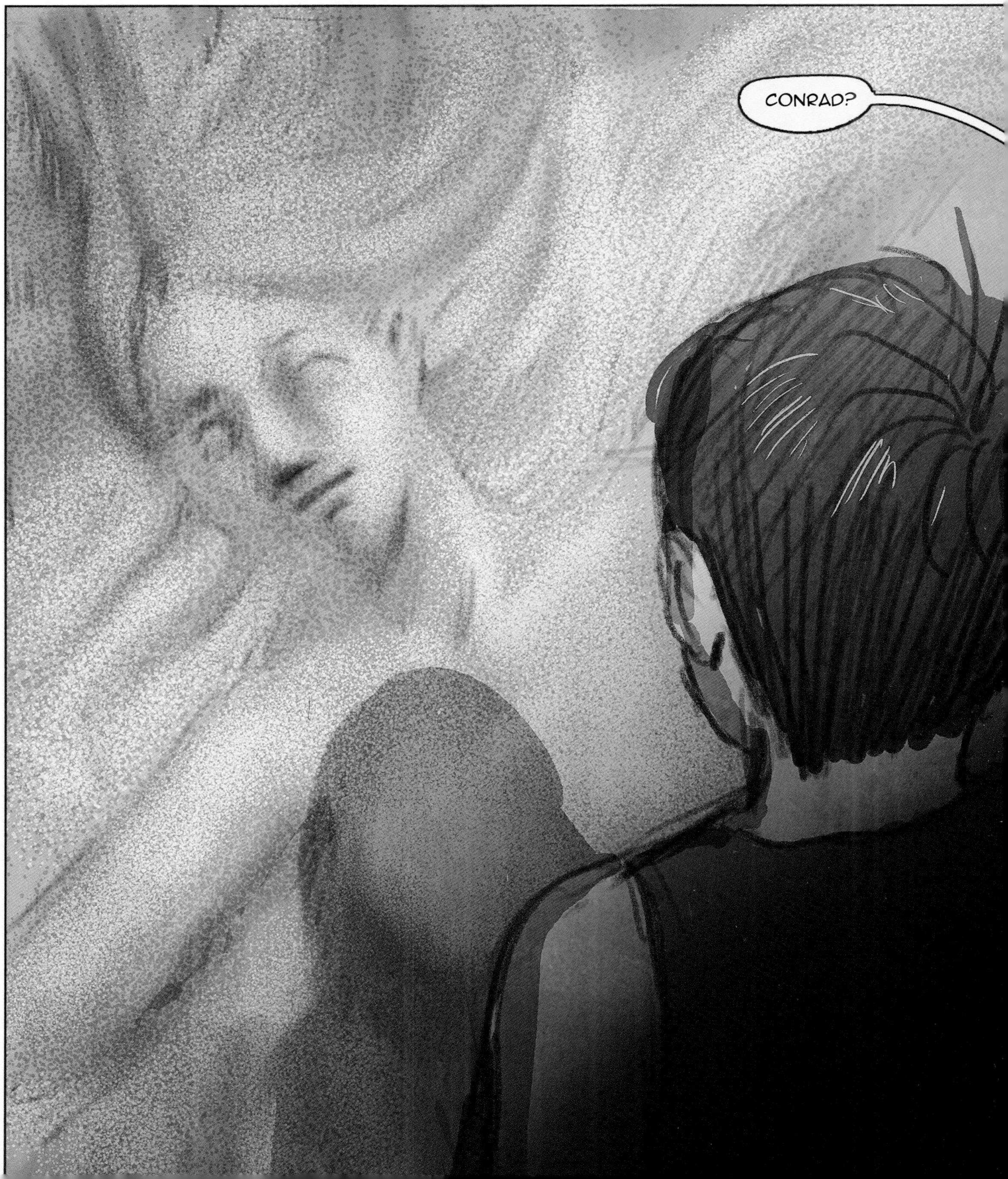
CONRAD?

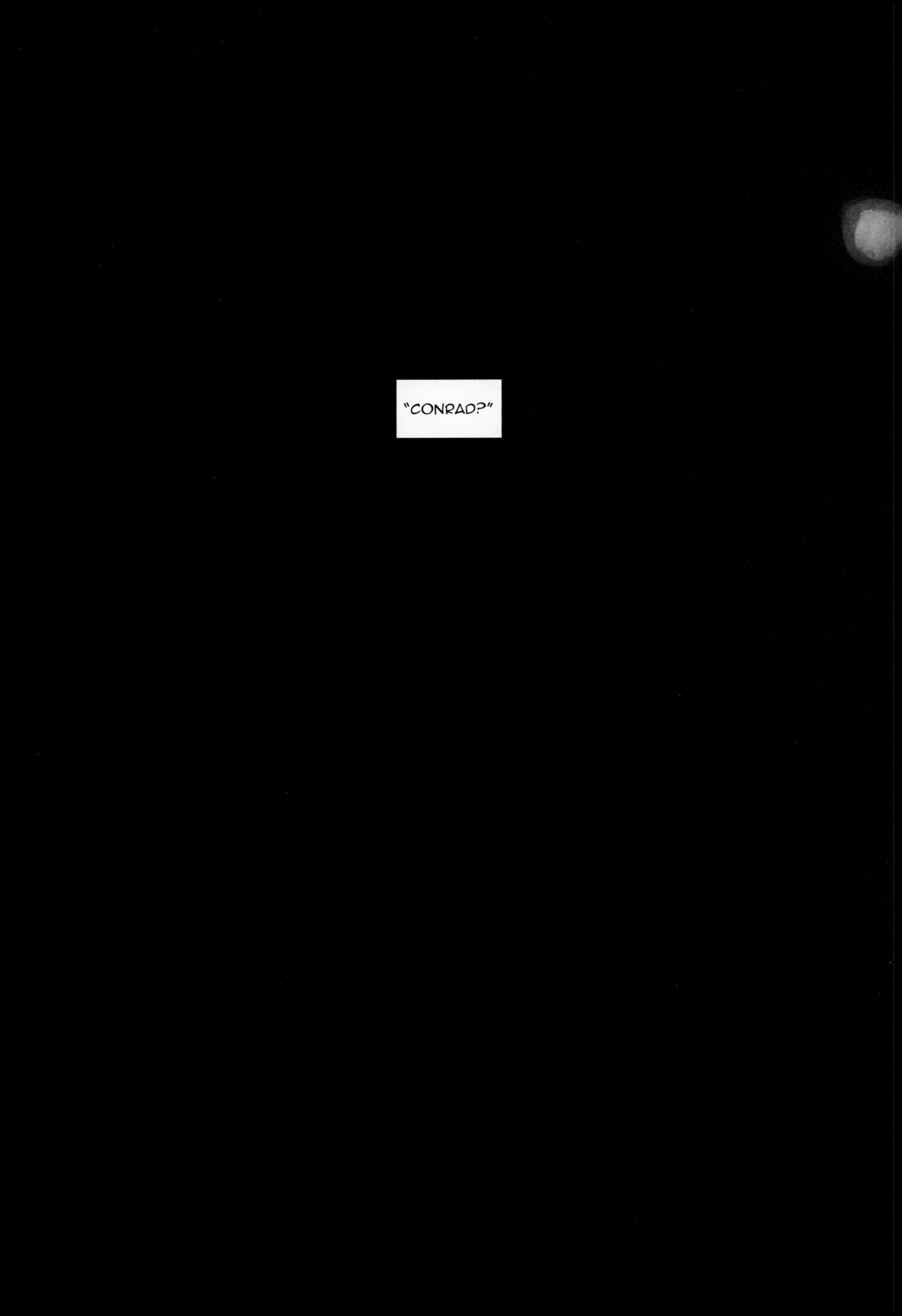
"CONRAD?"

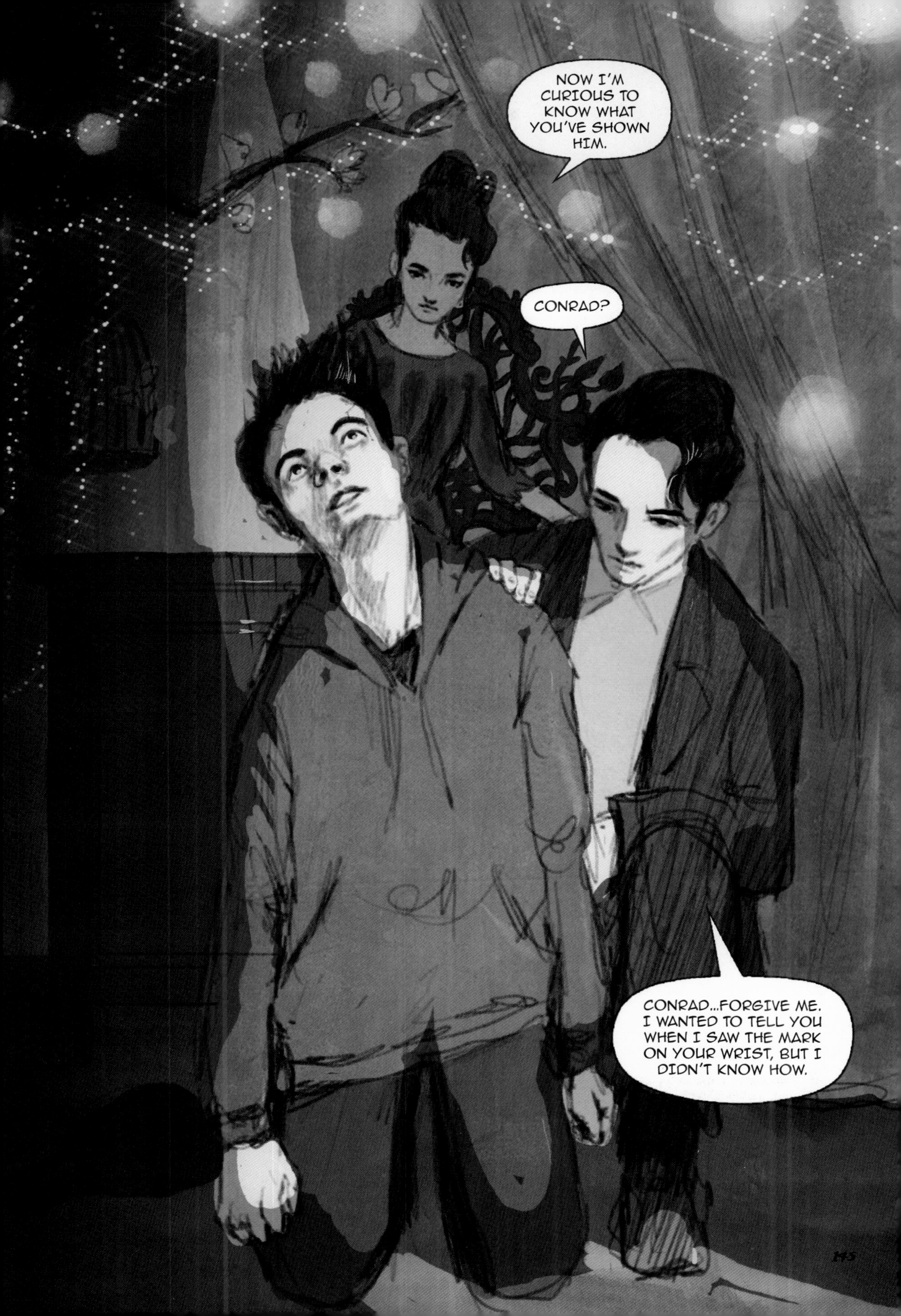
NOW I'M CURIOUS TO KNOW WHAT YOU'VE SHOWN HIM.
CONRAD?
CONRAD...FORGIVE ME. I WANTED TO TELL YOU WHEN I SAW THE MARK ON YOUR WRIST, BUT I DIDN'T KNOW HOW.

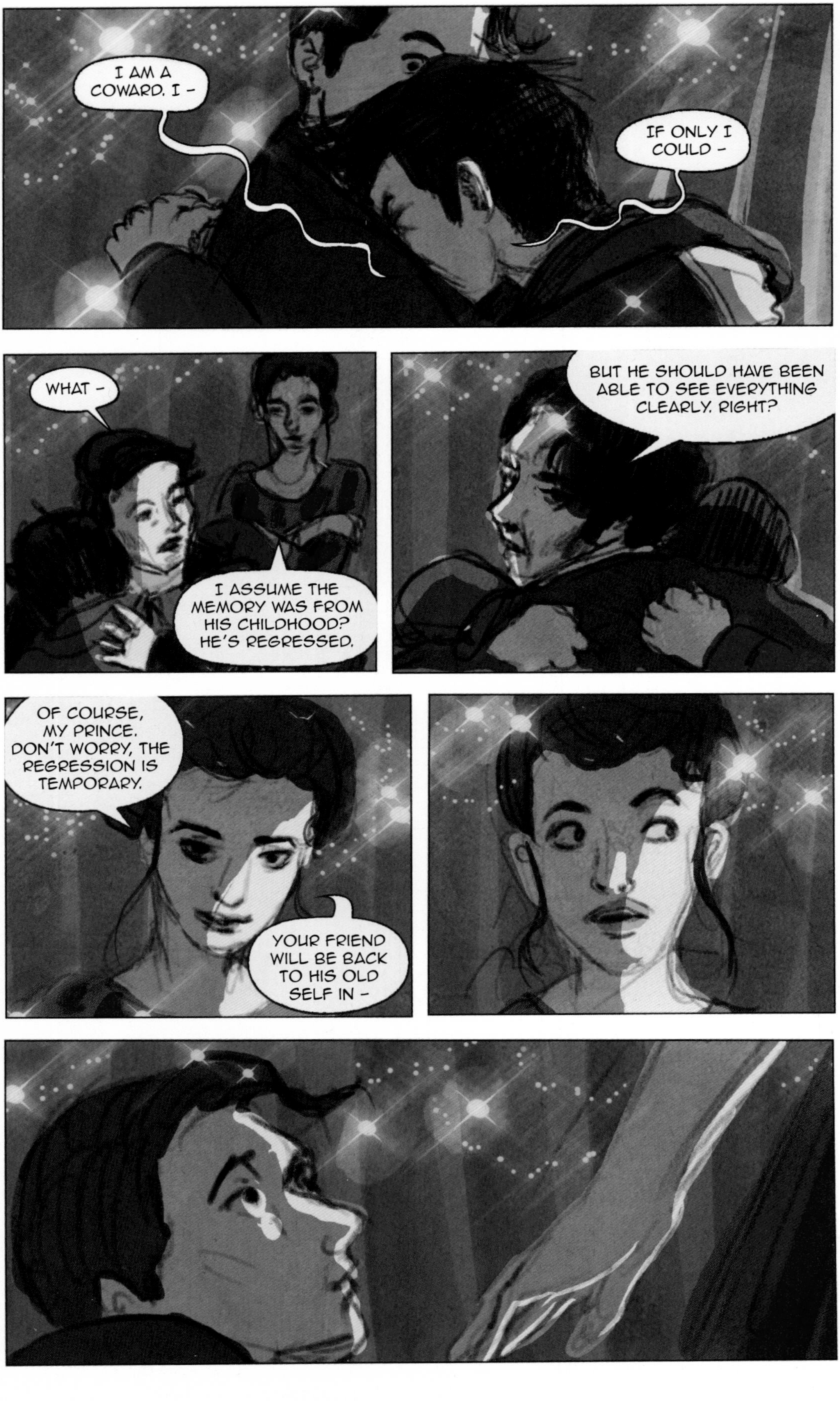
I AM A COWARD. I –
IF ONLY I COULD –
WHAT –
I ASSUME THE MEMORY WAS FROM HIS CHILDHOOD? HE'S REGRESSED.
BUT HE SHOULD HAVE BEEN ABLE TO SEE EVERYTHING CLEARLY. RIGHT?
OF COURSE, MY PRINCE. DON'T WORRY, THE REGRESSION IS TEMPORARY.
YOUR FRIEND WILL BE BACK TO HIS OLD SELF IN –

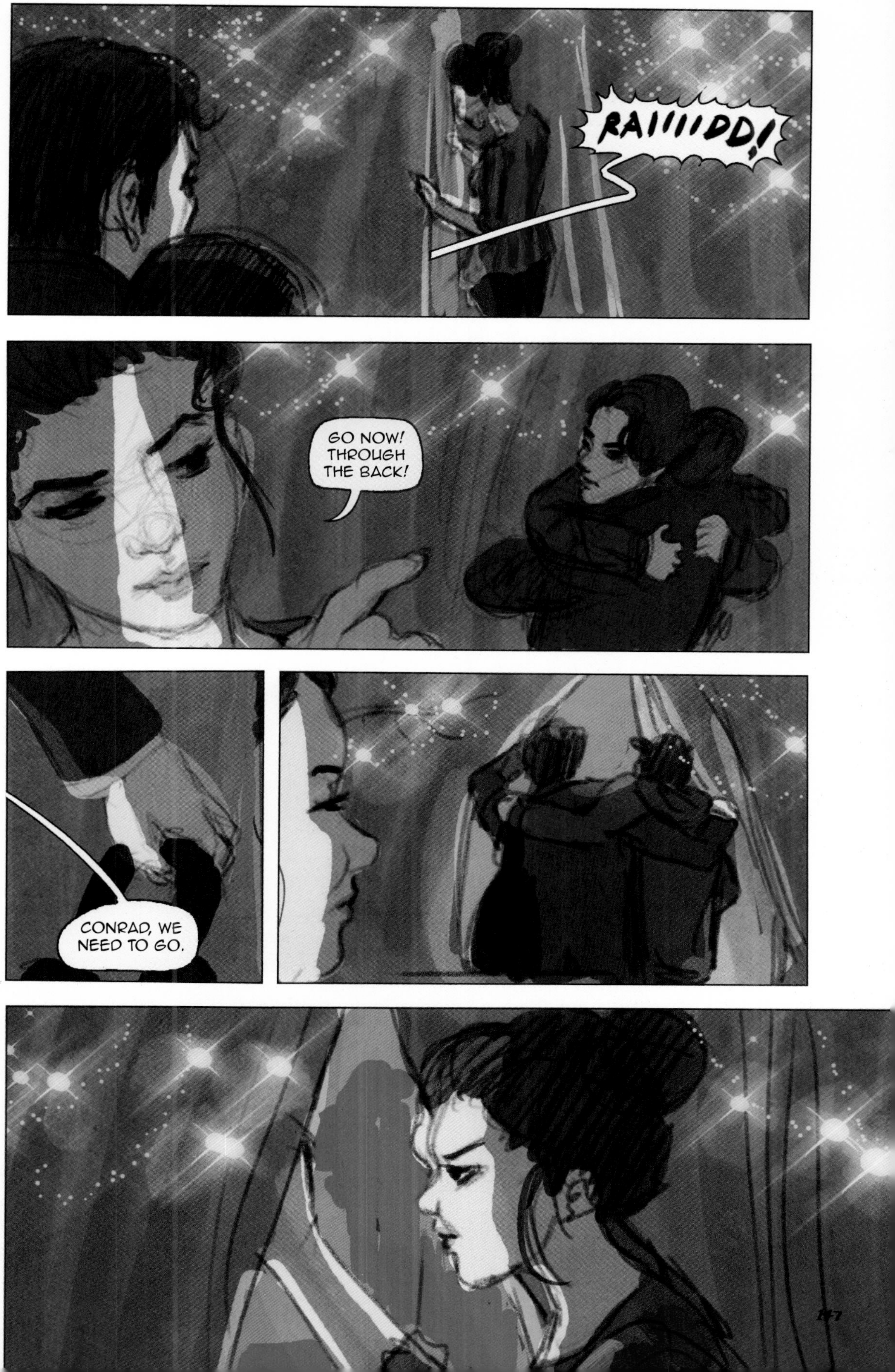
RAIIIIDD!
GO NOW! THROUGH THE BACK!
CONRAD, WE NEED TO GO.

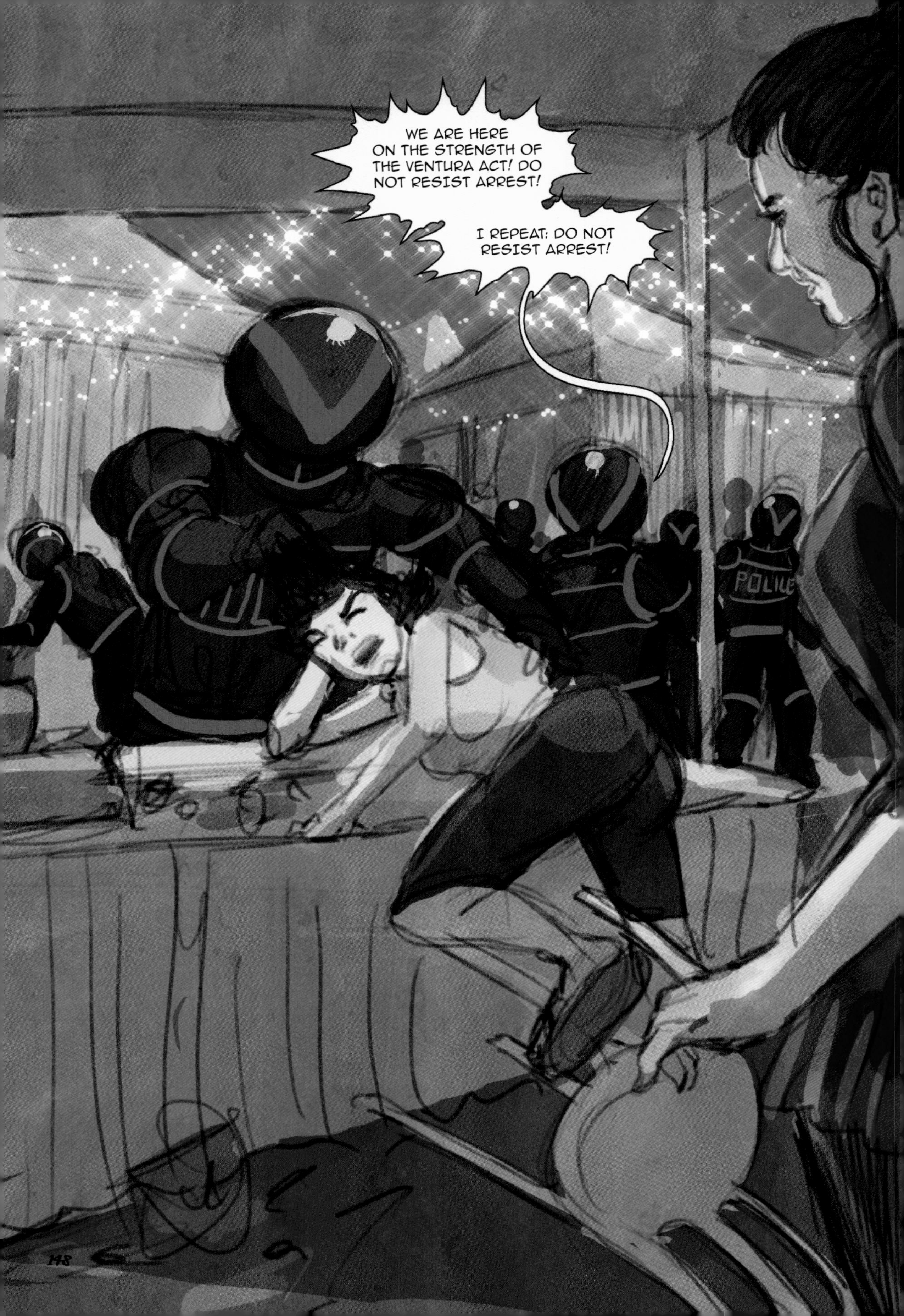
WE ARE HERE ON THE STRENGTH OF THE VENTURA ACT! DO NOT RESIST ARREST!
I REPEAT: DO NOT RESIST ARREST!
POLICE

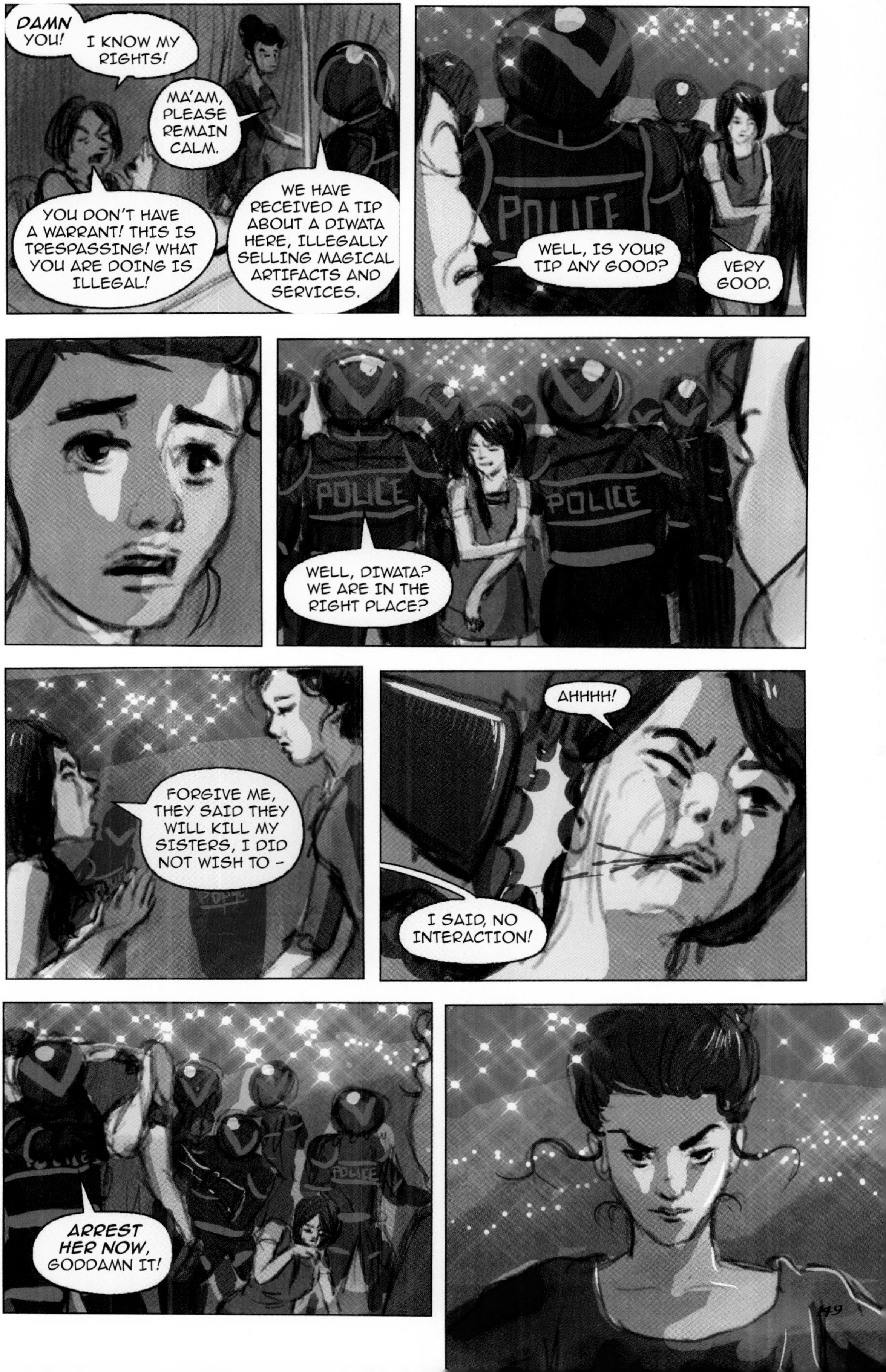
DAMN YOU!
I KNOW MY RIGHTS!
MA'AM, PLEASE REMAIN CALM.
YOU DON'T HAVE A WARRANT! THIS IS TRESPASSING! WHAT YOU ARE DOING IS ILLEGAL!
WE HAVE RECEIVED A TIP ABOUT A DIWATA HERE, ILLEGALLY SELLING MAGICAL ARTIFACTS AND SERVICES.
POLICE
WELL, IS YOUR TIP ANY GOOD?
VERY GOOD.
POLICE
POLICE
WELL, DIWATA? WE ARE IN THE RIGHT PLACE?
FORGIVE ME, THEY SAID THEY WILL KILL MY SISTERS, I DID NOT WISH TO -
AHHHH!
I SAID, NO INTERACTION!
POLICE
ARREST HER NOW, GODDAMN IT!

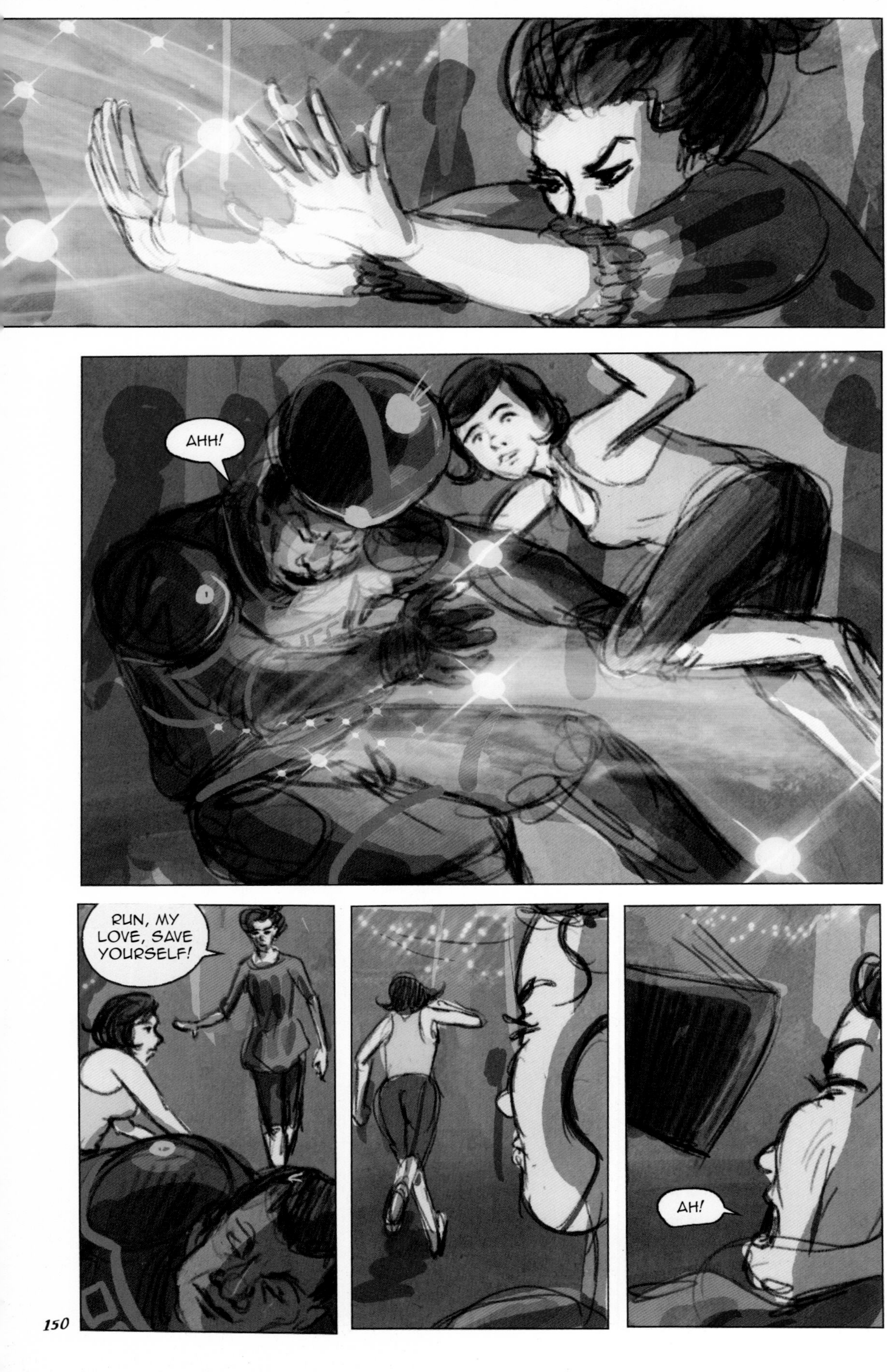
AHH!
RUN, MY LOVE, SAVE YOURSELF!
AH!

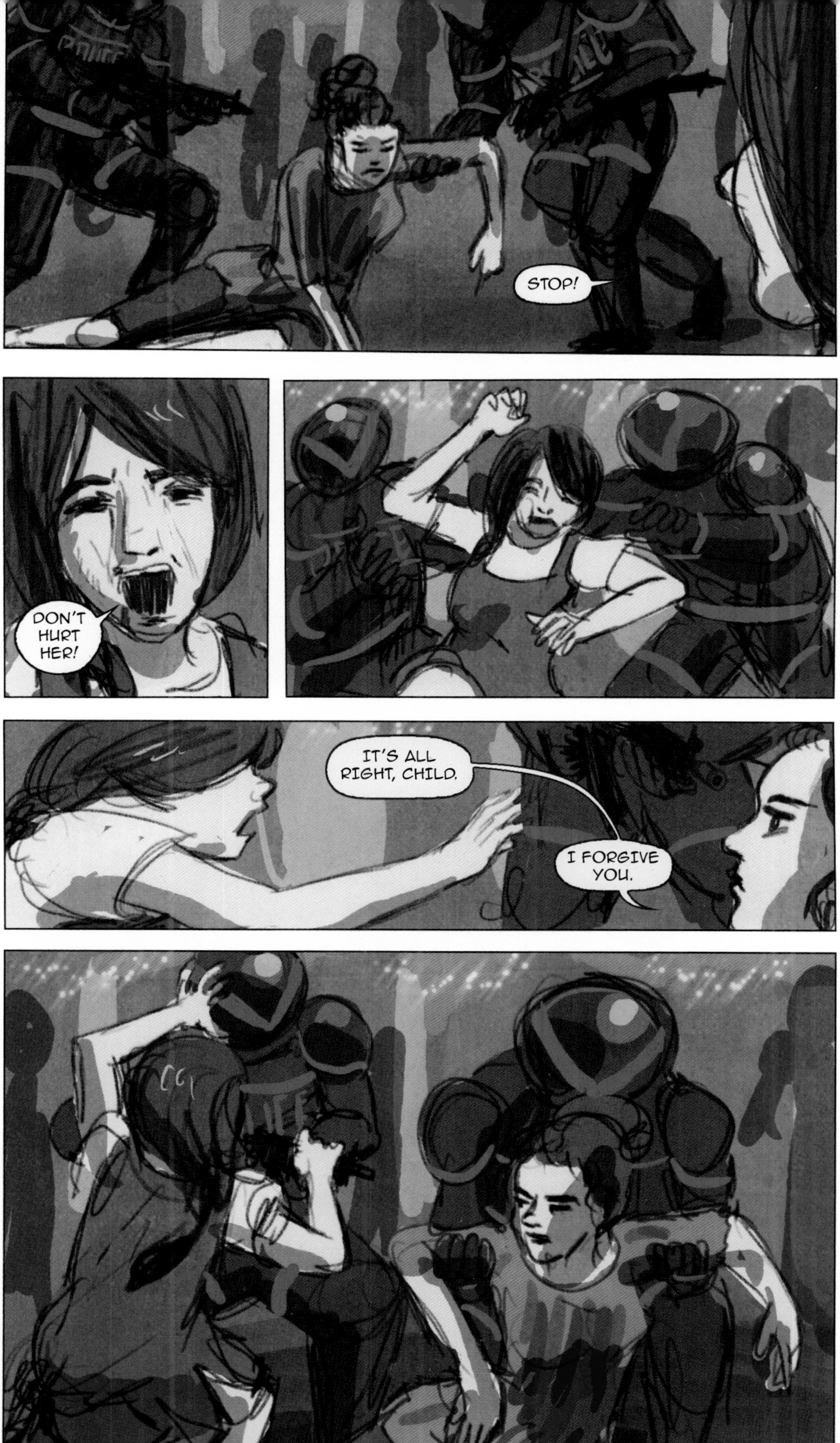
STOP!
DON'T HURT HER!
IT'S ALL RIGHT, CHILD.
I FORGIVE YOU.

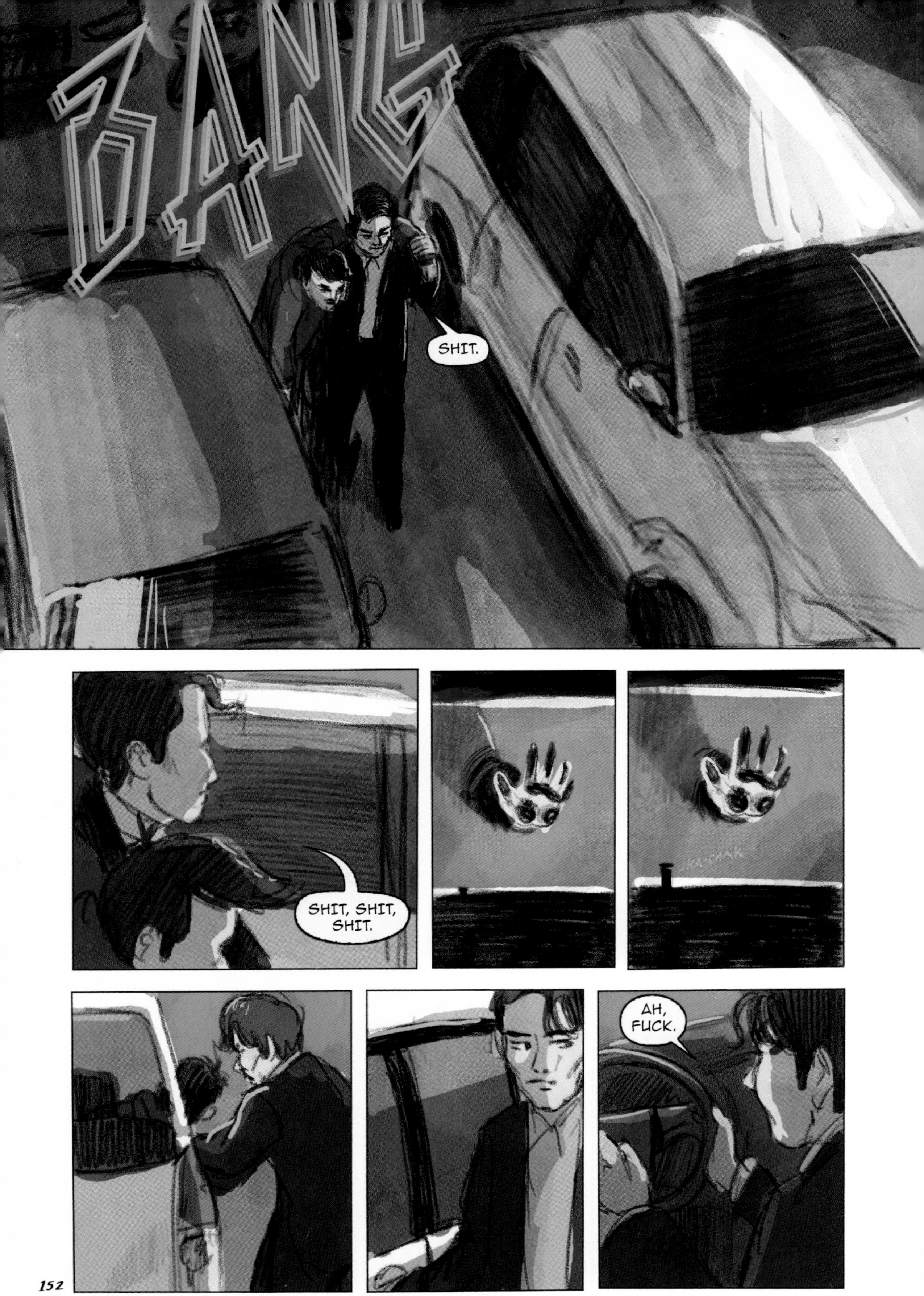

BANG
SHIT.
SHIT, SHIT, SHIT.
KA-CHAK
AH, FUCK.

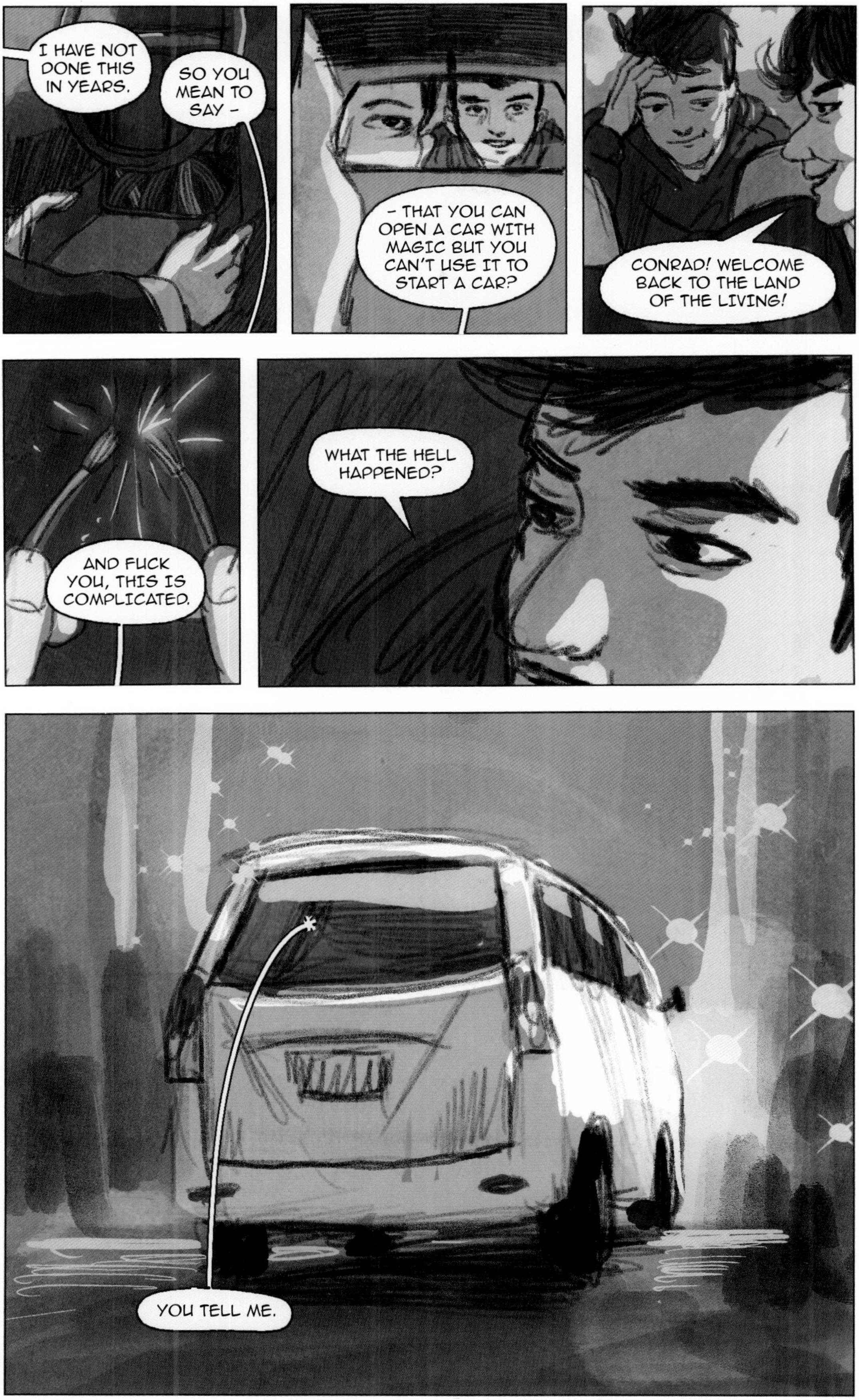

I HAVE NOT DONE THIS IN YEARS.
SO YOU MEAN TO SAY -
- THAT YOU CAN OPEN A CAR WITH MAGIC BUT YOU CAN'T USE IT TO START A CAR?
CONRAD! WELCOME BACK TO THE LAND OF THE LIVING!
AND FUCK YOU, THIS IS COMPLICATED.
WHAT THE HELL HAPPENED?
YOU TELL ME.

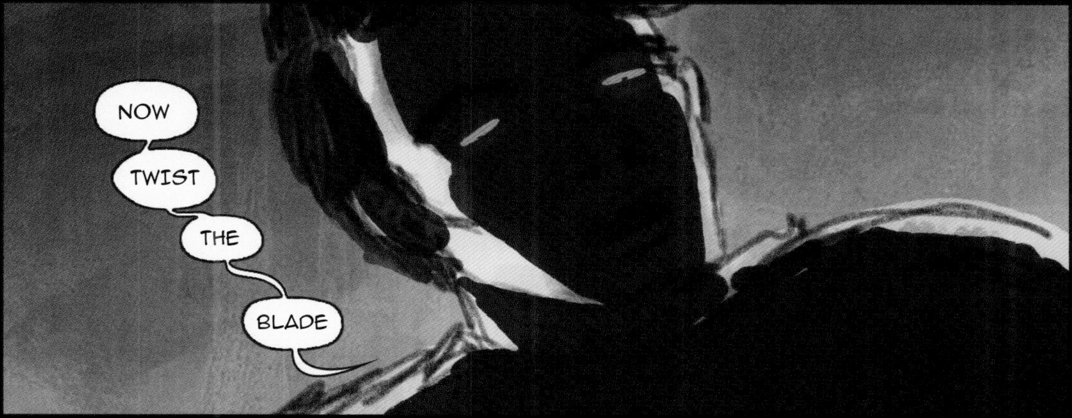
NOW
TWIST
THE
BLADE

SO YOU DIDN'T SEE THE MAN WHO TOLD YOU TO DO IT?

NO.

HIS FACE WAS BLURRY.

HM.

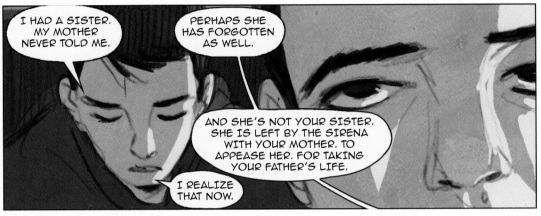

I HAD A SISTER. MY MOTHER NEVER TOLD ME.

PERHAPS SHE HAS FORGOTTEN AS WELL.

AND SHE'S NOT YOUR SISTER. SHE IS LEFT BY THE SIRENA WITH YOUR MOTHER. TO APPEASE HER. FOR TAKING YOUR FATHER'S LIFE.

I REALIZE THAT NOW.

BUT WHY DID YOU DO IT? WHY DID YOU BRING ME TO SOLEDAD?

IGNACIO?

I THOUGHT YOU MIGHT WANT TO KNOW.

THANK YOU.

I JUST WISH –

– I HAVE REMEMBERED THAT MAN'S FACE.

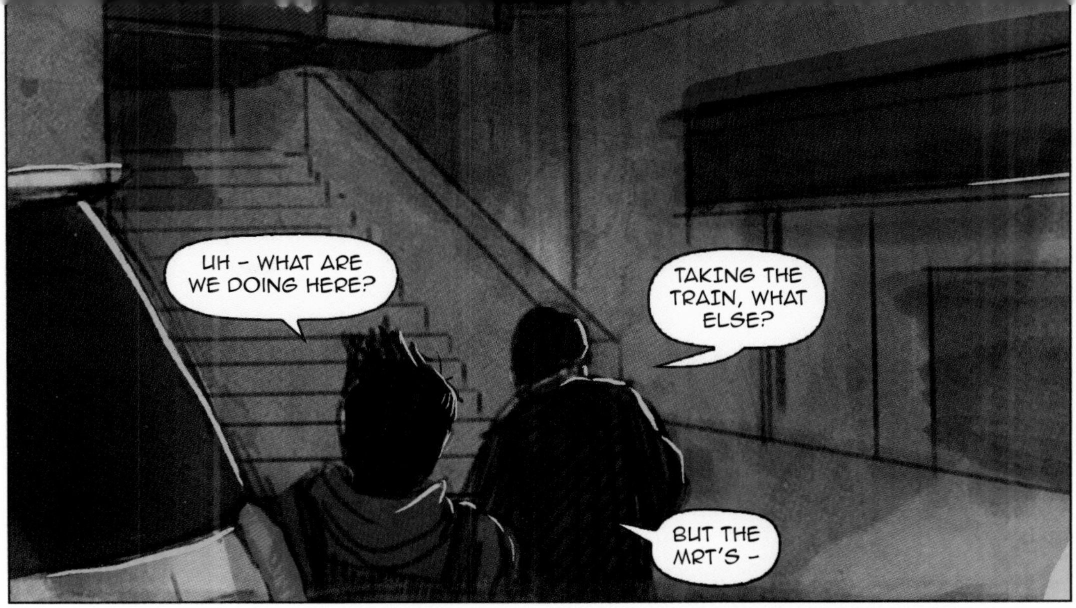
UH – WHAT ARE WE DOING HERE?
TAKING THE TRAIN, WHAT ELSE?
BUT THE MRT'S –

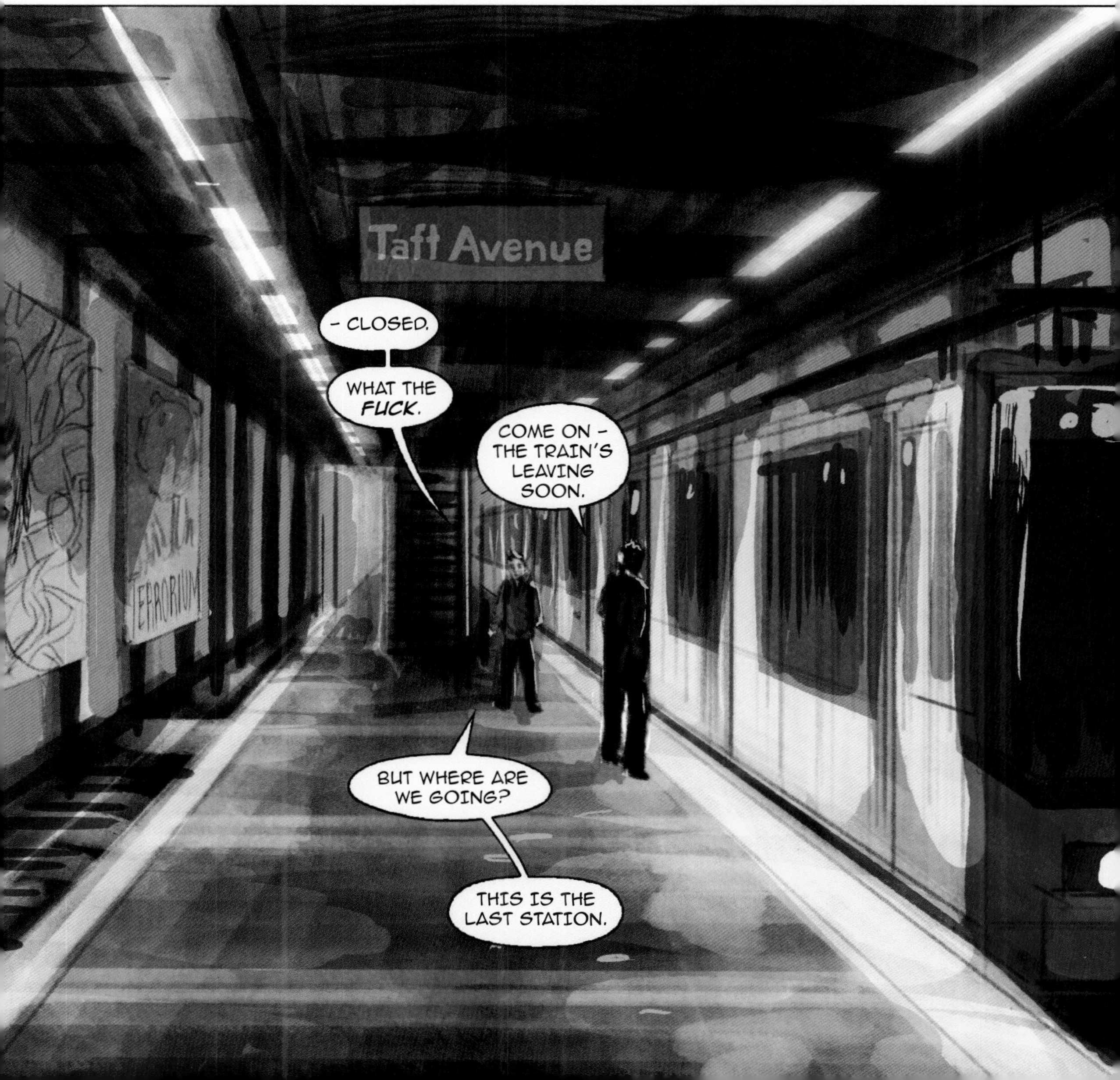
Taft Avenue
– CLOSED.
WHAT THE *FUCK*.
COME ON – THE TRAIN'S LEAVING SOON.
TERRORIUM
BUT WHERE ARE WE GOING?
THIS IS THE LAST STATION.

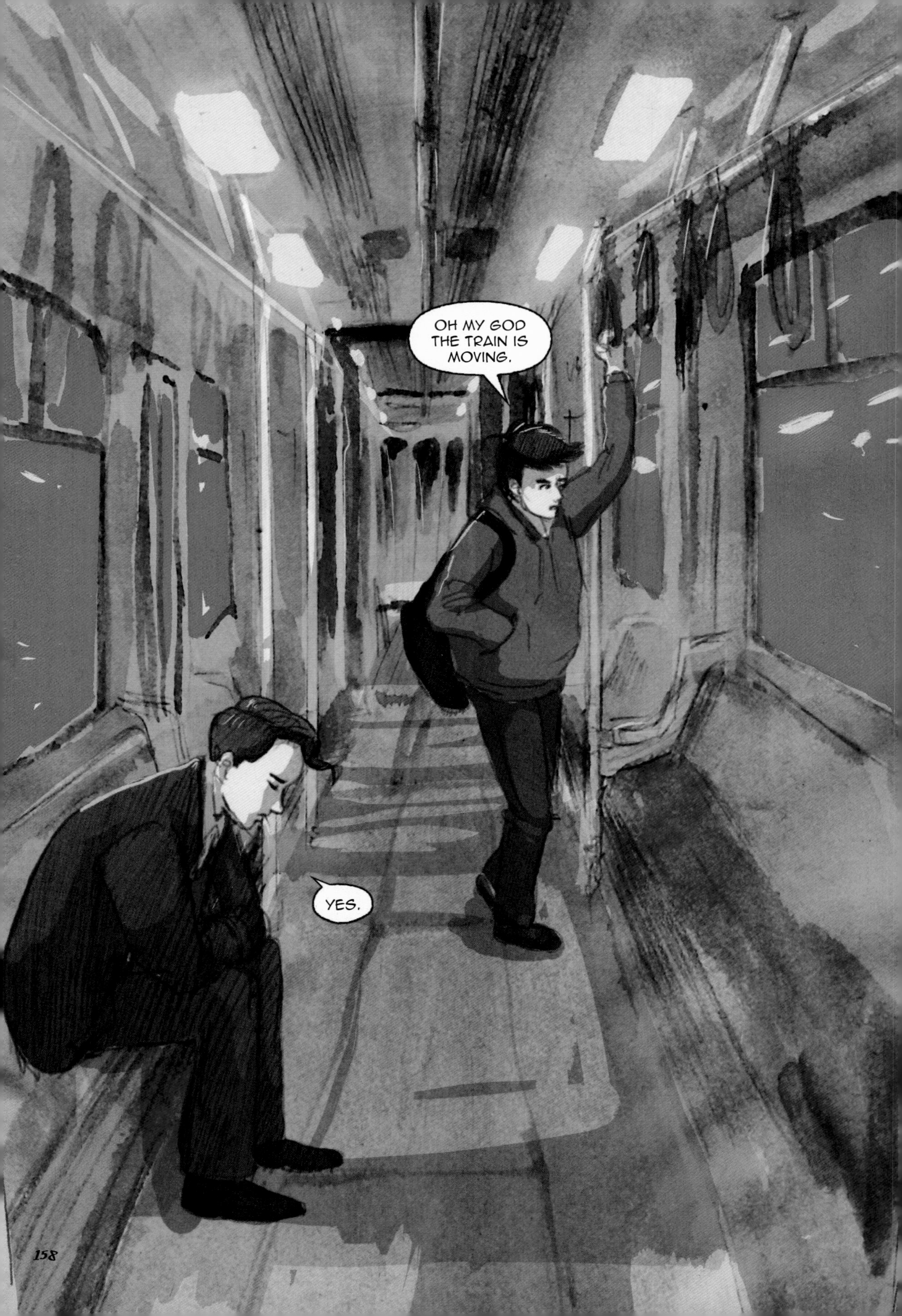
OH MY GOD THE TRAIN IS MOVING.
YES.

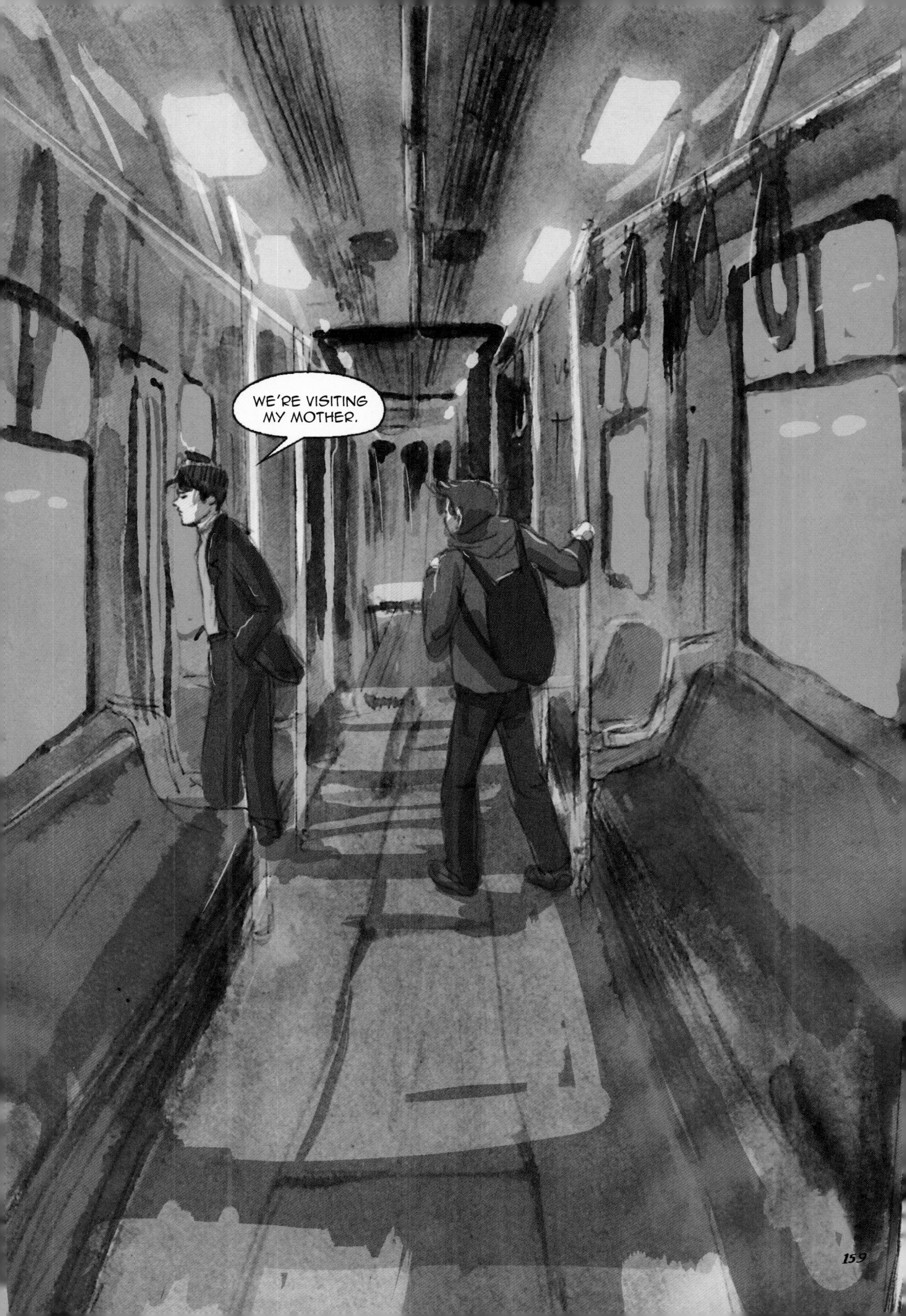
WE'RE VISITING MY MOTHER.

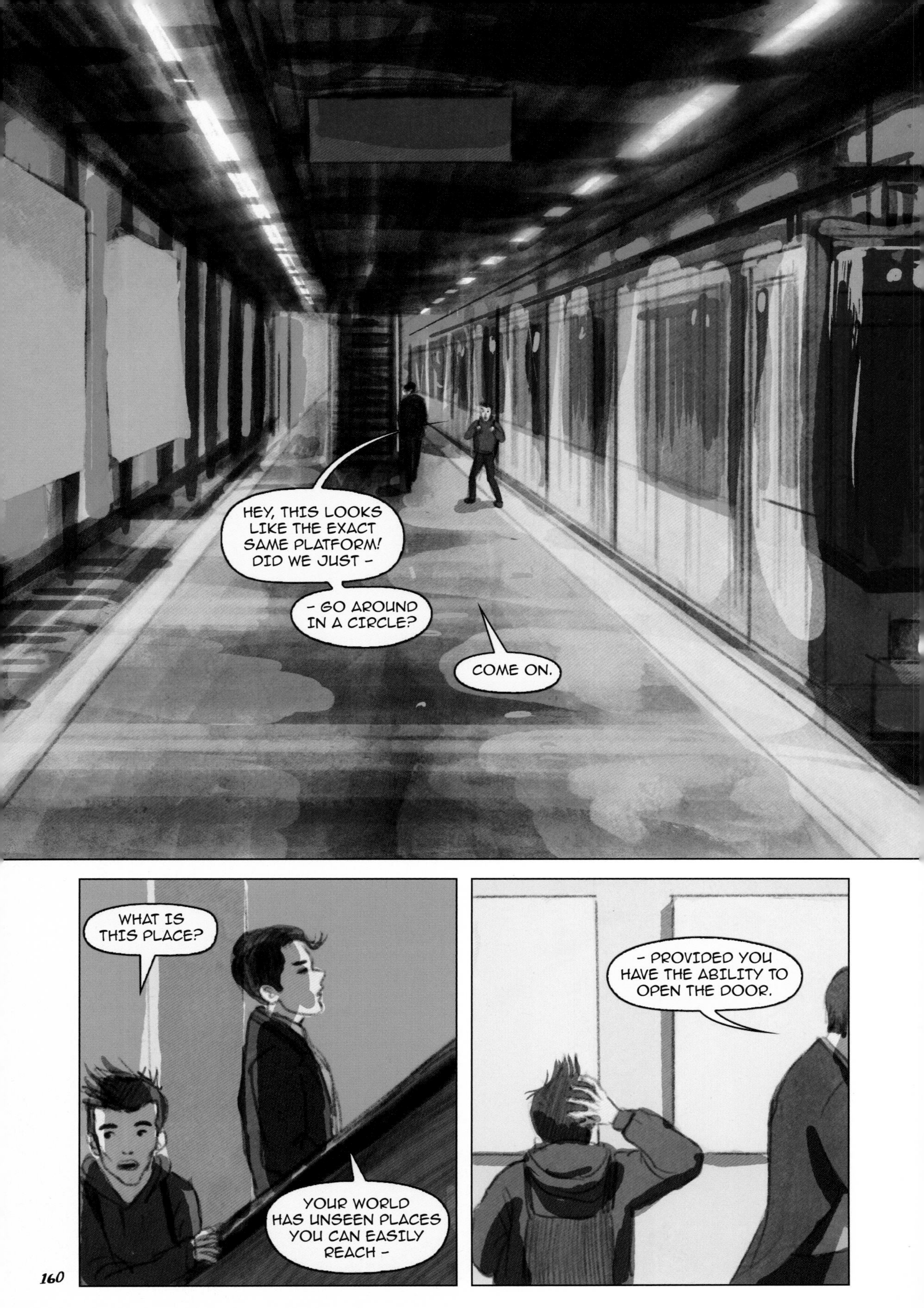
HEY, THIS LOOKS LIKE THE EXACT SAME PLATFORM! DID WE JUST -
- GO AROUND IN A CIRCLE?
COME ON.
WHAT IS THIS PLACE?
YOUR WORLD HAS UNSEEN PLACES YOU CAN EASILY REACH -
- PROVIDED YOU HAVE THE ABILITY TO OPEN THE DOOR.

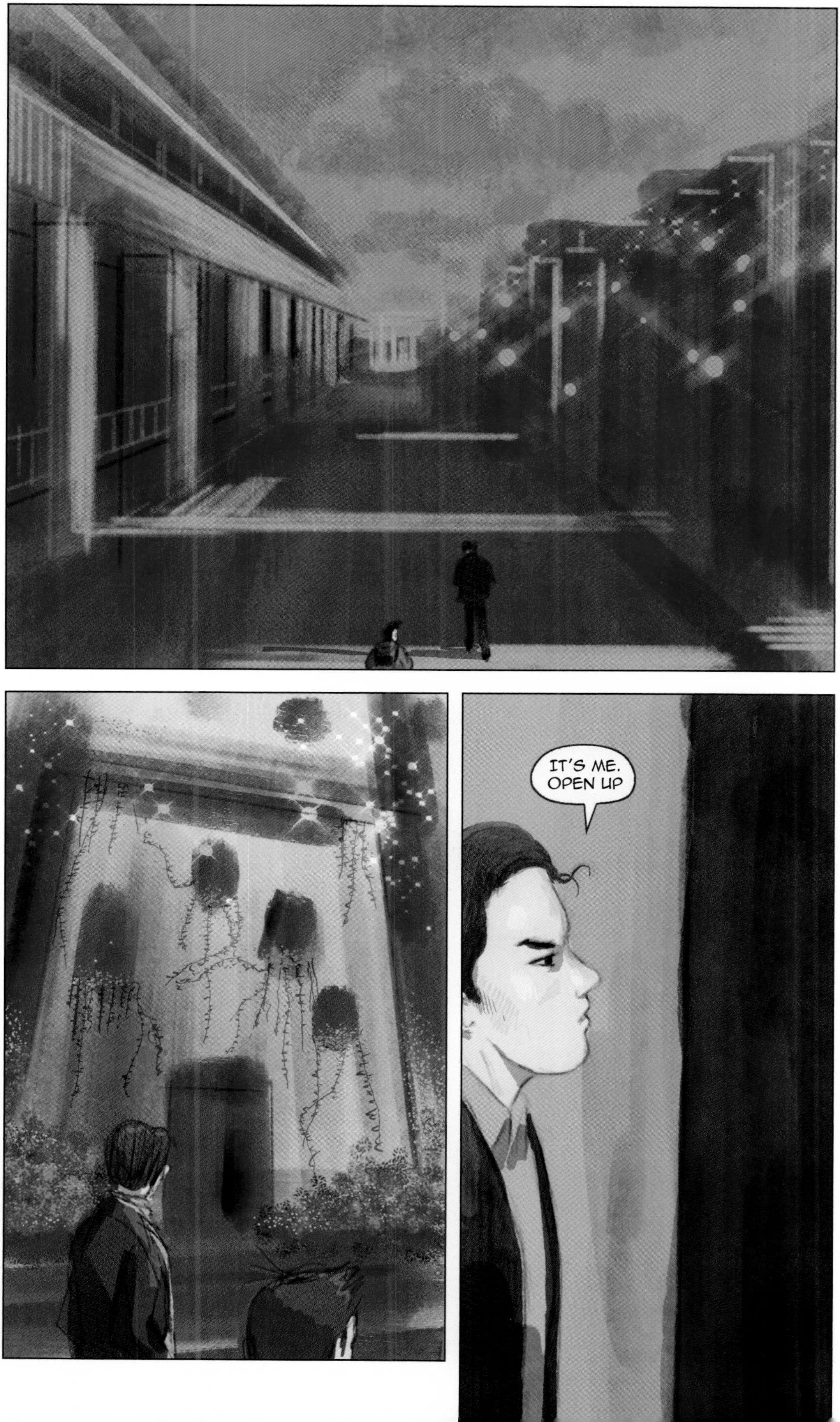
IT'S ME. OPEN UP

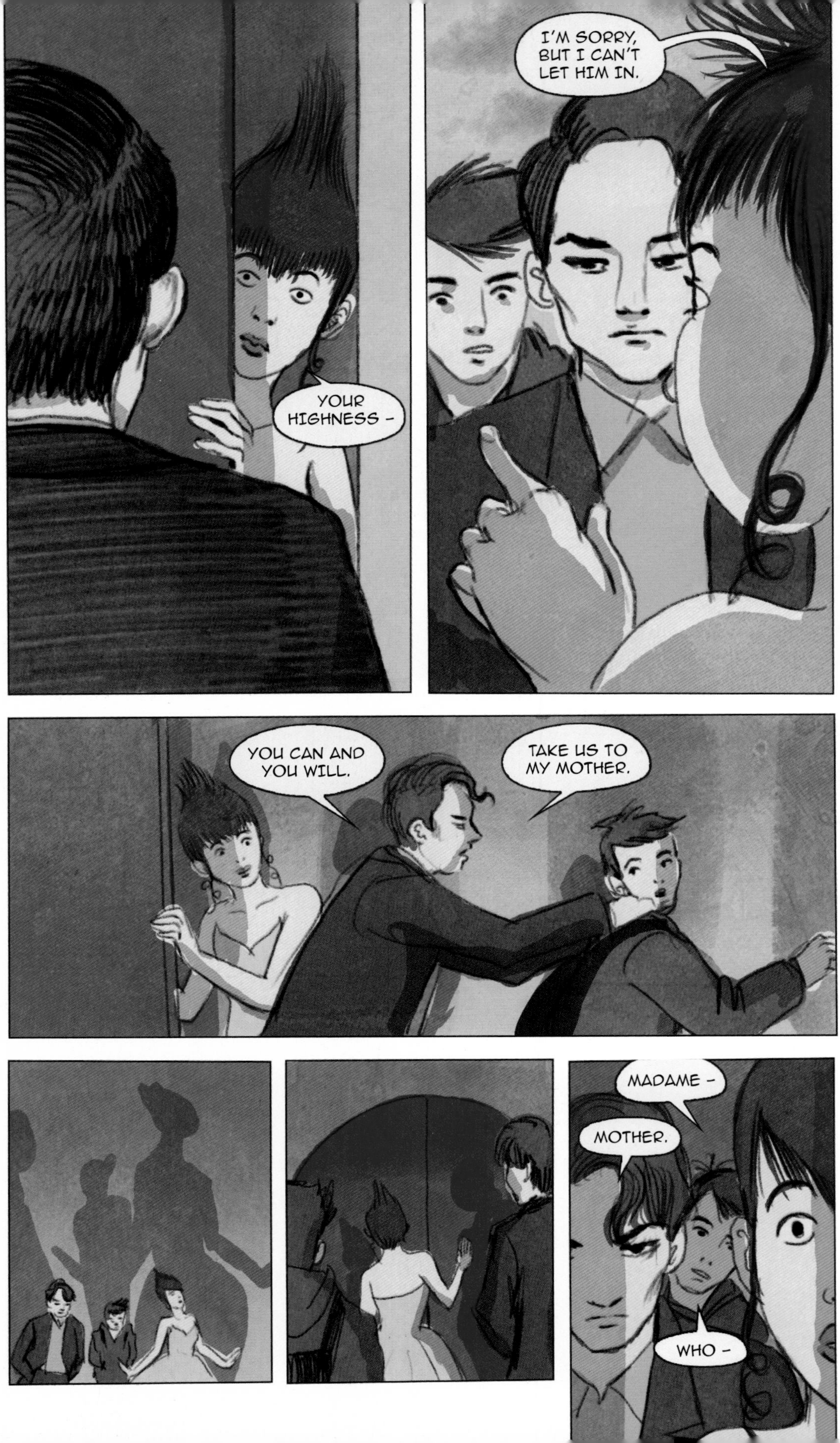
YOUR HIGHNESS –
I'M SORRY, BUT I CAN'T LET HIM IN.
YOU CAN AND YOU WILL.
TAKE US TO MY MOTHER.
MADAME –
MOTHER.
WHO –

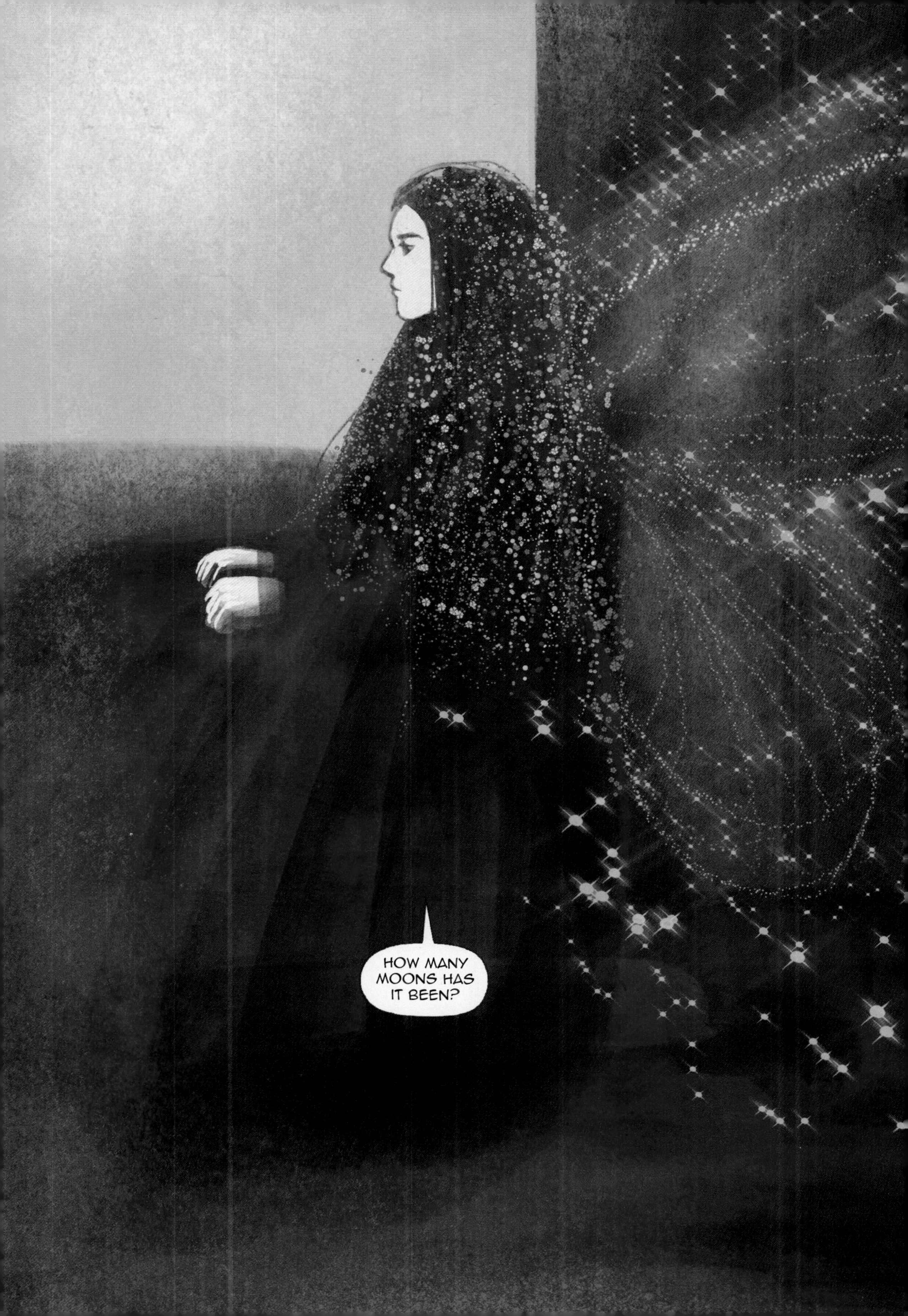
HOW MANY MOONS HAS IT BEEN?

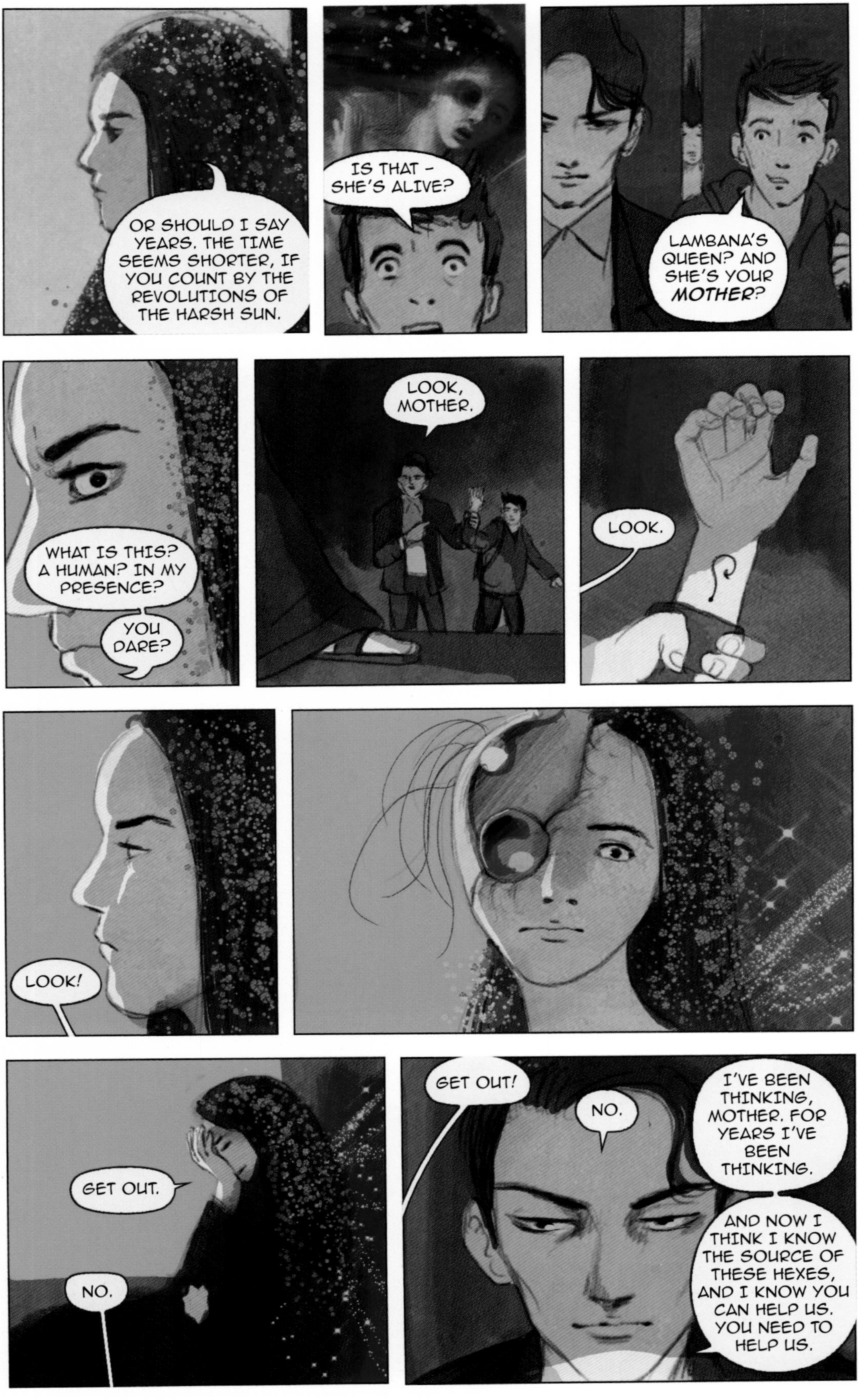
OR SHOULD I SAY YEARS. THE TIME SEEMS SHORTER, IF YOU COUNT BY THE REVOLUTIONS OF THE HARSH SUN.
IS THAT – SHE'S ALIVE?
LAMBANA'S QUEEN? AND SHE'S YOUR *MOTHER*?
WHAT IS THIS? A HUMAN? IN MY PRESENCE?
YOU DARE?
LOOK, MOTHER.
LOOK.
LOOK!
GET OUT.
NO.
GET OUT!
NO.
I'VE BEEN THINKING, MOTHER. FOR YEARS I'VE BEEN THINKING.
AND NOW I THINK I KNOW THE SOURCE OF THESE HEXES, AND I KNOW YOU CAN HELP US. YOU NEED TO HELP US.

BECAUSE HE HELPED US RE-OPEN LAMBANA!

WHAT MADE YOU THINK THAT I WOULD HELP A HUMAN?

WHY DO YOU THINK YOUR SISTER IS LEFT IN THE CARE OF A SIRENA?

THE SIRENA HID HER FROM US!

THE SIRENA HAD ALWAYS LONGED FOR THE DOWNFALL OF —

NONSENSE. THE CONFLICT WITH SIRENA WAS AN INSIDIOUS RUMOR, A FABRICATION — NOTHING MORE.

IT HAD NO BASIS IN REALITY. LAMBANA HAD A GOOD RELATIONSHIP WITH THE SIRENA. UNTIL YOU HAD ONE KILLED.

BUT I DID IT TO —

DON'T YOU UNDERSTAND?

I LEFT THE PRINCESS IN THEIR CARE.

I LEFT HER WITH THE SIRENA TO KEEP HER SAFE.

THE SIRENA DEEMED IT NECESSARY TO CLOAK HER IN HUMAN SKIN AND LEAVE HER WITH A HUMAN SURROGATE FAMILY, AND I ALLOWED IT.

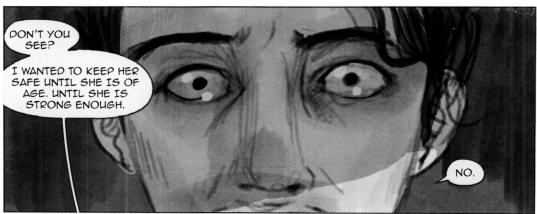

DON'T YOU SEE?

I WANTED TO KEEP HER SAFE UNTIL SHE IS OF AGE. UNTIL SHE IS STRONG ENOUGH.

NO.

YOU HAVE FIGURED OUT THAT THE HEXES CAME FROM LAMBANA.

THAT'S TRUE. BUT IT WAS FOR THE DEFENSE OF THE HEIRESS APPARENT.

THE HEXES WERE TO LEAVE LAMBANA AND ENTER THE HUMAN REALM IF THE PRINCESS WENT THROUGH THE THRESHOLD BEFORE HER APPOINTED TIME.

WHY DIDN'T YOU TELL ME THIS?

WHY WOULD I TELL ANYONE FROM LAMBANA THIS?

IF THE DIWATA KNEW A QUEEN'S DAUGHTER WAS LYING IN WAIT, DO YOU THINK THE HEXES WOULD DETER THEM?

DO YOU THINK THEY WOULD THINK TWICE BEFORE KILLING A SIRENA?

YOU DIDN'T.

EVERYONE WANTED TO GO HOME. I RECOGNIZE THAT.

I HAD HOPED YOU WOULD BE MORE PATIENT.

YOU SHOULD HAVE TOLD ME.

YOUR SISTER WAS TOO YOUNG.

SHE WAS NOT STRONG ENOUGH. SHE ABDICATED THE THRONE, OR WAS USURPED.

THE DETAILS REMAIN HAZY TO ME.

AND NOW HERE WE ARE, SON, EXILED. TOO WEAK TO EVEN AVENGE OURSELVES.

TO EVEN THINK OF VENGEANCE

I CAN CONVINCE HER TO RETURN.

I WILL CONVINCE HER TO RETURN.

YOU SHOULD HAVE TOLD ME.

WHY DIDN'T YOU TELL ME? *I AM YOUR SON!*

IGNACIO--

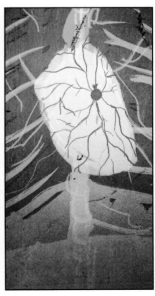

MOTHER, PLEASE. I HAVE RUINED THIS CHILD'S LIFE.

HELP ME DO ONE RIGHT THING.

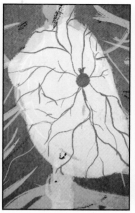

JUST ONE RIGHT THING, MOTHER.

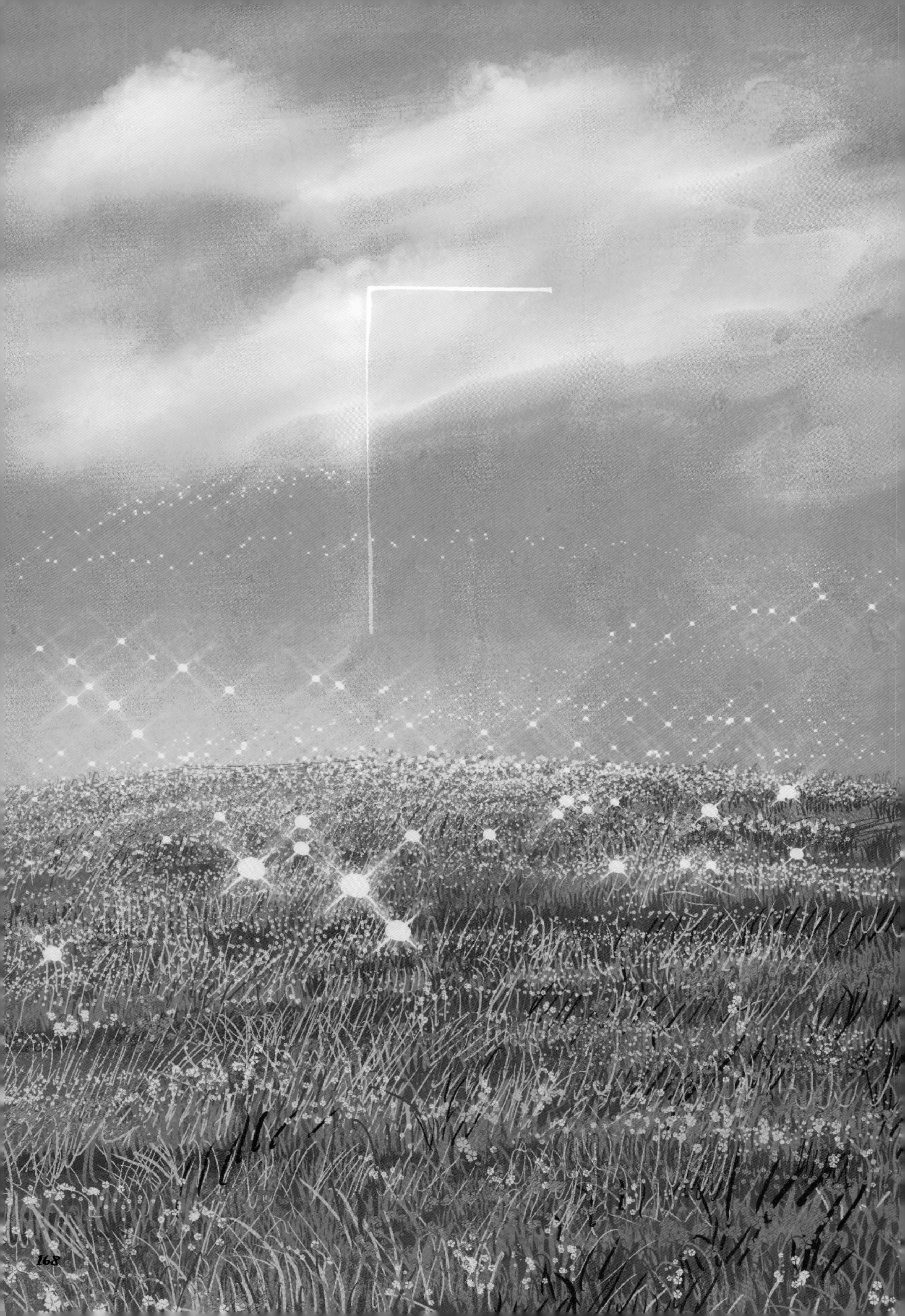

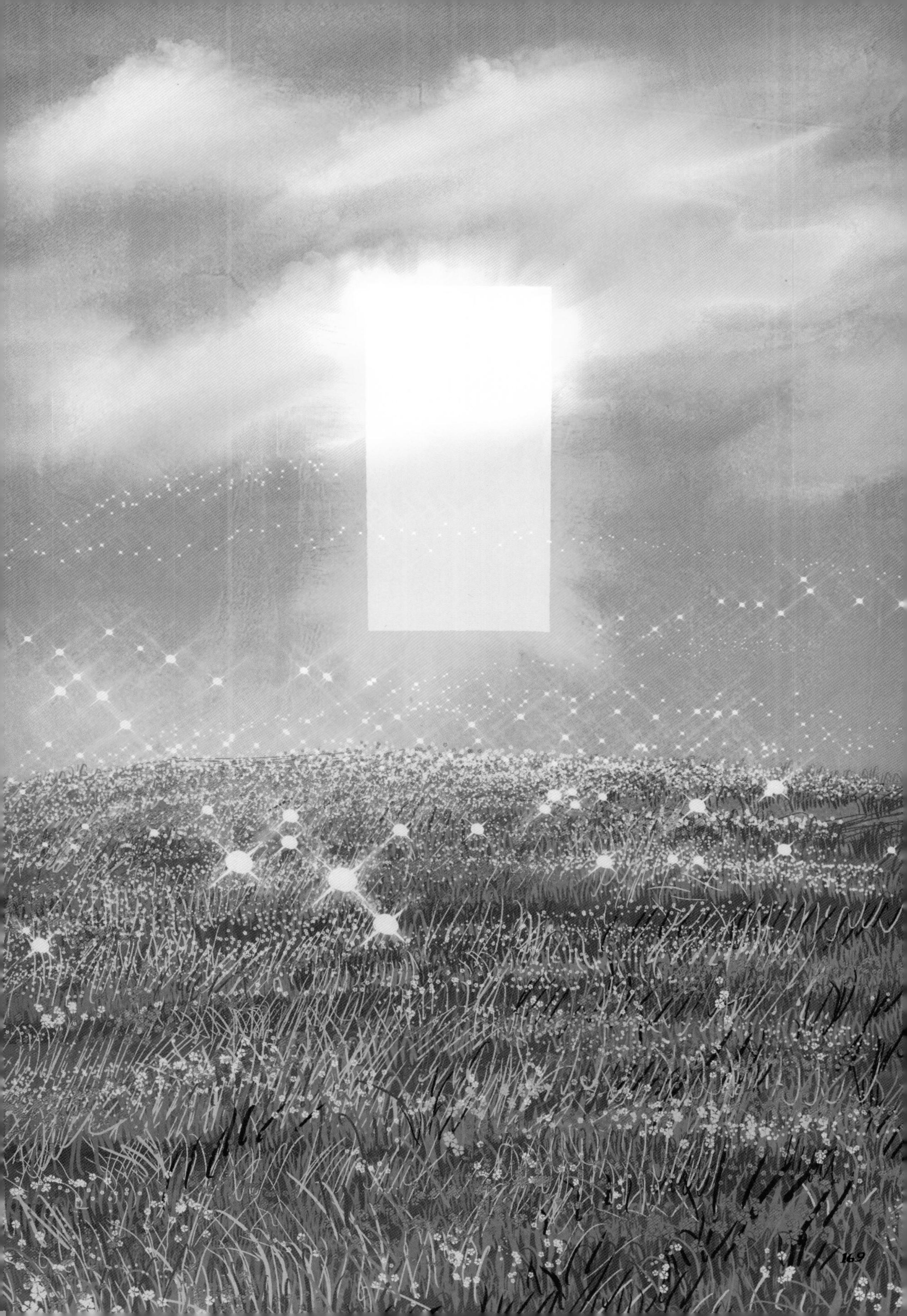

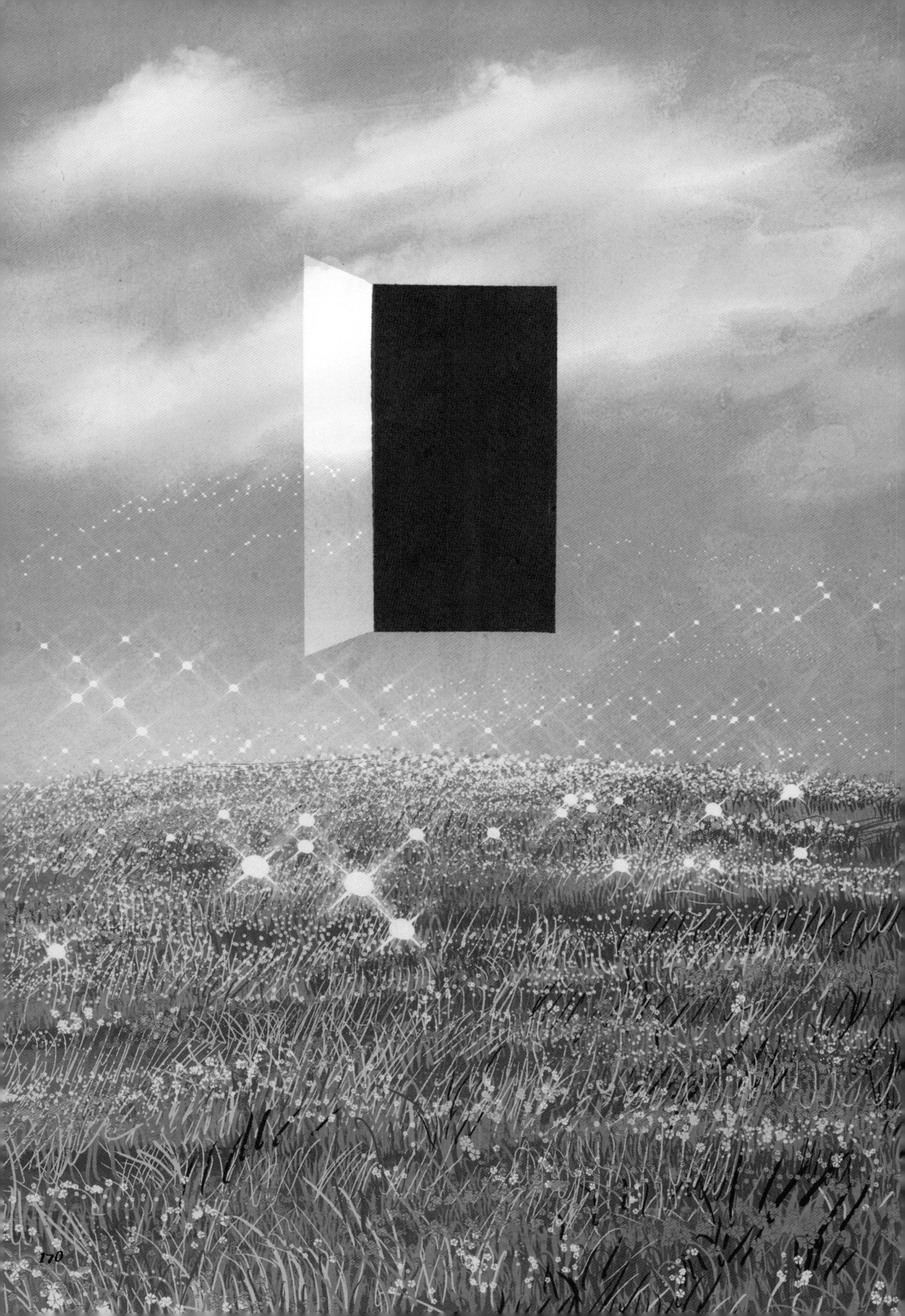

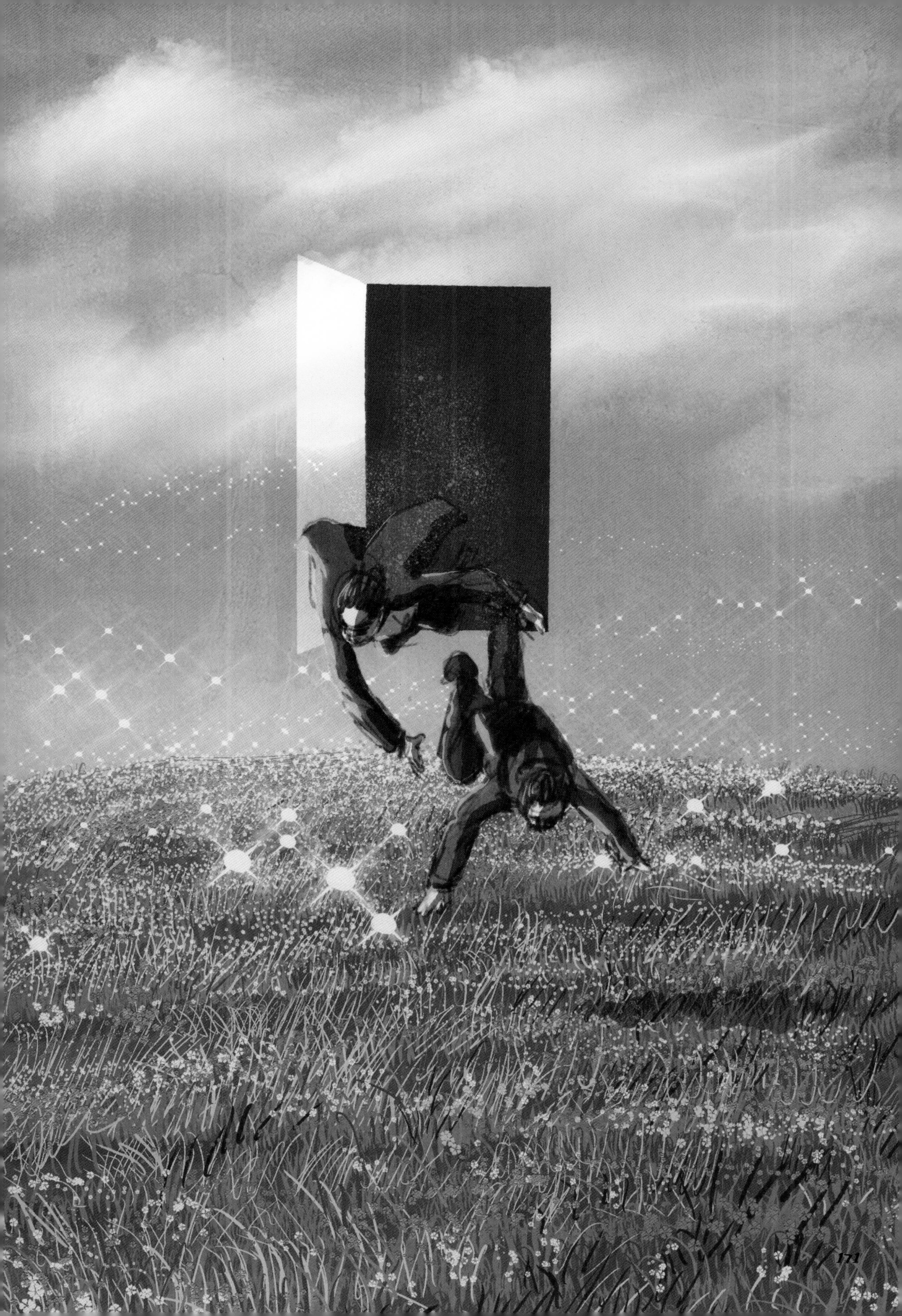

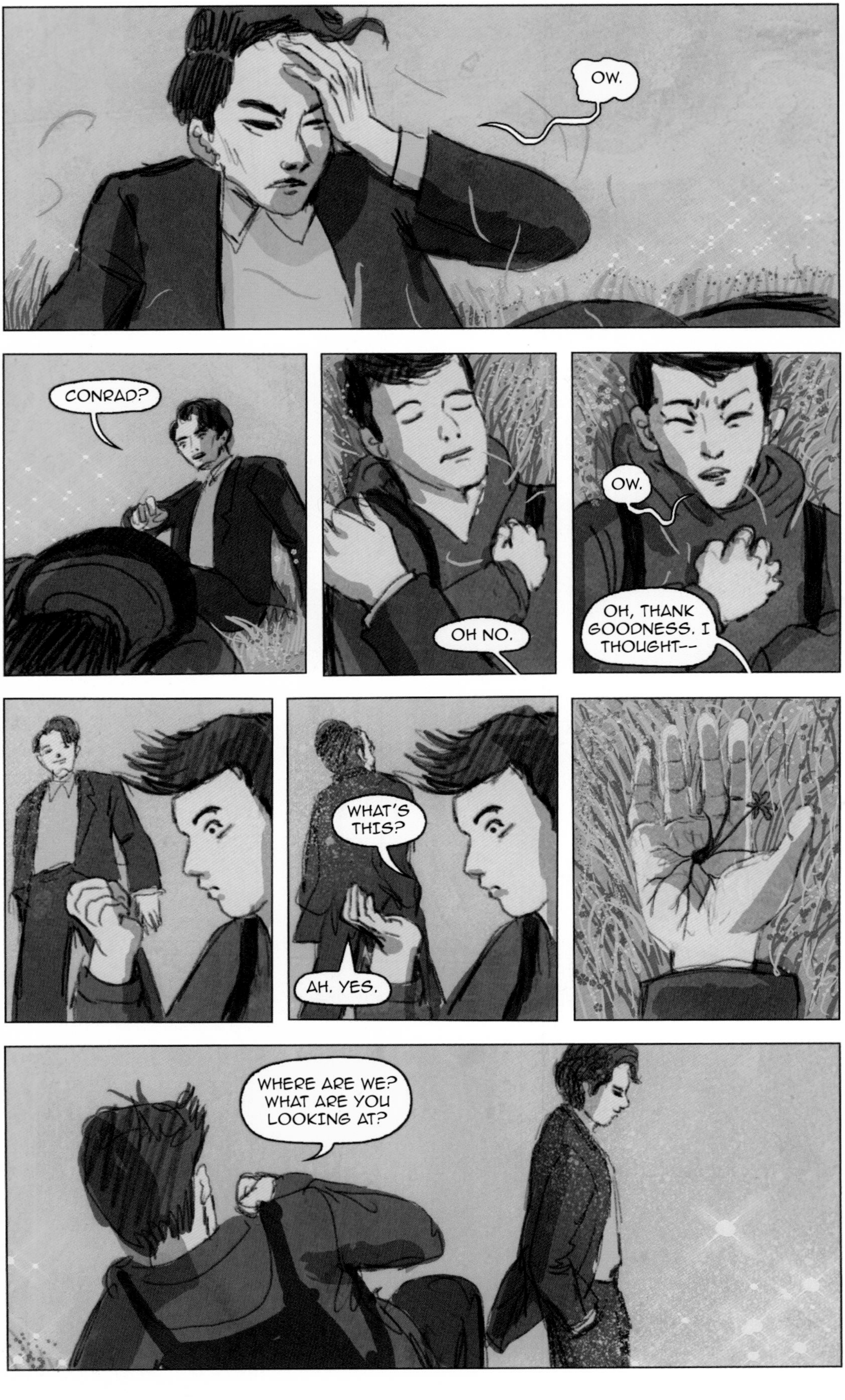
OW.
CONRAD?
OH NO.
OW.
OH, THANK GOODNESS. I THOUGHT--
WHAT'S THIS?
AH. YES.
WHERE ARE WE? WHAT ARE YOU LOOKING AT?

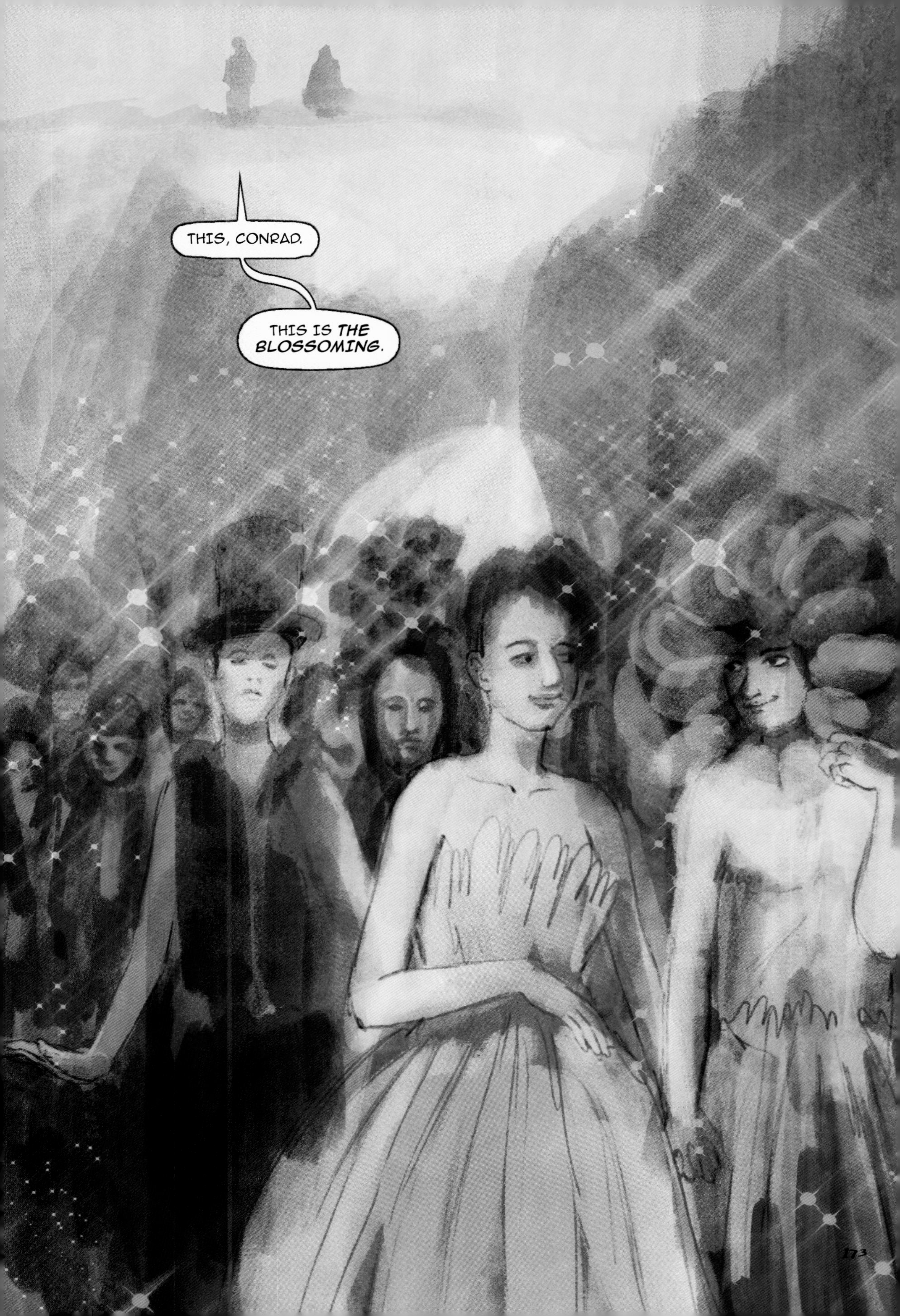
THIS, CONRAD.
THIS IS THE BLOSSOMING.

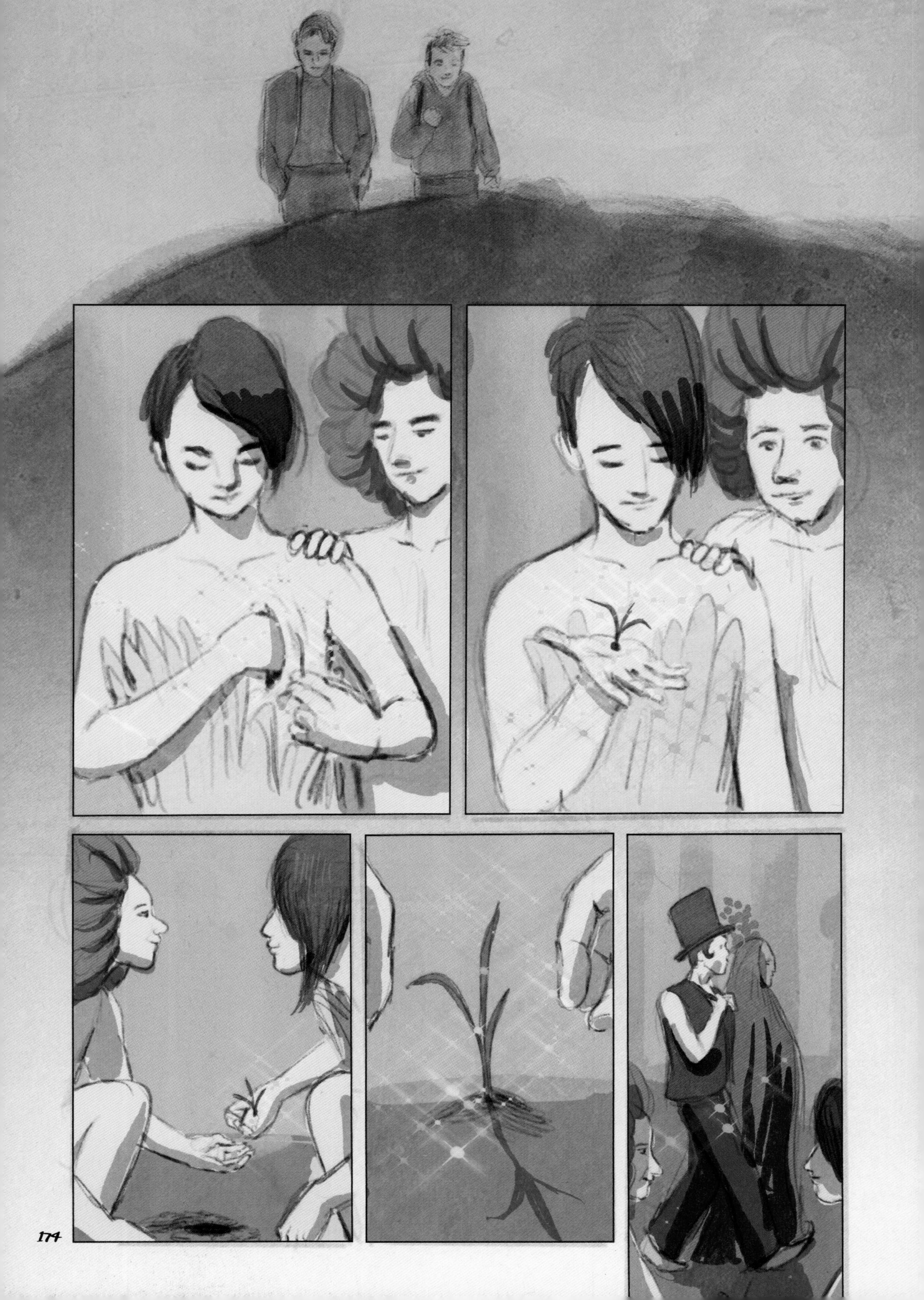

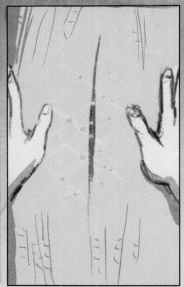

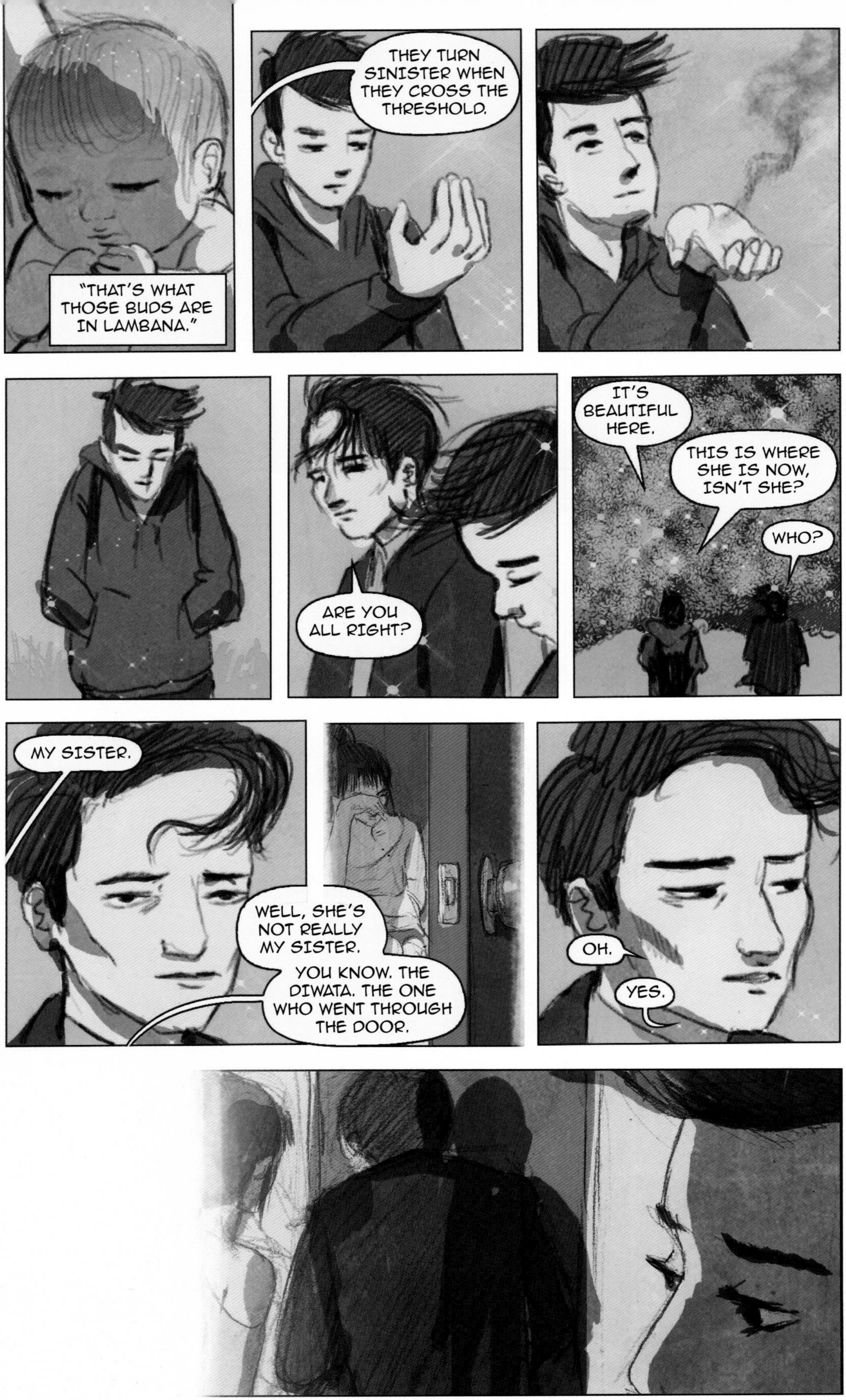
"THAT'S WHAT THOSE BUDS ARE IN LAMBANA."
THEY TURN SINISTER WHEN THEY CROSS THE THRESHOLD.
ARE YOU ALL RIGHT?
IT'S BEAUTIFUL HERE.
THIS IS WHERE SHE IS NOW, ISN'T SHE?
WHO?
MY SISTER.
WELL, SHE'S NOT REALLY MY SISTER.
YOU KNOW. THE DIWATA. THE ONE WHO WENT THROUGH THE DOOR.
OH.
YES.

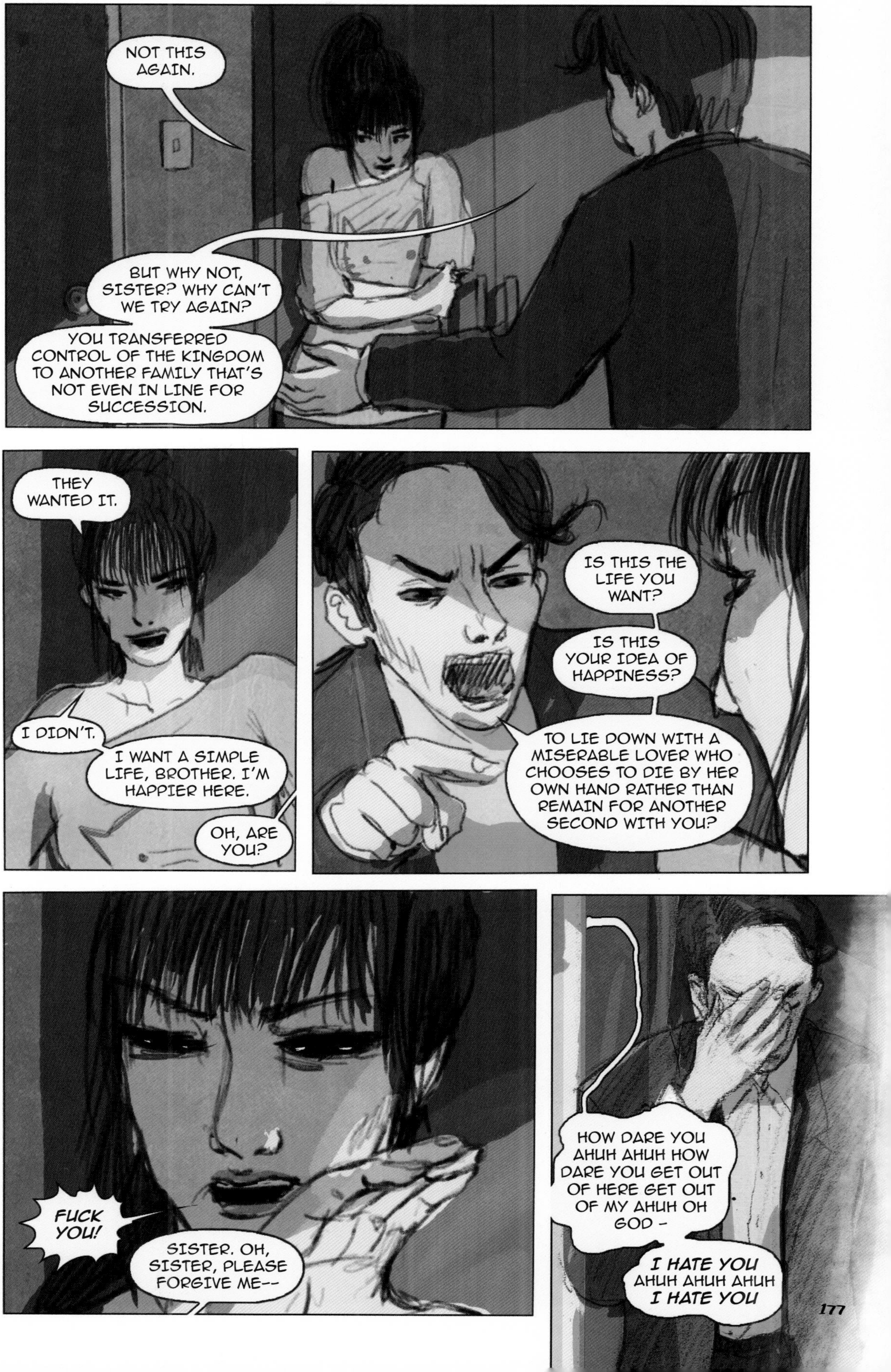
NOT THIS AGAIN.
BUT WHY NOT, SISTER? WHY CAN'T WE TRY AGAIN?
YOU TRANSFERRED CONTROL OF THE KINGDOM TO ANOTHER FAMILY THAT'S NOT EVEN IN LINE FOR SUCCESSION.
THEY WANTED IT.
I DIDN'T.
I WANT A SIMPLE LIFE, BROTHER. I'M HAPPIER HERE.
OH, ARE YOU?
IS THIS THE LIFE YOU WANT?
IS THIS YOUR IDEA OF HAPPINESS?
TO LIE DOWN WITH A MISERABLE LOVER WHO CHOOSES TO DIE BY HER OWN HAND RATHER THAN REMAIN FOR ANOTHER SECOND WITH YOU?
FUCK YOU!
SISTER. OH, SISTER, PLEASE FORGIVE ME--
HOW DARE YOU AHUH AHUH HOW DARE YOU GET OUT OF HERE GET OUT OF MY AHUH OH GOD –
I HATE YOU AHUH AHUH AHUH I HATE YOU

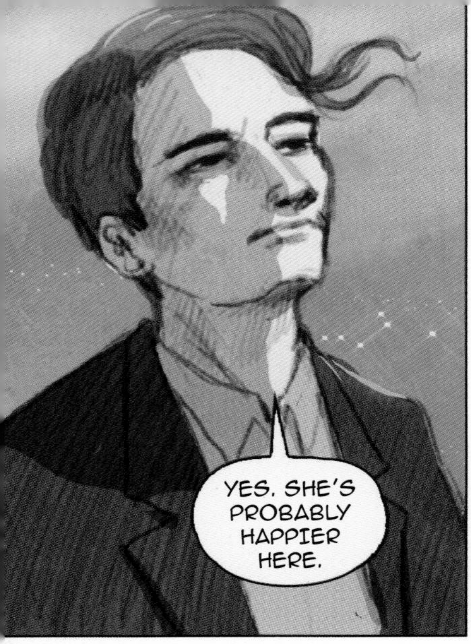
YES. SHE'S PROBABLY HAPPIER HERE.

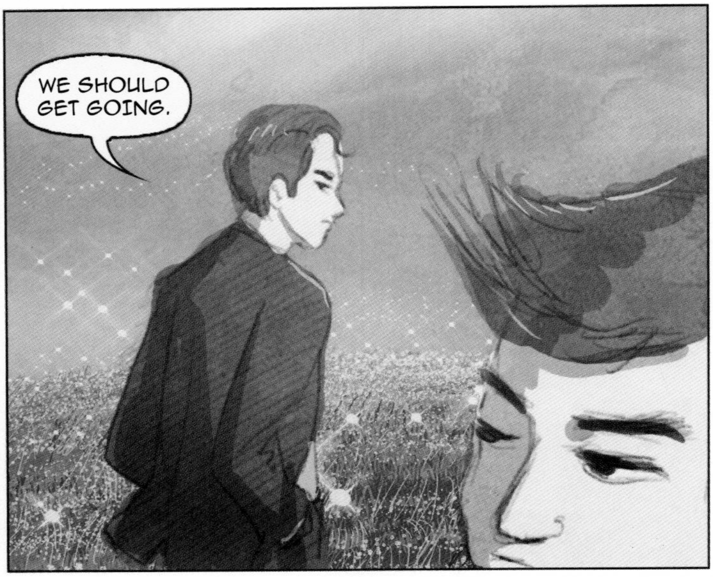
WE SHOULD GET GOING.

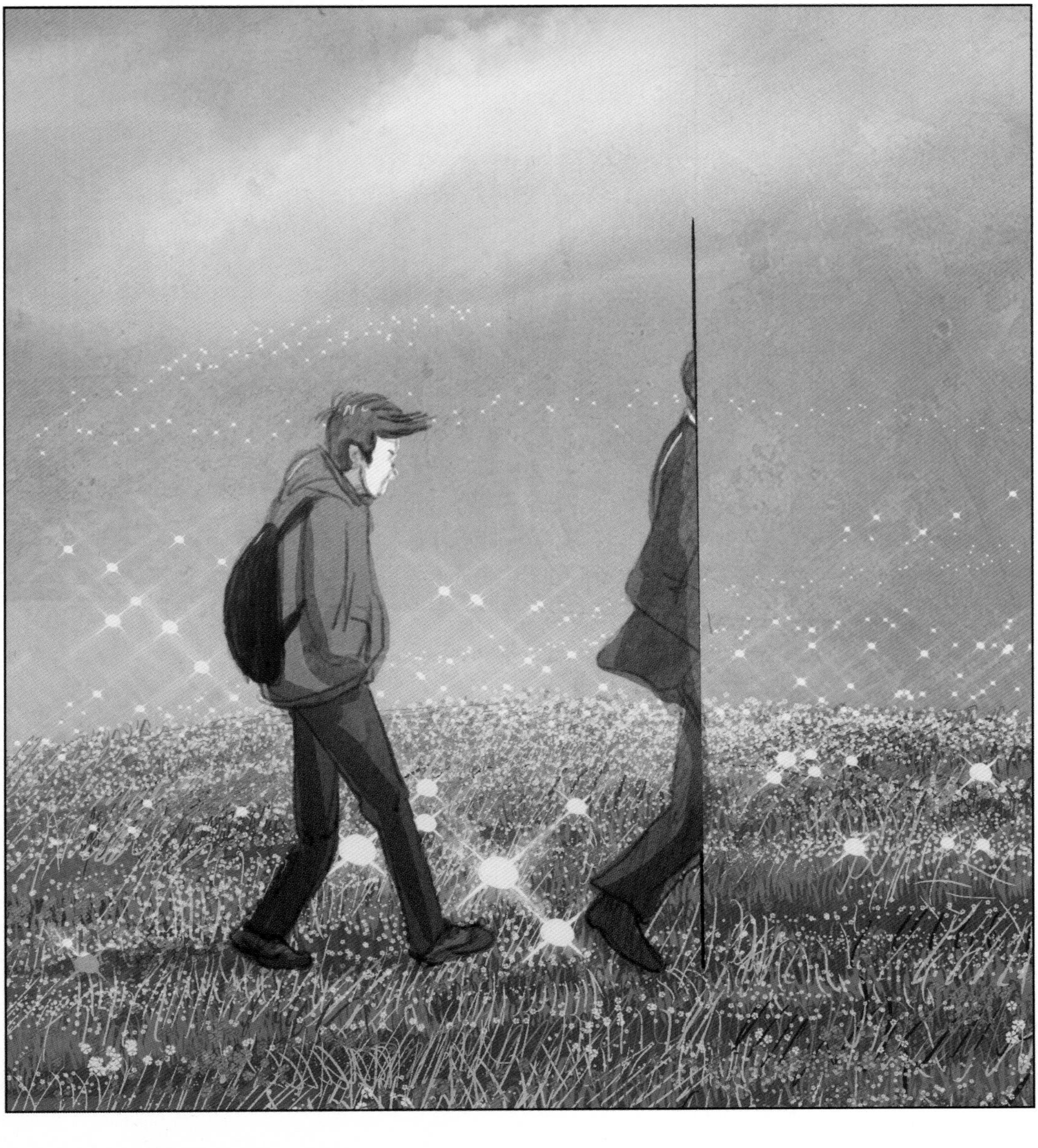

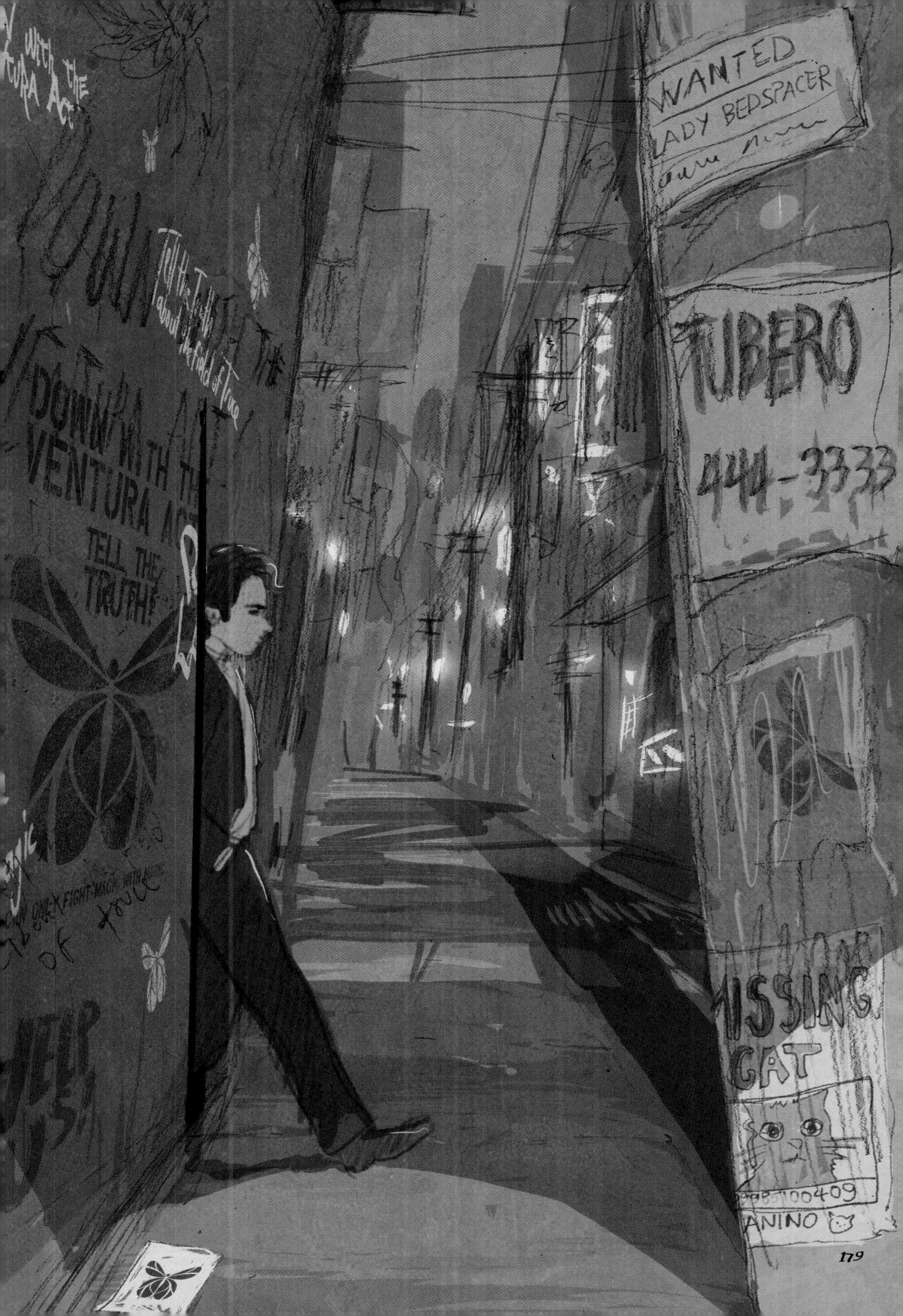
WANTED
LADY BEDSPACER
TUBERO
444-3333
DOWN WITH THE VENTURA ACT
TELL THE TRUTH!
MISSING CAT
ANINO

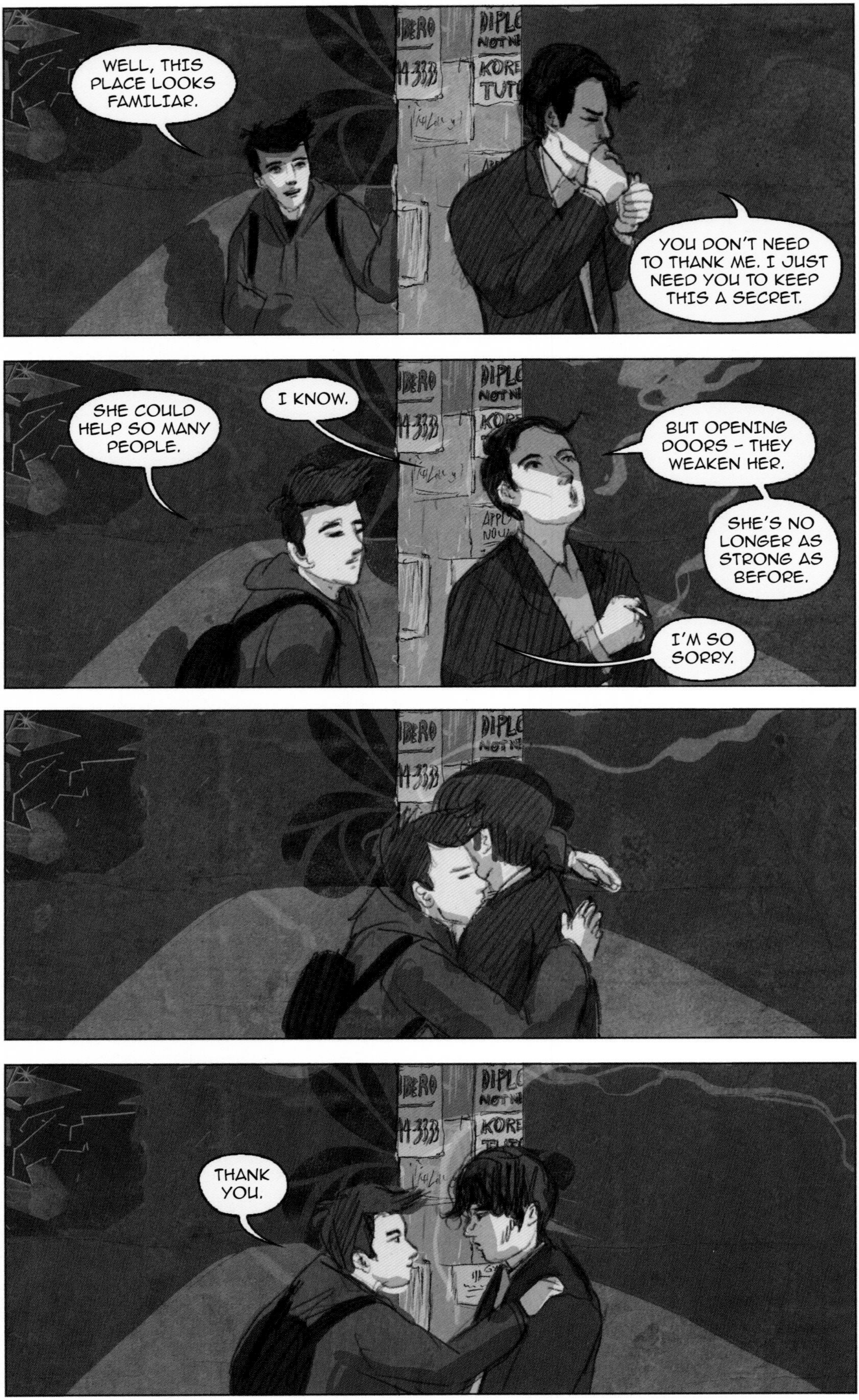
WELL, THIS PLACE LOOKS FAMILIAR.
YOU DON'T NEED TO THANK ME. I JUST NEED YOU TO KEEP THIS A SECRET.
SHE COULD HELP SO MANY PEOPLE.
I KNOW.
BUT OPENING DOORS – THEY WEAKEN HER.
SHE'S NO LONGER AS STRONG AS BEFORE.
I'M SO SORRY.
THANK YOU.

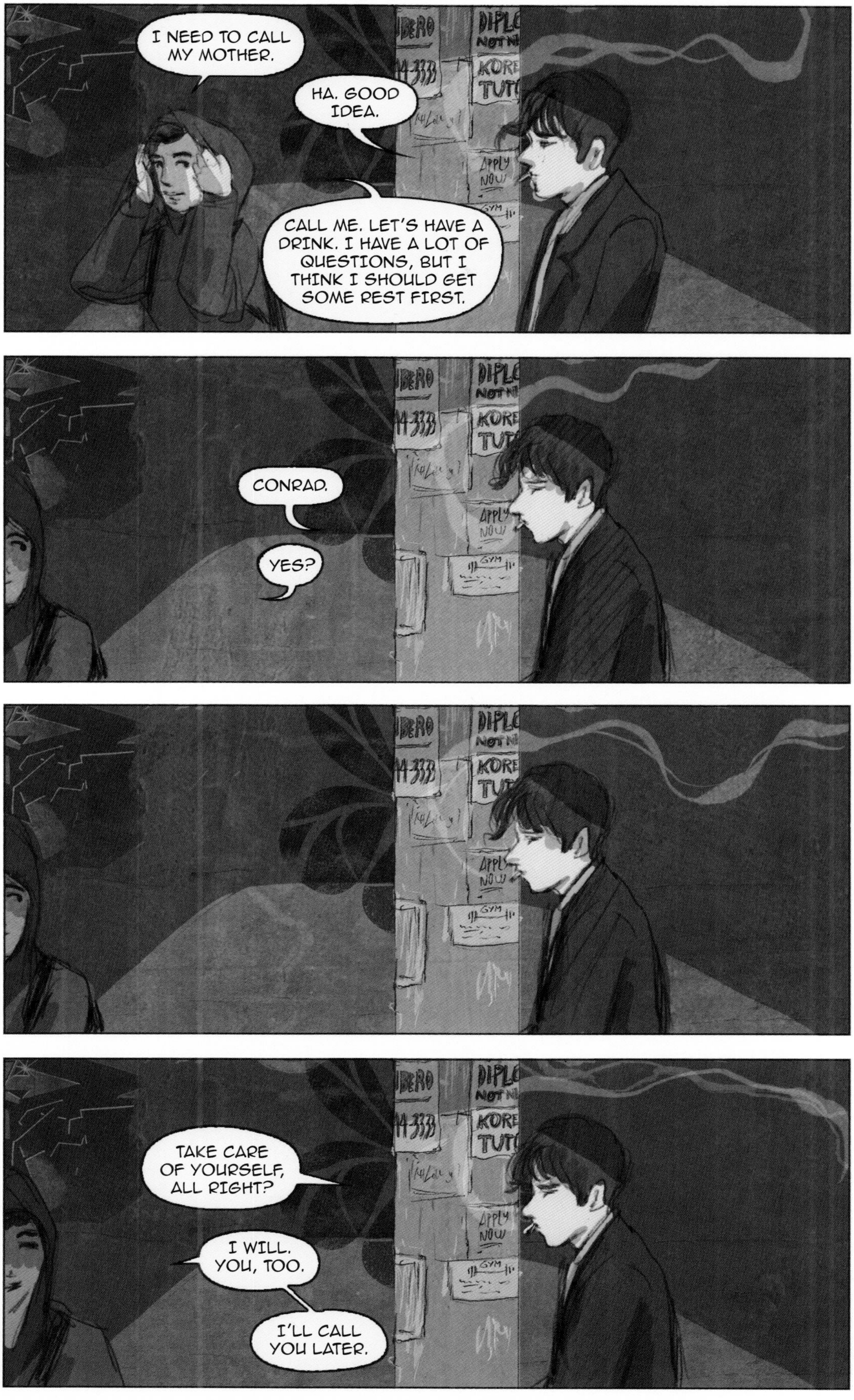
I NEED TO CALL MY MOTHER.
HA. GOOD IDEA.
CALL ME. LET'S HAVE A DRINK. I HAVE A LOT OF QUESTIONS, BUT I THINK I SHOULD GET SOME REST FIRST.
CONRAD.
YES?
TAKE CARE OF YOURSELF, ALL RIGHT?
I WILL. YOU, TOO.
I'LL CALL YOU LATER.

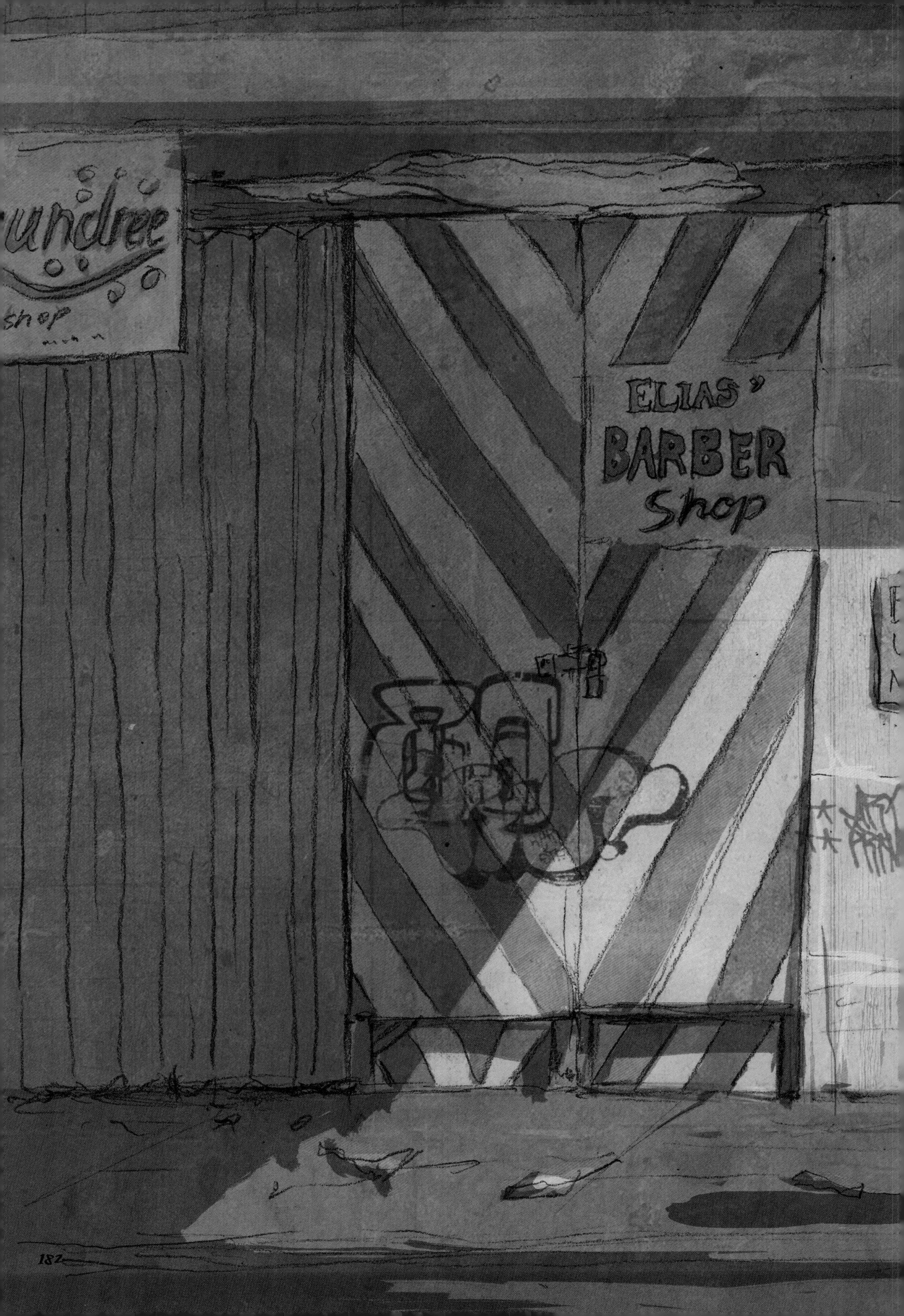
undree
shop
ELIAS'
BARBER
Shop

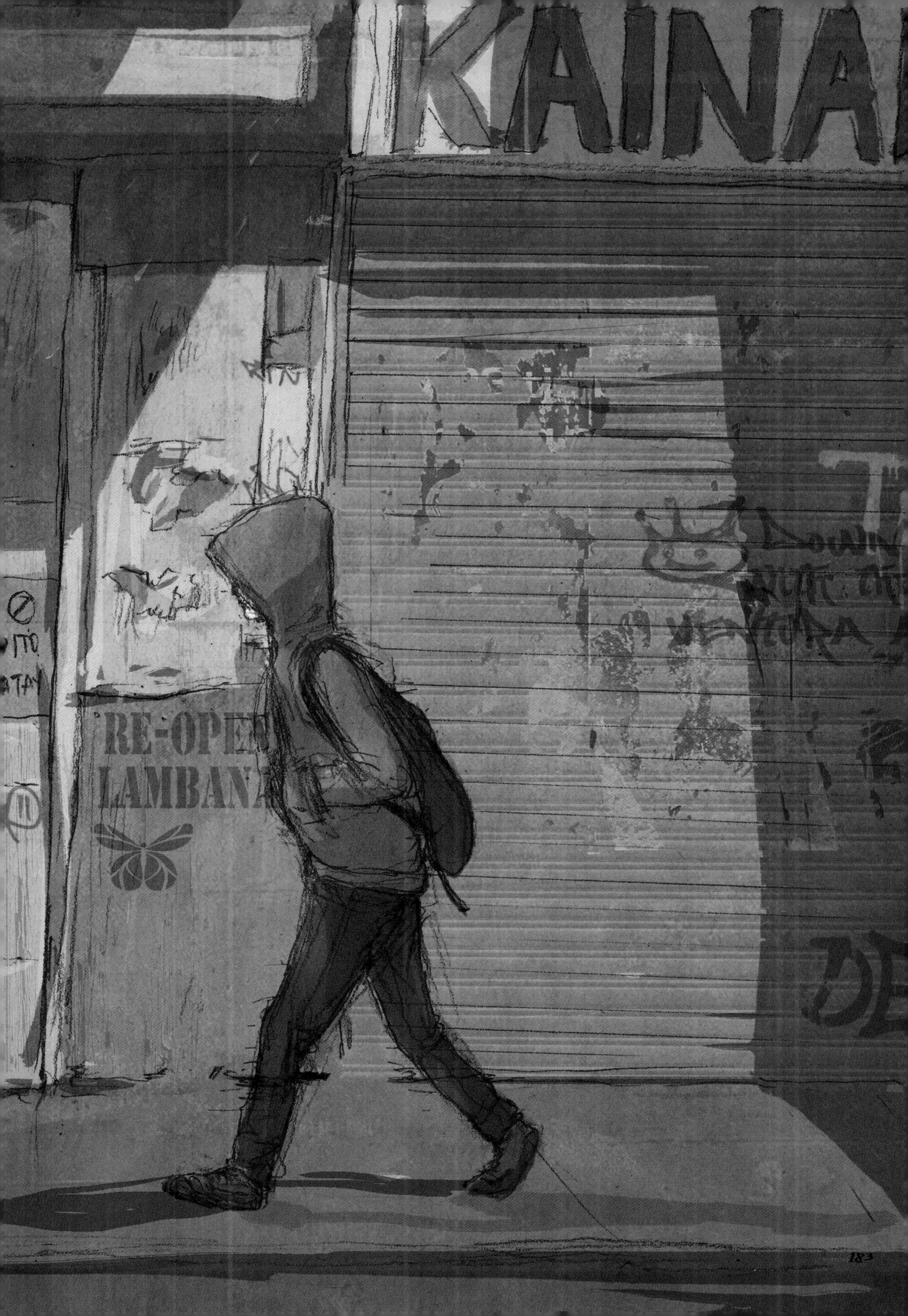
KAINA
RE-OPE
LAMBANA

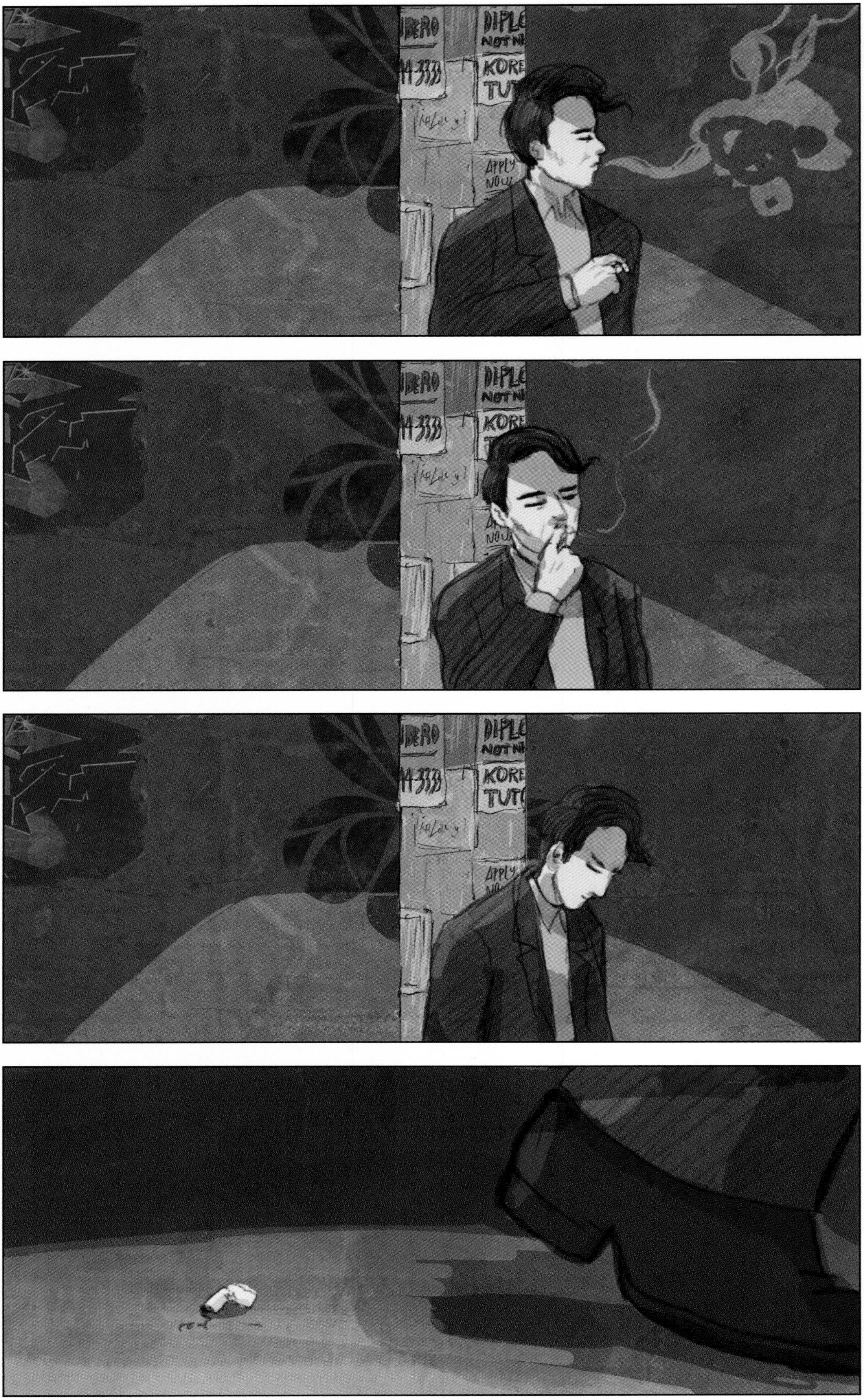
APPLY NOW

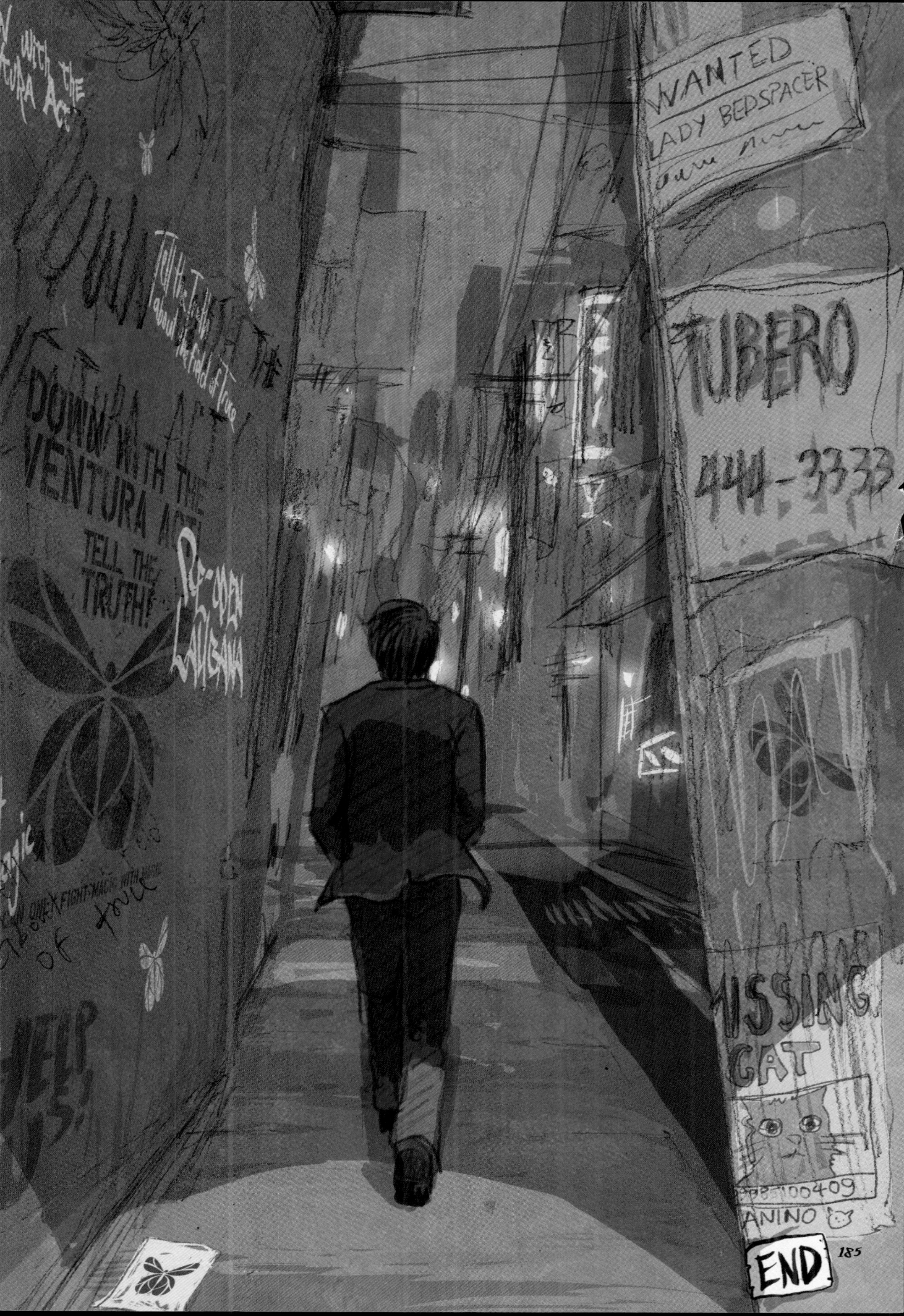

WANTED
LADY BEDSPACER
TUBERO
444-3333
DOWN WITH THE VENTURA ACT!
TELL THE TRUTH!
MISSING CAT
END

AFTERWORD

Eliza is not too fond of writing afterwords. Probably it's because she wants to let the work speak for itself, which is how it really should be. Or perhaps she's busy writing ten literary pieces at the same time. Avid readers of her works know how productive she is. But I for one love to read afterwords after I'm done reading a whole book, especially if the experience was good and I don't want it to end just yet. It's a way of cooling down or easing my way out of the world I have just experienced. I also love to see the process on how a book came to be. So if you are like me, this is for you.

(Just to be clear: it's better to read this Afterword after the story, as this contains spoilers.)

This project started in 2013. I have just released two issues of my ongoing comic series TABI PO that time. Since those were released, I received a bunch of emails and Facebook messages from authors who want to have their comic script illustrated and Eliza was one of them. I've read some of her short stories so I was excited to see what she was about to propose. The sample script for AFTER LAMBANA did not disappoint. I immediately liked it. There was a bunch of elements that were similar in both our works but there was enough differences as well. We both used the rich world of Philippine mythology as a source, but her story was set in the present, while mine was set mostly in the past. I liked this contrast in our work. I saw that it gave me a chance to draw different things than what I usually do in TABI PO - cars, trains, and buildings instead of trees. I was also excited in the visual imagery that I could contribute to the story. Eliza shortly gave me the complete script.

It isn't easy to illustrate a comic while trying to earn a living through freelancing, so it took me three years to finish it. My personal life was in chaos during those three years as well. I experienced a lot of hardships. I was heartbroken, healed, married, and became a father. To think that the events in this story happened in just one night! It also took a while because we do not want it to be released prematurely. We want to deliver a product with high quality so that you can enjoy it as well. After all, comics is an art form. It's a balancing of words and imagery to tell a cohesive story. I hope we are able to deliver that in AFTER LAMBANA. This is Eliza's first comic and this is my first complete comic because all of my other works are still ongoing, so there's a feeling of fulfilment for me as well upon finishing this. I hope you enjoyed reading this as much as we had fun creating it.

Mervin Malonzo

COLOR DESIGN

One of my goals in this comic is to experiment with colors. I chose to color code the different parts of the story according to the world they are in and whether it's on the past or present. The real world present time is red and green. The past is yellow and violet. The Lambana dimension is blue and orange. And the mirror dimension (my term; I do not know what Eliza calls it) where Alandra resides is the reverse of the real world - green for the light and red for the shadows.

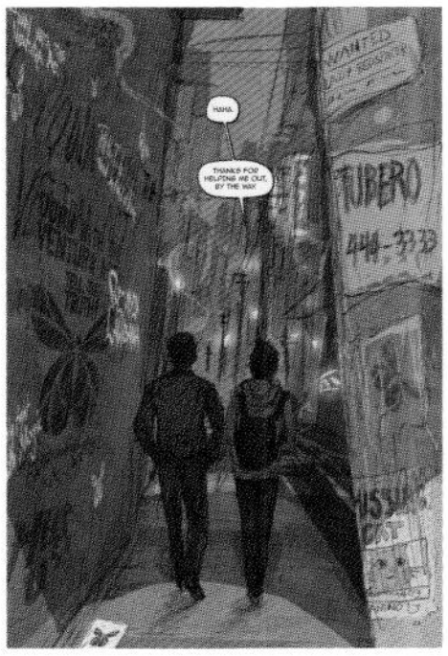
HAHA.
THANKS FOR HELPING ME OUT, BY THE WAY

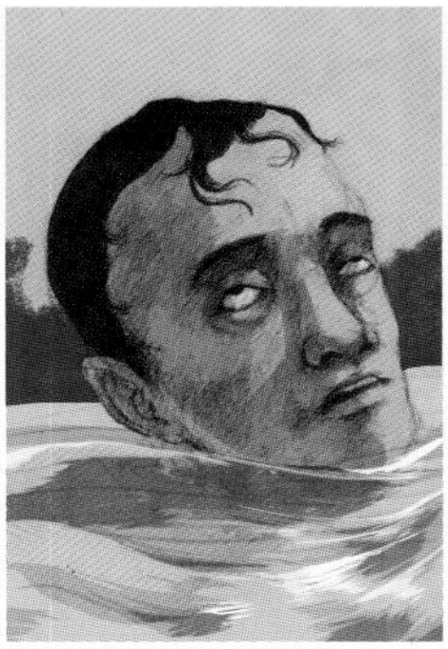

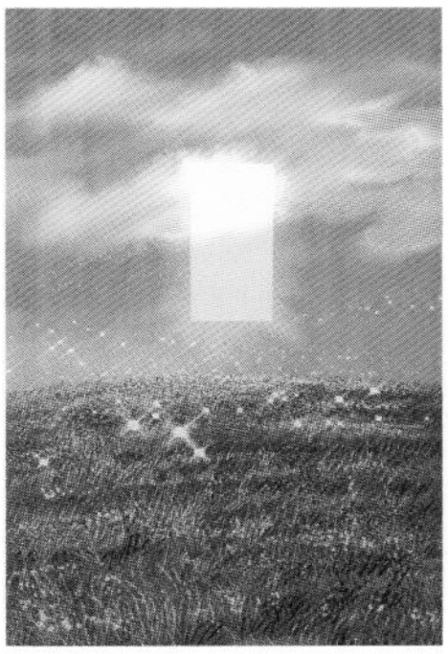

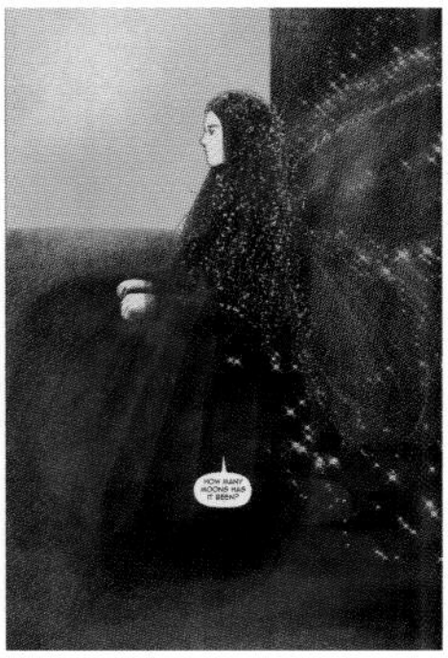
HOW MANY MOONS HAS IT BEEN?

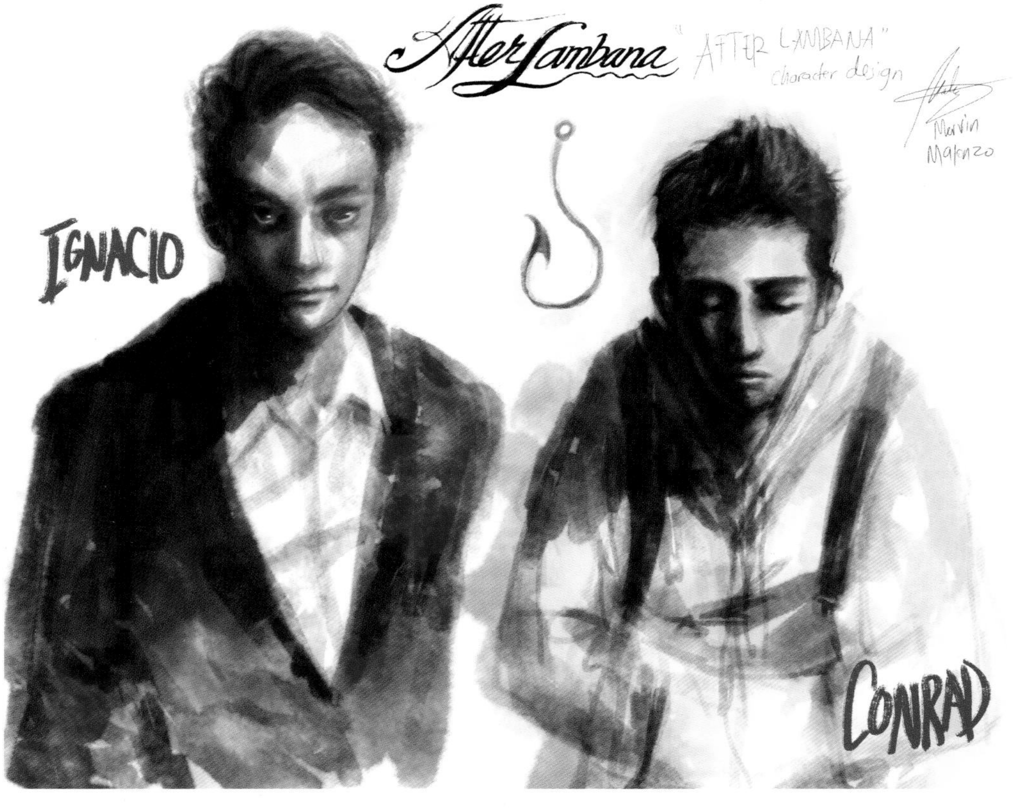
After Lambana
"AFTER LAMBANA"
character design
Marvin Malonzo
IGNACIO
CONRAD

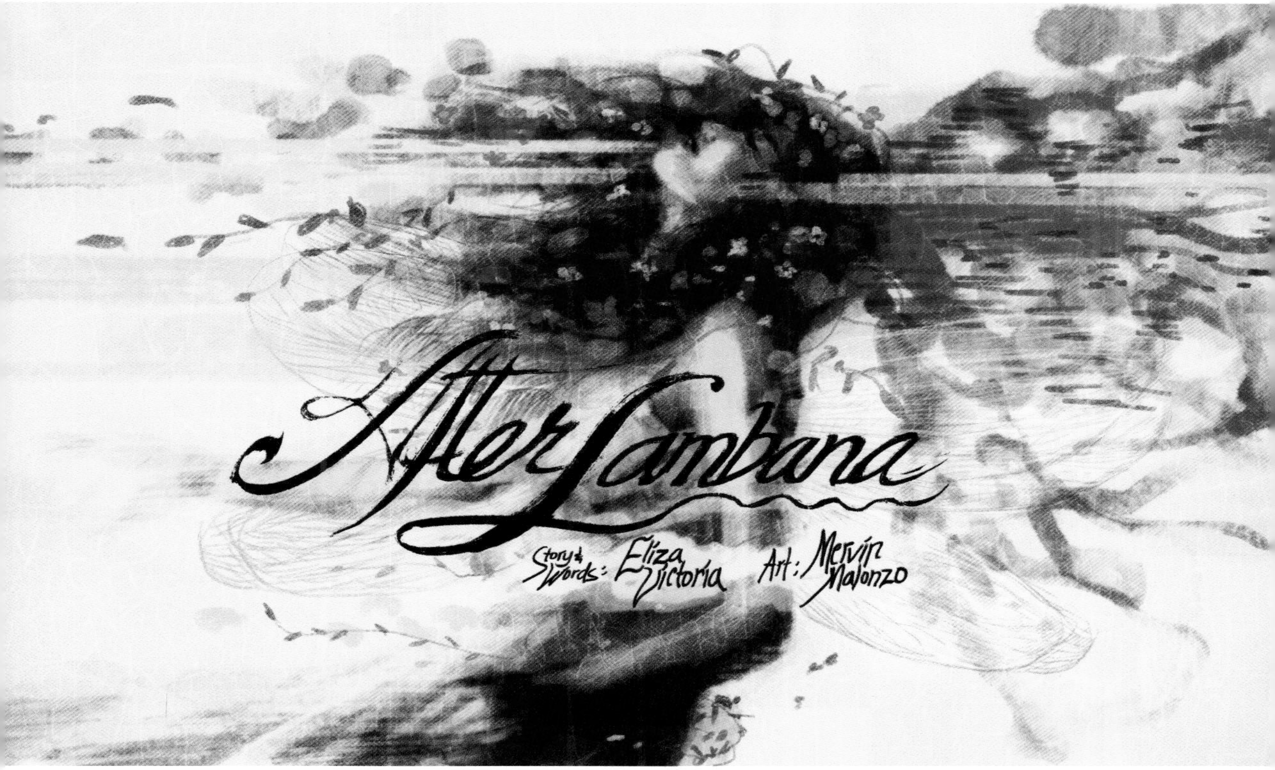
After Lambana
Story & Words: Eliza Victoria
Art: Mervin Malonzo

These are the first images I did for *After Lambana*

"BOOKS TO SPAN THE EAST AND WEST"

TUTTLE PUBLISHING WAS FOUNDED IN 1832 IN THE SMALL NEW ENGLAND TOWN OF RUTLAND, VERMONT (USA). OUR CORE VALUES REMAIN AS STRONG TODAY AS THEY WERE THEN—TO PUBLISH BEST-IN-CLASS BOOKS WHICH BRING PEOPLE TOGETHER ONE PAGE AT A TIME. IN 1948, WE ESTABLISHED A PUBLISHING OFFICE IN JAPAN—AND TUTTLE IS NOW A LEADER IN PUBLISHING ENGLISH-LANGUAGE BOOKS ABOUT THE ARTS, LANGUAGES AND CULTURES OF ASIA. THE WORLD HAS BECOME A MUCH SMALLER PLACE TODAY AND ASIA'S ECONOMIC AND CULTURAL INFLUENCE HAS GROWN. YET THE NEED FOR MEANINGFUL DIALOGUE AND INFORMATION ABOUT THIS DIVERSE REGION HAS NEVER BEEN GREATER. OVER THE PAST SEVEN DECADES, TUTTLE HAS PUBLISHED THOUSANDS OF BOOKS ON SUBJECTS RANGING FROM MARTIAL ARTS AND PAPER CRAFTS TO LANGUAGE LEARNING AND LITERATURE—AND OUR TALENTED AUTHORS, ILLUSTRATORS, DESIGNERS AND PHOTOGRAPHERS HAVE WON MANY PRESTIGIOUS AWARDS. WE WELCOME YOU TO EXPLORE THE WEALTH OF INFORMATION AVAILABLE ON ASIA AT WWW.TUTTLEPUBLISHING.COM.

PUBLISHED BY TUTTLE PUBLISHING, AN IMPRINT OF PERIPLUS EDITIONS (HK) LTD.

WWW.TUTTLEPUBLISHING.COM

LIBRARY OF CONGRESS CONTROL NUMBER: 2021951362

ISBN 978-0-8048-5525-9

STORY AND WORDS © 2022 ELIZA VICTORIA

ART, COVER, AND BOOK DESIGN © 2022 MERVIN MALONZO

PRINTED IN SINGAPORE   2201TP
25 24 23 22   10 9 8 7 6 5 4 3 2 1

DISTRIBUTED BY:
NORTH AMERICA, LATIN AMERICA & EUROPE
TUTTLE PUBLISHING
364 INNOVATION DRIVE
NORTH CLARENDON
VT 05759-9436 U.S.A.
TEL: (802) 773-8930
FAX: (802) 773-6993
INFO@TUTTLEPUBLISHING.COM
WWW.TUTTLEPUBLISHING.COM

ASIA PACIFIC
BERKELEY BOOKS PTE. LTD.
3 KALLANG SECTOR, #04-01
SINGAPORE 349278
TEL: (65) 6741-2178
FAX: (65) 6741-2179
INQUIRIES@PERIPLUS.COM.SG
WWW.TUTTLEPUBLISHING.COM